GRIMMGARD: HEIRS OF DESTRUCTION

TODD MIKA

First edition January 2024

Cover Art by Alex Albornoz

Map by Kier Scott-Schrueder

Grimmgard: Heirs of Destruction

ISBN-13 978-0-9909319-4-2 (Paperback Edition)

https://www.grimmgard.com/

"Life isn't about finding yourself.

Life is about creating yourself."

—

George Bernard Shaw

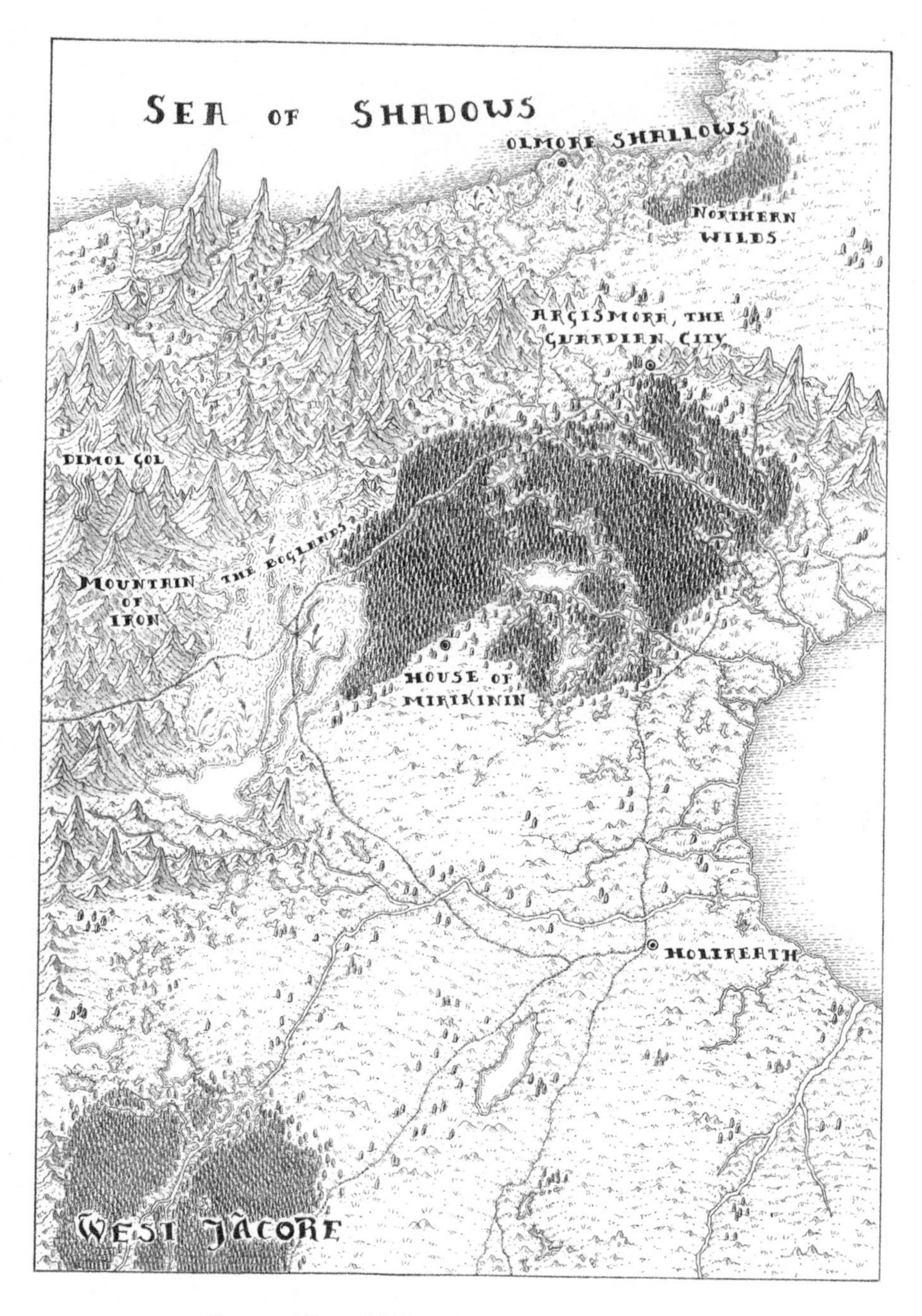

Jacore, Year 1801. The Winter Age.

NAME PRONUNCIATION

Argolvrecht – "Arr-gulf-REKT"

Chasmira – "Kaz-MEE-ruh"

Dimol Gol – "Dih-mull GAWL"

Emorya – "Eh-MORE-ee-uh"

Mirikinin – "Meh-RICK-in-in"

Nandrzael – "Nan-druh-ZELL"

Oczandarys – "Ock-ZAN-duh-riss"

GRIMMGARD: HEIRS OF DESTRUCTION

PART ONE

CHAPTER 1

Chasmira was nearly knee-deep in the mire. Her leggings and the hem of her dress were caked in green-black muck. Across the moonlit bog, she could see Hakon. His unmistakable black, pointed, pyramidal helmet rose like a spike. She heard the rumble of primordial force and a brief scream echoing.

These two had faced a hundred footsoldiers thus far. More would come.

Four hours ago, the two stood on opposite ends of a battlefield. Chasmira was dark seer to Magnate Argolvrecht and the scarlet-armored warriors that flowed like blood from a wound, out the gates of Dimol Gol. Hakon was grand executor for the Mad Prince Mirikinin and his hordes of hooded barbarians that bore spiked shields and saw-toothed warblades.

Argolvrecht was dead—torn to bits by Mirikinin's ironwolves. Mirikinin was also dead—skewered by a flurry of Dimol Gol arrows. There was no point in fighting when neither kingdom existed any longer. But the soldiers fought anyway, neither side knowing their lord was gone. When the battlefield cleared, there would not be enough standing warriors to lay siege to a chicken farm.

So they walked. The two sorcerers, through the marshland, making their way south and away from the battlefield. Deserters of a pointless war, and treated as deserters.

The chittering song of insects went quiet. Chasmira heard a burbling war cry as a hooded barbarian, covered in dark mud, leapt from under the water. His sword was raised to cleave her in two. Flames kindled in her eyes, but with a bright white flash and a roar of primordial force, the barbarian shattered like pottery before the seer could act.

"Art thou weary?" Hakon chuckled in a deep bass tone. The executor was like a wall of angular black armor over eight feet tall. He raised his iron staff back into an upright position at his side. Its three-pronged tip was still steaming.

The flames in her eyes dwindled back into their perpetual glow, each eye with a candle's flicker behind the pupil. "No, curious. I was wondering if he'd actually strike a lady unprovoked. Mirikinin's men have no manners at all."

"Nay, none. Like unto animals, all of them."

"You say that as if you disapprove of them. Are you of noble birth yourself, Hakon?"

"Thou art a jester."

"I felt like one these past six months, believe me." Entertaining Magnate Argolvrecht's mad ravings required a gentle hand and a generous amount of patience. Most of the time, her warnings were drowned in a court filled with bloodlusted barbarians. She was little more than another trinket in a trophy case, displayed to make him look impressive. "Confess. Whose courtier was your mother?"

Hakon scoffed, "Do wild boars of these very lands hold court?"

"You're kidding," she cackled, but only once so as not to wound him. "You were born here... Here, in these stinking pits?"

"Yea, a century ago, these marshlands were very fair. Feeding grounds for wild boars. Nomadic hunters did hunt and pitch here."

"How did they teach you the Arts?"

"They? Nay, not at all. When my powers did manifest, the hunters brought me to the Phrontistery of First Fire."

That was a name Chasmira had not heard in a very long time. Trudging in the thick mire, she stumbled. Her ankle had caught on a tree root for a moment. She caught herself, cursed, and placed her steps more carefully.

"The Sorcerers of the White Aegis didn't drop from the sky and into your hunting grounds?" she asked him.

"The White Aegis careth not to foster the weak. They descend where Chaos threatens, where it doth grow and then sprout out of young, rebellious hearts. For what cause doth one summon Chaos in their youth, but to destroy and control that which standeth in the way? It is this strength of spirit that draweth the White Aegis. They have crafted purposes for such, but not for someone such as myself."

"You, weak of spirit? I could hardly imagine, Hakon."

The compliment bounced off Hakon. "Thy power didst not draw the eyes of the White Aegis? Did they not send one of their own to find thee?"

"They did, actually."

"And?"

Chasmira rolled her eyes at the towering Hakon. "They should have sent two and not underestimated a little girl."

"Verily. Thy family should have brought thee to the Phrontistery as well."

"They might have if even one soul of them were left."

For a long minute after, the only exchange was the crackle of vines and squelching of mud as the two of them continued on without a word.

"Thy tale is befitting the long, dark road ahead," the towering executor said, breaking the silence. "Start with your birthplace, so that we may have enough words to match our steps."

"Ohh, now, now! We are companions of convenience. Don't fancy any thoughts that you and I will be bosom-friends when this is over and done. We'll eventually find the road that leads to Argismora—"

"Argismora? The Guardian City?"

"Yes and why not?"

"Thinkest thou—"

A loud clang sounded from Hakon's armor as a Dimol Gol arrow bounced off it. Chasmira turned, and a long stream of bright flame shot from her eyes into the cattails on her left. The scream of the archer was brief but shrill.

"Thinkest I—?" she prompted, blinking away fire.

"Thinkest thou, that thou shalt go to serve another lord? Thy reputation doth win thee easy hire."

"It is likely. The life of a courtier suits me. Even if I cannot sit upon a throne of power myself, the view from beside one is enchanting," she said, stepping over a log.

Hakon stepped onto the log and it snapped in half. "Thou

sayest. But methinkest thy desires are contrary one to another."

"Why would you say such a thing?"

"Because thy reputation doth not agree with thee. The view beside a throne is splendid indeed, but better befitting a pillar or a gargoyle. Thy mind is nought. Thy words are nought if all thou doest is agree. Wilt thou never rouse another up to let thee be heard?"

"No, I don't think I ever will."

"Why not?"

"Because I deny myself the vanity of fancying things that will never be." She heard a noise, and hot streams of golden fire burst forth again. Clumps of ashes scattered across the bog, flickering in the heat. Stinking steam rose from the spot. She did not even notice whether it was crimson armor or a black hood this time.

ψ

The bog eventually gave way to a road. It was man-made, insomuch as firm earth had been moved and reinforced with large stones to create a rise several feet above the steaming mire. The lumpy, moss-covered road snaked its way through the boglands, but one could not tell north from south. Neither sun nor sky could be seen, for the land was choked with vines and gnarled trees. Hakon and Chasmira looked one way and then the other.

"Which way?" the woman mused aloud.

"Betwixt the two of us, thou art the one going to Argismora. Thou knowest not thy way?"

She considered lashing him with fire from her eyes as she glared back at him. "I don't often detour through the stinking, pig-infested bog on my way to the main road, no. I'm not sure which way to go."

"We knowwww!" a choir of high-pitched voices shouted from the bog.

Hakon whirled about, bringing his iron staff down into both hands and aiming it at the source of the outburst. The three prongs at the forked tip thrummed loudly with a rush of primordial power, ready to destroy. His grip went a little slack, however, when he saw he was pointing it at a cluster of mushrooms growing between the stones of the roadside.

"Couldn't be..."

The mushrooms tittered and giggled, with tiny black eyes peeking open beneath their bulbs. It sounded like babies' laughter, and Hakon did not even draw back his staff from the surprise.

Chasmira tip-toed off the road and knelt on the mossy hillside. Lifting Hakon's staff gently away with the back of her hand, she spoke to the cluster of tiny creatures.

"Why hello down there! Did you say you know the way?"

The mushrooms giggled again, and all began to chatter at once. They were Cloven: tiny, endlessly playful little things who began life in clustered patches like these. Fully-grown Cloven sprout their own legs and arms and wiggle out of the patch to roam free, so these Cloven had to be mere children. They were small and pale with dark green spots on their bulbs.

Chasmira waved her hands frantically at the chattering cluster. "One at a time, please!"

"You want to go to the big city?" one of the tiny Cloven squeaked.

"Or the *bigger* city?" another whispered, and they all gasped.

"Oh dear," Chasmira said, clasping her hands. "Eh, I want to go to Argismora."

"Argie's Moors?" one of them mimicked, sounding confused.

"She said Argo's Moolah," said another, followed by more tittering laughter.

Chasmira groaned. "It's a city!"

The Cloven *ooh'ed* in astonishment. "Yes, we know about those!"

"You do?"

"We've never seen them, but we have heard all about them! Tall stone trees and many many people! Noisy things with wheels, all pulled by snorting four-legs with long hair! Going to the city!"

Chasmira clapped her hands, "Oh good, yes. When the snorting four-legs pulled the noisy wheeled things to the city, which way did they go?"

"That wayyy!" the Cloven all shouted in unison.

After a short silence, "Wait... which way?"

"That wayyy!" the Cloven all shouted in unison again.

The sorceress craned her neck, looking to the road. "North or south?"

"What's northorsouth?" the tiny mushrooms asked.

Chasmira looked up at Hakon with pleading eyes.

"I shall try," he sighed.

Hakon knelt down, his armored body casting a dark shadow over the tiny things. Before he could say more, the Cloven called up to him, "Hey, you don't have a mouth!"

"What? I hath a mouth," flustered.

"You have half a mouth?"

"Nay, a whole mouth!" more flustered.

"Where?"

"Under my armor!" most flusteredly.

"Can we have armor like yours?"

Chasmira rolled her eyes, "You know, if I didn't know any better, I'd swear you are a Cloven yourself under that imposing shell you wear. Confess now. It's all right, you're among friends."

The little mushrooms squealed with laughter.

Chasmira brushed off her dress as she stood up. "Alright then, look at me. The four-legged things walked upon this road. Tell me if the way I am walking is to Argismora."

"Argues Morning?" the Cloven puzzled.

"Oh you did say there were two cities, didn't you?" She fretted. "Hakon, is there a neighboring city larger than Argismora?"

"Nay," Hakon pondered, and then looked down to the Cloven. "I pray you, little ones, tell us from whence came the travelers through here? Camest they from afar?"

"The people on the wheeled things said they came from another place, a big city."

"And they were coming here, to a bigger city?"

The Cloven all thought for a moment before all shouting "Yes! They said the place they were going was bigger!"

"The highway from Holireath comes all the way north to Argismora! What other city could it be?"

Hakon nodded. "And Argismora would be the larger city?"

"I should know! I came all the way from home to find Magnate Argolvrecht here beyond the western flats!" Chasmira clasped her hands together and rested them on her chin. "Now then, little ones! Did they walk this way to the bigger city?" and she began to walk in large, exaggerated strides.

The Cloven all laughed and exclaimed, "No no, the other way!"

"Wonderful!" She turned on her heel and waved for her towering companion. "Quickly, Hakon dear, we are going to Argismora! Thank you very much for your keen guidance, my little friends! Goodbye! Goodbye!"

CHAPTER 2

They proceeded northeast. After more than an hour of walking, the dark, gnarled forest was far behind. The two sorcerers now walked a dirt road that wound between rows and rows of lush green fir trees. Silvery morning light shone between the trees, sending bright beams across the road in a light mist that persisted in the air. The moist air felt warmer now that the sun reached through the firs.

"So, thy home is Holireath. It standeth to reason now," Hakon began.

"Whatever do you mean by that?" Chasmira answered, swinging her arms as she quickened her pace ahead of him.

"Why thou fled thy home. In peaceful Holireath such power as yours is damnable."

Her arms lowered stiffly to either side.

"Thy parents dead, unable to send thee away. The White Aegis sorcerer also dead, unable to take thee away."

Chasmira's heart pounded. Her slender hands tightened in fists. "What of it, Hakon? What of it?"

Hakon hesitated. "Thou escheweth thy home now, yet thou lived there for many years. Thou didst live quietly, secretly... No one to ever discover you..."

"Yes. Yes, Hakon... no one ever discovered my sorcery," she snapped at his prying, whirling around to face him. "No one ever knew what happened or why I lived alone for so many years."

"Why didst thou?"

"Why didst I what?"

"Live alone," solemnly.

"I wasn't like you, whisked away to the Phrontistery of First Fire when my power arose," she exploded at him. "Love changed to fear in my parents' eyes! I watched it happen. They would keep me in the house but not speak to me, as if I were vermin. Fear drove them to this, though I did not understand at the time. In my outrage, I confronted them about how estranged they were from me, and in my outrage, I summoned forth fire that destroyed them. Foolish child that I was... I see now only in hindsight that they were not afraid of me, but of what others might do to me.

"When the White Aegis sent their sorcerer from the sky, it was not to rescue me. It was to put me out of my misery. It was to find the fires of Chaos burning within me and snuff them out. But if my home was a castle and I the lone sentry, the infernal power within me was the moat. I summoned the beasts of the field to prey on my enemy and tear him to pieces. And none ever suspected a little girl," she coughed out laughter at the irony. "They suspected a dark sorcerer had killed my parents and then met an untimely end."

Hakon stood still as a pillar while Chasmira's words beat against him.

"So yes I lived alone," her face taut as she chided him. "At home for as long as I could. The strange one, the bereft child, the orphan! I was pitied. Years passed before I searched for a higher purpose, for something greater than clinging to the memories left in my parents' humble little home."

Chasmira tore herself away from him, ashamed of her outburst. She did not know how she had let it all flood out, but there it was. It could not be unsaid now. Had she spent so many many months staring wordlessly beside the Magnate's throne that it simply needed to burst forth?

"Therefore didst thou leave. Thou left to become Magnate Argolvrecht's seer. But... why?"

The woman said nothing, but clasped her hands together and walked ahead of him.

"What awaitest thee in the Guardian City? Just another master to serve?"

She walked faster.

"Why not simply go back?" Hakon called after her.

"As I said to you earlier," shouting back at him, "I deny myself the vanity of fancying things that will never be... And I can never simply go back!"

No sooner had the words left her mouth then a blast of the purest searing white light erupted from the road ahead, throwing her backward to the ground! The forest shook with the force.

Chasmira sat up, eyes wide.

Two great wings spread from the tall, statuesque female figure now standing in the road. The feathers glistened like glass, as did the armor plates that clung to her body as if they were molded to her shape. Her shoulders were angular, her neck cranelike, her chin pointed. Her hair was as bright as a pearl. Her skin shone like clouds holding back the dawn. Her eyes glimmered like jade.

"Nandrzael..." Chasmira whispered.

Hakon froze, bathed in the white light. He knew this name: Nandrzael, a being of the realm above, an Angelic, and the patron guardian of Argismora.

"What.... happened, sorceress?" this woman demanded. Her voice echoed like the sound of war drums.

Chasmira stumbled and stood. Her knees were jelly, and she wobbled from foot to foot. "It all went as intended. Argolvrecht challenged the Mad Prince as you wished—"

"MIRIKININ IS DEAD, YOU FOOL!" the Angelic burst out, and the forest shook again. "They both are! I told you to lead Argolvrecht to the brink of war, not drive him over it headfirst."

She was one of the mighty Angelics that oversaw the fate and future of lifekind. A visit from an Angelic was normally a blessed event. It portended a blessing once you completed a task for them. Though the tasks ranged from the grand to the mundane, a task from an Angelic usually set in motion a chain of events meant to accomplish good in the world. The end result could be hundreds of miles distant or many years away. Only the Angelics knew.

Almost unheard, Chasmira replied, "I merely—"

"You merely fed the idiot crumbs that would lead him to follow their trail, yes, a trail that led to the horde of the Mad Prince Mirikinin. Once provoked, the Prince would strike and Dimol Gol would be no more. The conquest of these lands would cease! Instead, both kings lie dead and all for nought!"

"It was his own rage that drove him over the brink, not I," the sorceress answered more firmly now. "What difference does it make? Are we not all the better now that we are rid of those beasts?"

"Those beasts, like all beasts, have whelps! The children of

Mirikinin will hear of their father's demise. His blood calls to them out of the ground, and they will answer in time. They will shed the blood of thousands across these fair lands and all the country, and all because of you!"

Chasmira shuddered at the last three words. More blood on her hands.

"There is nothing now to be done. You have failed," Nandrzael pronounced in a grave voice.

"There is more yet to be done. You tasked me to move Argolvrecht to war and I did it. Give me the blessing."

The Angelic simply sneered. "You whispered to start a fire but did not shout to control it. Woman, your silence has made a madman into a martyr. There will be no blessing."

Chasmira clenched her fists at the last two words.

"Now there is only chaos," Nandrzael added.

"Argismora's lord may be swayed to seek Mirikinin's heirs and destroy them. The quest of an Angelic, or the prophecy of a sorceress—"

"Your theatrics have done enough."

"Please," forcing out the word.

Nandrzael looked pitilessly down at her. Her crystalline wings shifted shape slightly, and in a moment she was hovering 10 feet off the ground.

"No. No, sorceress. Our bargain was life forfeited in exchange for life restored. A king and his kingdom, for a father and mother. Your chance for redemption has been squandered, and now it shall take at least a hundred years to undo what you have done this day. Fool that I was, I entrusted this to *you*... someone given to Chaos since childhood. All you do is leave death and destruction in your wake. I thought I could use it as a tool, but I see now this flame cannot be controlled."

Chasmira shut her eyes at the last word.

The Angelic continued, "It can only be snuffed out."

Chasmira's eyes snapped open in time to see a shower of bright white sparks. Nandrzael's shimmering sword, seemingly made of frozen vapor, wavered inches from her face... restrained only by Hakon's great iron staff parrying it.

Infernal flame swelled in Chasmira's eyes. "No. Like the others, you will *burn*," unleashing streams of fire.

The gleaming Angelic moved like a blur to avoid the blast. A heartbeat later, Hakon swatted Nandrzael down with a twirl of his staff, leaving her facedown in the soil. He drove it downward between her shoulder blades to impale her, but in a blur she was gone.

"Where did she go?" he growled.

Nandrzael's wings carried her with great speed and also silence, for Hakon did not notice as she appeared behind him.

"Hakon—" Chasmira screamed.

The sword pierced Hakon's armored shell like a stinger.

Black blood trickled out and then gushed as the Angelic yanked the vaporous blade back out of him. She watched Hakon's towering form topple over. "I'd pity you, dark creature, if I could."

A wave of fire engulfed her where she stood. Nandrzael shrieked in pain and spiraled up against a tree, before another stream of fiery hate struck her. It sent her spinning. The streams scorched straight through the tree trunk in seconds.

"BURRRNNNN! BURN, BURN, BURNNNN!!!" Chasmira howled.

When the fires died down, the forest fell quiet. Chasmira stepped carefully through the streams of silver sunlight. Her breathing shuddered as she looked this way and that.

She listened through the whispering crackles of flame on the tips of the tree branches. She listened hard for any gust of wind that might give away the Angelic's flight. Nandrzael was wounded, but the wound only made her angrier. Chasmira was useless to her. She would not spare her.

Moving shakily, the sorceress edged closer to Hakon's body. She forced her knees to bend and knelt next to him...

The Angelic struck like lightning, with a flash of brilliant light and the thunder of indignant rage. The force flung Chasmira backward off her feet. She landed against a fallen tree log. Nandrzael was right on top of her before she could even draw her next breath. She raised that blade of frozen vapor. The tip pressed against Chasmira's chest.

"Murderous scum," the gleaming Angelic spat on her with each word. The flesh of her face and neck were still sizzling, blotched black on one side, and her wing was wilted like a burnt flower. Her jade eyes glowed. "You have bereaved this world ten thousand lives today, for nothing!"

Chasmira's trembling lips curled into a smile. "Then what's one more?"

The forest echoed with a roar of primordial force, and Nandrzael shattered into bits, like a broken pot.

Strands of smoke rose from the prongs of the iron staff. Chasmira's white knuckles ached from how tightly she'd held it against the Angelic's ribs. She thought to drop it but instead raised it to brace herself, leaning her cheek against the warm metal.

Hakon. His body lay prostrate on the path. The massive suit of armor was now his coffin, and the forest his noble tomb. There was no way to move him or bury him now.

"It is so strange to call someone friend, but what else can I call you? Thank you."

The ashes of the Angelic shimmered as the wind carried them away. Chasmira knew not if an Angelic could truly die. If not, it would take an army to repel the Angelic a second time.

An army...

Chasmira turned and walked off the path, through the fir trees. The sun was rising in the east before her, and she pushed through the light that increased with every step. Miles beyond the forest lay the jagged fields and deep grottos where Mirikinin's ironwolves were bred. It was only right that a firsthand witness brings the news of his death. By sundown the children of Mirikinin would meet a ragged sorceress with an iron staff and eyes of fire, summoning them to war.

Perhaps she would get to pay a visit to the Guardian City of Argismora after all.

CHAPTER 3

The fog that rested sullenly upon the plains was so thick, Chasmira could hardly tell where she was placing her feet. Some sort of grass or grain about knee-high brushed against the leggings under her dress. Her boots sank slightly into each step she took. The earth beneath her soles was very soft but not miry. Shrubs and boulders drifted out of the grey cloud as if they were boats moving through a lagoon.

Chasmira had never seen this part of the country before, and she was not seeing it now. She felt as if she was being watched, as if the land of Mirikinin was watching her just beyond the unyielding wall of grey. The dense forest was miles behind her. Her feet ached. She wondered how much farther she would walk before happening upon a village or a farm of the children of Mirikinin.

She had heard all about them in the Magnate's court as the preparations were made for war. The Mad Prince Mirikinin had a brother, three sons, and many cousins besides that inhabited the land. They had several vassals: owners of adjoining land who pledged themselves to the Prince in exchange for the protection of his mighty army. Chasmira knew not how much manpower existed within a land that had just sent five thousand warriors to their deaths in the bloodbath she escaped. What she did know, however, was that the wrath of Mirikinin was fierce, and his family's wrath was equal to it. Nandrzael herself had said so.

Nandrzael...

She was going to make the Angelic pay for what she had done: for dangling the promise of mother and father restored to life as a blessing in exchange for the Magnate's destruction. Did Nandrzael even intend to uphold her part of the bargain, or was she counting on Chasmira being torn to shreds like the rest of them? It was only Hakon's arrival in the middle of a hopeless war that created their opportunity to escape together.

Hakon...

She tightened her grip on the three-pronged iron staff she had lifted out of his limp hand just moments before killing Nandrzael with it.

Hakon... how many times you did you save my life today, yet I couldn't save yours.

Chasmira yelped as a loud dog broke the silence. The hoarse barking and growling echoed through the fog ahead, and it was joined by the sounds of men's voices soon after.

Out of the grey vapor walked a man about Chasmira's height. He was a bit past sixty years old, his face chiseled with deep squint lines spiraling out from his eyes. The man was dressed only in short breeches and a wide conical farming hat made of straw weave. His arms were mottled with deep tan marks and freckles.

"Hark! There's a penalty for trespassers," he growled to her.

"Oh? And what's that?"

"We break their legs with mallets, and then I set the dogs on them."

"My, that seems rather unsporting. How are they meant to flee?"

"That's the sport. They aren't," the man leered.

Around them, the fog thinned a bit. She saw the shapes of four other men approaching behind him, each holding a farming tool of some kind. The largest man shifted his weight idly from foot to foot to keep a firm hold on the huge growling dog. It was a hellishund: bat-eared, pug-nosed, and native to the dark grottos. Hellishunds' eyesight was poor, but they could hear a mouse rustling through the grass ten furlongs away. If these men had a guard dog with them, there had to be a farm colony nearby.

Huge round haystacks appeared out of the recoiling fog around them. The colony was not just nearby—she had walked into the middle of it.

"She's a pretty thing," one of the other farmhands said.

"Bit muddy, but I don't care," said another.

The dog loudly slurped its own drool.

"Lay a hand on me and you'll regret it," Chasmira snarled.

The men shivered in mock fear and shared a chuckle.

"A viper's slithered onto the farm!" The man in the straw hat called back to them. "Watch out for the fangs, lads! She'll get you!"

"Ain't you supposed to kill snakes, Terror?" the large man asked the dog. It viciously barked at her, seeming to agree with its handler.

Something inside her tried to pull her away, tried to make her step backward to get even a step away from the men. She silenced it, instead squeezing the iron staff in her hands. If she used it, they might back off… or they might beat her to death and feed her to their pet hellishund…

"Out of my way!" A commanding voice echoed from the fog behind them. A big, broad-shouldered man pushed his way into the middle of the scene. When one of the men did not step aside quickly enough, the big man shoved him down onto the ground.

The man's short beard was the color of hazelwood, as was his hair that he kept pulled back into a topknot. He stood head and shoulders taller than any of the farmhands, with huge shoulders that sloped down like hills. His surcoat of burgundy leather was long enough to touch his knees. His big hands tightened into fists as he looked around at the men and then at the sorceress in her muck-stained dress.

"What's the meaning of this? Who is this woman?"

"A trespasser," the man in the straw hat replied.

"Or a spy," said the one holding the hellishund's chain. "Look at her clothes!"

The big man grunted. "I'm looking at them."

The fog continued to lift, revealing the shapes of gabled timber pithouses and silos. Farther beyond, she could see the shape of a dark hill…

"Who are you?" he demanded, lumbering close to her and blocking her view of the land behind them.

"I bring tidings of your war with the Magnate of Dimol Gol."

"Dimol Gol? Of course," he said with a grinless chuckle. "I should have recognized the strange fashion of your dress, but the women of Dimol Gol are rarely seen outside their territory."

"No one wants diseased vermin on their land," the man in the straw hat spat.

Chasmira could not resist. "Oh? Just a minute ago you were practically bickering over who would get his turn with me first.

Whatever my disease, you're all certainly very eager to *spread* it."

The big man lifted the back of his hand, but Chasmira just stuck out her chin to accept the blow. She locked her gaze with his. He could see the satisfied smile in her golden eyes, and he lowered his hand.

The dog handler's face turned red with anger. "Shut it! I let this chain slip a little, and Terror will rip that mouth right off your face."

"Which is why you won't let it slip, Lart," the big man warned, and the handler backed down instantly. "Now, I did not catch your name, Woman of Dimol Gol. Who are you?"

"I am Chasmira, seer to the Magnate."

"Argolvrecht's enchantress?"

"In the flesh," she said with a curtsy. "And I bring news of his war with your prince."

"If you have fled the land to come here, then I assume my father was victorious."

So, Mirikinin's son. She wondered which one he was, though from the way he spoke to the farmhands she could assume him to be the firstborn.

She had to choose her next words carefully. The men already wished her harm and accused her of being a spy. Their master now assumed Prince Mirikinin was victorious, which made sparing her life a matter of total indifference to them. If she told them Mirikinin died, they would assume an army was coming to destroy them next. It would be as good as agreeing she was a spy.

Her gaze leapt from man to man. "I can only discuss this matter with the family patriarch. Is your uncle here?"

The five men looked at each other in confusion. If she bore

tidings of victory, why not just tell them? And if she was indeed the Magnate's seer sent to bargain for the fate of his land, where was her honor guard?

The big man scratched at his chin for a moment. "Are you alone?"

"Yes."

"Are you carrying any weapons?"

"Why? Scared, son of Mirikinin?" taking a step within arm's reach.

His mouth fell open for just a moment, and he saw that smile in her eyes again.

"Not of you." He turned his back to her and began lumbering back the way he came.

The men parted ways for him and then stared at her, waiting for her to follow. She lifted up her eyes and saw that the fog had dispersed while they were talking, revealing a great stone fortress at the top of the hill. Great obelisks stood as turrets along the black stone walls, and in the center stood a single monolithic tower. There were no rounded spires, no decorative columns, no embrasures on the walls… just flat surfaces of cold stone jutting out of the hill like hardened shadows. This was the great House of Mirikinin.

She pressed her tongue hard against the backs of her teeth. Though she did not betray it to the men around her, her chest ached from her pounding heart. She ignored the leering stares of the men and followed the prince's son up the hill.

Her feet ached worse after trudging up the steep hill to the front gate. The fortress' location guaranteed the high ground against any assault, and any invaders would be deeply disadvantaged by the grade of the terrain. The open land on all sides guaranteed a clear view of any flying beasts, which would undoubtedly be riddled with arrows long before they even got close to the turrets.

The front gate gave entrance to the bare inner yard, which sank down abruptly after the gate. Chasmira recognized this as a "dry moat," a pit dug around a castle to slow or trap any invaders who manage to break through the imposing outer wall. A drawbridge allowed them to cross over the sunken yard.

Wisps of white vapor left Chasmira's lips with each breath in the cold, damp air. An iron portcullis rose, and beyond it a huge slab of black stone slid slowly into the wall. She could feel the deep vibration from the moving stone in her front teeth. Following the prince's son inside, she glanced back and noticed the hellishund and its handler Lart were following them in as well. The dog's eyes glowed eerily in the dark hallway.

The House of Mirikinin was a masterpiece of brutalist stonework. Dark smoky marble, cut almost invariably in right angles, gave shape to imposing rectangular pillars, towering doorways, and islands filled with spider-like ferns. Everything smelt of fire from braziers of burning coals that stood or hung in every room.

The audience chamber was the most striking of all. It was square, with a perimeter on which to stand around all four sides of the room. The square center of the chamber, about twelve feet wide, was recessed lower than the perimeter with stone steps leading down to it. Four square pillars stood at each corner of the center square. Thin vines snaked around these pillars, and Chasmira would scarcely have seen them if not for the vines' small black flowers glistening in the firelight.

The prince's son descended the steps to the center, and Chasmira followed.

At the top of the steps directly before them was a throne of black marble, cut at the same brutal right angles as the rest of the house. Flames from a hearth leapt high behind it, framing it in fire and shrouding the one sitting upon the throne. Out of the darkness, Chasmira could only see his boots and the train of long fur robes piled around them.

The prince's son cleared his throat. "Lord Maram, I found this woman wandering on the western sward. She claims—"

"*You* didn't find her, Warrick," the hellishund handler interrupted from behind them. "*I* did."

Warrick sighed, turning his head to say something back at him but refraining. Tongue in cheek, he began again, "Your *cunning* son Lartham found her wandering on the western sward. She asked for an audience with you, Uncle."

"I wandered not but sought you out intentionally, to bring news of the war," Chasmira objected. "I am—"

"I know who you are," a voice rumbling out of the fire and darkness cut her off. "Chasmira… Argolvrecht's pet witch."

She fumbled the words she was about to speak.

A face and a pair of folded hands appeared out of the darkness as Lord Maram leaned forward to get a better look at her. The firelight flickered across his wrinkled flesh, which was tough and gnarled as olivewood. Upon his finger was a black and gold signet ring that glistened in the darkness. He stared through her condemningly. His hazy blue eyes twinkled faintly under the shadow of his brow, like a predator watching its prey from the shadows.

"And you are here to deliver the news that my impetuous brother is quite dead, are you not? Bewitched into walking off a ledge or sleeping facedown in his bath?"

By now Chasmira had abandoned her introduction and simply stood back, blinking at the patriarch. "Do you mean to imply that I somehow instrumented your brother's death?"

Lord Maram sat back a bit, and his eyes vanished under his heavy brow. "So I was right. He *is* dead."

"If it eases your suspicions, he died in battle. As did the Magnate."

"Well, of course he did!" Maram pounded his fist on the armrest. "That idiot Argolvrecht had dug his own grave already, keeping a magical harlot under his roof. You think me a damned fool? Why else would a man as powerful as Argolvrecht take a viper into his bosom except he thought her venom could be useful? Your very words are poison, witch. Your counsel probably guided him right to his doom, and it took my brother with him."

She grimaced. Her counsel was *supposed* to guide him to his doom. She had stirred him up with fantastic dark prophecies about the Mad Prince Mirikinin and the chaos his descendants would spread upon the world. Not all of it was fantasy, however. The Angelic Nandrzael pointed out many dark omens about the Mad Prince's wrath that made him the perfect tool with which to destroy Dimol Gol.

Warrick's shoulders rose and fell with tense breaths, restraining his emotions. Chasmira saw him blinking away angry tears.

She folded her hands and made sure her next words carried

nothing but the somberest respect. "To be quite honest, my lord Maram, Dimol Gol's destruction was fated. Mirikinin's death was not. Every crystal gazing, every rune reading, every moon ceremony from new to full… None of them showed so much as a hair of your brother's head lost."

"Then why did Argolvrecht not relent?" Mirikinin's son Warrick finally turned and said, looking down at her with reddened eyes. "If he and his kingdom were doomed—if you told him this—why did he fight against my father?"

"Because by then, both men had exchanged insults and the corpses of their scouts. Words cannot be taken back after they have been spoken, blood cannot be poured back after it has been spilled, and revenge cannot be uprooted once it has taken hold."

"You were his dark seer. You were his counselor," Warrick rumbled like a volcano.

"And my counsel was only heeded so long as it agreed with him."

"Spare us your lies!" Lord Maram stood from the stone dais in anger. His dark wrinkles deepened further in a scowl. "Even if Argolvrecht scorned your warnings and went to his doom, you have not explained why my brother is dead when all your divination said he would live."

She fought with her words for just a moment. "All I can surmise, my lord, is that some people are bigger than fate can control. Argolvrecht was destined to die, and in his wrath he played into destiny's hand. Prince Mirikinin was destined to triumph, but in his wrath he cut off destiny's fingers."

This answer did not satisfy Warrick. "You served the man who killed my father. The very fact you escaped without a scratch while his body is rotting on a battlefield somewhere, mocks us." He closed his huge hand around her wrist and drew his dagger with his other hand. "Destiny is not the only thing losing fingers today."

Enough was enough. From within Chasmira rose a fire that blazed brightly in her eyes. Warrick fell backward in surprise, and his dagger clattered on the stone floor.

"Warrick!" shouted Lart. The chain slipped from his hand. His hellishund bounded forward with jaws wide open to tear her apart.

Eyes still ablaze, she stared at the dog and pointed toward the floor. "*Obey*."

The walls of the audience chamber shook with a low bass tone. The charging hellishund stopped short. It grunted, sat down, and panted happily up at her.

Chasmira then fixed her fiery gaze upon Lord Maram. Her voice echoed in the harsh silence of the chamber. "I came here in hopes I could find asylum, and to bring the news of your late brother with compassion, not with scorn. However I see that you, like he, look only to make enemies. May I say that you needn't try so hard? Many enemies are ready to rise against you in the coming months, but make no mistake—" The flames in her eyes died down to a red glow like embers. "I am not an enemy you wish to make."

With that, she turned her back on Lord Maram and walked past the hellishund and its trembling owner.

"You said many enemies will rise against us," Maram called after her, his grating voice echoing in the chamber. "Who?"

Her fingers touched the edge of the doorway. The stone was neither warm nor cold to the touch. One step away from leaving the room, she paused there.

"Who?" he asked again.

She drew in a long, slow breath. "Your Mad Prince Mirikinin was feared throughout these lands for his unrelenting wrath and unforgiving heart. A man who tamed the savage ironwolves and turned them into his personal warbeasts. A man no one dared cross, save for a power-hungry magnate who now lies in pieces. Now, your Mad Prince is gone, and his kingdom no longer stands. It bows, waiting for the final stroke."

"It bows to no one!" Warrick cried.

"Oh, but it does. It awaits a merciful end from an eager lord's blade."

"An eager lord?" Lord Maram stood.

Warrick also rose to his feet, angrily refusing his cousin Lart's help. "What lord is so haughty to think they can threaten us while we have not even begun to grieve? The lords of Whiteshore? Farholdt? Who?"

The sorceress turned back to face them. "So now you want the venom from the magnate's viper?"

Lord Maram's cold stare could be felt across the chamber. At last he answered, "He had use for it. So do I. If it is asylum you seek, you may have it here in the House of Mirikinin."

Warrick protested angrily but quickly fell silent as his uncle lifted a hand. He glowered at the sorceress.

Maram leaned forward. "Now tell me, viper, what city's lord so eagerly imagines such evil against us?"

She scowled to stifle her urge to smile. "The Guardian City…"

Warrick's fists tightened.

"...Argismora."

CHAPTER 4

A single jade streak sliced through billowing cloudbanks, leaving a trail like a dew-kissed spiderweb in the golden light. An Angelic, reborn from the undying power of the stars, moved with the greatest speed through the highest heaven.

He is waiting.

Below lay the vast sea and the yawning bays of the wildlands, so far below that forests were as patches of moss. Such was the view from Stornheime, the celestial realm, home to the race that watched mortal life take its first wobbling steps.

He is waiting.

Nandrzael's crystalline wings left long vapor trails in the cold air as she hurled herself past tremendous glittering pillars and great walls of dark cloud. As the mortal world was made of solid land and sinking seas, even so the celestial world was made of solid clouds and sinking clouds. It was upon these islands of solid cloud, that shimmered like topaz stone with fiery orange and purest blue, that the Angelics built their fantastic estates.

Greatest among these was the sanctum of Oczandarys, the mightiest of all Angelics. Nandrzael's heart raced at the mere thought of him as she approached the sanctum. Oczandarys was one of the eldest Angelics, a generation of immortals created by the gods' own hands. For his great power, age, and influence, he was considered by many to be the ruler of Stornheime and the Angelics but this could not be true, for the Angelics have no ruler as mortals do. Still, there were Angelics who bowed the knee to him, insisting that he was a prince among them, even if he had no throne.

The chamber was immense, bordered with pillars eighty feet in height, and all of the purest white cloudstone. Beyond the pillars was Stornheime in all its splendor and unspeakable majesty.

"Is your task fulfilled?" His voice filled the hall like the sound of a waterfall when he spoke. It sent chills through Nandrzael's neck.

"Dimol Gol has been destroyed. They are little more than a scar left upon the earth. That accursed kingdom is no more."

Oczandarys turned. The sound of his great black wings sent a rush that echoed through the chamber. She clenched her teeth. Goosebumps rose across her skin in a wave from head to foot. She bit back against both excitement and dread.

He approached her slowly, her heart pounding more with every step closer he came. His deeply-muscled body shone with the brilliance of polished bronze. She could not look away from his eyes, from their glowing golden hue. A taut smile appeared on his face.

"Well done, Nandrzael. Aforetime, the mindglass showed me a future land ravaged by war, stained as red as the armor of Dimol Gol's warriors. Were I to gaze into the mindglass again… Were I to focus it upon the threads of time… what future would it show me? The lords of Whiteshore, Farholdt, and Argismora supping together? Clerics bowed in prayer at my Oracle at Himmelhoyd?"

Nandrzael tried to speak but could not force any word from her mouth. She could not make herself lie to him.

His smile fell. "Or will I see fire, Nandrzael? Will I see the blood of young and old pooled like rainwater after a storm? Will I see cities in ruin and hear their aching songs of lament rising up to mine ears?"

"It wasn't my fault!"

She bit her tongue as soon as the words left her mouth. Even bowing her head down, she could feel the intensity of Oczandarys' golden glare. She did not have to meet it.

With unfathomable speed, a single footstep brought him looming over her. He bent at the waist, slowly, lowering his face toward where she stared down at the perfect white floor.

"It wasn't your fault?" he echoed. "I showed *you* a glimpse of the centuries ahead. I pointed *you* to the origin—the very fault line—of a dark future. I told *you* the name of the king that must die. I placed death and life in *your* hands. So tell me, Nandrzael, whose fault is it?"

"The sorceress Chasmira," she spouted bitterly.

"Oh, the sorceress' fault. And who was it that chose her as *your* pawn?"

"She was the most reasonable choice—"

"No, she was the easiest choice!" His voice echoed like a church bell in the chamber. Nandrzael stood up straight immediately, unable to look away from him any longer. "The sorceress stood at Argolvrecht's right hand, giving him counsel day and night. An obvious choice, for you simply looked at where you would have wanted to stand and found *her* standing there. And so the fault is yours. She simply committed the folly in your stead.

Argolvrecht alone should have died. Now all the land will die with him."

Tears welled in Nandrzael's eyes, but she restrained them. She folded her hands at her waist sullenly, her fingers clenched so tightly the knuckles turned white. "If so great was the importance of this, why did you not just kill him yourself?"

"You know full well why not." Oczandarys spread his great wings and lifted off the ground. Carved into the domed ceiling were ancient murals. This one depicted warriors of all mortal races: Humans, Dwarven, Ogres, Cloven, Beastkin, Herdsmen, and many others. Among them were Angelics. She recognized the features and faces of some, including the eminent prince hovering in the air beside this intricate artwork.

"In the last age, all the world—Grimmgard—faced annihilation. Chaos itself descended from beyond the stars. Churning, gnawing, screaming Chaos," he said. The light that glowed from Oczandarys' brilliant bronze body illuminated the next section of the mural. Facing the mortal warriors was what appeared at first to be a storm cloud. The longer she gazed upon it, the details of the cloud appeared to be a tangle of horrific limbs, eyes, and horns. Studying it in awe, Nandrzael tilted her head, and with the change in perspective the cloud now appeared to be a raging fire.

"Chaos would have claimed and consumed the world as we know it. Lifekind knelt at the Oracles, beseeching us for help. They wept and begged and made vows. I heard every one of them." Oczandarys bowed his head. Nandrzael wondered if the mighty prince could still remember every sobbing word that rose into the heavens, even hundreds of years later.

"You commanded the heavens to answer," she said. "And it answered with holy war against this irrational evil. You rallied lifekind to battle! You held back Chaos until finally you could banish it from entering our sky and defiling their earth, ever again."

"Until..." Oczandarys lifted a finger and then turned in the air to face her. Slowly descending, he continued, "Until Chaos began to rise in the hearts of lifekind themselves. You see, I could not hear it clearly until the din of war had subsided, a peaceful stillness prevailed again, and these mortals—bored with such stillness—began to rob and betray and murder one another. And deep within the hearts of mortals I began to discern the noise of churning, gnawing, screaming Chaos again. We had not defeated it. We had preserved it, and all the while we lost brothers and sisters in that holy war... raising sword to save mere mortal lives."

The two Angelics stood so close now, she could feel the radiant heat from his bare chest near her face as she gazed up at him. She wanted to put her hand out and touch his gleaming skin. She wanted him to touch hers.

Her lips parted breathlessly as he leaned in closer.

His words were like rumbling thunder. "We will *never* make that mistake again."

All she wanted was to kiss him.

"Thus our people are forbidden to touch lifekind again with our own hands, to kill or to save. If they wish to deceive, defile, and destroy each other, they will do so for our purposes."

"Even if it means thousands must die?"

With a dour look, he simply stepped past her. "If it means millions will live. Thus it must be, and thus it has been for nearly three hundred years."

Nandrzael closed her eyes and softly panted for breath. Then, she felt his radiance again, glowing against her back.

"I trusted you with this," he crooned. "You were created to take the place of those we lost, to help make things right. If you cannot correct your error—"

She whirled about to face him. "I can. I can and I will. You will see, mighty prince."

"Will I?"

"You will. When next I bid you gaze into the mindglass and behold the threads of time, you will see peace restored to those lands. You will see a future crafted by order's design instead of Chaos' hunger. And yes, there will be prayer in the Oracle at Himmelhoyd. Prayers of praise to *you.*"

Oczandarys scowled, unimpressed. "I desire neither praise nor lamentation from mortal lips."

"What *do* you desire then?" she asked eagerly.

He strode to the circle of tall-backed white chairs in the chamber and sat down. His black wings folded back, but their long tips yet dragged across the floor at his feet.

"I desire peace… and *quiet.*"

Nandrzael bowed down low, her crystalline wings spread wide. Without another word or even a look to him, she quietly turned and flew between the great pillars of Oczandarys' sanctuary, out into the open sky.

CHAPTER 5

Chasmira woke to the sound of rain outside her window. She did not want to move. After trudging for a day and a half through bogs, forests, and fields, her aching body made its plea to remain in bed a while longer. She found no argument and agreed the plea was reasonable.

She turned on her side to watch the rain with her half-open eyes. It pattered on the edge of the window, a narrow rectangle carved out of the dark castle stone.

Years ago, the sound of rain meant sleepless nights alone trying to patch holes in the roof of her parents' house. Where she could not patch it, she would put a pail underneath to catch the water. Nights spent alone, cold, and miserable in a house where she felt she did not belong anymore. An invader in a place that she used to call her home.

She pulled the blankets up a little more, over her chin and up to her lips.

That place was far away and long ago. It was unworthy of remembrance.

At this moment she thought back on Hakon. She wished he was here, and the feeling surprised her. Until now, she knew not what it was about his absence that hurt so much. All he did was harangue her about her past, about the reasons behind every move she made. Chasmira had been lonely her entire life. But in the bog with Hakon, she felt *seen* at last… uncomfortably seen, but seen nonetheless. He was unbothered by her power, by her past. All he wanted was honesty, and all he offered was safety.

She was not a little girl in a cold, leaky, lonely house anymore. She was *now* a guest in a great fortress of stone and warm fires, and yet the last thing she felt was *safe*.

After she dangled the threat of new enemies last night, Lord Maram was quite hospitable. He surely valued her divination—among her other sorcerous abilities—but she knew he did not value her life. As with other warlords she had served in the past, she was merely *useful* to him. Useful but not indispensable. He had given her a room, a comfortable bed, and some dinner, but those things could easily be exchanged for a cold dungeon or a burning pyre once her usefulness ended.

Chasmira pushed away the covers and sighed, arm draped off the side of the bed. Restless thoughts made for poor rest, no matter how tired her body was. Changing into her dress and lacing her leather bodice, she ventured out of the room and began to explore the House of Mirikinin.

The smell of food lured her through the halls. It grew stronger until it led her into a dining room with a black marble table. At the back of the room was a curtained doorway that led back to the kitchen.

At the far end of the marble table sat Lart, shoving boiled eggs and chunks of pork into his mouth with such dedication that he did not even take notice of her. Beside him on the floor, his pet hellishund lay gnawing on a bone. The dog's large ears perked up as Chasmira appeared in the doorway.

She clasped her hands behind her back and entered softly.

A hoarse bark from the dog made Lart jump, nearly overturning his plate. The man nervously gripped his eating knife and stood. He had good reason to be afraid of her.

"Good morning," she offered.

"Mornin'."

The two of them stood still, staring, for a few long moments.

"The fire and such was just for show last night," she laughed, swaying from foot to foot. "You know, make the big man sweat..."

Lart smirked. "You nearly made Warrick piss himself."

"You couldn't blame me for being a bit miffed. To think I came all that way, and on foot too, just to be treated that badly by him and by your Lord Maram."

"Father was just upset, I think. Prolly upset about Uncle Mirik," he shrugged, fumbling the knife a little.

"That is quite understandable, and a lady never holds grudges. I will forgive you."

His crooked smile had a few gaps in the teeth. "You will?"

"Of course."

"No more fire?"

"No more fire."

Lart wiped his nose, sat back down, and resumed eating breakfast. "Listen, I don't know what you did to ol' Terror here to make him like you so good. He don't even follow *my* commands like that."

Terror sat and panted happily, thumping his stubby tail against the floor.

"You drag him around on the end of a chain," Chasmira scolded as she patted Terror's wrinkly head. "Anyone treated like that would fight you every step of the way."

"I couldn't rightly let him off it. He'd rip people's faces off!"

She squinted and smiled at him. "So you say, and so you keep saying as you strut about with a face-ripping beast on the end of your chain. Makes you *very* intimidating."

"Damn right it does," Lart laughed. He picked up a black bottle, poured a cup of frothy beer, and gave it a shove down the table in her direction.

She lifted it to her lips and raised her brows after smelling it. The drink was rich, sweet, and full-bodied. "Oh, a maple stout! How unexpected!"

"Says the most unexpected thing to walk into this house in years."

"I'll take that as a compliment, dear," raising the cup.

"S'not meant to be one." Grumbling, he resumed digging into his food.

"First you pour me a drink, and now you sweet-talk me?" She reached for a boiled egg. "Next we'll be sharing breakfast off the same trencher."

Lart slapped her hand away. "Hands off!"

Chasmira was preparing to deliver a scolding about getting between a lady and her food when suddenly Terror stood up and backed under the table with a whine. His sensitive ears flattened back on his head.

There was a crash as Warrick entered. He slammed the door behind him and stormed in. The huge man glared briefly at the two at the table, huffing disapprovingly.

"Morning poorly risen?" Lart ventured.

"Does it *seem* a good morning to you?" Warrick thundered. He cast a withering glare at Chasmira, the witch who had brought tidings of his father's death.

"Sorry, Warrick. I just asked."

"Well, you have your answer. Swallow it down with another helping of pig meat and stupidity, why don't you?"

"Sit and have a drink," Lart offered.

Warrick trundled up, grabbed the beer bottle, and pitched it across the room.

Lart rose inches from his chair, but then thought it wiser to stay seated and let this storm pass. A storm named Warrick.

"My father is dead, you dumb festering boil. Dead. You've not a care what it means for me. Not you, son of the reigning patriarch." He fumed like a boiling pot running over everything.

"Warrick, not in front of her."

The son of Mirikinin did not even look at Chasmira. He trembled with restrained emotion and said nothing more before he rumbled out of the room.

She let out her held breath.

"He's not always like that," Lart said.

"I hope not."

"Grief will do things to a man, y'know."

"It will do things to anyone," she countered.

"It's doing a number on Warrick. But he'll get over it. He'll probably give in to drink by tomorrow, after he's through raging and breaking everything in sight."

"And he won't rage and break things after drinking?"

"Oh he will. But his aim will be much worse," Lart said, again smirking boyishly.

Chasmira laughed. With the tension in the room finally gone, she sat down and pulled over her cup of maple stout. "Prince Mirikinin had three sons, did he not?"

"I wish he'd stopped after Warrick."

"I would know all the members of this great house," resting her chin on her fist.

"Right, so Uncle Mirikinin's got three boys. Warrick you've met, and then there's Wilvrey and Luthian."

"Wilvrey? Not the same Wilvrey the Serpent?"

Lart raised his brows and downed another mouthful of beer. "Aye, the same. Wil's just like his father: a warrior, mad and bloodthirsty as a Scarrlok with rabies."

"The Eastern Slither of Wilvrey the Serpent is a legend of yesteryear. Thousands were left dead in the Battle of Eppenhorn. Who knew that Wilvrey was The Mad Prince's son?"

"Anyone who survived," Lart explained between bites of egg and pork. "Ol' Wil's always been jealous of Warrick being the firstborn. Warrick's only been the faithful steward at home. He keeps the farmhands in line and watches the fields from seed to harvest. Wil joined the *koga*—the warband—and fought his way up through the ranks. Wanted to earn it, he said, to prove himself. So he carved himself a name in the flesh of his father's enemies."

"Middle child behavior, surely."

"Surely," clinking cups with her.

Chasmira swallowed too big a gulp of beer as a thought occurred to her. "Wait. Wilvrey was sent to Dimol Gol to fight the Magnate? Because hardly a man survived…"

"No." Lart shook his head and set his empty cup down. "He

stayed out east in Eppenhorn to build a new citadel after tearing their old one down. He ain't come home since. Just wait till he does. If you think Warrick is taking Uncle Mirik's death badly... well, let's just say we might need to lock ol' Wilvrey in Terror's cage for a few moons."

Terror perked his ears and whimpered curiously at his master.

Lart chuckled and rubbed the hellishund's head. "What's the matter, boy? You don't want to bunk up with Cousin Wilvrey?"

"Of course he doesn't," Chasmira agreed, bending over to tug on Terror's ear and scratch his chin. "Who wants to be in a cage? Cages are for madmen and monsters, and I've never met a more cool-headed gentleman in my life than you, Terror."

"Aye, damn right. He's got better manners than me now."

"I'd wager they've always been better than yours, Lart."

Lart spit on the floor and huffed. "Well if it's a stuffy buck what entices you, then you'll be tickled to meet Luthian. He's always got his nose in his books, avoiding people like he's a shadow on a library wall."

"You have a library here?" She sat up straighter, eyes wide.

He rolled his eyes. "Knew it. You're the kind what likes a man who can read. Ain't it always the way. What? Not happy until you've got a prince of your own?"

She smiled sweetly and sipped the beer, smacking her lips. "I don't need a prince. I don't need anybody."

CHAPTER 6

Chasmira's knees weakened at the earthy scent in the air. She did not realize how much she longed for the smell of books until she stepped into the dark library.

Her last footsteps up the stairway quickened. The library was on the highest level of the House of Mirikinin, but the climb up so many black marble steps was worth it. Surrounding her was a veritable maze of black oakwood shelves, each twenty feet tall and packed with hundreds of precious books. She allowed herself a few long moments to take it all in before entering the literary labyrinth.

It was so quiet, Chasmira became conscious of the sound of her own breathing and the soft clack of her footsteps on the stone floor. She felt like a ghost wandering through a graveyard—the bookshelves like looming mausoleums all around her, filled with dead men's words.

She stepped into a long stripe of daylight that stretched across the face of a bookshelf. Narrow slats in the walls, high up near the ceiling, permitted just a little natural light into the room. There in that beam of sun, she ran her fingertips across the spines of the books and read their faded titles:

Chronicela Cryptea: Inga's Silent War

Following of the White Sunset

Ylfred's Lost Travels

Seventy Dreams, Seventy Souls

Someone cleared their throat behind her, and she jumped.

Whirling around, she immediately saw a young man at a reading desk at the end of the aisle. He glared at her over the top of his book, clearly agitated at the intruder.

Chasmira leaned back against the bumpy row of books behind her and laughed silently, embarrassed at her own surprise. "My word! I'm surprised my ribs aren't bruised from how my heart leapt."

He lowered the book and arched an eyebrow at her. His long, smooth, angular features betrayed his youth in defiance of his heavy brow and stoic glower.

Tucking wild loose hairs back, she composed herself. "I did not even hear you back there."

He blinked slowly and returned to his book. "Hear me reading? *That* would be a talent."

"You must be Luthian."

"So my fame and reputation precede me," he quipped without looking up from the page.

"They do, and the tales I have heard were not an exaggeration."

He glanced up at her with a dry expression. "Oh?"

"Indeed. The myths spoke of wit keener than the sharpest sword and stealth that would make a sabrestag look clumsy as an ox."

"Sabrestags haven't stealth because of their swiftness and

agility. Their stealth is due to their ability to alter the hue and pattern of their fur to match their surroundings, effectively making themselves invisible to approaching prey."

"You've seen one in the wild?"

"Not as such."

"But you've read about them in that book."

"This very book, yes."

"*Jaul's Curiosorum*?"

Shaking his head, he showed her the book cover. "*Pilgrims and Predators*."

"Then you must have read that their antlers, which were once thought to be for mating rituals, are in fact for luring prey. When the sabrestag lies down in the tall grass, its antlers bear an uncanny likeness to the estorberry shrubs that grow in those lands."

"Not bad," he parted with the compliment like a miser parting with a copper coin. "You've read this too?"

"No," with a sigh.

"Seems you could have written it yourself," he complimented her, and then resumed reading with perfect coolness.

She tried, and failed, to repress her smile. Instead she crossed her arms. "How old are you, son of Mirikinin?"

"Sixteen."

"Liar."

"Got me. Seventeen."

"Why fib downward?"

"Upward begs questions."

She chortled, "Such as?"

"Such as why do I not attend to the fields with Warrick? Why have I not already courted and wed? Why have I not even tried to join the koga?"

"Because you don't want to."

Luthian snorted a laugh. "Simple answer but unacceptable."

"Unacceptable to whom? Your uncle, Lord Maram?"

"And to my father."

Chasmira bit back any words that came to her lips. She would naturally respond to youth's gripes about their elders' expectations by reciting a line about living for yourself and not for others, but this was a nuanced moment. A seventeen-year-old boy had just lost his father in a horrific massacre of a war. He was also the third and youngest in his family—surely he would not respond with Warrick's anger to coat over the sorrow and vulnerability.

"Parents have a way of expecting too much from us, of wishing we won't be as *human* as they are," she said.

"I am aware. I see that reflected in Warrick all the time."

"I was under the impression you didn't see much of anyone, squirreled away up here in the closest thing this house has to an attic."

"Oh I saw Warrick recently… or rather, I heard him. He came up here to let me know the outcome of the war with Magnate Argolvrecht. He called to me from the stairs, gave me the report."

"What did you say to him?"

"What's there to say?" Luthian answered tersely, looking into his book to avoid her eyes.

Chasmira sighed. "I am sorry, Luthian. I am sorry for all of you."

He stared into the book for what felt like several long minutes before forcing himself to look up at her. His eyes were the dark troubled blue of a stormy sea. It reminded her of the eyes of his uncle Lord Maram, but while Maram's gaze was bleached with the coldness and hardness of his soul, Luthian's was vibrant and deep.

"Thank you for saying that," Luthian said. "I know that you are just the bearer of the bad news, despite being so evil spoken of."

"Ooooh, 'evil spoken of' you say?" Chasmira tittered with excitement, biting her lip and sitting on the writing table. "A lady loves a bit of good gossip to tickle the ears, especially when it's about her."

Luthian put the book down and eagerly shared. "I heard Uncle Maram just fuming last night. He thinks you're going to turn him into a snake in the middle of the night."

"A snake? Oh, he doesn't need my help there. He's practically slithering already. All he needs is his arms cut off, and it doesn't take enchanting to do that."

"Enchanting… So you *are* a witch, like he says?"

She clicked her tongue. "I'm not a witch. I'm a sorcerer."

"Where lies the difference?"

"The difference is that a witch seeks out dark forces to make alliance with them. A sorcerer simply learns to use the powers that fate has gifted to her."

"Why then does Uncle call you a witch?"

"Because fate gifted to me a terrible power older than the earth beneath us or the stars above us."

Luthian's blue eyes widened. "Chaos…"

Chasmira nodded. "A power and presence that predates all there is and all we know."

"I've read about it. In the journals of Ædant Refactus, he speaks of Chaos as 'an infernal limitlessness, a bottomless well of self-destruction and self-recreation.' In one journal he said he believed that all mortal things have a tiny spark of this infernal devilry inside of them. I think he may be right. How else does one explain the mortal urge to destroy in fits of passion?"

"My my, Luthian, it is no wonder to me now why you and Warrick barely talk. I'm not sure the brute would understand more than three words of that."

He smiled and looked down, his bony cheeks flushing with color. "But am I right?"

"To be quite honest with you, I have never sat and pondered such things. It is one thing to observe it and another thing to wield it for yourself."

"So then, what does it feel like to you?"

She answered before he even finished the last word, as if all she needed was an opportunity to say it. "It feels precisely as he wrote: what was once a tiny spark turned fully into a roaring flame. At first the flame caught on everything and burned some very precious things, but since then I have learned to tame it… use it… summon it… and then command it."

"And this power is hated, which makes you hated too," he prompted, listening intently.

"No, it is not hated, it is *feared*. Your Uncle was fuming angry about something I hadn't done, because he was simply afraid of what I might do. People fear the unknown, the strange. People fear what they cannot control, and so they hide their fear beneath anger. That is why Chaos sorcerers are hunted down in many lands. They fear what we may do. They fear our—what did your Ædant call it?—oh, our infernal limitlessness. So we must always be guarded and wary."

"But not so wary as to hear my loud reading behind you."

"No, I suppose not," she laughed and then retorted, "Need I be more wary around you?"

His dry aloofness finally cracked into a mischievous smile. "The stranger need not be wary in strange company."

"Thank you, Luthian. I'm glad to have met you, and to find someone who welcomes my strangeness. You will let me know what sort of creature your uncle next dreads to become, won't you?"

"You can count on me."

ψ

The change from summer to autumn mixed the best of both seasons. The warm hazy sunlight quietly debated with the slight chill that crept into the wind. Some trees already had brilliant splashes of red and yellow in their crowns, making the green of the surrounding flora seem all the more like jealousy.

Nothing complimented this change better than the firstfruits of the harvest. That afternoon, Chasmira decided to explore the east fields and discovered a rather extensive apple orchard. Swiping a fresh pick out of one of the many bushels laid by the farmhands, she crossed the field and climbed over the roundpole fence with the apple held in her teeth. She savored a big bite of the crisp, juicy fruit as she walked through fields of golden oats.

Argolvrecht's domain was nothing like this. In the midst of three growling mountains stood his castle Dimol Gol, half-buried in treacherous snow, half cloaked in poisonous volcanic fumes. No glistening fields, no sprawling orchards, no quiet libraries.

I like it much better here.

Walking to the end of the oat field, she clambered over the fence and noticed that beyond it, the ground dropped down into a deep gulch. The gulch was nearly dry except for a brook that still persisted through the rutted riverbed. She noticed several men at the bottom, including Warrick and Lart, standing at the mouth of a cave and peering inside it. In front of the cave was an enclosure large enough to be a horse corral, made of iron stakes and bars. *What are they doing down there?* Stepping carefully, she made her way down the rocky hill to see up close.

"Warrick, someone's come to join us," Lart called.

The big man grumbled and stomped over in her direction. "Go back to the house. This is no place for women."

"Oh, but even women need sunlight and fresh air once in a while, Warrick. Like potted plants, except we talk sometimes and not all plants do."

"What are you even doing here?" he huffed.

"Well, as does a potted plant, I started to wither in the sun so I thought I'd come down for a drink of water!"

Lart and a few of the farmhands laughed.

Warrick rolled his eyes and growled like a bear. "Fine. Stay here but stay out of the way." He turned away and called out, "Lart! Have Terror bring them out now!"

Lart whispered a command to the hellishund, which then let out a long bay that echoed into the grotto. Moments later, three large creatures rushed out of the cave entrance and into the enclosure, sliding to a stop on the pebbly ground. They were wolves, but no ordinary wolves. These were much larger, with long, pale quills all over their bodies from snout to tail instead of fur. When the sunlight caught them just right, the quills gleamed like iron daggers.

"Ironwolves. Very impressive beasts," she complimented them.

"They make up a substantial amount of the koga," Lart explained. "We breed them here in their natural habitat and then train them for war. They'll bring down a horse and its rider in seconds."

"Why the iron fence? Afraid of them?"

Warrick interrupted, "It is because the ironwolf does not like to stay settled in one place. A pack may travel forty miles in a single day. Here in their pens, they grow restless day after day, unable to hunt and roam as they please. This restlessness keeps them agitated, fierce, and hungry."

"Your domestication of so vicious a beast is even more impressive."

"Domesticated? Ha! The ironwolf cannot be tamed and trained by humans. It neither fears nor trusts us."

Chasmira crossed her arms, awaiting his enlightenment.

Warrick obliged. "Typically, a pack of ironwolves is led by the patriarch, which prowls its territory to drive away intruders and keep the pack safe. We kill males that exhibit patriarchal behaviors at middle age, or about five years old."

"What becomes of the pack then?"

"In the wild, ironwolves will find and ingratiate themselves to a lone hellishund, usually bribing it with a fresh kill to establish their submission. They need him to find new caves to sleep in every night and also alert them to dangers. The hellishund adopts them and teaches them commands so that he may herd them, warn them, call them to attack prey, and so on."

Chasmira pursed her lips. "You could not tame the ironwolf, so you domesticated the beast that has already tamed them for himself. Even more impressive than I first said."

Warrick nodded and began to turn away.

"There is just one lingering question. You repeatedly said 'he' in reference to the hellishund. Must it be a male that takes over the pack?"

Warrick fumbled with his words at first. "Quite honestly, I have never seen a she-wolf doing such a thing, although I have no doubt that she could."

"What a wonder that'd be," Chasmira grinned, taking a big bite of delicious apple.

CHAPTER 7

The next day had scarcely dawned before Chasmira was summoned back to Lord Maram's audience chamber. Warrick was already there, hands clasped at his waist as he awaited the patriarch.

Maram laced his fingers and leaned forward. "I have weighed your words of warning and have decided the threat of Argismora attacking us is too great to ignore. However, greater yet is the threat of antagonizing them if you are misleading us, witch. You gave counsel to Magnate Argolvrecht and he now lies in bloody shreds."

Chasmira stared back at the "I assure you that my word is true. The Prefect of Argismora rules as the heavens bid him. The heavens will turn his sword against you."

Maram's lips curled back in a snarl. "You are but words until I see warriors assembled and banners raised."

"So send scouts to Argismora," Warrick interjected. "Let others be your eyes and ears, Uncle."

Lord Maram drummed his gnarled fingers on the stone armrest of his dais. "Your father's best scouts were lost at Dimol Gol, and there is not enough gold in all the world to pay a huntsman to spy the Guardian City for us. Therefore, Warrick, you will go and scout it yourself."

Warrick's mouth dropped open. "Me? Why me?"

"Have I not given you reasons already? Besides, they do not know you. In all your years you have remained here, gracing our land with your keen oversight."

"I agree it is cunning, but I am neither warrior nor scout."

"This task demands not stealth, but subtlety. If your ears can hear murmuring, they can hear treachery. If your eyes can count swine, they can count warriors."

Warrick hesitated a moment longer. He clearly wanted to argue, but had no words to do so. Instead, he nodded his agreement.

"And take her with you," Maram added.

"What?"

Chasmira was equally shocked at this command.

Maram merely arched his wrinkled brow. "You cannot see the benefit in having a living weapon sauntering beside you? Lart's hellishund has enough sense not to harm her. Perchance the men of Argismora have at least as much sense as that stupid dog."

Warrick stammered. "But what am I to do with her?"

Lord Maram pounded his fist on the armrest. "Damn it, Warrick, do what any man does with a woman! Keep her on your arm and pretend to care about whatever she talks about. And for Naru's sake don't *buy* her anything!"

"She has the fires of Chaos burning inside her," Warrick said through grit teeth. "You imagine that will not attract attention?"

"I *imagine* that a fire has covered many a spy's escape before," The patriarch replied with stone coldness. "Do as I say."

Chasmira felt a lump in her throat. It would be easy enough

for Warrick to expose her as a sorceress of Chaos. Just publicly accusing her would raise a mob demanding she be put to death. She raised her eyes to meet Lord Maram's—to discern anything about his intentions—but under the shadow of his brow he was as dark and expressionless as the black stone walls around him. Did he truly believe her but needed to verify it first? Or was he simply looking for a way to get her to willingly leave the castle so he could be rid of her?

Warrick sighed, "As you say, Lord Maram." He bowed his head reverently.

ψ

"So, what do you know of Argismora?"

Warrick rode in silence, ignoring her.

She cleared her throat loudly. "Argismora: nicknamed 'The Guardian City' not only for its towering walls, but because it was originally built around the Oracle of Ædant Aculus five hundred years ago. I'll bet you're just itching to know why."

Warrick said nothing.

"Because the Ædant opened the Oracle's doors to refugees from all lands, whomsoever needed a warm fire and shelter. It mattered not whether it was for a night or a season. When the chapel was full, the yard became a camp. The camp became a farm. The farm became a village. The village became a city… a city of safety."

"The Guardian City, I get it," Warrick said impatiently.

They rode in silence for a half a minute that felt like half an hour.

"What's an Ædant?" he asked without looking at her.

She laughed, and he shot her a glare that made her horse hesitate a step. Instantly she regretted it, for she had forgotten Warrick was foreman of his father's farm. He was clearly not as book-learned as his younger brother Luthian or as well-traveled as Chasmira.

She composed an apologetic smile. "Clerics of the Ædant religion, an old faith from the previous age… but a faith still followed by many living in the very cradle of Human civilization."

"The golden kingdom," Warrick muttered.

"Yes. They believe that the Makergods are nameless and benevolent, and that They only desire for mortals to show forth the same benevolence."

This time Warrick was the one who laughed, a dry sardonic laugh. "Easy for them to say."

Indeed, the northerners forsook these old beliefs long ago. They had migrated across badlands infested with plagues and monsters, and had settled in a land even colder and harsher. These hardships drove the tenets of the Ædant faith out of them. They named the Makergods to curse them or thank them: Tyor the god of necessity, Soth the god of war, and Naru the god of mirth. While the Ædants believed the Makergods to watch from a distance like loving parents, the northerners believed that Makergods hunched over the mortal world, gambling over whose will would be honored most. Sacrifice honored Tyor. Conquest honored Soth. Mischief honored Naru. All part of a game.

She continued, "The Prefect of Argismora follows the old faith of the Ædants. Whatever word descends from the heavens to the keepers of the Oracle, he will follow."

Warrick scoffed. "You believe the heavens speak to them?"

"You do not believe in Angelics?" she said. The Angelic Nandrzael was the patron of Argismora and had descended into the Oracle many times before. She had warned them of plague, murrain, and famine far in advance to shield them from catastrophe.

"I believe only what I have seen," he said.

Chasmira opened her mouth to speak but withheld. Maybe it was for the best that Warrick was skeptical. It would be easier to cast doubt on the Prefect if Warrick believed him to be a superstitious fool. She smiled politely. "Well, what matters is that the people of Argismora believe in them. The clerics could tell the Prefect anything, and he would believe it if they said it was received from a divine messenger."

Their horses squealed and stopped.

Both at once Warrick and Chasmira noticed the large hunched creature at the corner where the dirt path connected to the main road. Its flesh looked grey as mountain stone and just as strong. Even sitting down, it was eye-to-eye with their horses. Its heavy brow and jutting jaw were framed with flowing black braids.

"Ogre," Chasmira whispered.

"Perchance he merely rests and means no ill to passersby."

"Perchance. Carefully now."

The crossroad was surrounded by thick shrubbery, tree stumps, and tall grass on all sides. Even if the horses could be made to walk through it, there was no sure footing for them.

Chasmira dismounted her horse, leaving the reins in Warrick's hands. The Ogre sat on a log, puffing an enormous pipe. His arms were wrapped in leather mail and topped with round pauldrons upon his shoulders. The armor was marked with white scrapes and scratches, clearly from horns and claws. Little wonder, for no one would bother laying a blade to an Ogre. It is folly to attack with mere swords a creature that could easily tear an ox in two.

"Excuse me," Chasmira began cautiously, clearing her throat. "Good morning."

The Ogre's pipe bowl glowed deep red, and strands of smoke rose from the corners of his mouth. His narrow, beady eyes turned to her but he said nothing.

The woman knew Ogres were not be underestimated, physically or otherwise. While many were brutish as they were brutal, others were very cunning. Either he wished to simply smoke his pipe in peace, or he—unarmed and unassuming—lured antagonists to their doom.

"I pray you, Master Ogre, where does this road lead?"

"To many place," the Ogre mumbled.

"Would you happen to know if Argismora is one of them?"

"Morth not like big cities. Noisy, crowded."

The Ogre's tone was mixed with both annoyance and apathy, which Chasmira weighed mentally to see if one was greater than the other. On her back she carried the iron staff. She could use it if she had to, but she hoped with everything in her it would not come to that. The staff's power could disintegrate a man, but at best it would only wound and anger the Ogre. After using it once, the staff required time to cool down. Otherwise, it could melt or explode from the great power channeled through it.

Chasmira approached a step closer. "Understandable, Morth... I assume that is your name?" she proceeded diplomatically.

The Ogre nodded slowly, with the same grim side-eye at her.

"We simply wish to be sure of the way. There are opportunities for work and trading in Argismora, but we have never been there before."

"You leave too late." The leaves in the pipe bowl crackled and glowed bright red.

She blinked a few times. "Too late? Too late for what?"

"Sunset." Swirling smoke from the corners of his mouth punctuated his answer.

"I don't understand. What happens at sunset?"

"Night time," Morth replied. "You cannot make campfire then."

"No campfire? Why not?"

The Ogre looked away from her and toward the northern horizon. "The Eyes in the Night will find you. Better to leave tomorrow, at dawn."

Chasmira bit her lip. It had been difficult enough to convince Lord Maram that Argismora was a threat based on her vague, ominous prophecy. If they returned now and explained they were going to wait for an earlier start tomorrow to avoid hungry demons of Ogre folklore, Maram would surely throw her out right then and there.

"Many thanks for the words of warning," she said. "Our journey is urgent, however. We have a place to lodge come sunset, provided we may pass by without further delay. May we pass?"

The Ogre sighed so heavily, the ground beneath Chasmira's feet rumbled. He took the pipe from his mouth, laid down on his back, and shut his eyes.

She looked back at Warrick and the horses, who all seemed much more at ease while Morth feigned sleep. She motioned for them to pass by, and they did so quietly.

"Thank you," she whispered. She then hurried over to mount her horse and ride on northward.

The Ogre sat up and watched them depart. A wave moved across the tall grass in the cold wind, and he answered it aloud with a rhyme far older than he himself:

The starlit children always late,
Hurrying, hurrying in the light.
The Eyes of Night lie in wait,
Hobbling, hobbling in the night.

CHAPTER 8

The campfire hissed and crackled as Warrick laid another branch on it.

Chasmira gazed up at the moon. It was just a day or so away from being full. She had noticed its yellow color waxing while she still stood in the court of Magnate Argolvrecht, watching him make preparations for war. Her eyes drifted from the yellow halo to the dark around it as she remembered the war drums and the chants of warriors clad in scarlet…

"Full moon?"

It was a moment before she even acknowledged it was Warrick that spoke to her. She turned around to see him kneeling by the fire and jabbing a branch up at the moon.

"Nearly full," she smiled, looking back to the beautiful moon. "The Children of the Wood call this the 'Honey Moon' due to its golden color. They think it's a sign of bad luck, a time to stay inside and fast. A time for solemn thoughts upon fate and the future, and putting worries to rest."

Warrick chewed on that a moment. "Yes. Good for calving cows," and he went back to laying branches in the fire.

"Very romantic, Warrick. I bet you're an enchanting dancer as well, what with the goats showing you how to spin and kick."

"As if I've time for it," he countered. "My father cared nothing for reveling, strange as it might seem to one such as yourself."

"I might assume your meaning, but say on."

"Your Magnate was given over to spirited drinks, rumors tell. The courts of Dimol Gol are famed for violence and lewdness—sometimes combined," he said, sitting back. "Unless I have heard amiss?"

She laughed and shook her head. "Oh, I wish I could dispel such rumors, but they are true. The Magnate was a wild man. His court was like living in a den of frenzied flengers: pawing, slobbering apes packed so closely together you are practically choking from the heat and the smell."

"Hmm. Hard to envision my father riding into battle against such a foe: war-drunk barbarians, little better than beasts."

Chasmira simply watched as he pondered aloud. The campfire had reached a full blaze now, casting red and orange light upon his face.

"My father cast down King Nelfry Greyflesh in his youth. Cruel bastard, that Greyflesh. His warriors had taken all the fresh rivers in this land. When the people did not do as he wished, he dammed the rivers and made their villages thirst. My father could not let this stand, so he summoned the villagers to war. At first none would join with him, for none believed they could take on the warriors and flying beasts of Greyflesh's host. They called him a madman. A madman," he repeated, chuckling and sniffling. "They ambushed the dams at sunset, when the warriors and their beasts could not see them approaching against the setting sun. They then besieged the fortress by night, and by daybreak old Nelfry Greyflesh was drowned in the cold river water with my father Mirikinin's hands around his neck."

"Truly a madman," Chasmira complimented softly.

"Mad, indeed. My father accomplished much. He built a family and a great house, and he put me in charge of it."

There was something tense, something far from admiration in Warrick's voice. Chasmira could hear it, and her smile wilted a little. "He trusted you. You're his firstborn."

"And now he is gone."

Even the crackle of the campfire seemed to quiet itself somberly.

"You can treasure the time you had with him while he lived."

"Can I?" Warrick said, pained. "What time did I even have with him? A full week maybe, out of the month? And only for supper at that? My father was a man of war. The battlefield was always more important than the farms."

"What? Why, because he entrusted the one to you and not the other?"

"No, of course not. I'm no warrior. I have no place out there."

Chasmira lowered her gaze. "You wanted him at home, with you. And if he had not gone out to fight those war-drunk barbarians..."

Warrick's silence as he stared into the fire was the only answer she needed. She nodded and joined him in watching the leaping flames. Something inside her pushed to get out, to reach him.

"Your father Prince Mirikinin did not prowl the fields because what lay at home mattered little to him, but because it mattered much. You said it yourself that the patriarch ironwolf prowls its territory to drive away intruders and keep its family safe. You cannot imagine how strange men are to me, that their eyes can wander so far and yet their heart still remain at home."

Their eyes met across the campfire.

"The ironwolves also grow restless in their pens," she added. "When they want to hunt in the fields but cannot."

In that next moment, she could imagine Warrick as a young boy. The sadness behind a strong front, watching his father depart after so little time together. She imagined the lines around his eyes betrayed the heavy burden that the eldest child must bear.

He laid back and rolled to his side. "Goodnight."

Her shoulders sagged. The campfire suddenly seemed to do little against the cold she felt. She looked back up to the moon and its honey hue for company.

A time for solemn thoughts upon fate and future, she repeated to herself inside. *See now the reason why you ought to stick to divination and rune readings, idiot.*

ψ

It was midday the next day when they rode into Argismora.

The city hummed with activity. Packs of huntsmen loitered by the alleyways, leering at passing women through clouds of pipesmoke. Merchants shouted out clever rhymes about their wares, one after another as though they were reciting poetry from a stage. Fountains of water drew beggars who sat upon the stone edge with cups in their hands, asking those nearby for any coins they could spare. Women carrying baskets and water pots waited for the horses to pass. They stared up at the riders with eyes as green as forest moss.

Chasmira kept the hood of her traveling coat down over her

head, lest some passerby happen to notice the gleam of fire in her eyes. She could not, however, resist lifting her head to admire one particular sight…

The Oracle of Ædant Aculus was magnificent to behold. Its polished grey stone towers, rising high into the sky, were topped with brass-gilded spires. Even the dull sunlight of the hazy morning shone off the gilded shingles in long bands of light across the city. Winding vines covered in white buds, scaled either side of the huge arched doorway. From the street, Chasmira could see the shine of the marble pillars and brass basins inside the holy landmark.

"Doesn't seem like a city girding itself for war," Warrick grunted.

"Oh, you've seen many?"

"You know what I mean. No warbeasts in sight. No warriors in armor gathering for final farewells."

Chasmira grimaced. Warrick was right: the city was clearly not preparing itself for war. Was she mistaken? Nandrzael's best chance to destroy Mirikinin's land and family was to call upon an entire kingdom that bowed to her.

She pondered why the Angelic had not simply called upon Argismora to destroy Dimol Gol in the first place. Then, she remembered the tremendous host of scarlet-clad warriors that roared from the depths of the Magnate's castle. This city would not have stood a chance. Magnate Argolvrecht would have invaded and would now control *two* strongholds: Dimol Gol in the western peaks and Argismora here in the northern ridgeline.

"Wait here," Warrick said. "I'm going to find the central city tower and see if there is any sort of gathering there. You'd better be right about all this."

Lost in thought, she offered no rebuttal and simply nodded as he rode off. Chasmira sat a minute longer before dismounting her horse and tying it to a post under the shadow of the great spires.

"Blessings, sojourner."

Chasmira almost fell back. "Blessings," she repeated back reflexively, and then laughed at herself. "Good morning, I mean!"

The Ædant was covered head to foot in white veils, as was ever their custom. Only the shadows of their facial features were visible beneath the sheets of sheer fabric flowing over their body.

"Would you enter the sanctuary to pray?"

Just the thought of entering made Chasmira's veins burn with the infernal energy inside her. Something inside of her screamed *no* and she followed the urge.

"No, thank you. Some other time," she laughed it off.

"There is clarity in speaking to the Makergods."

"I know. And I miss it. But I don't think they wish to speak to me."

"Absence from the gods is estrangement from your soul," the cleric offered in a kind voice.

"Believe me, I know. The estrangement is acute the past few years," she yielded, but only that far. Even speaking of her yearning for a divine connection made the fire within her burn at her skin.

The Ædant's voice was soft and clear as a flute. "A mile to us is but an inch to the gods. Be not afraid to call upon them."

Chasmira melted inside. She grabbed the veiled cleric's hands tightly. "I am too weak in spirit to call upon them myself. I need intervention, for I am overladen in my transgressions. The gods will not hear me."

"I will pray for you," they reassured her, and whispered a supplication in the celestial tongue, the tongue of the Angelics themselves.

Chasmira could feel the divine energy shining into her. It felt like sunbeams breaking through clouds, like a storm interrupted by a prolonged minute of sun-blazen calm. The shrieking Chaos in her thoughts retreated, and something she had not heard in years spoke to her in the calm silence.

She smiled, lips trembling. "Thank you."

"Clarity is precious in the chaos of this life. I hope it will help you."

Chasmira nodded, still catching her breath.

Over the Ædant's shoulder, she took notice of a great brass statue in the shape of a winged woman that stood on a pedestal in the chapel. No doubt it was Nandrzael, the patron guardian of the city. She was depicted with her face looking upward and her wings stretched back behind her, as if she were lifting off to ascend back into the heavens. Chasmira's face flushed with anger.

This is where the Ædants would call to her and pray. This is where Nandrzael would descend and deliver her messages. If she had issued a call to war against the land of Mirikinin, surely it would have already come by now.

"So this is the great Oracle?"

"It is all but a gateway to the divine realm," the Ædant replied, looking up at spires high above them.

"Is it true that the divine speak to you, to give wisdom and warning?"

"Aye, it is."

"And which have they given recently? Wisdom or warning?"

The Ædant hesitated.

Chasmira did not. "I am a sojourner from the villages beyond the bogland. Blood has run red in the brooks that flow from the mountain. War has rumbled like the thunder of a looming storm. We only want to know if this storm is fated to break upon us, please."

Her performance seemed convincing, for the veiled cleric squeezed Chasmira's hands tighter in reassurance. "If such dispensation had been given, the Archvate—the head of the Oracle—he would know. I am only the Vate of the chapel."

"I understand. Please, could you ask him for me? I am unworthy of his presence…"

"The Archvate is not here presently," they said softly, apologetically. "He is ministering at the Prefect's tower today and will be back tomorrow."

"Tomorrow?" She sighed.

"I'm afraid so."

"I have traveled such a long way... I can wait a bit longer."

"Have you lodging for the night? If not, you are welcome to stay here."

"Oh, no no," Chasmira laughed. "Quite unnecessary, but very kind, thank you. I will return on the morrow and ask for the Archvate then."

She departed, cursing inside for the delay but grateful inside for the Ædant's loose lips. *They could have said no, that there was no word from the heavens, but they did not. They only said the Archvate is at the Prefect's tower. Why would he be paying a visit to the ruler of the land except to pass along Nandrzael's evil word against Mirikinin? Unless, of course, this is routine and the two of them meet regularly. But the way the cleric hesitated when I asked… They have received her revelation, I know it… No, you can't live off assumptions. You have to be certain. Too much is at stake.*

Warrick returned, a dour look on his round face as he halted his horse beside hers. "Just another day at the tower. What say you to that?"

She chewed her lip. Over the rooftops she could see the Prefect's tower, with its distinct reddish stone and small turrets jutting from the sides. The answers she needed were inside. "I say let's have a look."

CHAPTER 9

"This is impossible."

Chasmira ignored him and continued to study the tower layout. The tower itself was at least eighty feet in height, with smaller buildings clustered closely around it. A wall twenty feet tall surrounded the entire grounds and was topped with metal spikes to impale anyone foolish enough to try climbing it. The only visible way in was underneath a rather formidable gatehouse, where sentries stood in the turrets and an iron portcullis blocked the entryway.

"The Archvate is in there," she explained. "He's meeting with the Prefect to pass along whatever divine revelation he's received; I am sure of it."

"And you intend to interrupt him?"

"Not interrupt. More like... intervene. Especially if the message is in writing. We must take it and bring it back to your uncle."

"Would the Archvate really take the time to pen a message from an Angelic?"

Chasmira cocked her eyebrow at him. "Would you not write down a divine revelation?"

Warrick conceded her point with a grunt. "Your plan is only

good in theory, however. There is no way inside the tower, unless you know an enchantment that can turn you invisible and permit you to pass through those walls."

"Alas, no. Such enchantments do exist, but they are beyond my practice."

"Perhaps you could sprout wings and fly up to the tower in the cover of night, unless that too is beyond your practice?"

"I could make *you* sprout wings, if you'd like me to demonstrate," she smirked.

"I will decline and say I believe you."

She smiled victoriously and went back to studying the tower a bit longer. There appeared to be no way inside without extreme force to overcome the defenses, which would run counter to their entire purpose in coming: to discreetly and quietly discover Argismora's intentions.

They agreed that trying to force entry was out of the question. The Archvate had to leave sooner or later to return to the Oracle. The danger was in the delay: waiting until tomorrow meant the army could be assembled already and they would not know it. They could be left lingering outside the Oracle while an army marched on the unsuspecting House of Mirikinin.

Chasmira and Warrick noticed the road between the Prefect's tower and the Oracle adjoined to the marketplace they passed earlier. They needed to remain inconspicuous as possible while waiting, so they began to explore the wares under a canopy of colorful awnings. They would circle back to inquire at the Oracle before sundown. If they noticed the white-robed Archvate walking by, so much the better.

Small animals of all kinds were on display in cages, stacked on tables and hung from racks. They collectively chirped, twittered, squawked, and yowled at the pair as they walked past.

"Ooh, what about a new pet, Warrick? Something to keep you company at home?"

Warrick crossed his arms. "I've plenty of company at home, thanks."

"Who? You mean those leering imbeciles who work your farmland? Lart and the rest of them? Excellent companions. Kindred spirits if I ever saw."

He almost laughed. "Well, I certainly do not lack animals to spend my time with."

"Oh Warrick, don't be so obtuse," she chided him. "Swine and goats are not companions. You feed them, and breed them, and milk them, and then eventually you slaughter them. I'm talking about companionship."

"The likes of Lart and Terror?"

She tutted and clicked her tongue. "Not quite what I had in mind," peering closely into the cages.

Warrick rolled his eyes. He wanted to complain that this was a waste of time, but wasting time was exactly what they needed to do: blend in until the Archvate returned to the chapel...

"What about a glitzy?"

He sighed and walked to her side. She wiggled her finger though the cage at a small amphibian that hissed and gurgled like an angry kitten. Its flesh sparkled with every color of the rainbow as it backed against the wooden bars.

"You're just mocking me now. Glitzies shed their scales when they feel threatened! Scales like sand! There is no way I'm picking glitter off of everything I own for the rest of my days."

"You can't pick it off, it stays on anything forever," she muttered, pulling her finger back out of the cage. "What about a meowl?"

The three meowls huddled together, pressing their whiskered faces against the bars of their cage. Their huge eyes stared wondrously at Chasmira and Warrick. These round, furry birds were feline in appearance except for their wings and tails, which were very similar to those of owls.

"I haven't need for such things," said Warrick.

"Nonsense. We all have need for tender things to look after. Things that require our hands to be gentler and more careful. Go on, they won't bite you."

He put his knuckles against their cage and twiddled his fingers to get the meowls' attention. The white one pressed its face against the cage to rub its whiskers and jowls against his hand. The orange one trilled and leapt up to the top of the cage, hanging upside-down by its claws. The last one, grey and black striped, batted the white one aside for the chance to curiously sniff at his hand before meowing.

"I think this one likes you," she said, tickling the white meowl with her fingers.

Warrick rolled his eyes and huffed, turning his back to her.

"Scarrlok," he said.

She was sure she had misheard him. "What did you say?"

"Scarrlok," he repeated, not turning back to look at her. He squinted for a better look at the six little jabbering goblins making their way through the crowded marketplace.

The Scarrlok were overall small in stature, though they varied from one another greatly in height. The largest of them was nearly half the height of a Human, while the smallest would hardly come up to one's knee. They were all greenish in color, with pointed ears that jutted from the sides of their leather cowls. Most notably, Scarrlok had large shells like a tortoise and could draw their arms, legs, and head into their shells when in danger. Their eyes stared blankly like the eyes of goldfish, and each eye turned separately from the other eye, enabling the Scarrlok to see in two directions at once.

"I have never seen one with my own eyes," Chasmira remarked.

"Yes, very strange. Scarrlok do not roam free in these lands."

In the midland country to the south, these goblins were auctioned as slaves. They were stupid, obedient, and strong for their small size, which made them very valuable to the right parties.

Warrick nodded, still not taking his eyes off them. "Last year a slave merchant from the eastern midlands arrived with wagons full of the stupid little devils. He offered a price of five hundred gold a head. I told him to ride on, that we had not that kind of coin to spend."

"I should think not," Chasmira scoffed. "Who would?"

"Who indeed? In Argismora, a city of refugees and vagabonds, who would have the wealth to purchase Scarrlok slaves but the Prefect himself?" Warrick prompted with a sly grin.

"Well done, Warrick," she said, patting his arm as she went past to follow the Scarrlok.

The six of them waddled to an alleyway and entered, trying to look nonchalant. Subtlety was not their strong suit, especially with their superstitious habits: one Scarrlok licked his nose like a nervous tic every time someone walked past him, and another crossed his heart twice when he bumped into one of his fellows. One of them whistled an off-key tune and dawdled for a bit while the others slipped in behind him, before backing into the alley himself.

"This hasn't the look of a reputable marketplace sale to me," Chasmira said, creeping to the corner of the alleyway. She contemplated for just a moment, hoping that the Scarrlok had ventured far enough down the passage where they would not notice her following them.

She chanced it and stuck her head around the corner.

The six squat creatures were huddled around an open doorway about forty feet down the alleyway. One Scarrlok wearing a red sash apparently had some superstition about looking at the sunlight, for he had walked backward facing away from the light, and only turned around once he was standing in the shadow of the alley. He seemed to be in charge, barking something in their guttural language to whomever was in the doorway. Chasmira squinted, looking for any signs or wording to indicate what this place was…

Chasmira saw daylight flash off the eyes of a small Scarrlok that turned around. Stifling her gasp, she threw herself back around the corner and pressed herself flat against the stone wall. Had she been seen? She decided it was best to hide, retreating back under the shadow of the marketplace awnings.

Across the street, Warrick tried to look casual, but his eyes kept looking between Chasmira and the alleyway.

The Scarrlok emerged from the dark alley, scurrying back the way they came. No sooner had they turned the corner when from the alley hurried a long line of women all wearing identical short capes of marigold yellow, with hoods the women drew up over their heads.

The Prefect's lowest slaves escorting a troop of women? Ah, of course... Not a troop but a troupe. Without doubt he is in need of diversions for more guests than just Simon the Pure... either that, or the holy man is not as boring as his title claims.

Chasmira got an idea. She crossed the street and leaned against Warrick's side. "Quickly, I need a hooded cape just like those."

"What?"

She clutched his arm. "Forgive me, Warrick, but I've an important evening to attend at the Prefect's tower, and the dress code appears quite strict."

He groaned, hustling over to a clothier with a wide selection at their shop. Not even a minute later, he returned a few coins lighter but with a hooded cape in a similar shade of yellow.

Chasmira smiled, taking the cape from his hands and throwing it around her shoulders. "Wait for me at the inn we passed on the way here."

"I cannot believe you're seriously doing this."

"Desperate times," she quipped as she fastened the cape. "I'll try to be back by sundown, depending how late this event is going."

"Try not to go *too* late," he snarked back.

She only replied with that mischievous smirk and a scant glow like candlelight in her eyes as she ran out of the marketplace to catch up with the harem.

The squat, squawking goblins led the women down winding alleyways and narrow stairways, out of sight as they wound their way back to the Prefect's tower. There, tucked into a wall alcove, was a back door that appeared to be for the slaves' use only. A cart of liquor bottles stood beside the door, and a Scarrlok carrying an armful of such bottles paused to let the troupe enter inside.

Chasmira shut her eyes and remembered the Ædant's blessing upon her. Perhaps the god Tyor thought this all necessary, or perhaps Naru was laughing at the irony of it. In any case, it seemed the gods were showing her grace… either that, or the Scarrlok could not count higher than ten.

She questioned it no further, following the murmur of distant conversation and the sound of harp music.

CHAPTER 10

Chasmira spun slowly in place, gawking upward. The great vaulted ceiling overhead was covered in painted murals depicting some epic battle of old. The other women parted around her, attaching themselves to the arms of powerful nobles and handsome courtiers, while she stood staring upward. The figures of warriors contorted in battle entranced her. They were dressed in rags and robes, yet each of them bore upon their forehead a glyph that beamed with golden light.

"That's a beautiful color on you," someone said to her.

She said nothing.

"You're looking the wrong direction," another jabbed at her.

She still stared up.

"Strange, is it not, to see art of the dead?"

A smile crept onto her lips, and she lowered her gaze to the new speaker. Long curly locks of black hair framed the finely-chiseled features of the man who stared upward at the same ceiling murals. He had a jawline like the edge of a sword, accented with a shadow of dark stubble, ending in a round dimpled chin. One side of his mouth bent in a boyish grin, and he chortled loudly at the art above them.

"This mural depicts the three sieges of Gafral the Cyclops," he continued. "A century ago, in the deep of the Dragon's Winter, Lord Gafral thought to besiege this refuge. The Ædants thought that the guardians of the Oracle were their only defense, until the refugees stood up between them and the enemy. They raised blade and hammer with no banner, no armor, and no shield. None that anyone could see, at any rate."

Chasmira looked him up and down. "What happened?"

"They met Gafral's siege man for man," he laughed. "By the grace of Soth, the ragged vagabonds died off in droves, but they still decimated the siege forces until only Gafral himself remained. The Archvate summoned a thunderbolt that cleaved Gafral in two. The next generation that raised this tower painted this mural in memory of the courageous that laid down their lives to ensure theirs could go on."

She could restrain her curiosity no longer. "Who are you?"

"I am Boe, commander of the host," he said with a bow. He took her hand in his and kissed it gingerly. "Be the light to my shadow tonight?"

"Happily," she blushed. What an opportunity… to be the escort of Argismora's commander, who with a single order could call an entire province to war. As she walked with him, she could feel the strength in his arm, the strength in his very step through the great hall.

It seemed to be a gathering of the Prefect's advisors and dignitaries, about thirty in all. Chasmira turned this over in her mind. If this was a regular meeting for conversation and revelry, then perhaps there was no divine dispensation to the Archvate, and this infiltration would be fruitless. On the other hand, why invite the Archvate at all when a man of his standing would abstain from every indulgence this gathering offered?

Unless, she reasoned, *the Archvate's presence today is out of the ordinary.*

She needed to ask, but discretion was key. There was no reason to ask now.

"What's your name?" Boe asked casually as he made his way across the room.

Yanked out of her internal dialogue, she drew in a slow breath, stretching out the seconds to conjure up an alter ego. She smiled, "I'm Janessa."

He smiled back. "Not used to being asked your name?"

"You'd be the first in a long time to bother with such formalities."

"I sensed that, which is why I asked," patting her hand that rested on his arm.

"You sensed it? What else do you *sense* about me?"

"Hmmm... That you are not here just to have a good time."

Chasmira laughed a little, hoping to hide her nervousness that her front might not have been as convincing as she hoped. Next to them, one of the other women laughed overly loudly at a middle-aged nobleman's joke, faking a cough to get another goblet of drink from him.

She sighed. "You are a cunning man indeed, Commander. One cannot help but hope for more than just endless diversions. It all becomes a bit routine after a while, you know? The music all seems to sound the same. The drinks all seem to taste the same."

"And the men all seem the same too?"

"As I said: cunning."

Commander Boe walked the perimeter of the room with her.

"I know all about men, my sweet. I oversee two thousand of them. Most men are… unremarkable. No original thoughts, no anticipation, no creativity. What's worse, they put deliberate effort into making others believe they are all the same. It takes a remarkable man to stand out and make something more of himself."

She arched an eyebrow. "Are you speaking of yourself, Commander?"

"The simple fact you address me as 'commander' ought to answer that." Arriving at a couch, they sat down together. He rested his hand in the middle of her back, instead of wrapping his arm around her waist as the others did with their escorts.

Chasmira almost wished he would. Aside from the fact it would help her blend in, she also felt an unexpected ease and comfort in his presence. Commander Boe was handsome, strong, and well-spoken. *Remarkable*, she laughed internally.

"Have you lived in Argismora long?" he asked, brushing aside his dark locks with a swipe of his hand.

"No, not long at all. Not even one moon."

"I thought not. Your dress is a bit different from our fashions."

"Are you saying my dress is plain?" She clutched her necklace as if deeply insulted.

"Not at all," he laughed, seeing through her play. "Just that theirs are laced and bejeweled. Yours is like a shepherd's daughter."

"So it makes me look innocent?"

"So it makes you look *honest*."

She tucked her chin down at such a sincere compliment. "My

word, Commander, you are positively disarming."

"Years of practice. If I can disarm a charging barbarian, I would hope to disarm a lady with at least as much finesse," he replied, pausing to accept a goblet of rich blackberry wine from a passing servant. "So where *are* you from, Janessa?"

"Holireath, about two days' ride on the south road. Have you been there?"

Boe nodded, "Once or twice. Beautiful land down there, but too much farmland."

"What, not enough walls and towers and stone for you?"

"I must sound like a crude military man," he said apologetically. "I simply meant that such beautiful land should be guarded better. The people of Holireath are too exposed, too trusting of their neighbors."

She leaned against him coyly. "And what's wrong with trusting your neighbors?"

"Sometimes they haven't the best intentions," trading his goblet to the hand farther away from her.

Chasmira wanted so badly to speak of Mirikinin—to water the seeds of distrust in this man—but forcing the issue would have been suspicious. A strong political opinion would not make her pleasurable company, which is all she intended to be at this moment. Even this playful conversation was proving to be very informative.

Boe's lips hardly touched the goblet before he paused and then raised it in a salute across the room.

"Who was that for?" she asked.

"The reason we are all here today: the Prefect himself."

She immediately craned her neck to find the Prefect in the

center of a small crowd near the door. He was a elderly man, but quite tall and not at all hunched despite his years. Long robes, white as the stone walls of Argismora themselves, adorned him. His long silver beard was intricately braided and laden with brass rings that signified the divine guardianship over his reign.

The implications of this guardianship were a little haunting. The only person who could possibly remove him from power was the Archvate, as no one else in this room could ever challenge his integrity. It also meant that the Prefect could never lay down his brass rings so long as the Archvate insisted the heavens desired him to rule. The seemingly immutable power he had over this land was eclipsed only by the word of the Archvate, Chasmira realized. The Prefect was as much a slave to the divine as she once was.

As he neared them, they could hear the soft chime of his brass beard rings against one another. The Prefect leaned on his scepter and asked, "Enjoying yourself, Boe?"

"Your hospitality is unmatched, Sire. Who could not enjoy themselves here?"

Chasmira instantly noticed their rapport was that of two old friends: a tone somewhere on the line between genuine warmth and sarcastic ribbing, and only the two of them truly knew which one was intended.

The elder man's smile looked like a sneer. "Only you. That wine definitely will not quench a thirst such as yours. A thirst for war, or at the rumors of war to moisten your palate."

"Speaking of rumors, did you hear what I heard about the midlands?"

"Down in the golden kingdom? No, what did you hear?"

"Your spies did not tell you first?"

The Prefect rolled his eyes. "My spies listen for marriages and trade opportunities, Boe. Yours sniff out blood and smoke."

"Indeed they do, and they caught the scent of both in Volcini. Little province all the way west near Zünden."

"Well, what about it?"

"It's been overthrown. Just before last winter, some marauder and his band of zealots sneaked in and sacked the citadel overnight. He emptied out the entire treasury, saying he had no need for gold. Poured it all out onto the streets."

"Madness!"

"That's not all. Right afterward, he issued a proclamation that the land is now to be called Volgoth and declared himself the king of it."

"Poor thing. I don't want to imagine what the lords of the golden kingdom will do to him," the Prefect laughed.

"A battalion of knights will probably answer that question," Boe joined him in laughter, sipping on his wine before shifting subjects. "Any word about my warbling nightwing?"

"Warbling nightwing?" Chasmira interjected.

The Prefect jabbed at Boe with his scepter. "His pet bird may have injured its leg. You mean to say he has gone this long without mentioning them? This one's started quite the menagerie of exotic fowl. "

"Five is hardly a menagerie," Boe retorted.

"It's five more than I have," said the Prefect.

Chasmira's smile widened. "No, he hasn't spoken a word about them until now, I am quite flattered to say, for it is difficult to break a man away from his obsessions."

"Difficult would be an understatement," the Prefect said

before stepping aside to speak with his other guests. "You both have a good time."

She watched him depart. "Pleasant man."

"He's all right," Boe said into his goblet as he took another sip of blackberry wine.

"Oh? Is 'all right' not 'remarkable'?"

Boe simply smacked his lips in reply.

She laughed and swatted at him. "That's certainly no way to speak of the man caring for your warbling nightwing."

"No, I suppose not," he laughed sheepishly.

"Whatever is wrong with it? Not that I've any idea what it is."

"Oh, it's beautiful, just a beautiful bird. They're native to the deep boglands, and you can hear them in the trees at night, oh but only on the new and crescent moons. You see, the moonlight is toxic to them, and the sunlight is outright deadly. So you can only hunt them in darkest of nights, when the females come out to gather food and the males come out to mate."

She cast a glance over at another of the hired women gorging herself on wine, cheese, and pork leg. The man with her whispered something over her shoulder that made her blush and snort.

"How very unusual," said Chasmira.

Something then caught her eye as she was looking back toward Boe. Over his shoulder, at the far end of the room, a set of doors opened for the Prefect. Beyond them stood someone dressed head to toe in white silk like an Ædant but with an ornate brass circlet on their head.

"Is that the Archvate?"

"Yes, that's him. Archvate Simon, or *Simonas Parku*, the Ædants call him.

"*Simonas Parku*? What does it mean?"

"They say in the divine tongue, it means 'Simon the Pure.' Only the pure can receive revelation from the Angelics. In all his years, Archvate Simon has yielded to neither lust nor revelry nor temper. When the divine word descends into the Oracle, it enters no one's ears but his."

"That's a heavy burden for one man," feigning her admiration, remembering vividly how Nandrzael sought her out—a Chaos sorceress—to do her dirty work. *If the Angelics require only that much purity, might as well make me the next Archvate.*

The shrouded figure of the man was strangely still. It was not until the doors were shutting that Chasmira realized he may have been staring back at her across the room and she would not have known it.

ψ

Hours passed.

Boe proved to be an excellent companion. He was courteous, complimentary, and conversational—definitely not the kind of company she was used to. He regaled her with stories of battle against Beastkin marauders and Ogre grudges, the latter of which she listened to with healthy skepticism. One would require a small army to fight even one Ogre, let alone an entire grudge of Ogres. Still, he told the stories well, embellishing them with drama and even humor at the right moments. She would respond by answering his questions about herself, weaving simple lies about growing up in Holireath with a happy family around her.

While at first she feared it would pain her to speak of her

hometown, she quickly lost herself in the fiction. She was no longer Chasmira but Janessa: the daughter of shepherds who lived at the end of town and had neighbors over for brunch every Faderdyd, the first day of the week. Janessa would go visit her four cousins in Pan's Providence, a little village fourteen miles north of Hopewell, every other month. Except that is, in the month Curmared, when they would all come visit her instead to celebrate the Feasts of Curmared together.

It was a beautiful fantasy, one that Boe would listen to with wonder in his grey eyes, only interjecting a small question here and there. He would nod, sip his wine, and then offer another story of his travels up and down the sea coasts.

All of this, of course, was enjoyed with a clear view of the doors behind which the Prefect and the Archvate had hidden.

Boe was in the midst of a story about seeing a sea monster off the rocky coasts of Khon Dha when the doors opened behind him. The Prefect emerged, thanking the veiled Archvate for his company. Then, he circled the room once to check on his guests before arriving back where Boe and Chasmira sat.

"All I saw was the tail, but it was pale as an iceberg and larger than a frigate sail—" Boe paused and looked up at the Prefect. "Sire?"

The Prefect's smile was not the same sneering, sardonic look as earlier. It was calm and polite. *Diplomatic. Fake. Intended to give a pleasant appearance to onlookers.* Chasmira dug intently into a fruit bowl to appear distracted, but focused every bit of her attention on his next words. "Word has been handed down. I need a number by tomorrow."

A number?

"As you wish," Boe replied casually, with a tip of his goblet.

The Prefect's fingers closed firmly around the goblet, and he lifted it out of Boe's grasp. "By tomorrow," he repeated slowly before nodding in thanks, as if accepting an offering and walking off with it.

The commander set his jaw and paced his breath. Clearly the Prefect's order soured his entire evening. After a long pause, he stood and brushed off his clothes. "Thank you for your company today, Janessa. I hate to say I must retire early this evening, but other matters need my attention."

"Leaving me alone?" she asked with a sad look up at him.

That look alone nearly pulled him back to the couch. "I doubt you'd be at a lack for company," he replied, with disdain for the other men in attendance.

"Company that isn't yours is hardly company I desire." She rose from the couch and straightened her dress.

"Be content here."

"Here? I dare say I've already tired of staring up at this ceiling. Whatever you need to do, surely it can be done quickly enough, can it not?"

Boe hesitated a moment longer, drinking in the sweetness of her plea, the softness of her dress, and the scent of autumn wildflowers when she leaned in closer. He took a slow step and lifted her hand to his mouth to place a gentle kiss.

"Quickly enough, yes," he answered, his eyes meeting hers.

CHAPTER 11

Chasmira's foot sank into the lush red carpet. She had never seen such luxury as was on display in the commander's chambers. The floor was adorned with fine red carpet the whole breadth of the room, while the walls were decorated with ornate sconces made of various antlers and horns. From the soffits to the mirror frames to the bedposts, there was not a piece of dark wood in all the furniture that was not overlaid with gold filigree.

"My word, Commander…" she remarked breathlessly.

"The wooden pieces were handcrafted by a Khon Dhali furniture maker," he told her as he shut the door.

"You said you were a well-traveled man. I had no idea you were a collector of anything besides exotic birds."

No sooner had the words left her mouth than she was greeted by the soft, wafting, coo of a plump white bird in a golden cage. It ruffled up its plumage at the sight of her, making itself so large that the tips of its feathers stuck out of the bars on all sides.

She leaned in close. "Oooh, a puffercaw!"

"She's beautiful isn't she? As you know, the puffercaw's song grows slowly but surely louder with the coming of sunrise. I let her song awaken me, but then I must get out of bed to cover her cage before the sun is fully risen… lest she wake the entire tower too!"

Chasmira mimicked the white puffercaw's coo, and it let its plumage fall back in place. It sidestepped slowly on its perch and tilted its head almost completely ninety degrees sideways. It watched her walk over to the next birdcage, which was so tall it reached from floor to ceiling.

"What is in here?" she wondered aloud, squinting through the cage bars. The bottom of the cage contained a large water basin, out of which grew a tangle of leafy shoots that spiraled upward all the way until they clutched the top of the gold cage. At first it appeared there were no birds at all, until at last she caught sight of them, hidden in the foliage.

With their four wings tucked flat on their limbless bodies, these birds would wind themselves through tree branches much as a snake would, hunting for prey. Upon finding it, they would lash out with their serpentine tails and wrap around it to choke it, earning them their name…

"Blue constrictals," Boe said, looking into the cage beside her. "Elegant creatures. You should see a strangle of them in flight. It's truly breathtaking."

"Are they dangerous?"

"Not to Humans. They're far too small. They go after small animals such as frogs, lizards, or mice. If one were to wrap itself around your neck, it would be by mistake, by reflex, and they would quickly fly away."

She nodded, watching them in their cage. Their feathers looked like black scales, that is, until they would occasionally preen themselves. Then, the black scales rippled with splashes of glossy blue color.

A sudden noise from the back of the room made her jump. Near the window, beside the commander's wardrobe and his changing screen, stood the last birdcage, which was nearly five feet tall and covered in a black sheet. Chasmira put her hand to her chest and slowly approached. Between the exposed gold bars at the bottom of the cage, she could see red plumage.

"Why is this one covered?" she asked.

"Oh, that's my most recent acquisition: a blood-tipped gallowsbird."

"You mean a hangman's hawk?"

Boe laughed wryly. "They have several nicknames. They are also called noosebeaks, for after catching prey they will land and dangle it, neck clamped tightly in the bird's huge, crushing beak. Sometimes it will keep it like that for hours before finally breaking its neck and eating it."

"Frightening but fascinating," she replied.

"I'm glad to hear it. Most women wouldn't think so."

"Well, I'm hardly most women."

The room spun, and Chasmira felt the stone of the wall against her shoulderblades and the heat of Boe's lips on her neck. Her wrist was pinned back as well by Boe's hand, and his other hand gripped her jaw.

Oh no. No.

"You should feel flattered, Janessa, for it is no easy challenge to catch my eye. The Prefect spoke imperfectly earlier in the great hall. You see, my obsession is not collecting exotic birds. My obsession is capturing rare things for my own amusement."

Fire nearly rose from her eyes instinctively, but she fought it.

Attacking him would only doom her entire mission. Besides, it would have done no good, for she could not see him. Boe's rock-solid body was flat against her, and his head was crooked down to run his tongue along her collarbone. She put her free hand up against his shoulder, but pushing him away was not possible. She began to tremble.

"Me? Rare?" she gasped, voice shaking.

"But of course! A sweet shepherd's daughter with a mind for art and an appetite for the unusual? You are *very* rare indeed."

Panic clawed at her mind, but she resisted. Instead, she moved her hand from his shoulder into his hair, gripping a handful of dark locks.

"Please, Commander, I beg of you—"

"Yes, beg—"

"No, I beg of you, Commander, my dress!" she shouted in annoyance instead of alarm. She dropped her hand from his hair and stopped struggling against him.

Feeling her body go limp and unresistant, Boe stopped. His hand slid from her jaw and gently rested on her throat. He let out an exasperated sigh against her bosom. "What *about* your dress?"

"I have only this one dress. If you tear it, I will have no other," she pled as pathetically as possible. "Let me take it off before you rip it apart!"

He slowly rose up and rested his temple against hers. His hot breath panted against her bare shoulder before she heard him say, "Very well. But be quick about it."

Chasmira mumbled something in thanks, slipping out from between him and the wall. She took a few steps away toward the wardrobe near the window, turned away, and began to unlace her clothes. She could feel his eyes on her, watching each knot untie and fall aside.

A loud, hurried knock on the door forced Boe's attention away from her. With a hiss of frustration he turned to answer it, and Chasmira scurried behind the changing screen to hide herself. She was already not prepared to entertain an audience.

He yanked the door open. "What do you want?"

She heard the guttural squawking of a Scarrlok servant.

"Can you not tell I am busy?"

The Scarrlok clucked a sheepish reply.

Chasmira stood as still as possible behind the screen, overhearing the noise of a chair pulled out and Boe sitting. She turned and peeked between the slats of the wicker screen. Boe was hunched over his desk, quickly writing a note on a roll of paper.

"Take this to my captain of the guard," he commanded. "I need our army numbered by sunrise. Give it to no one else but him personally."

So that's the number the Prefect wants. He is calling upon his army after what the Archvate said to him, Chasmira reasoned. She squinted to get a better look.

Waiting at the door was the Scarrlok with the red sash from earlier, anxiously stepping from foot to foot as Boe finished the message. The paper was rolled, tied with twine, and then sealed with hot wax and a signet. Boe then put it into a leather tube, capped it, and shoved it into the Scarrlok's stubby hands.

"No dawdling, or I'll have your shell to use as a salad bowl," he warned, grabbing the Scarrlok by the ear. "Now get out."

The little goblin whimpered and nodded, taking the message and slamming the door shut as he left. Chasmira spun back around, turning her back to Boe as if still fidgeting with her dress. She needed that message to prove to Lord Maram that Argismora was rising up against them.

No sooner did her fingers pinch her dress laces again than she heard Boe behind her, "Here I was hoping you would be ready by now." She could hear the smile in his words, but she could also hear the clipped aggravation behind them. Chasmira squeezed her eyes shut and steadied her breath, which she realized had become more rapid.

Between the changing screen and the bookshelf was the window, just a few steps away from her. There was a wooden stool beside her, and with a single movement she could run to the window and swing the stool through the glass panes. She could probably reach it before he could reach her. She could make it in time. She could.

"Don't hide from me," he said.

But there was no point in escape. He would pursue her. If she wasn't caught at the window, she would be caught on the roof or in the courtyard. She would never get the message. She'd be forced to kill him and so many others. The captain of the guard would send soldiers to lock down the castle and the whole city...

The birdcage beside her rattled under the black sheet. The huge, caged gallowsbird could probably sense the tension in the room.

Chasmira smiled, fire kindling in her eyes.

"I'm ready," she called to him in a bright voice. "I'm sorry it took so long for me to *change*."

After her last word, the gallowsbird squawked, rattled its cage, and then squawked unnaturally louder and deeper than before.

The cage toppled forward onto the floor with a crash. A second later, both the sheet and the bars were torn open, and the red bird rose to its feet.

Normally an adult blood-tipped gallowsbird would stand waist-high next to an average Human, but this creature had now grown to twice its normal size in seconds. Its beak bent downward at a sharp angle like a boomerang and looked like it had the crushing force of a millstone. The bird blinked its yellow eyes, which were now level with Boe's own baffled stare.

"What the—"

Boe could not get another word out before the huge bird lunged onto him, knocking him backward and clamping onto his forearm. Boe fiercely pounded his fist against it, but the gallowbird was unfazed by the blows. It dragged him through the furniture, overturning chairs, breaking a mirror, and knocking over the white puffercaw's cage.

In the chaos, Chasmira darted from the screen to the door, flinging it open and then slamming it shut behind her. As she hurried through the halls, her skirt bunched up in her fists, she gloated smugly at the power she held over wild animals—to command them, calm them, and turn them into hulking monsters if she bade such a change.

Rounding the corner, she spotted one of the servants carrying an armful of empty wine bottles from the great hall. She fanned her flushed face, not attempting to make herself look any less disheveled. "My my, what a wild afternoon it has been!"

"If you say, milady," the servant replied meekly.

Chasmira minced up close, placing a hand on their arm. "No need for formalities, dear. I'm no more a lady than you are a flying horse. By chance, could you show me the way to the back door? I've got to get in a hot bath before my evening engagement."

ψ

Scarrlok were neither particularly swift nor subtle, but their small size made them difficult to spot. *How far could he have gone? You would think a red sash would stand out like a wine stain on a wedding gown,* Chasmira huffed as she twisted her head from side to side and craned it to see down the crowded road to her left. Two roads, leading in different directions, met at the Prefect's tower. She squinted into the setting sun, straining to see down the road on her right. The Scarrlok could have gone down either path.

No, no he couldn't. To her right was the setting sun, which the red-sashed Scarrlok refused to look at directly earlier. Would the little goblin really take an alternate route just to avoid it?

Of course he would.

She rushed down the leftward road, where the sun's red rays shone upon her back instead of her face. Scuttling through crowds and dashing past beast-drawn wagons, Chasmira ran until she had to stop from the aching in her sides. Then, the sunlight caught a flash of red ahead of her. The sash! The Scarrlok was ambling down the road about a block ahead of her.

She kept her eyes locked on him as she took a few more deep breaths and then took off running again. The captain of the guard could be right around the corner. She was only a minute or two behind the grimy little messenger, and she hoped it was quick enough to stop him.

The Scarrlok had no idea he was being followed, that is, until

Chasmira spooked a horse by accident. The animal reared and neighed, the Scarrlok looked back to see what was the matter, and Chasmira made direct eye contact with the little green messenger through the crowd.

Then, he turned and ran.

"The Scarrlok is a thief! Stop him! Stop the Scarrlok!" she shouted, desperate to get any passerby's help. A few people stepped in front of him to block his path, but the grungy goblin just rolled under their legs and kept going.

Her side was aching. She still pursued in long, limping strides, pointing and shouting, "Stop the Scarrlok! Someone st—"

Next thing she knew, she was on her back and elbows in the cold mud patch in the middle of the street.

She could not tell whether she had lost her footing or struck something, but it did not matter. She whirled about on her hands and knees, looking desperately for the Scarrlok. Which way were they even running? The sun had sunken beneath the tops of the buildings now. Someone passing by asked her a question, but she did not acknowledge them. They shrugged and led their ox past her, giving a wide berth as she stood up shakily.

"You should be more careful, milady," said a man's voice behind her.

Legs still wobbly, she turned around and then looked up at him.

Warrick stood with one eyebrow cocked and a fist on his hip. Chasmira's gaze sunk down to the muddy street, and her shoulders slumped. Then she saw it.

In the hoof-trodden mud laid a capped leather tube.

She blinked a few times in disbelief, crawled to it, and

uncapped it for just a brief moment. The paper roll was still inside! In his haste and panic, the Scarrlok messenger had unknowingly dropped it on the ground…

"What is that?" Warrick asked.

She drew out the note just enough to see the wax seal, then put it back, capped it, and smiled. "It is exactly what we needed."

"A message?"

"From Argismora's commander himself," she said in a hushed voice. "We must depart immediately."

Warrick squinted up at the autumn sky. "Little late in the day to set about riding home. The watchmen would ask why two strangers are leaving when nightfall is hardly an hour or so away."

She grimaced. "Is it safe to stay?"

"Safer than trying to leave, by my reckoning. Besides, the day is long spent. I cannot speak for you, but if I am to doze off, I would much prefer a soft bed over a horse's saddle. Wouldn't you agree?"

Warrick was right. Attempting to leave the city now would only get them questioned and searched. She had been riding the whole first half of the day and stalking the Archvate the second half. She was tired and aching, and her dress was scuffed with dark mud.

"I suppose a night in the Guardian City couldn't hurt," she sighed with a defeated chuckle as she walked with him toward the handsome building with latticed bay windows. "Besides, who would pass up a chance to spend that night in the Morning Glory Inn?"

CHAPTER 12

Argismora was host to many visitors during the harvest season. In addition to the farmers bringing the fruit of their fields, hunters came from the northlands with furs to sell for the coming cold, while merchants sold medicines to combat winter illnesses. As such, the Morning Glory Inn was nearly full except for one room. Circumstances being what they were, Warrick and Chasmira accepted the arrangement.

While he went to prepare a fire for their room, Chasmira washed at the well in the cobblestone court behind the inn. The cold water and open air felt good. She had spent all afternoon in stuffy chambers congested with pipe smoke and tacky perfume. She splashed herself again and looked up, letting the water run down her face and neck in cold trails. The sky overhead was a dark plum-colored hue, and the stars were just becoming visible in the twilight.

A bird crowed from the roof, and her heart pounded despite the way she kept still on the outside. It reminded her that she had left Boe in the jaws of the gallowsbird. She could not decide how she felt about that: relieved to have escaped, but for some reason guilty about having left him in such danger. Still, despite its savage reputation, it was far more likely he killed it than that it killed him.

He was a man of ferocity and passion, neither of which Chasmira wanted to experience at his hands. She also remembered that he was a man of charm and intelligence, and she hated that she remembered him that way. Her jaw still ached on one side from the way he had gripped it so roughly. She gingerly traced her finger along her jawline from chin to ear and back again, shutting her eyes when it felt sore.

She washed off her neck and chest twice before she felt fully clean.

The foyer of the inn was full of guests swaying in tune to a jaunty drinking song. She lingered for only a moment, taking in the view of their silhouettes against the hearthfire, cups in every raised hand. The warmth felt strange to her. Not the warmth of the literal fire, but the camaraderie of strangers gathered under one roof. She had never experienced that herself, instead living like a shadow on a wall. That is how she had lived and survived. Sometimes it was comfortable and safe, and other times she felt truly, painfully invisible.

The song swelled to a last crescendo. Voices and cups raised as high as they could go, followed by loud coughing, peeling laughter, the clank of tankards, and the splash of drinks on tabletops.

She smiled and leaned forward a bit out of the doorway and into the firelight.

A flurry of fiddling roused the crowd for another song, so the patrons began to pull the tables and chairs back to make some space for dancing.

Chasmira shrank back into the shadowy stairway and crept up the steps to find her and Warrick's room.

ψ

"Did you have something to drink?" Warrick asked as soon as he heard the door.

He was sitting on a wooden stool at the foot of a large bed draped with rabbit fur blankets. He smoothed out his surcoat, folded it, and laid it down on a stack of the rest of vestments on his knees. The red glow of hot coals in a metal floor brazier flickered faintly against the walls and furniture.

"No," she replied.

"Something to eat?"

"No. Why? Did you want something?" she offered.

"No, not at all," he said, moving the stack of clothes from his lap onto the floor. "I had something in the afternoon while you were still in the tower."

"Ah."

"Silly that I ask, really. One could assume you enjoyed plenty of food and drink."

Chasmira crossed her arms and clicked her tongue. "One could assume that, yes, but I was a tad preoccupied while I was there. It was not easy."

Warrick nodded and grunted in reply, unlacing the front of his shirt.

She could not help but laugh a little at Warrick. Between his size and his low grunts instead of answers, he reminded her of a big, grumpy bear.

"So there's only one bed?" she half-asked, half-announced. Grabbing a handful of the blanket, she squeezed the plush fur.

"Seems so," Warrick said without looking up.

"And where are you sleeping?"

"In the bed, where else?"

Her mouth dropped open. "I beg your pardon?"

"Beds are for sleeping, first and foremost," he said. "The night is cold and the fire is meager. I can sleep with my trousers on if it makes you feel any better."

She laughed incredulously, brushing her hair out of her face. "Gallant of you, I suppose! For a moment there I was certain I'd be curled up on the surround of the fire like Lart's hound."

He rolled his eyes in reply and pulled back the blankets to inspect the bedding. Chasmira turned around and stepped out of the firelight. She had never slept in only her chemise, but it was comfortable enough. She was not about to sleep bare next to Warrick.

She heard the bedframe creak behind her, and turned to see Warrick testing it for comfort. He was a large man, and no doubt he needed to consider furniture's sturdiness. The flickering light cast deep shadows across his broad back, showing thick muscles hardened from years of farm labor. He was well-tanned, probably from working in the fields during harvest. Warrick was evidently not the kind of man who left the hard work to others.

He nearly caught her looking, but she quickly turned away and reached for the laces of her bodice.

"Silly of me," she mused aloud.

"What is it?"

"It's still half unlaced," she chuckled. "I must have forgotten to lace it back up before I left the tower."

"Silly indeed," he grumbled before settling back into the bed. He put his feet under the blankets and turned on his side.

Chasmira removed her bodice and tossed it on the floor next to Warrick's neatly-folded clothes. Her dress soon landed beside it.

"Now don't mistake yours for mine in the morning, Warrick. You'll stretch the seams, and then what'll I do?"

He sighed. "Get in bed. Sleep."

Chasmira planted her hands on her hips. "Frankly, I don't know how we're going to get *any* sleep."

"Not with all this talking."

"You cannot blame me for being restless. We have something quite precious that we need to smuggle out of here and get it back to your uncle, without being pursued and caught."

Warrick's brow furrowed. "Who would pursue us?"

"The Scarrlok might have gone back and told them how I chased him halfway across town. They'll come looking for me."

"That Scarrlok won't breathe a word about it. He's a slave. If he failed to deliver the message and told them why, he'd be whipped. Now get in bed."

She sat down on the side of the bed. "Whipped? Do you think they really would?"

"I've seen Scarrlok *killed* for less than that. They're born in broods, you know, like chickens on a farm. For slave owners, there are always more Scarrlok to use."

"Fair enough," she conceded, getting up to put her bracelets on the bedside table. "He hardly even got a good look at me, honestly."

"Right," Warrick said, shutting his eyes again.

"And even if we *were* found out, we can split up. Then, you can just tell them I'm a witch and barter for your freedom if you reveal where I am. They'll run off to burn me at the stake or behead me in the square—"

"Why must you speak like that?"

"Only a minute more, I just wanted us to have this sorted."

"No, why must you speak *like that?*"

Chasmira was taken off guard by this. "Speak like what?"

Warrick was now sitting up in bed. "Like my uncle speaks about you. A beast… a harlot… a weapon… a bartering tool… Is that all you are?"

"To your uncle, yes," she said with a shrug.

"My uncle be damned, what about you? Have some dignity, woman."

"Dignity?"

"Yes, dignity. Not something best displayed as you were passing yourself around at the Prefect's tower this afternoon."

Chasmira bit back her anger. "You don't know what you're talking about."

"Don't I?" His words hung in the air for a long moment before he continued. "I have heard tales, how the women of Dimol Gol would debase themselves for a mere audience with the Magnate… much less be welcomed to live in his castle. Dare I imagine the price to stand at court with the Magnate himself?"

"You may imagine whatever you like," she snapped.

"I'd like to imagine you've a shred of dignity in you yet."

"Why? Why, Warrick? Does it keep you up at night, worrying if you're sheltering a royal whore in your castle walls? I've paid a price much higher than you can imagine, just to keep body and soul together."

Warrick stood. "You suppose I cannot imagine?"

"No, you cannot, how could you?"

"I'd put a copper on it."

She laughed bitterly. "I wouldn't bid higher with your pride on the line."

"Well then, you tell me. The same dark power that makes you perpetual prey for others, also marks you a predator for all to beware. So tell me the price of that fiendish fire that burns in your eyes. I haven't a care who has had your body but I shiver to think who—or what—named the price for your power. What was the cost? Your soul?"

Chasmira's eyes were the coldest he had ever seen them. "No. My heart."

He laughed once, scornfully. "I cannot imagine you ever had one."

"No. You cannot." She bent down, rummaged in the pocket of his coat, and took a copper coin in her fist. Opening the door, she paused and said, "This will pay for the bench downstairs, or a chair by the hearth if I ask them nicely. See you in the morning."

CHAPTER 13

She was only disturbed once as she lay barefoot on the hallway bench at the bottom of the stairs. She wordlessly held out the copper in payment, but the innkeeper shook his head and let her lie. The hospitality, or pity, was appreciated.

Flecks of firelight flashed across the ceiling above her. From the other room where once others sang and drank around the hearth, now the faint, drowsy, mumbled tune of a drunken man was the only sound.

As she lay there, a tear rolled down to her ear. She could not unhear Warrick's words. *A beast. A harlot. A weapon. A bartering tool.*

Have I heard myself described all of those ways so often, that I've become comfortable with it? Am I at ease with being a thing? Am I complicit with being used? Or am I simply quicker to suggest it so that others do not have the chance, so that I am the first to own my role? Do I do so to defy them, or unwittingly do I agree with them?

She gnawed at the inside of her cheek and squeezed her eyes shut. *Can I be valuable without being useful? Can a thing be useful without being used? Even a thing like me?*

She was useful to Nandrzael, who foretold that she would be useful to Magnate Argolvrecht. Now she was useful to Lord Maram. Her persuasiveness was valuable to Nandrzael. Her prophecy was valuable to Argolvrecht. Her power was valuable to Maram. However, it seemed that Warrick would not be happy with her, no matter what. In his eyes, her persuasiveness made her a whore, her prophecy made her a witch, and her power made her a monster.

It does not matter what I do. He hates what I am, and why I am.

Another hot tear rolled down. She watched the firelight on the ceiling. That would be her inevitable end. When all her usefulness ran out, she would be bound to a stake and burned. The fire inside her would at last be matched by a fire around her, equally destructive. Perhaps it would be a mob of angry villagers in a melodramatic display of public outrage. Perhaps it would be a mighty Alcimaean Slayer riding all the way from his golden kingdom to extinguish her flame of Chaos in the name of all that is good and pure and true.

And it was upon this thought she lingered as she shut her eyes. When she opened them, the innkeeper stood looking down at her. Again she held out the copper coin, and this time the innkeeper took it before putting something down on the floor beside the bench. She smelled hot porridge and looked out the doorway to see the hall aglow with soft dawnlight.

Chasmira sat up with a groan. Her arm tingled from sleeping on it awkwardly all night, and she flexed her elbow slowly to work the stiffness out of it. She picked up the porridge bowl and ate. It had the bland, vaguely nutty flavor she expected, but after a few spoonfuls she discovered some chopped dates mixed in for a bit of crisp sweetness. She wondered if the innkeeper put them in the entire pot or only in her bowl…

Warrick's thudding footsteps on the stairs made her abandon

the thought and put down her breakfast. He was dressed for travel already. He said nothing to her but lifted the leather message tube briefly out of his coat before tucking it away again.

She got up and walked to his side, pausing at the first stair. Coldly and quietly, she said to him, "Don't wait. Leave now so that we will not draw attention."

"No," he replied, walking under the stairs and folding his arms. He leaned back against a wood beam to wait. "We go together."

Without debate, she went upstairs to hastily get dressed. Every passing minute was a minute lost, a minute later returning to the House of Mirikinin.

Soon enough they retrieved their horses and rode side-by-side to the city gates. Chasmira fought the urge to look at every passerby to discern if any of them recognized her as the madwoman who tore through their streets last evening, chasing a Scarrlok thief. Instead, she kept her hood drawn up just as she had when they entered, and she focused on the sound of their horses' hooves. Their steps had a rhythm to them, and it kept her calm as she fixed her gaze upon the approaching gate.

The guardsmen on either side did not detain them. The watchmen atop the gate said nothing, only watching them pass under the stone archway.

That is when she heard it.

A single murmured word in the Scarrlok tongue.

"Did you hear it too?"

Warrick said nothing. He moved his horse to a quick trot.

"Did you hear it?"

He just grunted and rode on.

A half-hour into the ride, Warrick turned his horse aside off the road and moved to a canter gait across the field. Chasmira followed without hesitation. They were going to be followed, she knew it. By whom and how quickly, she did not know.

ψ

Nightfall came sooner than expected. They had pushed the horses as hard as they dared. Even though he rode the most suitable horse for his huge size and weight, Warrick needed to rest his mount more often because of it.

The day had passed wordlessly since departing Argismora. There was nothing more to be said. They both knew where they were going and that they were likely being followed. They noticed when the other was slowing down to stop. They did not make eye contact or say a single word. They simply did what they had to do.

The moon was hiding behind the overcast sky overhead. The horses had refused to move faster than a quick walk, probably due to fatigue or a fear of predators, Chasmira reasoned. They waited to find a safe glen where they could make camp. The horses could sleep for a while, and a quick bite of food would help everyone travel better through the rest of the night. After Warrick gathered enough wood together, Chasmira waited until he stepped away to whisper the word "burn" and ignite the fire in a flash.

Their dinner was some bread and dried meat he had purchased at the marketplace yesterday. The damp air made the chilly night more bothersome. Chasmira stayed close to the fire to absorb as much warmth as possible, knowing they would be riding again soon.

Warrick, stoic as ever, ignored the cold and busied himself with checking the saddlebags a third time. All the while, he cast watchful glances off into the woods to the north.

He caught a glimpse of bright, pale moonlight through the trees and sighed with relief. Riding without the moonlight would have meant trusting his horse to avoid any obstacles. However, as Warrick turned around to go back to the campfire, he thought it strange that the famously golden Honey Moon should appear so starkly white…

When he looked back at it, he saw not one but two pale orbs through the trees.

In fright he staggered backward, tripping and falling over a stone behind his heels.

"Warrick!" Chasmira leapt up from the fire and rushed to him, hearing him cry out in alarm.

He clambered up onto his hands and knees to look again, but all he saw was the darkness of the woods now. A chill went through him.

"What's the matter?" she knelt down next to him. "Are you hurt?"

"No," waving her off as she tried to pick the leaves, twigs, and other litter out of his clothes and his hair. "I saw something… something not right."

"Not right? What did you see?"

He shook his head and then stared off into the night where he'd seen it. "As if there were two moons, I saw eyes in the night staring back at me."

Eyes in the Night?

There was not a moment longer to think. Before either of

them could say another word, one of the horses let out a terrible noise. It was lifted up into the air by something massive hiding in the darkness. The horse screamed as behind it, two huge pale eyes opened and illuminated the woods with light greater than the brightest moon. Beneath the eyes was its broad, grinning mouth that drizzled blood from where its teeth were buried in the horse's middle.

It stood to full height, towering taller than a three-story house. Its body was hairless and wormlike, with two knobby legs under it and two tiny arms halfway up its torso. The horse's desperate screaming ended when the monster clamped down its jaws, and the front half of the horse fell to the ground with a loud, wet *crunch*. The monster swallowed the other half in a single gulp, and its innards churned loudly as they pulverized the mouthful.

"Get back," Chasmira panted before looking back at the slavering abomination with flames rising from her eyes. "And as for you, you will *obey*."

But the monster did not obey. It snapped boughs off the trees like twigs as it bent down over her, bathing her in the white light from its globe-like eyes.

"OBEY!" she shouted, but the monster only opened its mouth to devour her.

She felt her feet leave the ground as Warrick yanked her backward by her cowl. The monster's jaws snapped shut on the spot where she had stood just seconds ago.

"What is this?" Warrick demanded.

"A forest demon of some kind. The ogre on the road tried to warn us about the Eyes in the Night. It's killed the horses!"

"Just the one," he said, pointing to the other horse desperately pulling against its reins he had tied to a tree. Its shrieks attracted the attention of the monster, which stood only a few steps away.

"No!" Warrick shouted.

"BURN!" Bright streams of fire shot from Chasmira's eyes, lighting up the monster's fleshy back. It stopped mid-step and turned back. Despite the black scorch marks left by the flames, the monster's mouth was still a wide perpetual grin of jagged teeth.

Warrick gawked up at it. "If we can wound it, we can get to the—"

"We? It will kill us both before we can even untie the reins," she said as she backstepped. The monster lurched forward and then lunged for her. She dove left, narrowly dodging its crushing bite. Its head upturned the earth and toppled two trees. "There is no way both of us can leave, Warrick!"

"We go together!" He drew his blue-hilted dagger from under his coat and boldly stabbed at the back of the monster's leg. The blade bounced off it as if he were trying to stab an oak tree. He reared back, this time plunging it into the same place with all his strength. The dagger embedded itself deep, and white foam began to bleed from the wound.

The monster made no cry of pain, no bellow of rage. It simply lifted its foot and kicked Warrick backward with such force that his feet left the ground, and he rolled twice before coming to a stop.

She could not let it turn on him. Screaming, she poured thick billowing fire out of her eyes and into the monster's side with the greatest vehemence she could muster. It winced, shutting its great glowing globes in what appeared to finally be pain. The flames burnt away chunks of its flesh. Shreds of its hide fell like burning paper, and white foam bubbled from the smoking patches.

"Warrick!"

He was getting up, but slowly and unsteadily.

"The message! Take it!"

He wiped the blood running down his face and blinked blearily. He felt for the leather tube in his coat to make sure he had not lost it. The monster was already rising to full height again, and it stepped between the two of them.

"Warrick, go!" She shouted.

Rivulets of fire ran across the ground like cracks forming. Chunks of the monster's burning hide had ignited the dry litter of the forest floor, turning the glade into a fiery battlefield. The earth shook as it hobbled toward her, smoke streaming from its scorched flesh. Its mouth was still frozen in a haunting grin.

"I know not if you can be killed, demon. But I promise to make you *suffer*," and with that last word she flexed her hands, channeling the infernal energy inside her toward her fingertips. The bone in her wrists and hands began to glow red.

She heard the squeal of Warrick's horse and the sound of hoofbeats. *Ride, Warrick. As fast as you can.*

Chasmira took off running. The light from the monster's eyes behind her lit her path as she skirted past tree trunks and lunged over fallen logs, hoping to slow its pursuit even a little. The monster's crashing steps behind her neither slacked nor slowed. It toppled trees and crushed logs, focused solely on her.

She could also hear it sucking in short, panting breaths as it charged after her. When they stopped, she threw herself forward and rolled across the ground. Its open maw bit into a shrub and the ground around it, tearing it from the earth before spitting it out in a cloud of dirt.

A sharp pain shot through her lower leg from her ankle as she scrambled to her feet. She cursed inside. She could ill afford to slow down. Shuddering and shaking, she forced herself to run on the sprained ankle.

Seconds later, the woods were behind her. She had run into a clearing. Ahead of her, the terrain bowed down steeply into a fast-moving river. There was no crossing, but there was a large outcropping of stone that jutted upward and out over the river like a spearhead. The thunderous roar of the water seemed to call to her.

The monster butted a tree aside and broke into the clearing. It spotted her instantly and shambled forward, drool dribbling off its jaws and down its belly.

Chasmira ran as far up the outcropping as she could before she crumpled from the stabbing pain in her ankle. It twisted awkwardly as she fell into a kneel, and hot tears burned down her face. She crawled on one knee to get as close as she could to the tip of the rock.

It shook beneath her as the monster approached, looming over her. Every bone in her body felt like it was vibrating, as if her flesh were fire. She opened her hand, which until now had been squeezed into a tight fist.

In the palm of her hand there appeared a red molten orb like a ball of burning lava. It sizzled and bubbled, pulsing with infernal energy—Chasmira's infernal energy, drawn to the surface and made into a solid substance.

She had only done this once before. The strain felt like her tongue was being slowly torn out of her mouth. She clenched her teeth as hard as she could and molded the energy. Last time, she made a dagger…

The monster's mouth gaped over her for only a moment before it lunged down and closed around her.

The flesh between its eyes burst open, and out came a long red pike that sizzled like hot steel fresh from a forge. The monster stared at it, and tried to push down farther onto Chasmira. The serrated edge of the infernal pike only sawed through more of the monster's head, steaming against mounds of white foam that rose from the horrible gash.

It staggered forward another step, and Chasmira crawled out from under its jaws. She dragged herself between its legs, certain that it would topple forward into the thundering river below.

Instead, Chasmira gasped as a crack formed in the rock outcropping directly beneath her. The weight of the huge forest demon was too much for the narrow rock. She had only a moment before it would fully break in two.

In that moment, she saw the blue hilt of Warrick's dagger sticking out of the back of the monster's leg. She put her good foot up against its heel and yanked the dagger. It slid halfway out before the blade snapped off!

The breaking of the blade and the breaking of the rock fell upon the same moment. Suddenly Chasmira felt weightless, and the whole world seemed to be falling to its side.

Her foot still on the monster's heel, she pushed off it with all her strength, flinging herself off the falling rubble and toward what remained of the rock outcropping. Gripping the broken dagger tightly, she swung it to jam it into the cleft of the cracked rock as deep as she could.

It stuck.

Somewhere below, the collapsed rock and the terrible forest monster vanished, swept away by the rolling, white-crested current. She did not even look down. She put her forehead against the rock and shut her eyes.

There was no way to climb. While there were certainly edges big enough for her hand to grip, there was no assurance they would not give way if she tried to ascend. Her sprained ankle would be unable to support her even if she could find a foothold. There was no feasible way she was going to climb up the steep rock fissure using only her arms.

Chasmira forced herself to look down. She was nearly halfway across the river. Dropping down would mean death; even if she did not drown in the rapids, she would be dashed against the rocks. Climbing down was impossible, for the outcropping was concave at its base and she could not climb upside-down.

She took a few steadying breaths and then reached her left hand to the nearest edge she could find. It felt solid enough, but when she leaned more of her weight onto it, it gave way immediately. A shower of dark rock tumbled down, soundlessly vanishing into the river.

Chasmira clung to the blue hilt of the dagger as tightly as she did to her last hope.

She was that surprised when a length of rope was tossed from above, falling along the fissure beside her.

A voice above her called out over the sound of the river, "Climb!"

"I cannot," she shouted back. "I haven't the strength!"

"Then grab ahold of it and I will pull you up!"

Chasmira carefully grabbed the rope, tested it, and then wrapped her legs around it to transfer her weight onto it. As she began to be pulled up, she yanked the jagged broken dagger out from the rocks.

When she reached the top, she clambered over it, prepared to decline further help at all from Warrick. He had that infuriating way of being so hurtful and then acting chivalrous afterward. She threw his dagger down in the grass.

A second rope was thrown, this time looped into a snare that landed around her neck. She grabbed it, but the loop closed and caught her fingers between the cord and her throat. She tried to choke out a word to defend herself, but she could not as she fell to her side.

Ten soldiers of Argismora stood against her, and in the midst of them was Boe. His left eye had a bandage over it, and his arm was in a sling.

"A spy *and* a sorceress? You are a rare catch indeed," he sneered.

The soldiers rushed her, grabbing for her legs and arms to bind them with rope. She shrieked just one word before she was roughly gagged. It left one of the soldier's faces nothing but a scorched skull inside his helmet. His fellows seized her and angrily drew swords to cut her apart.

"Take her alive," Boe commanded.

Her arms were stretched to either side and tied to a wooden plank laid across her shoulders.

"The Archvate would like to meet her."

CHAPTER 14

Lord Maram peered coldly down at the unrolled message. Warrick shifted his weight from foot to foot, anxiously awaiting his uncle's reply. He opened and shut his fists to work out the tension.

His ribs ached. The entire ride home his head and his nerves had been miles ahead of his horse. It was only as he dismounted that he realized he had been riding with cracked ribs. He still had the metallic taste of blood in his mouth. He had not been struck there—he still had all his teeth—but his forehead had quite a gash and his nose was broken.

At last Maram set down the paper. "So the Guardian City is wary. It seems that even in the dim twilight of my brother's reign, his shadow still stretches out before us."

"She was right."

"Remarkably, yes."

"We must start a search immediately."

Maram blinked slowly. "Search? For what?"

"Uncle, if she's alive, she'll be moving during daylight—"

"And if not, we are spreading ourselves like sheep in a pasture when hungry wolves are about. Why take such a risk?"

"We cannot just leave her," Warrick nearly laughed,

incredulous.

"Why not? She has done as she promised. Her wit and wiles delivered into our hands the proof of her prediction, and now we are forewarned. Her usefulness is over."

"You don't know that! Perhaps she survived against the demon."

Maram snorted, "Survived? Against a Hobble? No one has ever encountered so terrible a creature and lived. Besides, we are all better off if she is dead. Had the men of Argismora caught her, she would surely tell them that we sent her—a Chaos witch—into their midst, and thus would she hasten our destruction."

"The only hasty one is you, Uncle—"

"In these chambers, I am addressed as Lord Maram," the patriarch shouted angrily, his words echoing between the black stone walls. "I should not have to remind you that your father is no longer here to rule what is left of his realm."

Warrick's shoulders sagged. "No. You should not have to." With a slow bow, the son of Mirikinin turned and retreated out of the room.

His father was dead. Why did he need to be reminded? Why was it so hard to believe, to accept? There was no emptiness, no hollowness, no vacant space that Warrick felt, as a mourning son should. There was no sense of loss, only confusion, for in his mind his father was not dead but merely absent, like someone who had simply stepped away. As if he would walk in the door again at any moment, put Uncle Maram in his place, and take his rightful seat upon that black throne…

That was not going to happen. He knew it in his soul, even if his mind was still in denial.

He walked the halls, contemplating. Maram had spoken of Mirikinin's shadow stretching before them, inspiring dread in all who saw it. Despite his absence, that still inspired fear. Warrick watched his own shadow upon the black stone walls. Would it ever inspire the same dread, or was the realm better off under Lord Maram?

Decades ago, Maram and Mirikinin strove against one another for that seat of power. Both were great men, men of war, so they agreed that the first to wed and produce an heir would rule. Warrick's very birth was a victory for his father. He now doubted if the rest of his life could honor his father's memory.

And if Maram remained in power, it would potentially mean his children would succeed him after his death. Warrick shuddered at the thought of that simpleton Lart attempting to rule from the black throne…

"Warrick?"

He jumped at the sound at Lart's voice behind him in the dark hallway. "Damn it, Lart, do not sneak up on me!"

"Soth's sake, Warrick, I didn't even know you were back!"

Warrick looked him up and down. "And I didn't know you pillage the cupboards at midnight in nothing but your breeches."

Lart chuckled, "Aye, no sense getting all dressed. I'm raiding a kitchen, not a castle."

"What did you have?"

"Last of the blueberry pie."

"Nyell didn't make blueberry, she made mulberry."

Lart smacked his lips. "Hmm. Might have been. I ate it fast."

"Shame. I hoped to get the last of it."

"You haven't eaten?"

"Hardly time for it. Not that I've any appetite left tonight."

"Oh no," Lart groaned. "What's the word from the big city?"

Warrick sighed deeply. "The Prefect of Argismora ordered his commander to number their army. Apparently the Archvate of the city has named us as a threat to him and they plan to pay us a visit."

"A threat? We've not even a standing army left after what—"

"I know, Lart," cutting him off there.

A somber silence hung in the air between the two cousins. Warrick sullen but restrained, Lart embarrassed and fumbling.

"Where's she?"

Warrick grunted, scowling at the floor.

"Warrick?"

"We were attacked in the woods tonight. I took the only horse left alive and fled. She stayed behind."

"Stayed behind?" Lart echoed, wide-eyed.

"It was not my choice, it was hers. Your father thinks searching for her is a fool's errand, but I do not believe she is dead. That woman has survived worse," he said, gnawing his lip in thought. The two men traded glances wordlessly before Warrick finally said, "I have need of Terror. He's a tracker. Fear not, I will bring him back."

"No you won't," Lart answered, "I will. Because I'm going along."

Warrick smiled in relief.

"Just… let me get dressed first."

ψ

While Terror circled the camp trying to pick up a scent to follow, Warrick and Lart walked the trail of upturned earth and broken trees that led them to the river.

"I ain't seen anything like it," Lart said, hunting bow in his hands.

"No, and I pray you never will."

The trail led them to the outcropping that overlooked the river, now bathed in the golden glow of the full Honey Moon in the sky. They had never seen the unbroken rock before, so nothing seemed out of place, and the trail appeared to end there.

A blue gleam from the ground caught Warrick's eye. He bent down to investigate more closely, and found his broken dagger in the grass, reflecting the moonlight.

"Lart, look here."

"Your dagger. But the blade's snapped in half."

"I had plunged it into the monster's leg before I was struck," Warrick explained. "I stabbed it in deep, till the crossguard touched flesh. It would not be lying here unless she had slain the monster and pulled it out herself."

"Or tried to, at least."

Warrick looked this way and that, searching for any clue as to where she had gone. There was no carcass, no bloody trail.

Lart whistled and called for Terror. He bounded to Lart's side, broad sensitive ears twitching toward every sound of the night. Hellishunds were famous for their hearing, but their sense of smell was just as keen. He pressed his snout to the ground where the burnt soldier had fallen dead before his fellows picked up his body.

Terror growled.

"He's found something he doesn't like," Lart said, watching.

Now following the scent of the soldiers, Terror circled where they had snared and bound Chasmira. He barked, calling the two men to the spot. Warrick knelt and ran his hands over the trod-upon clay to feel for tracks.

"Hoofprints. Horses," Warrick said with surprise.

Lart sighed, patting Terror on the head.

"And boots, too large to be only hers."

"How many?"

"Too many," Warrick said.

Terror sniffed at a clump of horse hair in the dirt. Lart pinched it between his fingers, held it to the dog's nose, and gave him a command to seek it out. The dog trotted dutifully onward, nose to the ground, before looking back and barking for them to follow.

Warrick grimaced. "And they lead northward. They are taking her back to Argismora."

CHAPTER 15

"Ah, you're finally awake."

Chasmira moaned and forced her eyes open. Sticky crust stretched between her eyelids. After a few seconds she could make out Boe standing in front of her, with his eyepatch and his polished armor.

Her throat burned and her teeth ached. Her tongue scratched against the rope wedged between her jaws to both bind her and keep her from speaking. Her hands were still tied to the wooden plank, as was the rope snare around her neck. If the ropes around her were cut or untied, the snare would catch her when she fell, breaking her neck as would a hangman's noose.

"She must have been tired," Boe said.

An unseen man answered, "All day at the plow handle of evil, sowing seeds of ruin... The field of Chaos is exhausting for its laborers to tread day after day."

Despite her bleary sight and throbbing pain, she still recognized the figure that stepped out wrapped in white silk linen and with a brass circlet upon his head: the Archvate Simonas Parku... Simon the Pure.

"You had nearly set your own bed ablaze, Commander," said the Archvate, his words dripping with scorn. "I am certain Janessa is not even her true name. Not that it matters at all, for the wild beasts of the field and creeping things of the darkness all die nameless as well."

Chasmira definitely felt like a wild beast. Her head swam somewhere between malicious urges and torturous pangs of hunger and thirst. Her hair was greasy, knotted, and matted down on one side. She did her best to ignore the scent of her own filth, as she had been left tied here all night and day until this hour. She was not even sure what hour it was. The sun hid behind dark autumn clouds that murmured with dull thunder.

She exhaled a hoarse noise, attempting to cast fire at him, but could not articulate the word with the rope in her mouth. Invocation required speech.

"Not here, creature, not here." The Archvate wagged a finger and turned his back to her, giving the soldiers room. They placed armful after armful of hay at her feet, and she only now realized she was mounted up in the bed of a wooden cart.

"The infernal fire of Chaos inside you should be extinguished with fire of equal virulence. It is the closest thing to purification you can experience. Fire from within has defiled you. Fire from without will wipe you away. Your ashes can be scattered to scatter your shame."

Boe stepped to the Archvate's side with a question. "Your Grace, I would have thought it better to execute her in the city, that the citizens should bear witness to this."

"And put in jeopardy the lives of every man, woman, and child inside those precious walls? Commander, while I appreciate such a sentiment that humiliates and publicly punishes evil, please understand that this woman could have set the entire tower ablaze with but a few choice words from her lips. She is a silent threat to everything around her. She is death, corseted and painted. She is destruction."

The soldiers continued to pack the wagon bed with hay.

The Archvate looked back to regard her. Through the white silk, he appeared as little more than a faceless, unfeeling specter of vengeance. "Thus I say no, Commander. She will burn in a wilderness as untamed as she, and her ashes will be lost in the mire. We will commend her infernal soul not to journey to the court of the dreaded death god in cold, cold Avgannon, but rather to the abyss of fiery oblivion to be erased forever."

"Well said, Your Grace. Let us not keep the abyss waiting," and Boe himself took the torch from one of his soldiers and walked up to her.

With her head lashed back, all she could do was groan something to him, her dry throat seizing.

He looked up, and Chasmira could see the torchlight glisten in his stony grey gaze as it met hers. "Such a waste."

The hay turned into a roaring blaze in seconds. Lines of fire crawled up her dress, engulfing her in flames that continued to rise.

The rope in her jaws did not even allow her to fully scream. Her wails—weak, wavering, raw—hauntingly filled the air. No other sound dared interrupt. The soldiers stood solemnly staring as she, damned, burnt there in front of them. Thunder rumbled through the sky overhead like the tolling of a great bell in the sky.

The first soldier to fall was the one beside the Archvate.

He had an arrow straight through his neck, its head protruding out a few inches on the other side. The blood sprayed across the white veil that covered Archvate's face, and he staggered back as he watched the soldier collapse.

The next soldier was trampled under the hooves of Warrick's horse as it ran him down, crushing him. Another soldier lifted a spear to hurl at their attacker, but he was quickly dragged down and mauled. Terror had gotten to him first, biting off a stringy chunk of his face before ripping his arm off with a few hard pulls. The huge dog then immediately lunged on the next soldier, who could barely draw his sword before he too was torn apart.

Boe, meanwhile, ran for cover as another soldier was felled by an arrow to the chest. Lart knelt some distance away, nocking another arrow in his hunting bow before taking aim at the scrambling soldiers.

With the soldiers in disarray, Warrick dismounted his horse and went for the wagon. The entire bed was a blaze large enough that he could hardly see her. Wasting not a moment, the burly man climbed onto the back of the wagon, slammed his hands down upon the burning plank, and threw himself backward with all of his might. He toppled backward, tearing free the entire plank and Chasmira with it.

He tore off his coat, patting her down as quickly as possible to smother the flames, starting with her head. Drawing his broken blue dagger from its sheath, he sawed through ropes around her hands and her neck before a soldier charged him with a raised sword. Warrick parried the blow with his dagger's crossguard and struck him in the eye, sending him to the ground.

The soldier rolled, clutching his bleeding eye. He cursed and screamed angrily, vowing revenge that he would never get to take, for just a few feet away, out from under Warrick's coat emerged

Chasmira.

She was charred into shreds of blackened flesh that flaked off her like dead leaves as she crawled. Smoke rose from her body and blood seeped from her shattered skin. Her mouth was lipless, her eyes lidless. She stared blindly but dragged herself to him as if guided by something else. What guided her was something she desperately needed in this moment: *life.*

The soldier was clambering for his sword when suddenly she shoved him down, jamming two fingers into his nostrils and breaking his nose. The man cried in terror as the disfigured sorceress growled from her scorched throat, "DIE."

His cry fell to a low howl. His skin paled and his cheeks sank. Atop him, Chasmira's burnt flesh fell away and fresh skin reappeared beneath it. Missing flesh reformed. Missing hair regrew.

"DIE," she hissed.

His howl faded to a wheeze. His skin rotted away and his eyes vanished into dry holes. Chasmira drank in the last of his life force with a snort and wiped her nose with the back of her hand.

The soldiers that remained took a slow step backward.

Before them, the woman that wailed helplessly in flames just a moment earlier now rose up on her feet, looking stronger and more vital than ever. Her mouth was twisted in a foul grimace, and her eyes burnt with streams of red fire. The Chaos within her had fresh fuel: the life of the unfortunate soldier now mummified on the ground.

A burst of fire from her eyes burnt the nearest soldier into a pillar of black charcoal. It twitched with his final whimper.

A second burst turned the legs of another soldier into ash that crumbled beneath him. He screamed and crawled away desperately before Terror silenced him with his jaws.

"*Tuhhus-walh!*" the Archvate shouted, and Chasmira turned to see lattices of radiant energy wrapping around him in the shape of armor over his blood-spattered robes. As they did, he knelt and picked up a sword that lay in the grass nearby.

"Coward," she accused him, flames leaping from her mouth with every word. "Is the ward of the divine too noble for lowly footsoldiers? They spill blood and gather straw for you, but even now you lift not a finger to help them."

"Hypocrite," he answered and pointed the sword tip at her in a middle guard stance. "As if their lives mean anything to you, witch!"

"There it is, that word again. You say 'witch' when what you mean is 'kindling.' Well, let us see how well *you* burn!"

Bright red fire shot from her eyes as the Archvate finished a mumbled incantation. Glistening with divine silver light, his outstretched sword split the flames into two fiery walls that curled around him.

He shouted over the roar of the flames, "Cruel woman, you beguile men to do your bidding and burn those that refuse!"

She replied with hard, coarse laughter. "That would make me no different than the Angelic you kneel to, Your Grace, except for one thing: I keep the promises I make." The fire in her eyes died down to a flicker.

The Archvate stumbled but regained his footing, keeping the sword raised.

"And I promise that I shall make her city *suffer.*" Her veins glowed, hot infernal energy pooling in the palm of her hand to use however she willed.

Lart loosed his arrow, aimed straight at the Archvate's heart.

With a whirl of brilliant silver strands trailing behind it, the sword struck down the arrow. Blade met arrowhead in a flare of sparks.

A long, sizzling, infernal spike burst from the back of the Archvate's cowl. Dark crimson ran down his white veils, and he crumpled within them onto the cold earth.

Chasmira had struck true. Smoke still rising from her hands, she stepped forward to glower down at the body. The long spike she created dissolved away into a swarm of chittering red beetles, no longer held together in a solid form by her will.

Warrick came to her side, panting in the heat of battle. "You are… unharmed?" he asked, looking her up and down in shock. While her dress was a blackened, tattered mess, her exposed skin was whole and fair.

"Chaos gives me command over the fire that burns in my soul. It can destroy, but it can also consume. And when it consumes, it sustains me." She let out a low laugh. "They should have beheaded me."

Warrick scanned the bloody carnage. "Idiots."

CHAPTER 16

Idiots!" Maram bellowed in rage.

Warrick and Lart stood silent in the center of the audience chamber. The fire behind Lord Maram's throne seemed to burn higher than normal to match his temperament.

He continued railing at them, "The two of you set off into the night like feral cats and now you wander back an hour till dawn, licking your wounds? I would expect this of you, Lart, but Warrick? Our entire livelihood depends on you! We depend on you. We all trust in you, and here you up and leave over what? That churlish woman?"

"My ears are burning, which means I am being well spoken of," Chasmira said as she strode into the chamber behind them. The hellishund accompanied her, unwilling to leave her side after almost losing her once.

Maram's pale blue eyes looked like they might pop out of his head. "You live! I had been told rumors of your demise—"

"Rumors that have been greatly exaggerated," she interrupted, stepping in front of Warrick and Lart. "Your son and nephew came back for me. In this, they showed greater mercy than either you or the Archvate."

"The Archvate?" Maram exclaimed, tottering backward to sit

upon the black throne. "What malice did he unto you?"

She shook her head, chuckling. "A better question would be what malice did he *not* unto me, but that is all water under the bridge now. Argismora's divine leader is as brainless in death as he was in life. The fowl have his body now, if they even want it."

"Death? You mean—"

"It's true," Warrick interjected. "He is extremely dead."

"He was a prick too," Chasmira added.

Warrick nodded. "Doubtful anyone loved him."

Lart snickered.

"Silence, all of you!" Maram fumed. "Do you realize what you have done? You have murdered the head of the Oracle! If the Guardian City had reason to fear us before, you have given them doubly reason to hate us now."

Chasmira stepped closer to the throne. "What does it matter? Attack us tomorrow, next week, next moon? This was inevitable, Lord Maram. The evil word descended, the message was sent, and now blood is spilt. Better that we know it is coming than being ambushed unawares, lounging without preparation for war."

"War? You need two armies to have a war. My brother is dead, and our army with him. We have nothing to defend ourselves but these walls."

"Then they will have to be enough," she said earnestly. "Because they are coming. You have at the most three days. The warriors of Argismora are rising up, and they are coming for you."

ψ

The rest of the day was spent in preparation. Servants stacked pots of tar in the gatehouse above the main door, which would inevitably be the most vulnerable point in the defenses. Sentries with warbows were posted upon the fortress walls, and the weaponsmiths whet every blade in the armory. Every guard was pulled into the courtyard and drilled on what they might expect: Argismora's army had not taken the field in many years, but history testified they were a fighting force of some renown. They would likely ignore the walls and attack the main gate, trying to make for a quick victory with minimal time for the guards to respond and thus minimal losses. Mirikinin's guards were formidable, but they were nothing like the thousands of great barbarian warriors that once rode with the Mad Prince.

"Forty-two men on the walls," Warrick said, looking over the defenses from the wall, "And twenty footmen bearing pikes and swords."

"Your uncle has little faith that we can defeat whatever army Argismora sends to us."

"Defeating them is hardly an option. They will outnumber us greatly. If we are lucky, they burn the fields and then come straightaway to take the main gate. We may inflict heavy enough casualties that they are forced to retreat and at least delay their return. If fate looks upon us darkly, they will encamp outside our warbows' range and capture any caravans bringing us supplies over the next few weeks..."

"Until we starve," Chasmira said grimly.

Silence prevailed after that. They simply stood side by side looking over it all. In the fields outside the walls, the farmhands hurried back in wagons loaded with their hasted harvest. In the courtyard within the walls, the guards gathered tools of war. It was as if the bushels, bales, and barrels were coming back to be magically changed into pots, pikes, and poleaxes.

"Thank you," said Warrick.

She did not answer right away, thinking at first that she imagined him saying it. "What for?"

"For warning us, else we would have no idea they were coming. You fled Dimol Gol and could have gone anywhere but here. You could have gone westward to the Dwarven guilds or southward to fairer lands than these. The comfort of Holireath's pools or even Oxhaven's vineyards could have driven out the memories of war from you."

Chasmira nodded, blinking away the wind. "I could have."

"Instead you risked yourself coming here and you risked yourself saving my life. Why?"

She lowered her gaze in thought and then searched the horizon before answering, "Because everywhere I have gone, I have left the dead behind me. Yes, armies upon their battlefield but also family, and the only friend I ever had. There is—" and she choked on the next words before she could say them "—no bringing them back. All we can do is protect what we have. Once it's gone, it's gone."

Warrick looked down at her wordlessly.

She dared a glance up at him. "I saw the chance to save lives instead of take them. It has been quite a while since my last good deeds, but I see that such deeds still do not go unpunished."

"Yes, that part of life has not changed."

"I would like to think all of this honors my friend."

Warrick set his gaze upon the horizon toward Argismora. "Despite all the good deeds and intentions, the House of Mirikinin may still be fated to fall."

"Perhaps. Perhaps not. You have your father's blood in your veins, Warrick. Some people are bigger than fate can control."

CHAPTER 17

The sun had just set upon the third day. The sky was a deep violet, striped with clouds that turned from gold to black in the vanishing sunlight. As the stars emerged from the growing darkness, so too did dozens of torches emerge from the woodlands.

Fire blazed across the fields and the apple orchards. It did not matter that the crops had already been harvested. This was not a strategic destruction of enemy supplies but an act of intimidation, for all inside the fortress' walls to watch their livelihood burning around them, for them to see the starry twilight obscured by clouds of smoke.

From the red ash and smoke appeared the warriors of Argismora. Clad in white armor with black war paint streaking down from their helmet visors like tears, they looked like an army of weeping ghosts. Sleek swords and shining shields were in their hands. This army, over a thousand strong, gathered at the west base of the hill.

Warrick stood at a corner of the wall, flanked on either side by footmen holding shields ready to cover him. They were the only three people visible upon the black stone wall, for the sentries were all knelt behind the embattlements. His deep voice echoed through the night, "Warriors of the Guardian City, you burn our fields like wild marauders and trample our land like migrating swine. Why?"

A horse stepped through the smoke and walked to the front of the battle line. Upon its back was a single rider in armor like the others, except for a black sash on his right shoulder. He removed his helmet to reveal long red hair that framed his pale, aquiline features.

"Children of Mirikinin," the man shouted, "You harbor within your walls a woman of Dimol Gol. She may be your prisoner, or she may be your guest. Whatever she is to you, know this: she is a Chaos witch and will only bring doom to you. Open your gates and deliver her into our hands, so that we may do our duty to destroy her."

Warrick let the words hang in the air before he spoke again. "You know with certainty that she is in league with Chaos?"

"Aye," said the man. "She has killed our Archvate Simon the Pure and for this she must die. Deliver her to us, and we will trouble you no more."

"You have brought quite a host. Does it take a thousand men to destroy one woman?"

"No, just one. I have brought the other nine hundred and ninety-nine to help you see reason."

"Then you have mistaken me for a reasonable man," Warrick replied coldly. "The woman is mine and I will do with her whatsoever I please. Go, return back, and tell your Prefect not to disturb us again."

The man scowled, and his voice turned sullen. "I will ask only once more. Open your gates, deliver the witch to us, and we will spare you."

"I am not such a great fool as to open our gates while an army waits on our doorstep. If all you wanted was the woman, we could throw her down to you from this wall. No, you are here to make an end of the House of Mirikinin and destroy his heirs. If there is anything I dislike more than threats, it is trickery."

"Very well," the man said, "No more trickery. If you will not open your gates, we will open them ourselves." He placed his helmet back upon his head, turned his horse around, and rode back across the smoldering field.

Warrick turned his back, his two sentries closing their shields behind him. As he descended the stairs, he took a few slow breaths to slow his pounding heart.

At the bottom Chasmira waited, listening to every word traded over the wall. She wrung the fork-tipped iron staff in her hands, bracing herself against it. When Warrick arrived next to her, he made eye contact only to show her the tension in his gaze. She opened her mouth to speak, but Warrick beat her to it.

His voice rumbled so low that only she could hear him. "I'm a farmer, not a warrior."

"Your farm is in flames," said Chasmira. "Such actions have made many farmers into warriors before."

He stared down at her for a long moment. Her words put fresh kindling beneath his self-doubt. He did not want to fight. He did not want war. He did not want this fire-eyed sorceress to encourage him.

"Shall I take a position on the wall?" she asked.

"No. You will draw far too much attention. Stay inside the walls. Should they somehow breach the gate, your powers will be needed at the bottleneck. And if the sentries need to fall back, they will need you to cover their retreat. Do not put yourself in harm's way any more than necessary."

The huge man brushed past her, across the drawbridge, and into the black stone fortress. He was likely reporting to Lord Maram.

If the sentries need to fall back. She thought about his words. Warrick did not assume for a minute that his guards would lay down their lives defending his home. He thought they would do their best and then run when the battle got too intense. "We go together," he had said to her in Argismora and again in the dark forest. Sacrificing others was not even on the table for him.

Warrick returned outside and shouted, "Sentries! A volley please, to remind our guests that they are invaders on our land!"

The sentries all nocked arrows, stepped from their hiding places, and drew back their warbows. Their volley found the gaps in the warriors' armor. Thirty or so men dropped to the ground with arrows driven deep into their shoulders, legs, and eye sockets. As the screams of the wounded rose, so rose the roars of the other warriors, who rushed to form a shield wall. The next volley pelted against the interlocked shields of a battle line.

Warrick was about to order another volley when a dark shape came hurtling out of the smoke through the air. When it landed in the fortress' sunken inner yard, it shattered into wooden planks and a huge splash.

A water barrel?

Indeed it was, and left on the ground amid the debris were six round shapes that had been inside the huge wooden barrel. Next to them also lay random swords, mallets, and hooks…

Chasmira's eyes widened. "SCARRLOK!"

Arms and legs sprouted from holes in the six round shells on the ground. The Scarrlok's faces were hidden under splint armor masks of leather and iron that only left their green pointy ears exposed out the sides. They scurried to their weapons and charged toward the gate.

Warrick bellowed a command to the confused sentries, while over their heads two more water barrels came crashing down in the yard. The masked goblins inside them grabbed their weapons and squawked a warbling war cry. Arrows came down from all directions, but most of them glanced off Scarrlok's shells and armor. They cackled and ran for the gate like dogs scrambling for a scrap of meat. Four footmen stood at the front gate, but they would quickly be torn apart by the goblins.

Chasmira crossed the drawbridge from the fortress to the front gate. "Raise the bridge!"

Warrick replied with a hard stare. "Get back here!"

"Raise the bridge," she repeated.

He growled in frustration, grabbed the nearest guard's pike and shield, and crossed the drawbridge to join her. "Raise the bridge," he commanded over his shoulder.

The guards protested, "But Sire—"

"DO IT!"

Warrick was hardly two steps off the drawbridge when it rose, leaving him and Chasmira separated from the main fortress. Together they stood—the six of them—against a growing horde of snarling Scarrlok. Another trio of barrels landed in the yard, doubling their numbers.

"Sorry now that you didn't take the slave merchant's offer?"

Chasmira quipped to Warrick.

"Shut up and burn them already."

Streams of flame shot forth, turning a cluster of the Scarrlok to smoking hunks of meat. Undeterred, the rest of the horde still charged. Warrick and his footmen drove their long pikes down into them, piercing through scaly skin and carapace, but more Scarrlok simply climbed over their skewered fellows.

One of the footmen was too slow to raise his shield. Several Scarrlok grabbed hold of it, together tearing it from his hands while another one swept a mallet across his legs. He cried out as he slipped down the side of the pit and was repeatedly stabbed with swords and hooks. Flames from Chasmira's eyes sent his attackers flailing backward off him, and Warrick pulled the bleeding man up.

"I've got you!" he shouted over the din of weapons clashing and the squawking of bloodthirsty goblins.

Chasmira blinked away flames and turned, hearing a sound behind her. A small Scarrlok had slipped past them and was tugging at the heavy drawbar that held the main gate shut. Brandishing the iron staff in her hands, she speared him between two of the sharp prongs and flung him from the door. The Scarrlok spun on the ground, hissed, and drew out a nasty-looking, saw-toothed blade.

It was stomped down immediately by Warrick, who pinned it with his foot before cutting its head off. Her smile in thanks was brief, for a second later a bright red explosion threw her to the ground.

Warrick felt around for her blindly in the black smoke. "Are you alive? Say something!"

Coughing was her best reply as she grasped his hand, and he pulled her to her feet. Her ears were ringing loudly. Even the clash of weapons behind Warrick sounded like dull, distant bells.

"What happened?" he aloud.

A sentry from the wall cried out, "Sire! They're bombarding the gate! Get down!"

Warrick did not hesitate. At the sentry's warning, he threw himself to the ground and pulled Chasmira down with him. She was not wearing a helmet—for it obscured her vision and would melt in the heat of her fiery sight—leaving her vulnerable to flying shrapnel. An iron shard or a chunk of wood could easily strike her in the head.

"ANOTHERRRR!" the wall sentry shouted in warning.

A second red explosion rattled the gate with a deafening blast. Crumbs of black stone and wood rained down, and a wave of black smoke spread over them. Straining, Chasmira pulled her arm free from under Warrick and leaned up on her elbow. In the smoke, she could still see the shapes of the footmen stabbing and swatting Scarrlok in the melee.

"Bombarding the gate?" Warrick coughed incredulously. "How?"

"Blast potions. Magic potions that explode and *burn*," she answered, sending a long stream of fire that scorched a Scarrlok into a mound of black ash. Beads of sweat dripped off her face, and she panted for breath. "Likely affixed to an arrow in place of a normal arrowhead."

"I need to get us back inside."

"No. You need to kill those bloody goblins before they rip your guards apart!" She shoved him off and rose up into a knelt position, scooping his sword out of the dirt in her trembling hands. She pushed the hilt into his grasp. "Take your damned sword, get up, and KILL THEM!"

Her screaming words were punctuated by the blast of a third bombardment that tore away a chunk of the thick wood planks. Warrick did not even look back at the gate. He locked eyes with her, a look that clearly expressed his shaky hopes that she knew what she was doing. With an angry bellow he then charged into the fray alongside his brave footmen.

With Warrick no longer in the way, Chasmira could see straight out the hole in the door. Outside on the hill, hundreds of warriors advanced with shields carefully raised. Arrows bounced off the shields, which all bore the same insignia as Commander Boe's seal.

They have not charged the gate, near as they are. Which means it must not be damaged badly enough for them yet. They're staying back because the blast—

And behind the warriors, she saw a small red dot leap up into the night sky in the distance.

I knew it.

Blast arrows were aimed upward to then fall in a curved path down upon their targets. The arrowheads were not pointed blades but pointed glass caps, filled with explosive potions that had devastating effects on a battlefield. She had seen them used against Mirikinin's soldiers at Dimol Gol.

Chasmira ran to the gate and looked out the hole. Above the warriors she saw the red dot coming directly for her…

"*Burn*," she shouted. Flames shot forth upward—over the warriors instead of at them—and met the incoming blast arrow just ten feet above their heads.

The bright red fireball engulfed dozens of white-armored warriors, and the blast knocked at least a hundred of them flat on the ground. The sentries on the wall wasted no time: they loosed arrow after arrow into the fallen warriors to kill them where they lay. The rest of the front line scrambled in disarray, half of them trying to reform the shield wall.

A voice shouted over the noise of the battle. Chasmira could not discern his words, but she discerned his voice and that was enough. It was the red-haired man who traded words with Warrick before the battle. A lump formed in her throat, and she paused in silence as he issued his next command:

"TAKE THE GATE!"

Her heart shuddered.

With one voice his army roared, and with one accord they charged. Still hundreds strong, they were not wasting any more time. She backed away. Nothing stood between her and the gate. Through the hole in it, she could see swords waving in the air. They were coming fast, and if they broke through…

Warrick and his footmen were shin-deep in guts and green blood. They were missing pieces of their armor where the Scarrlok had crawled onto them like ticks crawling on dogs, ripping off metal and cloth to get to flesh. The men looked tired. Their arms looked heavy.

Another trio of barrels came down in the yard. *The bowmen must not be able to find those catapults in the smoke. Damn these goblins!* Chasmira growled and trudged toward them, away from the gate, next to Warrick.

"Sentries!" She pointed to the Scarrlok. "Tar them!"

"The tar pots are to defend the gate," Warrick objected.

"I *am* defending it, Warrick."

She had lived through war. He had not. "Do as she says!"

The sentries obeyed. They hefted the tar pots and hurled them down into the yard. The pots shattered, spilling their sticky contents all over the squat, green, walleyed invaders. Tar pooled around their feet, making it difficult to walk. The Scarrlok squawked and cursed. The last thing they saw was the sorceress crouched like a beast, drawing two lines of flame from her eyes to the tar.

They went up in a plume of red flame so tall, the army outside could see it billowing up over the wall. Some warriors gawked upward at the sight and the black smoke that followed. Most pushed forward all the more urgently, eager to kill whoever had done that.

Chasmira's legs shook and buckled. She panted, sweat dripping off her eyelashes and the tip of her nose. She expected to feel her knees hit the ground, but instead she felt weightless when her legs went out from under her. Warrick bore her up with one arm and let her lean on his shoulder.

"Take a moment. Breathe," he said.

"I've got plenty of fire left in me."

"That's what I'm afraid of. You look red as hot coals."

"Nonsense," she snapped in denial. She had never summoned up this much inner fire this quickly, and she did not know if it would have any ill effects. She only knew one thing. "That gate won't hold."

"I know. We should get inside… now."

She scoffed. "We can't. Lower the drawbridge now, and they'll be through before you can raise it. We may as well just open the gate for them and *let* them in."

Warrick stepped back and took in the entire scene. The inner courtyard was a field of burning tar, green blood, and the twitching corpses of scorched Scarrlok. Upon the wall, his sentries were trading arrows with archers on the ground outside. One of them took an arrow to the neck, falling limp from the unbreakable black stone walls. A throng of Argismora's warriors were beating against the main gate while, above them, sentries in the guardhouse tipped cauldrons full of boiling water onto the invaders. The din of shouting and screaming began to sound muffled to Warrick, as if he were sinking underwater.

He snapped out of it when a bleeding footman clutched his arm to steady himself. His men were growing weary and three of them lay dying on the ground. This had gone far enough.

His hand did not fumble as it grasped the horn from his hip and raised it to his lips. The sounding of the curled horn was a haunting note like the howl of winter wind.

From the east, distant howls answered.

The warriors outside did not stop their advance. They did not check their flanks. Why would they? They were the aggressors and needed only look forward toward their target. Why would they turn to look back?

One warrior only did so when he saw long streaks of blood spatter across his fellow's back. Behind him was an ironwolf, shaking another warrior's mangled body around in its jaws like a dog playing with a rope. He could not move or react. He could not even form his next thought before he himself was seized, dragged, and flung through the air by another of the huge, snarling war dogs.

The rearmost positions collapsed immediately. Warriors screamed as they fell to ironwolves that darted out of the smoking fields. The firelight glistened off their metallic fur, giving them the appearance of fiery, red, four-legged demons. Their ferocity was unyielding. They tore shields from hands, hands from arms, and arms from shoulders. Ahead of them ran Lart's hellishund, directing the bloody havoc across the back of the battle line. Lart and Warrick had run this drill with Terror and the ironwolves more than thirty times in the last three days.

Warrick fastened the horn back on his hip and listened. Argismora's warriors were dying by the dozens. Their screams and the growls of the warbeasts echoed together like a grisly duet.

"Did it work?" Chasmira asked, beads of sweat upon her face.

"It did," said Warrick. "But I know not how well, or for how long."

The gate shook with the force of the warriors outside still pounding loudly against it. The ironwolves were tearing through the army but would never kill all of them. Not that they were intended to; they were meant to scatter the warriors and terrify them into retreat. They were legendary tools of fear, thanks to Prince Mirikinin.

Warrick had no more time to dwell on it. The next charge at the gate cracked the drawbar that laid across the doors. He willed the wolves to drive further into the ranks, but all he could do was listen to the carnage outside the walls. He twisted the sword in his grip. It hurt.

"They're coming through," Chasmira said. Her voice was ragged and dry.

"They won't."

"They will."

"No, they won't." He gripped his sword tighter.

She reaped strength from his words. She licked the sweat that dripped onto her lips and tossed her hair back out of her eyes.

They heard the chilling howls of ironwolves out beyond the sprawling army. Had a few warriors leapt onto the backs of the ironwolves, driving their blades between the iron quills to draw blood? An ironwolf's armor could stop an arrow, but the beast was not invincible.

Another roar from the army outside. They were not stopping. They charged the gate once more, and the drawbar cracked further. The doors budged open a few inches.

"Warrick, get behind me," Chasmira growled.

He knew better than to question her.

The army chanted ferociously, seeing the gate doors finally giving way. They raised one final shout and burst open the gates in a final charge.

There was no stopping all of them. The sentries on the wall had shot and burned them. The ironwolves had torn and ravaged them. Now it was her turn. Veins bulged in her face and forehead as Chasmira let loose her infernal fire in a final onslaught. The jets of flame from her eyes burnt white-hot, lined with lapping flares of bright gold. The very ground between her boots and theirs burnt like red hot coals as fire filled the open gateway. The nearest warriors burnt into curled pillars of black ash. Behind them, men screamed as their armor turned into deathtraps of molten metal pouring into their eyes and mouths. By the time the flames died down, dozens of Argismora's warriors lay dead upon the scorched earth.

The remaining army inched toward the open gate. Between them and the House of Mirikinin stood Chasmira. Her eyes burned like torches, with fire that rose above her head. Her red flesh glowed so intensely it was nearly transparent, revealing the dark outline of her skull underneath.

"Come if you dare." Her voice echoed as if something infinitely sinister were speaking right along with her. "Come burn with me."

They shivered in hesitation. That is, until one warrior broke and charged with a loud war cry. The rest followed.

Chasmira felt the fire surging in her now. She howled with the rage of something unearthly. The more she allowed it to move through her, the less she could control it. The less she controlled it, the more it controlled her. The more she surrendered to it…

A new sound broke over the raging screams of the burning battlefield. The long bray of war horns sounded through the night, and every warrior of Argismora stopped exactly where they stood. Desperate voices shouted from the back of the battle line, voices that called the men to take positions.

The warriors backed away quickly. Some of them ran to get back to their positions. The positions they took, however, did not make a battle line. They made a defensive circle.

Dumbfounded, Chasmira looked wordlessly to Warrick for an answer. His slack-jawed stare was his only reply.

The answer came in the form of a dozen pale beasts that charged the circle. They were goatish in appearance, with white fur and curling ram horns, but their strides were long and quick like horses. Metal war helmets were affixed to their heads. These were not wild beasts, but war mounts.

"Ivrits," she gasped. Ivrits were common war mounts of the eastern tribes, but what were they doing here? What force would have traveled all the way from the peninsula to adjoin itself to this fiery battle? She staggered to the broken gate to see.

The war horns brayed again, and the ivrits galloped away to the top of the hillocks. There, they joined a hundred more of their kind that stood at the ready. On every one of their backs sat a dark hooded rider decked in fur and iron scales. The light of the waning moon gleamed on the lances they lowered into position for a charge. It gleamed also upon the quills of the ironwolves that emerged from the northern forest.

The warriors of Argismora desperately tried to reposition themselves into a battle line. They had not the time to do so.

A single voice sounded the charge. Not a war cry, not a word of command, but a voice of echoing laughter in the lead before the rumble of the charging cavalry filled the air. The rumble even drowned out the screams of Argismora's army as the ivrits, snorting with rage, plunged into their ranks. Lances pierced armor. Hooves crushed bone. Ironwolves mauled flesh.

The sentries on the wall leaned forward for a better view, training their bows on any fleeing warriors on the battlefield. Even so, the ironwolves fell upon them so quickly that half the sentries' arrows did not even get the chance to find their marks.

Chasmira and Warrick continued watching from the gate. What had started as a fiery siege was ending as a bloody massacre right before their eyes.

"I cannot be hallucinating, Warrick. What is all this?"

His fist tightened. "He's returned from Eppenhorn."

Chasmira's eyes widened, still watching the carnage.

"My brother... Wilvrey."

The western sward was a bloodbath. Ironwolves tore the men of Argismora into pieces like puppies fighting over scraps of meat. Ivrit riders ran down their foes at will. Their tactic was to circle the survivors, wearing down their defenses and forcing them into tighter and tighter formation. By the end, the last of them were fighting atop the fallen bodies of their fellows, bleeding down onto those who bled before them. Argismora's army was left little more than a mound of corpses in the field.

Only ten of the warriors were spared. The hooded riders dismounted their beasts, seized the warriors, and stripped them completely naked. They then dragged the captives forward and kicked them down in front of the corpse mound. Trembling, the ten dared to look up at the bloody pile and saw a man standing at the top.

Two green eyes glowed under his hood, which he then drew back with his bloody, gauntleted hand. The firelight illuminated a cruel grin on his angular face, framed by a wild beard that twisted like the tails of snakes. He crouched for a better look down at the survivors.

"Do you know who I am?" he leered playfully.

One answered, "You're *him*. Wilvrey the Serpent."

Wilvrey replied with a humming laugh.

"Why spare us? What do you want?" Another of the men demanded, his voice trembling despite his brazen tone.

"Why? I need you, obviously," he said. "You see, I need a message delivered back to Argismora."

The men shuddered. Their hooded captors stepped back and

left them there kneeling before Wilvrey.

"Prince Mirikinin… my father… is dead. Without doubt, the lords of the land look upon us now as sheep that have lost their shepherd—lost, aimless, defenseless sheep—but I assure you, they are quite mistaken. We are not sheep, but wolves. Wolves that kill when hungry or threatened. You may tell your Lord Prefect that thanks to the fresh meat he has provided this night, the Children of Mirikinin hunger no more."

At first they sat in fearful silence, before one of them rose to his feet. "We will not be your messengers to spread fear in our home!" The other warriors then also stood, uniting in their defiance.

Wilvrey's lip slowly curled back in a sneer. "You're right. What was I thinking? I have neglected to provide an incentive for your help." He stood, brushed off his cloak, and then stepped aside to reveal a slavering ironwolf that came to stand in his place.

The ten men turned to flee, only to find two more of the huge beasts behind them. The ironwolves pounced, and for a few moments there was a tempest of fangs, blood, and screams. Wilvrey watched it all, his green eyes gleaming with delight. He then held up his fist, and it all stopped. The naked captives lay scattered on the ground, groaning in pain. As they shakily got to their feet, they each clutched a bleeding bite wound on their arms or shoulders.

"Before it was famous for being our warbeast, the ironwolf was infamous for only one thing: *ironbite.* It is a terrible disease, let me tell you. Within just a few hours your bowels begin bleeding horribly. The blood starts running out anywhere it can and it will not stop until you bleed out and die… unless of course, your guts swell up and rupture somewhere in the middle first. The disease is carried in the saliva of the ironwolf, and all it takes is one bite to infect you."

The captives' eyes bulged in horror. "How long do we have?"

Wilvrey stroked his beard and squinted upward as if trying to recall. "I seem to remember a story where ironbite infected a herd of goats. They all bled to death in about two days," concluding with a wicked smile.

"Two days!? Please—!"

He simply laughed and mocked, "Please what? 'Please, Wilvrey save us'? Oh, there's no medicine to cure you here, but if memory serves, there are some *very* good physicians back from whence you came. Surely not all of you will last the whole way home, but I think the very swiftest of you might get there just in time."

They shrank away from him, turned, and fled. Ten naked men frantically fleeing across the fields they'd set aflame not even an hour ago.

The second son of Mirikinin stroked the ears of his ironwolves as they licked the blood from their fangs. He smiled at the fleeing warriors as they disappeared into the night. "Run and tell them Wilvrey the Serpent has returned home."

CHAPTER 18

Chasmira had never set foot in the room behind the black throne. The great hearth that blazed behind it gave light and warmth to a private chamber for the sitting ruler: previously Prince Mirikinin and now his brother, Lord Maram. The room was bordered with couches covered in thick furs and furnished with a huge table of black marble at its center. All along the walls were mounted the tusks, teeth, and horns of great beasts, many of which Chasmira could not even begin to guess their origin. Were these all Mirikinin's? Maram's? Did the brothers hunt together? Or did these belong to his sons and Mirikinin kept them to mark their accomplishments? She could not help but wonder.

A shadow crept onto the wall. The profile was long and menacing, with jutting shoulders and a neck that bowed like a snake lurking after prey. She followed the length of the shadow to where Wilvrey stood at the hearth with his back to her.

She studied him. He shared his brother Warrick's height and hazelwood hair, but their similarities ended there. Where Warrick was wide and brawny, Wilvrey was sculpted and lean. If Warrick were a bear, Wilvrey was a panther. He even moved like a predatory creature: he hunched when he walked, stalking forward as if prowling through the woods, but when he was at rest he was still as the black stone walls themselves.

He ignored her. After dismissing the terrified ironbite-infected warriors, he had swept into the front gate without even acknowledging Chasmira or Warrick. "I will speak with my uncle" was all he said to the guards and servants. Any further questions and Wilvrey would act as if they had said nothing at all, as if he could not see or hear them. He had walked directly past the throne and into the chamber, and she simply followed.

She did not need to touch her face to know it was gristly with dirt, dried sweat, and ash caked onto it. Her hair looked like strands of dried seaweed and she had bruises around her eyes from relentlessly casting fire. Chasmira was as silent as Wilvrey's shadow upon the wall. Did he even notice she had followed him?

Out of the black of the audience chamber, Maram appeared. He was wrapped in his black robes and appeared as little more than a floating face in the doorway. "Wilvrey?"

"Hello, Uncle," he answered with eerie calmness. "I'm flattered to have received your invitation, but I wish our reunion were under better circumstances."

"You've saved us, boy."

"Yes, it would seem I have," he said, tilting his head as he regarded the way the flames leapt upon the hearth. He warmed his hand over the fire.

"I was uncertain if you had gotten my message."

"Your messenger raven has not failed you yet, old man."

Chasmira watched Maram's face. She waited for anger at Wilvrey's disrespect, but it never came. Not a single wrinkle moved.

"Nothing else?" Wilvrey added with brisk sarcasm. "No warm

welcome? No wine bottles cracked in my honor? No hug?"

Maram remained stoic. "Your brother missed you."

"Which one? I know Warrick didn't. Or do you mean the little one? Where is the lad anyway, little Luthian?"

"Probably in the library."

"You know, it's not healthy for him to sit in there all day with the dust and the spiders. Now and then you really ought to lure him out with some cheese on a string or something." Wilvrey laughed at his own wit and looked back into the hearth flames.

"The night is spent, Wilvrey. Take some wine, and wash the blood and carnage from your brain. You look like you are chasing sleep."

"I need not sleep, but answers," he replied through grit teeth. "There is no road from Eppenhorn to these scorched fields, Uncle. Three days I rode wondering how my father, the great Prince Mirkinin, could have fallen. Needed I wine, I would have ridden to the southeast coast and raided the wine cellars of Castle Wolvmonte. No, I need answers and I will have them. Whose counsel was it to war with Dimol Gol? Who assured him the skull-faced mountain would yield? Was it you?"

"No, of course not! He took Hakon, the grand executor, as his council. No one knew war better than he, or so the prince believed."

"And where is the grand executor?"

"He's dead," Chasmira said, breaking her silence at last.

Wilvrey whirled about as if the very stone of the walls had come alive and answered. When his eyes settled upon her, a smile crept onto his lips. "Who is this fair little lamb?"

"She's no lamb," snorted Warrick, appearing in the doorway

behind Lord Maram.

"Big brother!" Wilvrey laughed. "Has the simple farmer's life bored you so badly, that you've picked up some cute slag to—"

"Shut up, Wilvrey."

"Oh, it's good to see you too. I admit I was surprised to see you out there, sword in hand, pretending that you could defend our home from a siege. Very brave."

"At least I was here," Warrick said directly in his brother's face.

"Yes, you were here. So were the haybales and the fenceposts, just as useless to stop them and just as silent when Father rode to war. Tell me, Warrick, did you speak up at all? Did you tell him not to go?"

"As if you would. You would have volunteered to lead the army to Dimol Gol yourself."

"Maybe, and maybe I would have won."

"You would have died, you fool."

The two brothers stared each other down. Warrick scowled angrily while Wilvrey leered coolly back at him. The younger brother shattered the tension with a laugh. "Come on, Warrick, who is she really?"

Lord Maram answered, "She is the last survivor of Dimol Gol: Chasmira, their dark seer. She fled the battle and came to warn us that our neighbors conspire against us."

"Argismora is just the first," Warrick added. "The lords of the land are turning on us one by one."

"Is that so?" Wilvrey cocked his eyebrow and walked up to Chasmira, gingerly taking her chin in his fingers. "What a selfless thing to do! What more proof need we that the gods are watching over us, than that you have come here to help in our hour of need."

Chasmira pulled back, but Wilvrey held on and leaned in so close she could feel the warmth of his breath.

"But what's that I see in your eyes, Chasmira?" Wilvrey licked his lips and chuckled. "I see unholy fire in you."

Chasmira chuckled weakly, then wickedly. "Your eyes have not failed you, Wil. What more proof need you that the gods have forsaken you, than that something far older than gods now watches over your father's house?"

Wilvrey's wry smile soured, but only Chasmira could see it. He stepped back to let his green gaze take her in twice from head to foot. "I like her, Warrick. Keep her, and let me know if you get tired of her."

Warrick stepped to her side. "Forgive my younger brother's sleepless prattling. He has asked for an audience with Lord Maram, so let us not delay him any longer." He then turned and walked out, hoping Chasmira would follow.

She did. She could feel Wilvrey's eyes on her the entire time, trying to pierce her skin like a dagger to see what might bleed out. She gave him nothing but her side profile as she left the room. The moment she was free of his gaze in the audience chamber, she allowed herself to shiver, shaking out the chill that rose up her spine. There was something in the way Wilvrey looked at her, his eyes filled not with revile, lust, or disdain, but with something else. The cold, condemning stone of the audience chamber was comforting by comparison.

"My brother makes light of your help." Warrick's voice echoed somberly in the chamber. "Ignore him. If it were not for you, we would all be dead."

"And if not for you, *I* would be dead. You saved me from the Archvate's pyre."

"And you saved *me* from the Hobble."

"Debt is unsavory, Warrick. Let's call it even, hm?"

They both lingered on the steps, looking at each other in a silent exchange. Warrick looked as if he would speak, but just nodded instead.

"You know what, Warrick?"

He braced himself for a barb. "What?"

"I think you're alright."

He scoffed and turned away. "*Alright?*"

"You're brave, dedicated, and it's quaint the way you think I whored my way ahead in life."

Warrick hung his head. "I spoke out of spite and a lack of sleep. Forgive me."

Chasmira laughed. "Forgiveness granted. You may be out of line, but I'd dare say you're the closest thing that passes for a gentleman around here."

A grunt was his only reply as they continued walking. He did not look at her. He had apologized too quickly, she thought, which meant he wanted to change the subject as soon as possible. Perhaps she had teased him too hard, or perhaps he did not apologize for thinking so badly about her, but just for saying it aloud…

Her stomach gurgled and growled. They had both eaten lightly a few hours before the battle and were starving after such a long evening. Without so much as a single word about it between each other, they both turned the corner toward the dining room. Surely there would be a pot of something simmering on the fire. She could think over everything much more clearly with food in her stomach.

They were both surprised to see Lart there, but more surprised to see the girl who was with him. She knelt over Terror, rubbing his belly, scratching his chin, and letting him playfully nip at her fingers. When the dog sat up and barked happily at Chasmira, the girl turned and stood to greet them.

She was maybe twenty years old, with all her hair shorn down to a few days of stubble, and she bore a circular scar around her right eye, as if someone or something once tried to carve it out. The wound had healed very poorly, for the scarline was grey and jagged. The girl seemed to bear no shame about this disfigurement, for she approached with a smile so bright and beautiful that her scar seemed invisible next to it. Her exposed arms were tanned and tightly muscled. Clearly, she was a warrior of the highest caliber.

"I'm Emorya," she announced, thrusting out her hand for Chasmira to accept.

"Chasmira. A pleasure to meet you, Emorya. You're with the warband then, I take it?"

"Warmaiden, yes. Second in command," she bragged.

"No, you're not," Lart sighed.

"I might as well be," Emorya shrugged. "I was brought along to negotiate with Eppenhorn, to see if the poor bastards could agree to anything that would save them from our army."

"Wil's army," Lart sighed.

Chasmira arched an eyebrow. "And they could not agree?"

Emorya clicked her tongue. "I sat at a table outside their gates for ten hours in knee-deep snow, discussing terms in the middle of a blizzard. They assumed I would yield in the cold and wind. They assumed I was weak."

"Foolish assumptions, to be sure."

Emorya flashed that bright smile of hers again, and Chasmira could sense something like satisfaction in the smile. Wilvrey the Serpent's massacre at Eppenhorn had avenged her for the humiliation and trouble. The scarred woman went to the hearth and ladled hot stew from the cauldron into a bowl for herself.

"This one's quite a piece of work," Chasmira remarked.

"She's Uncle Maram's daughter," Warrick whispered before walking to the hearth himself.

"Daughter? Really!" Chasmira's mind began to turn over the possibilities. Emorya had connections to both the warband and the throne. She sauntered over beside her and took her arm. "Emorya dear, you must be exhausted after such a journey and then a battle."

"On the contrary, I never feel more awake than after battle," she replied, blowing on the stew before eating a spoonful. It was still hot, and she smacked on it loudly as she juggled it in her mouth.

Chasmira snort-laughed but quickly contained herself. "Good to know ravaging foreign lands with Wilvrey doesn't damage one's sense of humor. He takes himself quite seriously."

"Oh no," she said mid-chew, "Wilvrey's *lots* of fun."

"Is he now?"

She nodded, gulped down the mouthful of stew. "Oh, yes. I know all the things he enjoys and all the things that annoy him to death."

"Do tell! What's something that gets under his skin?"

Emorya laughed, almost too loudly. "Warrick, do you all still make dandelion jelly every year?"

"Of course. Perfect with bread in the summer and autumn," he replied, sitting down beside Lart with his own bowl of hot stew.

"They used to make it when we were all children, and I'd eat it when Lart and I came to visit. Wilvrey can't *stand* it. The taste, the color… just the mere smell of dandelion makes him want to gag. He used to say it would give me deatheye or blood shivers if I kept eating it, and eventually I said I believed him just to humor him."

The laughter was a great relief after such a day. Emorya would make a fine companion and a great insight into the inner workings of Mirikinin's family—a family that seemed more complicated every day. Not that she disliked it. In fact, there was something wonderful about sitting in the middle of siblings and cousins sharing a meal, laughing over childhood memories. She had never had that—as a child or an adult.

She nestled shoulder-to-shoulder with Emorya. "So that's what annoys Wilvrey. What about the things he enjoys?"

Emorya smacked the last bit of her stew. "Oh, I couldn't very well tell you all that, Chasmira."

"Why not?"

She licked the spoon. "Why, that'd be very unladylike."

PART TWO

CHAPTER 19

There was one place in all of the celestial realm Nandrzael loved above all others. It hid beyond seemingly endless forests of white apple trees, every one of them bright and pure as porcelain. It lay across a lake of water so perfect and still, it was like a mirror. It rose from an island of crystalline cloudgrass like a colossal dome. She was sure the majority of the structure was beneath the celestial soil, hidden by the lake around it. This construct was the Criterion, which housed the most sacred of all Angelic relics: the mindglass itself.

A great courtyard lay at its entrance, with many winding stairs that led from one patio to the next until at last one reached the entrance. Despite the grandiosity of the forecourt, at the top of the stairs stood a doorway quite narrow and humble, for only a select few were ever permitted inside.

It was upon this forecourt that Nandrzael lighted, tucking her wings behind her. The familiar cold touch of the banister filled her with happy memories, memories that never lost their luster over the centuries. She tired not of the long, swaying boughs of the white willows which lined the courtyard, nor of the glorious dark blue sky in which stars glittered at all times of the day.

"Nandrzael!"

It was the voice of an Angelic man who hovered down the steps, landing at her side soundlessly as a falling leaf. He had wings the color of the midnight sky, his hair was sandy red like the color of autumn itself, and his eyes glittered like diamonds beneath a heavy brow. Every word he spoke was tender and soothing as violin music. "Nandrzael. What a pleasure to see you. How long has it been?"

"Too long, but the fault is on you," she smiled brightly, greeting him with a hug. "You are never around anymore. Busy saving the world, noble Vametheon?"

Her smile brightened his even more. "You could exaggerate more and it would not tell half the story. Our labor is never done. So many like yourself are patrons of mortal civilization, but others constantly attend to the threads of time."

"The greatest of us bear them both," she said, thinking of Oczandarys. He was probably there inside the great hallowed place, his mind adream with visions of the future. "Some of us can hardly bear even one."

"You are speaking of yourself?"

"Yes," she said, making no pretense about her shame. "I failed him. Now Oczandarys will give me no more dispensation about the future until I have proven myself again."

Vametheon held her hand consolingly. "Do not torment yourself. You are spirited and cunning. He will see it soon enough, for daily he looks upon the future."

She squeezed his hand, grateful for his encouragement. Nandrzael had so much admiration for him, for he was so many things she was not and could never be. "You are like him, one of the originals of our kind. You are privileged to enter in and see it for yourself, so tell me: what is it like to gaze into the mindglass and behold destiny laid bare?"

Vametheon leaned on the staircase banister and looked out across the flawless lake. "It is beyond even the words of our divine tongue to describe, for there is no one metaphor that could capture it all. It is like sitting within an hourglass, placing the grains of sand in the right order before they fall away. It is like looking up at a tree, whose boughs and branches divide more and more the higher up you look. It is like creating this lake by hand, by placing each drop of water perfectly in its place. It is like sleepwalking on a battlefield against all entropy. It is Order itself."

She found herself breathless. "I can barely comprehend it."

"Few can," he continued. "Imagine the mortal mind, with no capacity at all to comprehend how one event cascades into another, how all points in time connect. Last month, I commanded a man to travel five hundred miles to Dajncastle, simply to shake some apples off a tree. It seemed like foolishness to him, naturally, but the entire fate of the golden kingdom has been saved by this act. No one will know it until many years hence. All celestial matters are foolishness to those blinded by the petty confinement of their own lives, for they cannot perceive a greater will at work."

"It is so frustrating," Nandrzael said through clenched teeth.

"Patience, Nandrzael. Therein lies your fault. You cannot blame them for their mortality. You must learn how to use it." he gently admonished before smiling. "But I am glad you can confide that in me."

She joined him at the banister, overlooking the lake. "You are the only one who understands me."

"To be understood is a rarity."

A strong breeze rippled across the tops of the trees bordering the lake. White leaves, taken by the wind, trickled through the air and touched down on the water, sending long ripples in all directions as they drifted.

"Vametheon, have you ever… lied to a mortal?"

They both watched the white leaves dancing on the lake's surface.

"In what way?" he asked.

"Oh, I don't know. Have you ever offered a reward for their obedience, that you knew you could not fulfill?"

"Such fiction can be destructive."

"But it was highly motivating."

"Go on."

"What if I told you that I shared a new revelation from the mindglass with a mortal, and showed them their divine purpose?"

A smile crossed his lips. "I would tell you that's not possible, as you have received no such revelations from Oczandarys."

"And you would be correct. But what if I did? What if I took advantage of their fascination with destiny, that craving inside every mortal for their existence to be validated that it is part of a divine plan, part of some enigmatic prophecy? What if I… what if I lied?"

Vametheon gazed up at the sky, his smile widening. "Then I would take back what I said a minute ago. You have learned more than I thought."

CHAPTER 20

"We cannot challenge them," Warrick said in resolution. Wilvrey rolled his eyes and Maram chewed his lip in thought. The three of them sat at the black marble table in Maram's private chambers. The great hearth blazed beside them, and Wilvrey's shadow rose across the table as he stood from his chair.

"Why shouldn't we? We are sons of Prince Mirikinin, he who broke the ironwolf! Its teeth were his swords, its quills were his shields! Father left us as an inheritance the secrets of ironbite: a pestilence we may mete out to anyone who dares stand in our way."

"To what end, Wilvrey?" Maram objected. "What do we win?"

Wilvrey scoffed, circling the room in laughter far too long before continuing. "I concede there is no tribute to be taken from the pundits of the Guardian City, and no gold to be wrung from the seaside tribes northward. But such barren land can be cultivated into rich soil. We will seed fear. We will rain terror. The dread of us will fall from the sky, and they will take shelter from it. It will drench their cities, it will soak their land! And from such, in time we will come and harvest. We will arrive not with sword but with sickle in hand. We will reap blood and cries for mercy, sweet as strawberries plucked from the creeping vine."

Warrick recoiled, his eyes locked in a hard stare at his brother. Wilvrey was practically salivating at the thought of razing the seaside cities. One of the commanders who returned with him from Eppenhorn reported that Wilvrey took a handful of the blood-soaked snow and savored it after the battle as if it were a hunk of cake. Warrick ignored that in the moment, but now could not get it out of his mind.

"Let us call upon our vassals," Wilvrey continued. "Able-bodied men and women to rebuild our army. We shall train them in the winter and have them battle-ready by the spring thaw."

Maram shot a glance to Warrick. He agreed, but reluctantly. Warrick crafted his reply in measured seconds. "It is reasonable. Long have they benefited from our father's protection. It is time we called in their show of loyalty: to salvage all that remains of the broken kingdom."

"You'll need a show of strength, Wilvrey," Maram added. "Something to assure them that they are sending their children not to die, but to fight."

Wilvrey regarded his glass goblet in the firelight, toying with it and swirling the contents. "I'll bring the sorceress."

"What?"

"The sorceress Chasmira. The woman could destroy half the warband herself. What greater show of strength than to march her in there like a trained dog at my side?"

"You try it. She'll burn you to ash and kick you into the wind," Warrick warned him.

"Oh, I don't mean it like that," Wilvrey chuckled and sipped his drink. "I mean that the very sight of her on our side is enough to impress them into compliance. A sorceress of Chaos was enough to provoke Argolvrecht's enemies—perhaps she is enough to provoke Father's allies as well."

"Very well, Wilvrey. Take her with you," Maram concluded.

Warrick seethed. "Lord Maram, you cannot mean for her to go with him!"

"What good is she here, Warrick? Is she to flip through books with Luthian in whatever shadow he's hiding in today? Or perhaps she is to follow you like a puppy while you oversee the rebuilding of our land after Argismora burned it right before our eyes?"

"No, milord," Warrick said with a loud sigh.

ψ

Like unto animals, all of them.

Hakon's words rolled through Chasmira's mind like distant thunder. She smiled at the memory of his commentary on Mirkinin's men.

She sat upon an old mossy log at the edge of the north field. It had been there for many, many years, marking where the family territory ended and the land given to their vassals began. Behind her were fields striped with ash, and before her were lush woodlands speckled with the colors of autumn.

Animals indeed, she mused. The savage fury of the ironwolves was matched only by that of their masters Warrick and Wilvrey. Without doubt they will raze Argisomora to dust, and the chapel of that treacherous Angelic Nandrzael will scatter away into the wind. *What will she be then? What will Nandrzael be, without anyone to love her? What are the immortals without their worship and adoration? What would any immortal life be, if lived without love?*

A gust of wind tossed her dark hair. She looked up to take in the sight of the woodland trees rustling in the wind all around her. She watched them stir and sprinkle down yellow leaves from their highest branches.

"A change in the wind," came a small, high-pitched voice from under the log.

Chasmira did not hesitate. She swung her legs back over the log, lay over it on her stomach, and peeked underneath. There sat a small, chubby Cloven that stared up at the swaying trees. Their bulb was green with white speckles, and a smaller bulb protruded from their crown as well.

"Hey, I know you! You were looking for northorsouth," the Cloven exclaimed, blinking and pointing at her.

"Yes, yes I was."

"Did you ever find it?"

"I did. It was… charming," she laughed, shaking her head.

"Good! Good, good, good-good."

"My name's Chasmira. What's yours?"

"My name's Wisp! I was the oldest in my patch and the first to leave. You probably don't remember me."

"You'll have to forgive me for that. Amidst all your siblings you were very difficult to pick out."

"Peeeeep," said another voice from under the log.

Chasmira raised a hand to her lips in surprise. "Oh goodness, do you have someone in there with you?"

They turned, revealing a smaller mushroom sprouting from their side. "My little brother is here with me!"

"Oh my, he is little indeed! What's his name?"

"Peeeeep," said the small sprout adjoined to Wisp. The sprout had a tiny mouth and one arm as slender as a blade of grass.

Wisp giggled. "That's all he says, so I guess that's his name! I don't know if Peep will ever get feet of his own."

"Peeeeep?"

"What will you do if he never does?"

The tiny Cloven rubbed their head in thought and then shrugged. "Nothin' I guess, which is all good-good with me! I don't mind having him around with me all the time. Maybe I'd be lonely without him."

"Peeeep," the sprout cooed, hugging Wisp.

"Well then, you two had best stick together." Chasmira smiled, tickling Wisp with her finger. "Don't let me ever catch you without him, got it?"

"Got it! Do you have a brother too?" The Cloven waddled out from under the log to see if she also had an adjoined sibling.

"No, I'm afraid not. It's just me."

Wisp blew a loud raspberry. "Bad-bad. You gotta have a brother too. I know! I'll be your brother!"

"My goodness, I'm flattered! You want to be *my* brother?"

"Yup! And you can be *my* brother!"

Chasmira laughed so hard she rolled backward in the warm grass. "I… I don't think that word means what you think it means."

Wisp looked at her with puzzlement but was quickly distracted by a blue glimmer in the grass. "A sapphret!"

As if recognizing its own name, the small blue locust leapt out of the grass high over Wisp's head. The sapphret glimmered a brilliant blue like the color of sapphires. Its wings sparkled the way morning dew sparkles in sunlight. Wisp squealed and ran after it to catch it. Chasmira lunged to cup her hands around it, but the sapphret bounced away to another sprig

Their peals of laughter could be heard far across the north field. Chasmira pushed back her disheveled hair so she could see as she dug her hands through the foliage. The sapphret's blue glimmer was not *that* hard to find in the golden grass…

Wisp shouted, "It's in your hair!"

She screamed with laughter, tumbling backward and shaking out her dark locks to get rid of the tiny invader. Wisp and Peep rolled in the grass, giggling uncontrollably.

"Lady Chasmira?"

She drew back a breath and held it. Behind her stood Wilvrey, craning like a vulture.

"Lady Chasmira, I have need of you."

"Need of me?" she replied as she shooed away the sweet little Cloven. "I dread to think what for, Wil, but say on."

"Dread? You dread? Now *that* is something I hope persists as long as possible," he laughed and licked his teeth. "I wish for you to escort me tonight."

"Escort you? Traversing frightening woods, are we?"

Wilvrey ignored that. "We will be paying a visit to Lord Ovis, my father's vassal. His clan has lived under our protection since the days of my grandfather. Four generations of his family have risen since. The Ovisites are many and strong."

Chasmira perceived his meaning perfectly. The Ovisites were indebted to Mirikinin's family, and Wilvrey meant to call in that debt. "Who else is coming along?"

"Emorya, my second-in-command, naturally."

"Naturally."

"And my savant brother Luthian, if he doesn't scorch in the daylight after all this time."

She sighed, stood, and brushed the flecks of grass off her dress. "Very well. How soon do we depart?"

"I have sent a messenger ahead to inform Lord Ovis of our arrival. I presume you will need time to look presentable for a formal occasion, so let me know in a few hours."

"A few hours?" She scoffed. "Are you implying that I don't look presentable now?"

He clicked his tongue loudly. "We are attending a ball, not a cattle auction, sorceress. When you enter beside me, you had better smell of rose, amber, and pomegranate... not sedge and wildflowers."

Biting her lip, she stood wordlessly. She gave a brief bow of the head before flouncing past him toward the castle. She could feel his eyes on her back, that bright green gaze with something infinitely vague and unknowable behind it. At first she shivered, but then knotted her hands into fists. She was not going to be perfumed and paraded around the way she was at the Prefect's tower. No, she had something much different in mind.

CHAPTER 21

Amber haze filled the forest that evening. The setting sun cast long beams between the towering fir trees, striping the dim forest with bright light. Nine riders on horseback vanished in and out of sight as they rode through the forest, bound for the ball at Lord Ovis' villa.

Chasmira blinked and squinted every time she passed through a beam of sunlight. She was already thinking ahead to the ball, anticipating every way this Lord Ovis might receive them. She knew much about Prince Mirikinin, but next to nothing about the vassals that lived in his kingdom.

In the twinkling glare she suddenly saw the silhouette of Wilvrey nearing to ride beside her. His napped leather doublet was the color of the night sky, and draped over his shoulder was a white fur pelerine he brought with him from snowy Eppenhorn. He called out to her, "Don't you look wonderful, Lady Chasmira!"

His green eyes gleamed as he drank in the sight of her. Her dress was a masterpiece of black and crimson ruffles, with puffed sleevelets and a broad neckline that bared her pale shoulders. Wilvrey's gaze hungrily traced over her collarbone and chest, and instinctively he rode closer to her, drawn like a moth to a flame.

"I wondered what my brother saw in you. I think I see it now."

She sighed. "I haven't the faintest clue what you mean by that, Wilvrey. You couldn't possibly see what Warrick does in me."

"Perhaps not," he recoiled with a shrug.

That hurt a little.

Before she could assemble words into a scathing retort, he changed the subject. "Now be careful not to breathe a word to Lord Ovis about my father's demise."

"What? Why not?"

He looked at her as if she had two heads. "Because we don't want him to know."

"Yes, I grasp the basic concept, Wil, but *why* don't you want him to know? The entire point of our engagement is to ask for him to help, to bolster your weakened army."

"And there is where you demonstrate that you know nothing of the politics at play."

"Apologies, I was raised by wolves, not snakes," she replied with the most searing sarcasm she could muster. "What's your cunning plan in deceiving our host?"

"Really? 'Host' is being overly gracious. Ovis and his kin do not serve us. They serve my father. What servant would not immediately run for freedom the instant they learnt their master was dead?"

"And that is not a chance you're willing to take?"

He chuckled scornfully at the very idea. "Absolutely not."

She nodded.

Then, Wilvrey leaned in closer and curled his lip. "What is that you're wearing?"

She shrugged and picked at the ruffled fabric. "Oh this? Just a little something your uncle's servants dug up for me."

"Not the dress," he snarled. "What is that I smell?"

"Oh, that! It's a special fragrance, made with essence of dandelion oil," she chirped, "Just as you asked for."

His response came back through grit teeth. "I... gave you... very clear directions..."

"Did you? Oh, I must have misunderstood entirely. Silly me! I hope this doesn't mean I can't be at your side when we enter. I was so looking forward to you strutting in with me wrapped around you like a cat stuck in a tree."

Wilvrey missed none of her meaning. "Well played, sorceress. Doubtless you have spirit. When we arrive at the villa, you may enter behind me."

"I'm surprised you even felt I was necessary. Is the reputation of Wilvrey the Serpent not enough to inspire fear in them?"

"Fear is not our goal here, just as pity was not. Intimidating them into agreement will only erode their trust in us. Our allies must believe that we are building, not begging."

"So it is a show of your strength."

"Precisely."

She sighed. Yet another warlord keeping her around like a trinket in a trophy case. "You know, Lart keeps Terror on a chain to make himself seem stronger, too."

"I didn't need to chain you."

"As if I'd let you."

"I said... I didn't *need* to chain you."

Chasmira let their gazes meet. That cold, penetrating green in Wilvrey's eyes met the warm, flickering fire in hers. There in the north field that afternoon, he had merely asked and she obliged. No, he had not even asked. He had stated his need and something inside her leapt to meet it.

She chastised herself for this. At the moment, she had not even realized it. Something about his very presence challenged her, provoked her. She wanted to prove him wrong about something, something he had not even said out loud. She strained to put into words exactly what that thing was, but could not.

Wilvrey said nothing more. He simply rode on ahead, leaving her to think on this for the remainder of the trip up the hillside. There, at the top, rose the regal spire of Lord Ovis' villa.

The spire, lined with wooden gargoyles all around it, was the crown of the house to be sure, but the rest was no less impressive. It topped a four-story stone turret with latticed windows and vines that wound beautifully up its entire height. The spire rose from a longhouse that, at its northmost corner, continued the same length eastward. Redbirds hopped along the black slate shingles of the roof, which was lined with their nests along its ridge. A broad archway welcomed the visitors into a cobblestone courtyard, where a row of footmen waited to receive the horses.

The footmen were white-furred Goatkin. Like all Beastkin, they bore every resemblance to their quadrupedal ancestors, save that they had opposable thumbs and stood upright on their hind legs.

Chasmira smiled as she dismounted, taking the footman's hand and handing him her horse's reins. The cool autumn air had been giving her a chill on the last leg of the ride, and she was glad to be done trotting through it. As he helped her down, her ear caught the sound of string music from the open doors of the villa. The long, sweet notes warmed her like a blanket. No such music warmed the cold, black halls of the House of Mirikinin.

True to his word, Wilvrey entered in front of her. The change in his demeanor was remarkable, she thought. Where she had only seen him storming through the castle and leering like a hungry wolf, Wilvrey now behaved like the most poised, dignified man she had ever met. He kissed hands, gave witty compliments, and flashed a broad smile to everyone who greeted them.

The great hall was magnificent to behold. Chasmira stared up at the domed ceiling, which was overgrown with green leafy vines that covered it all except for a few scant patches where the pale, cracked plaster was exposed. Among the hanging vines, hundreds of fireflies danced like tiny, shimmering, golden stars.

There were over a hundred people in attendance, almost all of them Beastkin of one variety or another. While Ovis' family were all Goatkin, Chasmira noticed a couple of massive Oxkin and a large family of Weaselkin that scurried past her. It behooved small and herbivorous Beastkin to group together, forming communities against the presence of carnivores who would happily kill and devour their natural prey. Prides of Lionkin roamed the southern plains, and Wolfkin packs formed warbands that battled each other in the Western Woods. Despite the fact the Beastkin had risen to walk upright, the natural order very much still prevailed.

She immediately identified Lord Ovis in the crowd. The old Goatkin was clothed in fine satin robes, and his long white beard was braided with rings of mountain silver. With one of his hands he leaned on an ornate scepter that aided him like a cane. Its top was curled like a shepherd's staff, a detail that Chasmira found amusing. Lord Ovis approached and bowed his head to Wilvrey in greeting.

Wilvrey gestured back with an outstretched arm. "Allow me to introduce Lady Chasmira. She once advised the Magnate at Dimol Gol. Now, she serves *us*."

She curtsied gracefully, and Lord Ovis reached out to take her hand and kiss it. Then, he paused abruptly and tilted his head, lingering close to her as he stood upright. "My word, Lady Chasmira, ye are perfumed like the bygone summertime I miss so badly. Just standing in your presence, I can practically smell sedge and wildflowers."

"Your senses do not deceive you, for I wear the essence of dandelion. I prefer the outdoors to stuffy castles," she quipped, smiling sweetly.

His face brightened with a smile. "Then surely ye must sit beside me at the ball tonight. We will be nearest the windows, practically like eating outside in the night air."

"That sounds splendid, milord."

Ovis placed Chasmira's hand upon his, upon the hand that held his scepter. "I hate to bereave ye of your companion so early in the evening, Wilvrey. I simply cannot resist."

Wilvrey replied with the broadest smile, "She is here at our pleasure. I would hate for her to feel neglected." She could not help that Wilvrey was both glad to see her make a good impression, but also equally happy to be rid of her. He was so aggravated. Emorya was right: it was *lots* of fun.

The old Goatkin then led her across the great hall. All around her, in the dim candlelight, sparkled the eyes of a hundred other Beastkin as they turned and showed their reverence to the patriarch. Every Goatkin great and small gave a bow of their horned heads, and a bevy of Otterkin bowed at the waist in unison.

She gave a nod to each as she went by.

"You must be a great ruler, to command them that are not even your own kin," she complimented him.

"I do not understand your meaning, Lady Chasmira."

"Why, look around! There are so many who clearly are not goats, but all manner of kin live under your roof, and all bow to you."

He chuckled, "That part I understand. But ye said I must be a great ruler, when in fact I am no ruler at all. I lay no laws or commands upon those who live upon all this land, for I am not the owner thereof."

"But you are called Lord—"

"An honorary title to be sure, bestowed on me by Melyr the Iron Prince, Mirikinin and Maram's father. At first it was just my family and I tending the land for them, until the first kin arrived seeking shelter from the Blood Moon, and it was in the power of my hand to provide it. Every year more come and I welcome them. This is a refuge for them, but I am a guest here as much as any."

It then began to dawn on Chasmira precisely what the old Goatkin meant to them all. He was not a superior, he was a savior. His family's alliance with the House of Mirikinin meant peace and safety for all of them. It meant a place of refuge, music, joy, and laughter. He could have kept this privilege—this gift—entirely to himself, but instead he chose to share it freely with any and all who would come in need of it. The gratitude and humility of the crowd moved her.

She began curtsying deeply to them in response. She was no nobility; she was nothing special to them just because she walked holding Lord Ovis' hand. She was their guest, but as esteemed a guest as she was, it was *her* honor to visit such a place and see what faithful generations could build when they had the opportunity, when power was used to protect rather than destroy.

A servant drew back the chair at Ovis' right hand and Chasmira sat down. His word was true: it was practically like sitting out in the night air. Goosebumps ran down her arms until another Goatkin sat beside her, shielding her from the chill.

Wilvrey watched them, silently seething.

The sun retreated fully into slumber for the evening, giving the candlelight its full effect in the great hall. Those who sat at Lord Ovis' table had a higher vantage point to watch the crowd dine and mingle before them. Ovis spun great tales of his ancestors surviving the Dragon's Winter, and both young and old alike stared attentively as they drank in every detail. Chasmira stared and drank with the rest of them, wonder in her eyes equal to that of the youngest child.

The music swelled and accelerated. Like a siren's call, it drew the guests from the halls and tables to dance. As the crowd assembled, Chasmira began to stare upward at the ceiling, for even the fireflies moved in tune to the music, holding their own ball up among the hanging vines. As she watched, a pair of fireflies flitted down and danced in the air in front of her face. Their golden glow matched the glow in her own eyes, and for a moment she realized they might have been attracted by her stare. She laughed and waved at them to shoo them away, and when she put her hand down again, she saw him.

Wilvrey.

The green-eyed warlord sipped from a chalice. "This is all wildly impressive! You do me and my guests a great honor this evening."

"The honor is mine. When ye called on me, I thought: how better to welcome ye and your father back from war? How fares your latest conquest in Eppenhorn?"

Wilvrey laughed and smacked his lips. "Eppenhorn is a dry bone. I have sucked the last of the marrow from it and now I crave fresh meat."

"I can see the hunger in your eyes," Lord Ovis replied, watching the twirling dancers instead of Wilvrey.

"My eyes betray not half of my hunger, believe me. I have set my sights on Argismora."

"The Guardian City?"

"They have already whet my appetite. Fresh blood spilt, and now I must have more. My army and my father's army are now one, and after the spring we ride north to set the siege. It will be a great conquest, one to be remembered forever."

"Truly your name would be immortal."

"Mine need not be the only name," he said, stepping in front of Lord Ovis to get his full attention. "You have a host of hardy kin here, Ovis. The Guardian City is a challenge I happily undertake, but together we would topple it like a sandcastle."

The old Goatkin nodded like a weary parent whose child was telling a long joke with no punchline. "I couldn't possibly, Wilvrey."

"Of course you could! Your people number in the hundreds. A fine addition to my battalion."

"They are not warriors. They'd be no good for your purposes."

"No good *now*, you mean. Anyone can lift a sword and—with

time and training—become a fine warrior. Swear me but five hundred of your kin," he said, smiling and lifting his goblet, "And together we can toast to the coming summer's war."

Chasmira and Wilvrey shared a glance as quick as two swords striking. Clearly, he was counting on the glories and spoils of battle to entice Lord Ovis. She had her doubts about this, but dared not let that glance betray any of them. He needed her to display confidence in him. She took a casual sip from her chalice, but her heart was starting to pound.

Ovis shook his head. "I could not swear five hundred to this end."

Wilvrey did not relent. "And right you are, for five hundred would be far too many to craft armor and arms when my cavalry will need their own smithing too. Yes, I agree. I'm sure three hundred would do, especially they of your strong Goatkin stock. They farm in the hard clay of the meadows, growing sprouts and cabbage."

Ovis shook his head again. "I could not swear three hundred."

This time Chasmira saw the momentary flash of anger in Wilvrey's expression. He blinked a few times and sniffled, wrinkling his nose to mask his reaction. Clearly he was not used to being denied.

"Perhaps," he began calmly as he could, "I have not made myself clear. In eight months we go northward to take the Guardian City, a victory long overdue. I am inviting you to be my partner in this endeavor, winning honor and infamy for both our families that will last for generations. Will you not join me?"

Chasmira glanced back and forth between them. The backdrop of the whirling dancers behind Wilvrey gave him the appearance of a hungry alligator, staring with eerie stillness in the middle of a choppy river. Dull and dispassionate, Ovis stared back for what felt like a full minute. He then licked his lips, cleared his throat, and smiled politely.

"Master Wilvrey, I ask ye not to speak of bloodshed at such a time as this. The Honey Moon wanes only now, and not two months hence waxes the Blood Moon. All my kin are sore afeard in such a season of dark omens."

Wilvrey's lip curled back to sneer but he repressed it with some effort and concentration. "Understandable, my friend. Surely you can join me after the Blood Moon, when this troubled season has passed?"

Ovis' stare hardened. "I have thrown a grand ball this night. Why not go and enjoy it with the rest of them? Dance a little, drink a little. Tell your father I said hello and good luck in Argismora."

Wilvrey answered nothing. He lifted his chalice in a salute and slunk back into the crowd.

Each breath of Chasmira's was taken and released carefully as she watched their exchange. As Wilvrey departed, she caught herself halfway standing to follow after him.

"Ye probably should see to him," Lord Ovis said.

Unsure whether that was a dismissal or actual goodwill for Wilvrey's mental wellness, Chasmira rose fully from her seat. "You are gracious, milord," she said before hurrying down the length of the table and into the corridor.

She looked this way and that. She imagined she would surely find him conscripting young kin by grabbing them by the neck and stuffing them into a burlap sack he would then toss over his shoulder to take home. Instead, she found no trace of Wilvrey in the crowd, which was no great surprise. Wilvrey the Serpent was renowned for vanishing in the midst of battle and reappearing where his enemies did not expect him. After the way he sneaked up on her in the yard earlier that morning, she could testify to the truth behind the legend.

"Chasmira!" Out of the crowd appeared Emorya, elbowing herself a path to get through. She was a strikingly elegant blend of courtesan and warrior, for about her neck and shoulders was a black metal gorget with ribbed pauldrons, which paired beautifully with her dark blue gown. She tilted her head, noticing the concern on Chasmira's face. "What on the earth is the matter?"

"Wil's politics were not welcomed as warmly as he hoped."

"He went right for the throat as is his nature?"

"Yes," grimacing.

Emorya rolled her eyes and sighed. "Fret not over him. If I know Wilvrey—and I do—he's not off to lick his wounds. He's circling the herd looking for a better opportunity. Do you honestly believe he's the kind that would tuck his tail and run after one harsh refusal?"

No, he is not. She knew this, but she still went after him. This was so important to him. She could feel the disappointment and the frustrations and something in her wanted to ease it. She knew not why and did not want to think about it any longer.

"No, he is not. I know this, but I still had to make a good show in front of our host, to ensure he can feel the disappointment and the frustration. Perhaps he will do something to ease it. But come now, let's not think about it any longer," Chasmira said.

Emorya lifted her chalice in a toast. "It's a ball, so let's have one!"

Chasmira took her arm and the two of them returned to the grand hall. The music soared and leapt, as did the dancing crowd. With hands held or arms interlocked, they danced in lines and sometimes circles, vocalizing along with the wild melody. The two women were welcomed into the line, and soon they were singing along with the rest of the crowd. All evening they laughed and danced and drank from chalices filled with sweet, smoky mulled wine.

CHAPTER 22

The ball at the villa seemed endless. It was as if the moon lingered in its celestial valley to hear the music and watch the dancing. Platters of fruit were borne around the room for guests who needed to catch their breath and sit for a while, lest they tire out completely. Many of them abandoned the floor to sit in a chair with a ripe apple or a halved melon. Chasmira and Emorya did not. The two women whirled and leapt in time to the music, each with a chalice of wine in hand.

Chasmira could not even remember when she last had such a good time. "You've got stamina, Emorya!"

"I've fought in deep snow," she replied proudly. "It builds the endurance!"

At last the sorceress slowed, holding a stitch in her side that was becoming unbearable. Emorya mimicked her, sending Chasmira doubling over onto the floor with laughter.

Emorya put her hands on her hips. "Do you like it better down there?"

"I do. I might have to sit this next one out."

The other guests joined in the laughter. Emorya helped her up and over to a chair before looking disappointedly into her chalice. "This wine is starting to taste like water to me. I'm going to find something a bit stronger, if I can."

"Indulge yourself. I'll come find you when I can feel my legs."

She gave a smile and a shoulder pat before sidling through the crowd and out in the villa's halls. Chasmira, meanwhile, folded her hands in her lap and watched the ball. The shimmering candle flames seemed to float in midair between the faces in the crowd. Here, an Oxkin flirted drunkenly with his own wife beside him. There, a tired Goatkin nodded along to the music with two sleeping kids in her arms.

She slipped away, through the crowd to look for a quiet place. Much as she was enjoying the dance and revelry, it was becoming a constant din, a dull roar inside her head. Maybe the wine had something to do with it too. Either way, she needed a reprieve.

From an alcove ahead, she saw a servant stepping out with fresh bottles of ale in hand. *That must be the buttery*, she thought. *Perfect.*

She smiled politely to the servant as she passed them and then strolled in. Once inside, she was that surprised to learn that she was not alone, for sitting there between the huge wooden casks was Luthian with a book in his hands. He looked up at her with a defeated expression, like a child who just lost a game of hide-and-seek.

"Luthian? What are you doing here?"

He lifted the book in his lap. "Reading."

"I can see that," she sighed, "but why?"

"I like reading," he smirked.

"I mean why are you reading in the buttery? There is a ball thrown in our honor tonight, happening right now."

"Incorrect. There is a ball thrown in *Wilvrey's* honor."

Chasmira conceded, chuckling and sitting down beside him. "I suppose you're right. Still, the food is quite good."

He was lost in the pages already, his dark locks hanging over his face. "Really… What have you eaten?"

She chewed her lip for a minute. "As I was saying, the dancing is quite good. Do you dance, Luthian?"

"Oh, no. Absolutely not," he laughed.

"What? A man of culture like yourself does not dance?"

"Dances are for joyous celebrations… for weddings and holidays. It's pretentious to have a dance for anything else."

"We *are* celebrating. Your brother Wilvrey is home again."

He stared. "Why would I celebrate that?"

"All right, you've got me there." She tucked her knees and leaned her elbows on them as she thought hard. "Well, the army from Argismora failed to burn your home and kill you all. Now, is that not worth celebrating?"

Luthian drummed his fingers against his mouth and nose in thought. "I suppose it would have been a shame if all my books burned…"

"Honestly, Luthian!" she laughed and slid down till she was lying on her back, looking up at the ceiling of the storage room.

"Why do you want me to dance so badly?"

"Because you cannot simply save all your joy for joyful moments. You must practice joy in ordinary moments, too."

He closed his book slowly and set it in his lap. "Where's your dance partner gone?"

"Emorya's gone off to find a drink of suitable potency."

"Emorya does not strike me as much of a dancer."

Chasmira scoffed. "I thought the same thing, but the blisters on my feet have convinced me I was mistaken."

"She always tried hard to be better than us at things, when we were all children. She thought she had something to prove."

"Did she not?" Chasmira asked. "One girl, surrounded by a family of boys?"

"If she had anything to prove, it was not to us. It was to Uncle Maram. Lart was such a disappointment to him—never competing with us, never pushing himself, never doing anything with much passion. I think, in a sense, she was trying to make up for that. Anything we did, she went at it twice as hard. She was never as strong as Warrick or smart as Wilvrey, but she made up for it with loud, clear effort."

"I would never have thought that of her, seeing her now."

"We were children. We grow out of things like that."

"What was Wilvrey like at that age?"

He laughed wryly, "Have you forgotten I am the youngest? I don't remember, but I heard that Wilvrey was quite impossible. No matter what punishment he received, he smiled through it like he knew something they did not."

"And Warrick?"

"He was never in trouble. Always keeping us in line, always following Father's rules." Luthian stopped and looked down at her as she laid, her black hair splayed in swirls upon the floor. "What about you?"

"Me?"

"Yes, you. What were you like as a child?"

Her eyes vacantly admired the ceiling before she answered. "Oh, I was any typical little girl. I loved dogs and always wanted one of my own. I loved to pick flowers and bring back little useless bouquets for my mother. Mostly lilac, because they grew plentifully where we lived. When I was eleven I stopped bringing them back home."

"Why?"

"No one appreciated them anymore," she said wistfully.

"I would have," Luthian offered.

"You're very sweet. Are you quite certain you will not dance with me tonight?"

He sighed and ran his hand through his dark, curly locks. "I suppose one dance couldn't hurt, now could it?"

They returned together to the ballroom. Luthian walked in with her on his arm, both of them looking poised and aloof to any attention they drew. The last dance was concluding, and as Luthian and Chasmira took their positions, a lively tune began. It was a line dance and it moved quickly. Luthian was not a very quick dancer, but his legs were long and it helped him keep up. He only stepped on her feet twice.

She had never danced with any man like this. No roaming hands, no roaming gaze. When he was not glancing down to awkwardly check his footwork, he was watching her eyes and her smile to be sure she was having a good time. She felt like she was walking on air the entire dance.

As the music wound down, Luthian stopped abruptly in answer to a hand placed on his shoulder.

Wilvrey.

"You're unexpectedly light on your feet, little brother."

Luthian chewed his lip. "Thanks, Wilvrey."

"Mind if I have this next dance? Your partner has been in high demand all evening," he said, his emerald gaze locked on her.

Luthian wordlessly looked to Chasmira. She stared back at Wilvrey with a blank expression on her face. He looked hungry, like a lion on a hunt. Her only answer was a nod as she stepped forward and into his arms for the next dance.

He was a strong lead, in the way he kept his hand firmly against her back but not too tight. His other hand was palm-to-palm with hers, as was the fashion of the dance. She felt at every moment that he was too close somehow, even when she leaned away a little to get some space. Perhaps it was not his closeness but his attention that felt suffocating, despite the fact he was not even looking at her. The two danced for a full minute before Wilvrey broke the stoic silence.

"You know, if you're going to seduce my brother, at least have the discretion to seduce only one at a time."

"Is that your idea of a compliment?" she replied icily.

His laugh was throaty and clipped. "My idea of a joke. Apologies if it is ill-timed. I merely meant that both my brothers are quite soft for you, and I hate to be the odd one out."

"On the contrary, Wil, I think you enjoy being the odd one out."

He sighed and searched the walls of the room for how to respond. "All right, I concede that. But here is my riddle: if given the choice to stand out from the crowd or blend in, why choose the latter? Why settle for being the rain when you can be the thunder?"

She left the question unanswered for a long moment while she danced, deep in thought. "You pose a fine question but I am a poor respondent, for I was not given such a choice."

He clasped her hand tighter as they stepped to the tempo of

the music. "We are both the odd ones then."

As they danced, she pondered why she felt so strange with Wilvrey. She had readily agreed to accompany him to the ball, yet she was defiant about such a petty detail as the fragrance she chose. She readily accepted his offer to dance, yet she resisted playing along with his banter. Were these petty displays a way to assert her independence despite following his lead every time? Or perhaps her way of creating space when it seemed every moment that she was the sole focus of his attention. It was not even the way he stared or leered. He simply seemed *aware* of her, of her every move.

"It seems I underestimated your enchantments, for you have put quite a spell on our dear Lord Ovis."

"Have I?" she asked, snapped out of her inner musings.

"He walked you around the room like a peacock at auction and then let you dine at his table. Meanwhile, he has me practically loitering at his gates like a drunk beggar, at least compared to the royal treatment you have received."

"It's nothing truly surprising, Wil, what happens when you offer someone a little softness in this hard world."

"A sorceress on a mission of vengeance, offering softness? Be careful that you spend not all of what is in short supply."

She huffed at his barb, as it reminded her of Nandrzael's treachery. "Nothing you need concern yourself about. As I have already demonstrated, I am quite tactful."

He pivoted, clasping her hand. "And that, my love, has put you in a very auspicious position."

"Am I a friend of the drunk beggar, on the inside of the gates?"

"Precisely," he said, and he slowly dipped her backward, kneeling with the movement to bring his lips to her ear. She felt a warm tingle on her shoulder and then her neck as his beard brushed along it. "Open those gates for me. I am not taking no for an answer."

Goosebumps rose across her skin. "You're desperate."

"I'm determined."

He lifted her upright again, amid applause from the other dancers around them. She sighed, smiling politely to the crowd and then looking back to Wilvrey. She had seen him retreat sullenly earlier that evening, but reemerging he seemed more confident than ever. Confident not in himself, but in her. The opportunity to gain his trust had arrived.

"I'll speak to him," she agreed, curtseying to her partner as he bowed deeply in response.

Chasmira began making her way out of the crowd and toward Lord Ovis, but soon felt lost in a new debate within herself. Ovis had coldly resisted Wilvrey's call to conquest and glory, and if she repeated the same call she might see the same resistance. Appealing to his compassion by begging for help could yield a different response, but Wilvrey expressly said he wanted a show of strength. Exposing his weakness, needfulness, and also his deception too? Ovis would never join him then…

"Lady Chasmira," Ovis said, startling her. Lost in thought, she did not expect him to address her so soon. "Are you alright? Come, sit with me."

She smiled pleasantly at the kind old Goatkin and rounded the side of the table to find her seat. Her hand touched the top of the chair but she could not bring herself to sit down. What she had to say was too important. She continued standing, and noticed a single black firefly that flitted over the table. A small comfort.

Ovis' expression was touched with worry. "My spring flower, you look exhausted. Too much dance and wine? I'll have fresh water brought for you right away."

"You're so kind, milord, but water could not wash away my trouble any more than a river could wash away the Mountain of Iron."

The Goatkin's brow furrowed. "Trouble? What trouble?"

"Wil's, for whatever troubles him troubles me."

"Oh," Ovis said, clicking his tongue, "I mean no dishonor toward him or your loyalty to him, but Mirikinin has filled his son's head with wild ambitions. The boy thinks he can disturb the peace of the Guardian City upon the northern ridgeline? Typical of a young, hotheaded warrior thirsting for blood and glory, thinking they will satisfy him."

Her face flushed at his dismissal. His reply was aimed at Wilvrey, but she could not help but feel she had just taken the blow for him. She had not worked so hard and gone through so much to be thwarted now. "Obviously you would thirst not for such things, for you are a protector and not a warrior. Perhaps you would be satisfied with something more."

"What do you mean?"

"What is greater than blood and glory? Greater than they both is the truth, milord. And the truth is that Wilvrey has omitted entirely the news of his father's death."

Ovis' eyes widened. "Mirikinin… Prince Mirikinin is dead?"

"It is better for it to be out in the open. I am sorry to be the one to tell you, and that Wil could not bring himself to say it. You see, he is readier to believe that your family is loyal to his, only out of fear and not gratitude."

"My word… but why would he think that?"

She swallowed back the pain of her next words. "The death of a parent changes you. It makes you doubt things. It makes you afraid of things you were never afraid of before, as if only once they are gone do you realize what silent reassurance their life gave you. There is a strange despair after loss, and that despair brings out a different side of us."

"And so Wilvrey wishes to start another war, only to avenge his father's death?" Ovis asked, his tone somber now.

Her expression was stony. "Is it less worthy a cause to avenge the fallen than to protect the living? Will you grant peace to your oppressor in order to keep your own? I desire neither an answer nor any discourse, but simply to ask the question and be gone."

"Could I not persuade you to give me your counsel on this?"

Chasmira answered, "I only counsel *rulers* on such matters."

The Goatkin nodded sadly. He reached out to take her hand, but she had already turned away and left.

ψ

The garden behind the villa was a sweet reprieve from the constant din of music and voices inside. The glimmer was gone from the evening now, and all Chasmira craved was solitude among the winding hedges and towering poplar trees.

Her steps were slow, aimless. In her mind, she retread her conversation with Lord Ovis again and again. She had spoken out of her fiery conviction, caring no longer if her words won or lost the night for Wilvrey. She had spoken in defense of him, but also of herself as well. Stoking the flames of vengeance in the hearts of Mirikinin's children was her goal, but she already felt her own inner flames were burning hotter than ever. It was as if she could feel burnt, frayed edges inside—at times making her rougher than she intended and other times softer than she realized.

She breathed deeply, absorbing the spectacular night sky overhead. traced the constellations. She counted the six gold stars that made Androxes' Shield, and found the twinkling Blue Serpent that dipped over and under the southern horizon like waves.

And that was when his voice broke the silence of the evening.

"Wandering in the garden at night? Such aimlessness does not befit you, Lady Chasmira."

Wilvrey.

She continued walking clumsily through the garden, leaning from side to side as she looked upward. "Aimless to you, perhaps, but if you can find Androxes' Shield in the night sky, you are never lost."

Wilvrey followed, hands clasped behind his back. "I would not have taken you for a stargazer."

"When you want to see something more interesting than yourself, look up," she replied. "Besides, stars are for much more than navigating, Wil. Ever look at a thing just because it's so beautiful you can hardly believe it's natural?"

"Rarely," said he.

"Really," she laughed, shaking her head as she still looked upward, drinking in the night sky. She sounded a little let down. "Do you not ever pause to regard something just for its beauty?"

His footsteps stopped in the grass behind her, and she

stopped as well. She dared a glance over her shoulder, and caught the green gleam in Wilvrey's eyes as he looked up at the stars right along with her. "Hm. The stars may seem beautiful, but there is something tainted about them."

"Tainted? How so?"

"Because according to the old legends, the Angelics picked stars from the sky, harvesting them like grain into a silo. They did so to sustain their own immortality, to use the power of the stars to fuel their lives eternally. Don't you see? The heavens themselves have been tainted. They are a vineyard that's been picked at by hungry birds. The night sky bears the marks of petty, greedy creatures violating what once was perfect."

Her stomach turned. The last thing she wanted to think about was Nandrzael's immortality, about her looming inevitable revenge that was long overdue. Dance and drink had driven it all out of her mind, and she did not want to welcome back the fear and failure. She failed the Angelic in allowing Argolvrecht and Mirikinin to wade into war and kill each other. She failed to win back her parents' lives. Chasmira suddenly became aware how vulnerable and careless she was to be standing out in the open alone. She hugged herself and retorted, "Imperfect things are still beautiful."

"To a point. I can appreciate many things for their imperfection, but I couldn't find beauty in them. Beauty is untouched… unspoiled."

She nodded, looking back to the sky and trying to forget he was there. His words burned her insides.

"You want to ask me if I think you're beautiful," he said.

She drew in a long breath. "Why would I care?"

"I was wondering the same thing myself, but you want to ask me all the same. I know you do."

"I don't, but since you've volunteered, fine. Do you?"

"Do I what?"

"Do you find me beautiful?"

"No, I don't."

She saw it coming—she asked, knowing already what his answer would be—but it still hurt. Something inside her wanted him to subvert her expectations as he seemed to enjoy doing so often. Maybe she was not so much hurt as infuriated that he would ruin her peaceful moment in the garden, and ruin her enjoyment of the night sky.

Stuck in her thoughts, she realized she was beginning to taste blood from gnawing the inside of her cheek. The frustration over how to respond was rising to a boil. Finally Chasmira choked out, "I don't know what sick game it is you're playing, Wil, but I hope you find someone better suited for it than me."

She was gone faster than he could respond. The maze and the yard moved around her in a blur. Her hands balled themselves into fists. She did not want to be in this place anymore. She wanted to be anywhere else: away from this villa, Wilvrey, and the tainted night sky with its stolen stars.

Outside the doorway to the back yard, she collided with someone in the darkness.

"Chasmira!"

"Emorya?" she replied, fumbling to hug her around the shoulders. "I'm so sorry!"

"What's the matter? You sound ragged, like you've just chased off a pack of flengers."

"I might as well have. Please, could we… could we leave?"

Emorya stepped back and nodded. "Yes. Yes, absolutely," she replied firmly, taking her by the hand and leading her around the house rather than through it. "We'll take my ivrit so that we can both ride. She's stronger than that stock horse you rode here."

The crunch of leaves beneath their feet seemed deafening to her. She felt a pang of regret for leaving Lord Ovis without thanks for his hospitality, and for leaving Luthian to skulk behind pillars and corners all night.

As Emorya untied her wooly ivrit, petting its pale fur and climbing onto its back, Chasmira cast one last look up at the night sky. A shooting star leapt from cloud to horizon, and a hot tear burned in her eye. She bitterly reflected, *Has the sky lost another one?* before accepting Emorya's hand to climb atop the warbeast behind her.

The two rode together under the tainted sky. Through glade and dale they rode, and did not stop until they saw the House of Mirikinin's black stone spire.

"I don't want to go in yet," Emorya said with a sigh. She leaned back in the saddle, and ivrit slowed to a stop about a hundred paces from the front gate. "Let's walk the rest of the way."

Chasmira lingered, jarred out of her thoughts. The entire ride back, she'd been lost in her thoughts, remembering the evening from start to finish. Now she stared at the landscape around them somberly. The fields were scorched to the dirt. Trees were burnt down to black, rounded stumps. Argismora's vengeance had followed her here, and only Wilvrey's army had chased it off. Wilvrey, whose words she had let wound her.

Emorya coughed, and she could see her breath in the

moonlight. The air was damp and cold, but neither of them seemed to mind it.

Chasmira slid carefully from the saddle onto the bare ground. "I don't know how you could stand to be around him a whole day, much less a year in Eppenhorn. I'd have killed him."

"I bet you would have. Thankfully, I was not his only company during or after the siege, and there was much work to be done."

"I thought you said he was lots of fun," she said, puzzled.

"I did, and he was, and he is, but there's a lot more to him than—" and Emorya stumbled, supporting herself against the ivrit. Chasmira immediately bent over to help but recoiled when she noticed the other woman's breath stank of wormwood moonshine. "Off, off, don't help me! You want to know the real story?"

"About what?"

"About Wilvrey," Emorya coughed, and for a moment Chasmira feared the girl was about to vomit. She paused and then belched instead. "The truth is that he's a monster."

"I could have told you that already. Come dear, let's walk."

Emorya's expression grew dark and sullen. "You have no idea. You have no idea what he did out there in Eppenhorn, the atrocities he committed. He did not just conquer that land, Chasmira. He did not just defeat their army. He tortured their families right in front of their eyes, just to hear them beg him for mercy. He locked them away and let them out when he wanted to watch them fight and kill each other like dogs in a pit, for his sick amusement. They were no longer people to him. They were *things* to be played with and discarded."

"Em, stop. I've heard enough to understand."

"It's not about you understanding. I'm sure that you do. But it has been my burden for the entire year's passing and now… now I can unburden myself at last. You see, he must not be allowed to rule."

Chasmira shook her head. "Lord Maram sits on the throne now."

"Not permanently. My father is only lord regent until one of Mirikinin's sons gets his blessing. What if it's Wilvrey?"

"He won't rule. Warrick is the firstborn."

She grabbed Chasmira roughly by the arm, suddenly overtaken by drunken frustration. "Then why has he not already taken the throne, huh? You know why? Because Father will abide by the same agreement he and my father had: that the first to marry wins the right to rule. Maram will bless the first to wed!"

It made sense. If the strife between brothers was thus resolved between Maram and Mirikinin, why would it be any different among Warrick, Wilvrey, and Luthian?

"He mustn't marry, do you understand?" she insisted.

"I understand, dear, but I cannot imagine what manner of woman would think Wil to be a suitable husband."

Emorya shook her head. "Don't underestimate him. What Wilvrey wants, he will find a way to get."

Chasmira grasped Emorya's hand, which now trembled. She gently lifted it off her arm and gave it a squeeze. "Don't worry. I promise you, I'll scare off anyone I see making eyes at him. And if I catch him holding hands with a girl, I'll burn her to a crisp just for you."

Emorya smiled and sniffled blearily. She stumbled a step and

Chasmira caught her around the shoulders.

"Come on, dear, let's go inside where you can sleep."

"I was brave at Eppenhorn," Emorya mumbled.

"Yes, you were."

"I fought in the snow."

"And you're a wonderful dancer because of it!"

The pair entered past the main gate and into the yard, escorted by a guardsman carrying a torch. No sooner were they inside than a familiar figure rose to meet them.

"Warrick?" Chasmira said, so surprised that she let go of Emorya, who toppled to the ground limply.

He cleared his throat. "I wanted to be sure you returned home."

"You were worried?" She started to smile, but the sound of Emorya wretching in the grass ruined the moment.

"Is she all right?"

"She will be," Chasmira grimaced. "She got into some moonshine that can put a Bearkin to sleep, and now here we are."

Warrick looked past her at the main gate. "Where is Wilvrey?"

"Back at the villa. His ruse was ill-received, and Lord Ovis refused to help us. I took the liberty of helping in the only way I thought to be right—I told the truth. In so doing," hanging her head, "I have probably ruined it for Wil, and for all of you by extension."

"I'm sure that's not true."

"No, I'm sure that it is," she sighed. When she looked up, she looked right into Warrick's brown eyes. "Were you really worried about us returning home tonight?"

Warrick crossed his arms over his chest. "We almost lost you in Argismora not even a week ago. You can hardly blame me for being protective."

"Feeling guilty because I saved your life?"

"Feeling *grateful*," he amended. "And don't tell me that I have paid you back. This is not about debt."

He really cares, she thought. What hour of the night was it anyway, that he was still awake to see her return?

Emorya moaned in the yard where Chasmira had let her fall. Warrick snapped into action, helping her up as gently as he could. As he stepped back into the torchlight, Chasmira spied something blue and familiar in his hip scabbard.

"Your dagger. I hadn't noticed until now that you found it again."

He glanced down at it. "Oh, yes."

"But it's broken. Why carry it?"

"Perhaps I like to keep it as a reminder."

"But it's useless."

Warrick smiled. "Oh, I don't think it is. It may not serve its original purpose, but that doesn't make it useless." He drew it out with one hand, looking at where the blade had cracked off diagonally just a few inches past the crossguard. He turned it over in his hand. "Some things become valuable to us for different reasons, besides whether or not they are useful."

She saw deep earnestness in his eyes, and everything inside her wanted to pull her gaze away from him. Everything inside her wanted to recoil and reject his sweet words. Instead, she held his gaze and nodded and let his words in. "Yes, I'm sure that's true."

He held out the dagger. "Here, take it."

Without understanding why, she accepted it.

"Perhaps you need the reminder more than I do," he said, and then took Emorya inside.

ф

Chasmira was already awake and looking out her bedroom window when Wilvrey returned home. The crunch of hooves in the morning frost alerted her, and she set down her book to watch him ride in the front gate.

She stood, still wrapped in the black ramskin from the bed. The ride home during the night left her with a persistent chill, and the cold morning did nothing to remedy it. At her bedside table, hot tea had been left for her to drink when she awoke, but she ignored it.

When the house's great stone door rumbled aside, Chasmira was there waiting for Wilvrey. Her hair was unkempt and her face naked, baring the grey circles around her eyes from the long night and uneasy sleep.

Snowflakes glinted in the hazy morning sun outside behind him as he stepped into the shade of the doorway. He tilted his head to one side. "You should have stayed. Lord Ovis was a very obliging host, and the bed was very—"

"You were counting on me."

Wilvrey replied only with raised eyebrows.

"You were counting on me, and I let you down."

His surprise was replaced with calm amusement. "On the contrary, Lady Chasmira, the meeting with Lord Ovis was a rousing success, even more so than I expected. It seems he had a change of heart and has pledged the five hundred that I asked for.

They will arrive in twelve days to begin training… Speaking of which, may I assume Emorya is in the house?"

Chasmira could hardly speak. Ovis had changed his mind, no doubt thanks to her sharing the truth with him. She cleared her throat and answered, "You may, and she is. Although I would knock softly at her door if I were you."

"Ahh, let me guess. She drank too much last night. Well, she has twelve days to recover from her revelry well enough to begin drilling these beasts on the art of war. Summer comes swiftly, and Argismora is waiting."

CHAPTER 23

The next month was Lomna, the "Month of Abundance" and the ninth month of the year. While the land glowed with golden hues, the sky glowered with the threat of snow constantly. The wind bore a freezing bite that every farmhand felt as they busied themselves reaping in the fields. Commander Boe had burned all the harvest of Mirikinin, but these fields belonged to Lord Ovis. Thanks to the renewed alliance between them, both families shared harvests from now on. Wilvrcy had never thanked Chasmira, for he remained oblivious that her honesty had won this for him.

Only Warrick knew.

Here on this cold Lomna day, he and Chasmira walked through the fields of golden grain as the farmhands worked.

"Fonio," he began, running his hand across the tops of the thin, fine grain stalks. "It has fed both man and beast in this land since the time before kings. Three hundred years ago, when the Dragon's Winter froze the continent solid, millions starved in the icy famine. The desperate migrated southward looking for signs of spring, and they died along the way. But not my ancestors. We stayed right here in the highlands."

"You say 'we' as if you were there with them," she quipped.

He smiled, looking off across the fields wistfully. "I feel as though I was, the stories were so vividly told."

Chasmira nodded, admiring the field but also watching the wind play with his hazelwood hair. It was getting longer. While he normally kept it tightly pulled into a topknot, he was wearing it down, and she had not realized how wavy it was. "How did they survive?"

"They rationed their reserves as long as they could. They hunted anything that moved: wild oxen, ice mammoths, snow hares, and even mountain flengers when there was nothing else left."

"Flengers?" She grimaced. "My word, can you imagine the taste of fresh snow ape?"

"Tastes like survival, I wager. Generations came and went without ever knowing the feeling of sunlight. They lived in deep caves near the last remaining hot springs—the faint heartbeat of a world whose death they awaited. But it never happened. The summers slowly began to wear away the snow, and when the sun finally touched the naked earth again, it brought forth wild fonio. No one had to plant it."

"It simply rose from the earth by the gods' mercy?"

"Or for their mirth," Warrick snarked.

"Yes. Perhaps Naru the god of laughter planned it all as a great practical joke. I couldn't imagine the looks on your ancestors' faces as food popped out of the ground, practically waving at them."

Warrick laughed, and for the first time without any scorn or sarcasm to it. She had never heard him laugh like this, with this deep, hearty laugh right from his belly. The sound of it was no surprise, for it clearly matched that booming voice of his, but what surprised her was how relaxed and unguarded he was. He explained, "We continued farming it in the highlands to show our gratitude to the sun and earth every year, that we did not take this good fortune for granted."

"Fortune? Ah yes, I nearly forgot. For a moment there you sounded like you believed in the gods as much as anyone."

The two of them reached the end of the fonio fields and kept walking, greeted by a beautiful forest of alder trees. In the sunlight, the bright yellow crowns of the alders would normally cast a golden hue in the forest, but on a cloudy day like this they cast a dark bronze canopy overhead.

"Why do *you* believe in the gods, Chasmira? You do not even serve them, nor can you enter into their holy places. If anyone is estranged from such faith, I would think it to be you."

"To acknowledge them is one thing. To serve them is another."

Warrick's gaze wandered the ground as they stepped over branches and stumps. "You serve no one, I see."

"That role is quite played out for me. Those I have served treated me like a weapon or a tool, just as you said to me in Argismora. I may seem like I am fit for the role, like a glove fit for a hand, but I am on a different path now. I do not need others' permission."

He nodded, stepping over a large, mossy log and waiting for her on the other side. "Nor do you need their help."

"No," pausing and holding out her hand. "But that does not mean I don't want it, or that I am too proud to ask for it."

He smiled and took her hand to help her over the obstacle. Rather than stepping over it, she stepped onto it, and suddenly she and Warrick were eye-to-eye. "That is a new perspective," he said.

"Is it?"

"Yes." His brown eyes were locked with hers. "It is certainly something I was unprepared for."

"Is it?" Her footing on the mossy log was a bit unsteady, so she put her hands on Warrick's big, broad shoulders.

He reached up and closed his calloused hands around her wrists gently. "Yes. But it's not unwelcome."

"I thought you said you were unprepared for it, yet you welcome it?" She leaned closer. She could feel her cheeks becoming flushed and warm, and she tried to steady her breath against the pounding of her heart.

He could smell the gentle essence of dandelion that she wore every day. At first the scent reminded him of his childhood. Lately, however, he had come to expect her to walk by every time he breathed in a hint of it. A lock of her long black hair fell over her eye, and he lifted it aside, brushing her cheek with his fingertips…

An arrow struck the tree beside them. Birds screeched and scattered from the brush, and Chasmira whirled about with flames in her eyes to torch their attacker.

Instead, they saw Lart standing across the glen with a shortbow in his hands and a disappointed look on his face.

"Damn it, Lart, are you mad!?" Warrick exploded.

"I almost got it," he whined back.

"Got what? You nearly killed us!"

"I wasn't aiming at you! I was aiming at that big ol' buck I've been tracking since dawn."

"A buck?"

Terror trotted up, looking expectantly up at his master. Lart scratched the dog's ear and then trudged over to them. "He was right on the other side of the tree from you, and you both were standing there so quietlike, you didn't even spook him."

Chasmira and Warrick turned to each other and stared for a few seconds before bursting into laughter. Lart, completely befuddled, holstered his bow on his back beside the quiver. He sighed and waited for them to compose themselves.

"Never change, Lart." Warrick said, patting Lart on the arm. "If you will both excuse me, I ought to go oversee the threshers. These new hands we hired may not know to dry out the grains after they have been sifted."

"What'sa matter, Warrick? Scared off like that buck?"

"If only I could move that fast," he chuckled as he walked off.

"Always busy," Chasmira called after him.

"Someone has got to keep this place running."

She stood for a minute, watching him lumber off through the woods back the way they came. Warrick was so huge, so strong, and yet continued to prove himself so gentle when given the chance. If only he had been given more chances…

"So you and Warrick seem to be getting along pretty good," Lart said, stretching his arms above his head.

She wanted to clobber him, but sighed and let it go. "Yes, we are indeed."

"He's been so bad-humored, I'd almost forgotten what it looked like when he smiled."

The wind rustled the treetops. Chasmira closed her eyes and let the wind toss her hair as she began walking with Lart. "He is always so greatly laden with responsibilities. I am genuinely happy when he takes a little time for himself."

"He doesn't take any time for himself. He takes time for you."

She looked down at the ground to hide her smile. "That's good then. If I can persuade him to escape his preoccupations for a while, I am glad to be of help. We go walking together, though I rarely get him past the end of the fields. Today we went even further and actually got past the treeline."

"It's progress."

"I'm working on it," she laughed.

Terror paused and flattened his ears against his head. He whined at first, sniffed the air, and then growled.

They both paused and sniffed the air as well.

"Smoke," Lart said.

"Brushfire?"

"Or campfire," he said, drawing his bow and nocking an arrow.

They crept through the brush, staying downwind and hopefully out of sight of whatever lay ahead. They tiptoed through an open glen and paused behind a tree. The smell of burning wood was getting stronger, but soon was overpowered by another smell.

"Meat?" they both whispered in unison.

A heartbeat later, the tree was torn straight out of the ground. Terror yelped and began to bark wildly.

"Meat!" a monstrous voice boomed overhead.

"Ogre!" Lart yelled, blindly drawing and loosing the arrow at the towering creature that leaned over them. The arrow ricocheted off the Ogre's grey hide like a pine cone thrown at a stone wall.

"Morth?" Chasmira squinted upward.

The Ogre hesitated, squinting back at her with the uprooted tree still held in his hands. She recognized his long braids and banded leather armor covered in scuffs and marks.

"Morth, who so wisely warned me about the Eyes of the Night?"

"You listened," Morth replied, lowering the tree.

"We didn't," she laughed with relief and shushed Terror, who was still barking fiercely. "But we got very lucky. Thank you for warning us. We should have listened to someone who lives in these very woods. After all, you did say you don't like big cities."

"Morth *hates* big cities," he affirmed, turning and dragging the tree with him. Terror, convinced his ferocity had routed the monster, followed after him and continued barking.

Chasmira took a step to follow but then glanced back to see Lart peeking out from behind another tree, his bow and arrow trembling in his hands. "Come out, Lart! He's a friend! He won't crush us or eat us!"

He blinked twice and then began to nervously follow. "How do you make friends with every growling giant you meet? First Warrick and now this thing?"

Morth led them into a clearing, where an entire tree lay burning, stripped of its leaves and broken into an impressive stack of wood. The trunk of another tree, cleared of its branches and cracked at the top to make a sharp point, served as a cooking skewer for an entire animal over the fire. Morth walked to the trunk and rotated it to turn over the cooking meat.

Lart looked down at Terror, who sniffed at an antlered head and pile of bloody deerskin on the ground. "Hey, that's my buck!"

"It not yours if you not kill it," Morth said as he walked over, leaned down, and snatched the antlered head off the ground. "This make good armor."

Chasmira followed next to Morth. "What are you doing here anyway, hunting on Prince Mirikinin's land?"

"Prince not own land. Prince dead."

"And where did you hear such a thing?"

"I told himmm!" Wisp's squeaky voice was unmistakeable. The little Cloven giggled and shyly stepped out of the tall grass.

Chasmira stifled her laughter and crossed her arms. "Oh, I see! And where did *you* hear such a thing, little sprout?"

"I was climbing in the apple trees and heard the grumpy man in the funny straw hat. He said, 'oy I can't believe the Prince is dead' and I said I couldn't believe it either. He got scared and looked around and asked if I was a ghost, and I said I didn't think but I wasn't sure. Then I asked him if he was a ghost and he didn't explain. He just ran away."

"Peeeep," Peep peeped.

"Peep heard it too," Wisp explained.

"And two mushrooms cannot be wrong," Chasmira smiled, her scolding act quickly falling apart.

"Cloven know many things for being so small," Morth said, settling down next to the fire to watch his meal cook.

"Yes, sometimes a little *too* much. Still, Morth, that does not explain what you are doing here."

"Winter coming soon. Morth needs to build house."

She had never considered that an Ogre—a creature so seemingly unaffected by fear, danger, or even weapons—would need a home. But all creatures, great and small, do. The winters were dreadfully cold, and the longer she thought on it the more obvious it was that the deep Jacorian winter would claim even the mightiest of creatures without shelter.

"Well, that simply will not do," she said, placing her fists on her hips. "That will not do at all. You were nothing but kind and helpful to us on the north road. Lart, the western sward is totally empty, is it not?"

"Aye, it's all burnt away. No fences, haystacks, or fields." Lart squinted suspiciously at her. "What's in your head, woman?"

"Why, there isn't a reason in the world why we should leave him to the glens and thickets to live like an animal," she scolded, and then looked up at the grey-skinned giant. "Morth, you're coming home with us."

Morth nodded his acceptance of her offer and then shot a glance at the skewered buck dangling over the fire. "Morth may eat first?"

CHAPTER 24

Winter's arrival chased off the precious warm days as if summer were merely a fleeting dream. All of Grimmgard once nearly perished in the teeth of the Dragon's Winter, and every year was a reminder how narrowly it had survived. Days of relentless storm left such deep snow behind that it hardly had time to melt before the next. Many years, the cold was persistent enough that some started to believe the spring might never return.

The only benefit was that war quieted in the shadow of winter. Few warbeasts could travel in such bitter cold. Even the ones that could would scarcely find an army willing to accompany them, to say nothing of the prospect of a drawn-out siege. All the land rested from war.

Chasmira was far from idle. When she was not in the fortress, she ventured out into the western sward to visit Morth, Wisp, and Peep. The Ogre had built an impressive hut out of stones and logs, complete with a crude hearth, a boulder for a table, and uprooted tree stumps for chairs. She visited regularly on Fufedyd, the second day of the week, when there was always a simmering cauldron that came to be called Morth's Sleeping Stew. The aroma of juicy venison, along with potatoes, carrots, dried tomatoes, garlic, cloves, and parsley, provoked the growling stomachs of the wall sentries far away. Chasmira brought juniper berries and red wine to add, creating a final recipe that left them all sleeping in their chairs with full bellies after.

She and Morth would trade stories of their travels. The Ogre made a yearly journey northward over the mountains to the Sea of Shadows in the summer, and then back down into the forests between Argismora and the House of Mirikinin in the autumn. Puffing his pipe, Morth spent long afternoons telling her about the taste of wild honey, fresh venison, and river salmon, and he talked of great blue lights in the sky over the north sea. He had never journeyed farther south than Mirikinin's land and had no desire to. The vast golden kingdom of Alcimaea was far too densely populated for his rustic taste.

She would reminisce about running up the grassy highlands outside Holireath, where she could see all the way to the coast. There, distant white-crested waves would carry in the trade ships, and little Chasmira would watch to see what color the tiny sails on the horizon would be. White sails meant lumber from savage East Jacore, red sails meant furs from wealthy Silvany, and blue sails meant spices from mysterious Khon Dha. The estuary port where they dropped their cargo was a haven for merchants and fishermen.

Morth hibernated during the winter, as most Ogres do. On any other day than Fufedyd, he was in a middle state somewhere between fully asleep and fully awake. Conserving energy was best for creatures that large, for food was too scarce in winter for any more activity. Wisp and Peep stayed indoors at all times, for it was far too dangerous for the little Cloven. They needed only water to survive, but this made them especially vulnerable to the cold. As Cloven never sleep, Wisp and Peep kept watch over the slumbering Ogre and would wake him up fully if necessary.

In thanks for the hospitality, Morth would go out and make a walking path after every snowstorm. The huge Ogre trod the snow down all the way from the front gate to the northern fields and the edge of the forest, exactly where Chasmira and Warrick had walked together in the autumn. Much to their delight, they would be able to continue their walks long into the winter.

Another fast friend she acquired was Nyell, the housekeeper. She was about fifty years old, plump and sweet, with long, silvery hair. Nyell had once been the cook, but over the years she took on more and more responsibility until finally the Prince appointed her head over the servants. Despite this, she was still happiest in the kitchen, treating Prince Mirikinin and his family to her latest culinary concoctions.

"You don't find it tedious?" Chasmira asked, following behind her and peeking under the lid of the cooking pot. She swiftly received a swat to the hand with a wooden spoon.

"Absolutely not," Nyell said, playfully scolding. "The House of Mirikinin is nothing more than strict, rigid timing. Guards come off shift every five hours. Bedding is changed and washed every Anndyd, and the plants are watered every Fufedyd. It would feel like a prison if not for the freedom here, where I can create what I please, whenever I please, and everyone had better be grateful I do."

"I've never heard it put quite like that. Cooking has always been something of a test for me, one I have always failed. Everything I make tastes like the color white," Chasmira laughed.

"That's tragic indeed. If the kitchen is your canvas, seasoning is your paint. A good roast, or a perfect maafé, is a work of art."

"And you are the artist. Fascinating."

Nyell arched an eyebrow. "Would you like to try your hand at it?"

"If you want the fortress to burn down."

"I would not have imagined you of all people, to be afraid to play with fire," she said with a grin.

Chasmira had no retort, neither had she the willpower to resist a challenge. She started joining Nyell in the mornings, helping make the servants' breakfasts before the ruling family was even awake.

Such quality time was not available with Emorya. Wilvrey put her in charge of training the beastkin that Lord Ovis pledged to the warband, and every day she was in the south reach at dawn, making them into proper warriors. Now and then Chasmira would rise early enough to join her, bundled in warm furs and watching the warmaiden at work. Over half of the horde were Goatkin, all male, likely the descendants of Lord Ovis himself. The rest were a mix of long-horned Oxkin and grumbling Boarkin. She ran them through combat drills using all manner of martial weaponry: swords, axes, polearms, and spears, though Emorya noted they all seemed to favor the axe.

"They are all strength and no skill," Emorya would comment, and she was right. While the hearty beastkin wielded their weapons with brute force, they were slow and undisciplined. Still, believing that practice would make progress, Emorya continued to run them through their drills every day without fail.

When they were not training for combat, they were

conditioning for endurance. Whole days were devoted to marching from the south reach to the snowy lowlands, the cramped woods, and even the stinking boglands. "You must be ready to make any terrain your killing field," Emorya would repeat. She was a hard taskmaster. Those who came up short were put through additional paces. Those who complained were punished.

One particularly frigid morning, they were loath to complete their drills in such foul conditions. The piercing cold and howling wind made their bones ache just at the thought of getting out of their beds. Emorya was not taking no for an answer.

"Get up," she commanded, standing in the barracks doorway.

One brazen bull withstood her: Guff, a highland rogue who owed Lord Ovis a debt of servitude. The long-horned Oxkin towered over her, his thick red fur rippling in the fierce wind. "No rest, not even in this weather? What are ye trying to do, get us killed?"

She just laughed scornfully. "Are you mad, Guff? I'm trying to save your lives. I gave you a command, not a choice. If you believe you have a choice, you will always take the easiest route, and that I cannot allow. *That* will get you killed."

"We *do* have a choice, and we cannot endure this."

She stepped forward without a shred of fear in her. "Aw, did you really awaken this early in the morning to confess to your weakness? Perhaps your mother will wipe your tears away, little veal. I know exactly what you can endure. I faced the deadly cold of Eppenhorn and far worse, in my pale Human flesh. If you are too frail for the cold then go home. The last thing this army needs is weaklings." She turned on her heel and left them there.

Guff, unsure whether he had won or lost the confrontation,

walked to the door to shut it. The biting wind felt like a warm breeze compared to Emorya's icy words. Before he could shut it, another shape appeared in the doorway: Chasmira, her black hair whipping in the wind.

"Lady Chasmira," Guff said, startled. The big Oxkin gave her a short, awkward bow. "Forgive us—this is not a good time."

She looked around and narrowed her eyes in confusion. "Is it not already the seventh hour of the day? I thought that I was running late. Where is Emorya?"

"She has come and gone."

"And you are all still abed?" she asked, suspicious now.

"She has given us a day of rest. The weather is too foul." An unconvincing lie.

Chasmira narrowed her eyes. She knew full well Emorya would not have done such a thing. More words could be said, but not to him. Instead, she returned his short bow. "And so it is. Good morning," she said, excusing herself to find Emorya.

On the north side of the black stone fortress was the armory and forge. They let out into the inner yard through a hall big enough to stand fifty guards in formation. On this day, the only thing standing in the hall was a trio of melee training dummies and Emorya in the midst of them. The warmaiden walked herself through slow, practiced steps, with a shortsword in one hand and a battle axe in the other.

Chasmira entered from the yard, the wind blowing stripes of snow across the floor around her. She shook the white flakes off her cape and lowered her hood as Emorya's combat drill captivated her.

The three dummies—stakes with wooden arms and hay bales

around their middles—were arranged to simulate an ambush from all sides. Emorya launched into her battle sequence with the agility of a cat. Without even looking back, she swung her axe, cut off the arm of the dummy behind her, and then kicked it over. She lunged forward and dropped into a roll, coming up with a stab straight through the abdomen of the next dummy. She spun it around, moving with it until she faced the third target. In a single smooth movement, she hurled her axe to bury it in the last dummy's face and yanked her sword free from the stabbed hay bale.

"You're a natural-born killer," Chasmira complimented with a slow clap from the end of the hall. "Your trainees would be lucky to be half the warrior you are."

Emorya rolled her eyes. "They'll be lucky to be warriors at all. We should have never wasted our time bidding on meat from Lord Ovis' stockhouse."

"Now, Emorya, be patient with them."

"Patient? They're animals."

"That is very unkind, dear, but I know you're frustrated. Even so, animals can be trained, too."

"That I know. I've trained animals before," the warmaiden said, yanking the axe out of the dummy's face. "When we were children, I trained a ratter meowl to steal the bacon off Warrick's breakfast plate. It would roost up in my room and wait for me to come upstairs so we could feast upon the spoils together."

"A bit of second breakfast, eh?"

"Never hurt anyone." Emorya tried and failed to repress her bright smile. "Also, stop it. You're spoiling my angst before I've had the chance to enjoy it."

"Sorry, did you want to savor it like stolen bacon?"

"I did, in fact, yes. Brings back happy memories."

"Must not have been too happy for Warrick," Chasmira laughed, turning to admire a polished set of sentry armor on the wall. She thought back to Argismora's warriors surrounding the walls, and to Warrick defending it among his valiant sentries. "Warrick's not a warrior either, you know, but when it came time to fight, he proved his mettle."

Emorya arched an eyebrow as she hung her weapons on the wall of the armory. "You're saying I should trust them to become warriors in their own time? I hate to remind you that we are on a timetable..."

"I was about to say that you should also trust yourself. Warrick did not train for war, and yet I saw him ankle-deep in green Scarrlok blood the night of the siege."

"At least Warrick's fought before. He's basically more beast than man," Emorya chuckled.

"The point is, sometimes things happen because they must, not because we push them and pull them along."

"You sound like a priest of Tyor, talking like that. 'What is meant to be, shall be.' Has the god of duty and necessity tasked you to speak his holy wisdom?"

Chasmira smiled and shook her head. It was not often that someone returned her snark blow for blow, but Emorya was as capable with words as with weapons. "Are you certain you are trying to prove them, and not prove yourself?"

"Not at all. I already know what I'm capable of," the warmaiden answered curtly. "I need not prove myself to anyone."

"Of course," Chasmira said, deciding to end the verbal

sparring and let the matter lie. "But trust me, you are doing a fine job with your herbivorous menagerie, even if they are a little... bull-headed."

"Har har. You could be my father's court jester." Emorya planted her hands on her hips and sighed. "I appreciate your encouragement, truly."

Chasmira let the sweet gratitude linger for a few silent seconds longer before replying, "They are taking a rest day. How about you?"

"*Rest?*" She pronounced it with all teeth, as if it were something vile. "I never touch the stuff."

"Well," slinging her arm around Emorya's waist, "I have another word from great, holy Tyor for you."

"Do you now?"

"Yes, he spoke to me just now. He said there are other things more necessary than training for war."

Rolling her eyes, "Oh? Name one."

Emorya's stomach answered the question with a loud, hungry gurgle. She bit her lip, trying her hardest to stifle any response. The moment she saw Chasmira's eyes, wide like the stare of a frightened horse at the sound of her angry gut, both women burst out in breathless laughter.

"Come on now, there's plenty of winter left. Argismora can wait until after breakfast," said the sorceress.

Worn down from the laughter, Emorya finally relented, and the two of them went arm-in-arm to the dining room. The rest of the morning was spent amid platters of scrambled eggs, bowls of salted pork stew, and steaming mugs of sweet mulled mead, and Emorya did not mention the Beastkin even once.

ψ

The snow and bitter cold gripped the land for a night and a day, but by the next sunset there was not a cloud in the sky. Warrick complained of the worsening cold it portended, but for Chasmira it meant something quite different. At twilight, she walked the inner yard with the crunch of the fresh snow to keep her company until sundown, when the stars appeared.

Tracing the constellations gave her peace. The brilliance of the night sky was breathtaking enough, but the quiet steadfastness of the stars in their journey across the sky every night was oddly reassuring to her. *If only everything could be so certain as looking for a star in its assigned place and always finding it…*

Wilvrey's words scratched at the back of her thoughts: *The heavens themselves have been tainted.* She pushed back against it. Surely he could not know the way the stars symbolized this security, this reassurance for her, and could not have meant to defy that. Surely he was stating a simple, cold fact and unwittingly treading on her toes.

She thought of the Angelics stealing the stars away, of celestial beings streaking across the night sky like shooting stars, leaving a tragically beautiful trail of stardust in the sky behind them. She thought of them cracking open the stars like melons and scooping out the pure light and goodness inside of them to devour it.

She thought of Nandrzael, blasting across the sky with malevolent glee and unimaginable speed, snatching a star in either hand and biting into one like an apple. Nandrzael, who would throw away mortal lives in fulfillment of her prophecies, in the name of peace.

Chasmira noticed the wall sentries were huddled together upon the wall, looking south and pointing. She ascended the ladder to the wall walkway and joined them for a good look.

There in the south reach, a huge bonfire blazed in the middle of the open field. Around it were the silhouettes of Beastkin gathering for some sort of ceremony. Music could be heard across the flatland, amplified by the biting cold air but too indistinct to be truly enjoyed. Curiosity got the better of her. A few minutes later, she was walking through the south reach toward the massive bonfire. Every single one of the Beastkin, five hundred in all, were present and stood around it. A sextet of flautists piped a somber tune over the entire scene, and the whole crowd swayed along with the music.

Chasmira watched them in wonder, lingering at the back near a lumber pile.

"Do ye wish to join in the ceremony?" asked a young goatkin.

"Oh no, I couldn't. I'm clearly not one of you," she said sheepishly. "I would be so obviously intruding."

"No, ye wouldn't. It is the day before the full moon, the Harmony Moon. Today is Harmony's Eve. In our culture, it is the last day of the year that ye may rightfully avenge yourself on someone who has wronged ye."

She arched an eyebrow. "Why the last day?"

"Because it is a day of cleansing, of renewal. The Harmony Moon is always on the fifth day of the week: Baldyd, the day of sacrifice. Ye must sacrifice part of yourself: your pain, your anger, your loss." The goatkin picked up a stubby log about as long as her forearm, and set it down in front of her. "Think of someone ye hate, that ye once sought revenge upon for the wrong they did ye. If ye have not taken revenge for the wrong, then write their name on one of these logs. Throw your log into the fire and let it burn away. Put the hatred to rest forever."

Her gaze wandered across the crowd. Logs, hundreds of them, were cut and laid out in a spiraling pattern that went around and around the central bonfire. Only now did she realize many of the Beastkin were knelt down, etching letters into the logs with their knives or hatchets.

Something inside her knotted itself like a fist. *If only forgiveness were so easy. If only pain could be etched on a piece of wood and be cast away with a simple gesture.* She smiled politely and took a step back from the proceedings, but just then, she also noticed a member of the crowd with unmistakable long horns and red fur. Guff stood swaying with the rest of them, yet she perceived how he moved off tempo from the music. Instead of departing into the night, she moved through the crowd and to the Oxkin's side. Before them, The other Kin were starting to approach the fire with logs held reverently in their hands.

Guff noticed her almost immediately, shifting uncomfortably. "Lady Chasmira! Uh, pleasant night, is it not?"

"Pleasant only when near the fire," she replied, wrapping herself tighter in her cape to keep warm.

"Yes, right ye are. I oft forget, Humans haven't the fur or the fat to endure the night outdoors."

"Some of us are more resilient to the cold," she said pointedly. She did not have to mention Emorya's name. She was certain he knew, and that he was still preoccupied with the incident the previous morning.

He hesitated at first, and then nodded. "Aye. Some of ye."

The crowd swayed along with the piping, while Chasmira and Guff stood still in the middle of them. One at a time, sometimes two at a time, the Beastkin delivered their contributions to the pyre. A few of them paced, struggling with their decision, but ultimately they let go of the logs and let their grievances burn away. Some knelt down and watched the log catch fire, while others wept as they turned away.

She broke the silence between them. "Funny, isn't it?"

"Hm?"

"So many ways the heart handles forgiveness."

"Every heart is different."

"Are they really, though? What is the difference between yours and mine, Guff? Same chambers, same heartbeat."

He took no time to ponder a reply. "Mine is twice the size of yours, at least."

Neither did she. "So it can hold twice as much. Twice as much hurt, twice as much care."

This time, he pondered but had no reply.

"It must be a burden to hold all of that inside your chest. Why not lighten it while you have the chance?"

The huge Oxkin shook his head, then nodded, and then shook it again. He chewed his lip as he fought with the idea. "Why? Because it is wrong to care so much?"

Chasmira turned to him with the most earnest look, placing her hand upon his furry forearm. "No. It's not wrong at all to care. But maybe some burdens are only meant to be carried a short while and then put down."

"So ye think I should—"

"Who, me?" She laughed and resumed staring at the pyre

ceremony. "My opinion does not matter. I'm not throwing any logs in there. No, I'm just making polite conversation while I keep warm." She bundled herself tighter in her cape and swayed in time to the pipe music.

Guff snorted his frustration, but after a pensive moment he leaned down to pick up a log. Drawing his axe, he began cutting into it. Chasmira could hardly restrain herself from smiling when she saw the name "*EMORYA*" carved into the wood before Guff tucked it under his arm, stood, and shuffled past her.

She continued watching as he became a small, humble silhouette against the massive blaze. He fidgeted reluctantly with the log, looking around to his fellow Kin for the strength to finish what he started. Then, with one hand he lifted the log over his shoulder and chucked it into the fire. She inhaled sharply as a cascade of red embers swirled upward into the night, joining with the stars in the beautiful sky overhead.

Guff returned amid the congratulatory back-patting and applause from the Beastkin around him. He looked embarrassed but lighter, more relaxed. Chasmira joined in the applause, but her smile was bittersweet. *Can pain be etched on a piece of wood and cast away with a simple gesture?* She, too, applauded him, for he was able to do something she could not:

Forgive.

CHAPTER 25

"So I have been reading about Chaos."

Chasmira shut her book and craned her neck over the back of her chair. "Have you now?"

The two sat the room's width apart from each other, separated by hundreds of books in stacks of various heights on the floor. Luthian and Chasmira had spent weeks reorganizing the library: scaling the great oakwood bookshelves, carefully emptying them from the top down, and debating for hours whether to refill them in order alphabetically or by subject matter. The debate was never settled, and the books they took down were far too interesting to neglect, and so their project remained half-finished. In the meantime, the two of them had grown quite comfortable with this setting, and it remained to be seen if either of them would ever return one of the books to the towering black shelves.

Luthian placed an old, triangular book onto the armrest. "I have been reading the *Pyramidia Gamalgald*, and it says here that Chaos was once studied as the purest sorcery a thousand years ago. Ancient masters from the Phrontistery of First Fire even believed it to be 'the innate core of the Arts of True Sorcery.'"

"It was that very belief that divided them," she said, taking a sip of wine. "A powerful sorcerer by the name of Muluvero left the Phrontistery's inner circle and created his own school: the Sorcerers of the White Aegis. Their mission was to foretell the rising of Chaos within gifted people and head it off."

"Head it off? How?"

"Well, they would either induct them into their school, or destroy them with prejudice."

Luthian grimaced at the thought, but still seemed confused.

"Where to begin? One's connection to the primordial forces manifests itself during late childhood, or sometimes early adolescence. It can manifest in a few different ways: mumbling words from an unknown tongue in their sleep, or unconsciously controlling water with their thoughts."

"Water?"

"Water usually, but also stone, or sometimes a kind of metal. Elemental sorcery is common, rudimentary even. Hardly used even by sorcerers who manifested it in their youth."

"Wow." Luthian's elbow slipped off his armrest as he stared in fascination. "The book described 'primordial languages.' Are those the same tongues you are referring to?"

"They are. There is the Elder tongue, the language of the Makergods themselves. Others speak with the Divine tongue of the celestial Angelics. There is also the Odic tongue of the sky that can summon great storms, and the Macabre tongue that mimics the voice of death itself. Children who can speak and understand these languages can commune with the power primordial. They are sorcerers."

"What about the tongue of Chaos?"

Chasmira watched the flickering light of the candles beside Luthian. "Chaos speaks with every tongue. It may be exercised in any language and with but a single word. We simply bid things to change, to die, to burn... and they do. That is how the White Aegis finds us and destroys us before we are strong enough to defend ourselves."

He nodded in somber understanding. "But you can understand the primordial languages?"

"No sorcerer can understand all of them. If you are gifted at all, you are gifted to understand one of them, or at most two. I never mumbled in my sleep or read from a grimoire."

"And so the White Aegis never found you. You were lucky, then."

"You could put it like that," she said, as if only to herself. *Lucky* was certainly the furthest thing from how she felt.

Luthian could tell from the sound of her voice that there was more behind those words than he knew. He idly flipped through the book pages, allowing her a few more moments with her thoughts before he asked, "The book also speaks of magic staves and wands. That iron staff you have, with the forked adornment, is that one such thing?"

"It is," snapping out of her inner thoughts. "It is a staff of destruction, and a powerful one at that. Not that I know much more about it."

"Did you not make it?"

"No, I did not. I inherited it from a friend of mine, who could not escape the war as I did: Hakon, your father's grand executor."

Sadness washed over his expression. "I'm very sorry to hear that, for us and also for you. Father trusted him with the most important tasks. I had no idea you two were friends."

"We were, but I wish we had been friends longer."

Luthian could see her slipping back into those inner thoughts again. Perhaps the long day was wearing on her. He wished he knew what to say, and how to comfort someone who had suffered so much loss. One thing he did know was how to keep distracted from the consuming thoughts…

"So do you think you will ever craft a staff of your own?"

She knew what he was doing, and smiled at his question. "Oh, I don't know. If I did, it would not be a staff, I assure you. They are much too large and heavy. Perhaps a wand... Is there anything in your book that tells us how to make one?"

He flipped the book shut. "Unfortunately, it is more of a history book than a grimoire."

"So then, fellow bookworm, surely you have burrowed into some arcane titles on these shelves. Where to look?"

Luthian ran his hand through his dark locks. "I believe those shelves back there, the last or second-to-last row… Fourth shelf, maybe? I recall them being roughly eye-level or a little higher."

She slid out of her chair and groaned as she stood up. *Sitting too long again,* she chided herself. It was so easy to find a comfortable spot and not move an inch for hours at a time when reading. She sauntered down the row of bookshelves with the manner of someone already full from dinner but seeing if dessert looked appealing.

"If only all the books with arcane knowledge were in the same shelf," she called out across the library. "That way, I would not have to walk from one end of the room to the other in search of my book's companion?"

His voice echoed in the chamber, "How will you even *know* where to find the book you are searching for, if they are not alphabetical?"

"How would your alphabetizing help when we do not even know the title?"

There was no answer.

She shook her head. "Perhaps we should have gone with my original idea."

Luthian almost fell out of his chair. "Putting them together in groups of similar height and color? You *are* a creature of Chaos."

Finding nothing useful on that side of the bookshelf, she came up the other end of the aisle and paused to admire the vast collection once again. "Where did all these come from anyway, Luthian? Your father was a great man, but he was not renowned as a scholar."

"Not my father but my grandfather, Melyr the Iron Prince. He acquired most of them during his raids of the southeast coasts. The old Oracle of Ædant Otzana contained a huge library, about half of what you see here," Luthian explained. "In an ironic twist, Otzana came by neither the Oracle nor the library legitimately. She was of Alcimaean birth, you see, and she was what they would call a *virago*, a warrioress of the sea."

"Really! The old girl was a pirate?"

"Please." He laughed sardonically at her crassness. "She was a woman of fine taste, for she counted books as treasure equal to silver and gold. At any rate, she and her loyal treasure hunters violently acquired the Oracle and used it as their refuge."

Treasure hunters, she snickered as she plucked a few choice books from the shelf. "How in the world did she ever get away with that?"

"That's the best part. When next a group of pilgrims arrived, she donned some cleric robes and introduced herself as Ædant Otzana. The rest is history."

"Whose Oracle was it really?" Chasmira asked, walking in and out of the shadows between the shelves.

"Who cares about that? What have you found?" he knelt in his chair, elbows on the table in eager anticipation.

"Luthian, sit back. You're going to drool on them." She set the books down on the table reverently, and then lifted the first book to show it to him. It was a handsome-looking tome with a gilded leather cover. "*Confessions of the Magus*. The author was a nameless scribe who sat at the feet of Magus Yfilim in the Tenth Century. Supposedly he shared blasphemous secrets of the arcane, exposed scandals about kings of the time, and spoke of the world beyond the Outer Gates."

"Do you think him a credible source?"

Chasmira shrugged. "The man lived nine hundred years before you or I saw the sun. He could claim whatever he wanted and we could not prove any of it."

"Fascinating nonetheless," said Luthian. "Even the wildest tales are based on a nugget of truth. What's the next book?"

"This *Cursed Chronicles, Book III* caught my eye."

"I can tell you books I and II were most definitely cursed."

She looked up to see if the disappointment in his face matched that of his voice. It did. "Fiction?"

"Worse. *Youth* fiction."

She grimaced and scooted the book aside using another book, as if it would spread leprosy if she dared touch it.

Luthian's eyes gleamed as he took in the third book: a dark, nameless, dusty, old book bound in leather that had seen centuries pass by. The iron clasps that once held it shut had been broken long ago. "I had forgotten this existed. This is a relic from my grandfather's time," he said, his voice tinged with excitement. "He showed it to me once. According to him, it was written by strange nomads that ran with packs of wolves and wore the bones of the prey they killed together."

Chasmira ran her fingers over the book's worn surface, intrigued by the aura of history that clung to it. "A fitting prize for such an expedition. Tell me more."

Luthian's voice dropped to a hushed tone, as though the words alone held great power. "He received his scouts' report, and the nomadic mystics in the snowy wastes were said to be more beast than man. They possessed powers that no one could fathom. My grandfather's men brought back this tome, but its contents were equally unfathomable. The language in which it was written, was impossible to read or translate as if it were from another world. This book has remained a mystery, Chasmira. Think of the secrets it holds."

She smirked. "And you've never picked it up since? I find that difficult to believe."

"I was a little boy when my grandfather showed it to me, and as we have well established, this library is not the easiest for finding things. Besides that, an unreadable book does not exactly top my reading stack."

"Fair. In that case, I think it has been neglected long enough," she said, rubbing her hands together eagerly. "Shall we?"

Together, they slowly opened the nameless book. The spine crackled, which made them gasp and then continue all the more carefully. The pages were the color of sandstone but felt like cloth, and they turned with a rustling sound like treetops moving in the summer wind. Every page was bordered with ornate knotwork art, no two pages the same.

Chasmira's brow furrowed in confusion. "What is this?"

"What do you mean?"

"Are you quite sure this is the same book your grandfather showed you? The very same book?"

"It is," he answered with no doubt. "Why?"

She looked back at the pages and sputtered a breathless laugh. "Because I can read it."

Luthian's blue eyes widened. "You can?"

"Yes! This script… so old… It is the language of the sky, of thunder itself. Odic. I know not how to explain... It feels like a memory from another life, surfacing in a dream too vivid to be just a dream."

He kept looking back and forth between her and the old cloth pages. "What does it say?"

She started to read aloud, and as she read she felt she could not stop reading until she had finished the entire passage:

Thou commandest now the strength that lived before a word could describe it, with storms and tempests at thy command. Understand that thy mortal spirit is ever-changing, ever-shifting, like the clouds that arise in the night. The storms slumber deep within thy soul, ready to rise at thy command, untamed and wild, dancing to the furious drums of thunder. Thou art the whispering zephyr, a bridge that joineth earth and heaven, a spirit both mortal and celestial, in a dance where power and peace doth intermingle, and the world unfoldeth before thee like a scroll.

Chasmira leaned back from the book slowly, catching her breath. "This is a grimoire, Luthian. No mere book of history or fiction, but a true grimoire of Odic Sorcery."

He looked afraid to touch it. "What should we do with it?"

A puff of dust arose when she flipped it shut. "Nothing to do but keep it and use it, but I cannot take it. Surely your uncle is having me watched and my room searched regularly, since he suspects me constantly of evil. Keep it here in the library, Luthian, somewhere safe where it will not be disturbed."

He nodded and took a few short breaths to steady his nerves. Stacking it on top of the other two books, he carried all of them back to his reading desk and stashed them underneath in the cabinet.

Chasmira's mind raced with the implications of this. She was not all fire and fury after all, but something more she did not realize. How ironic that such a transformative thought would plant itself in her just from opening a book and reading it... Ironic because that is what every bookworm believes a book can do but only experiences it with the right book.

"There. It's safe," he said, returning to her and cracking a smile.

She bit her lip with excitement and cupped his face in her hands. "We did it, Luthian. You have no idea what this all means, what this means for me. We must go through that book, page by page, until we have learned all its secrets. But we must be cautious, lest your uncle learn I am summoning such power under his roof."

"I cannot wait to see the mighty Arts of True Sorcery in practice before my very eyes," he said, still breathless with exhilaration. They could not contain their excitement. They hugged and leapt like children who had stolen a bag of candy.

"What on earth are you two doing?" Nyell interrupted them, her head poking up the edge of the stairway. "I told you a half hour ago there was fresh white bean spinach soup, Luthian. Your brothers have already eaten, as usual. If you want a bowl, come get it yourself."

The lad stifled his laughter. "Sorry, Nyell, I meant no disrespect to you or your outstanding cooking."

She absorbed the compliment with a flustered laugh.

He shot Chasmira a knowing glance. "You know how it is when you pick up a good book: you just lose all track of time."

CHAPTER 26

Chasmira vanished for long hours into the library almost every morning and every other night. Pouring over the Odic grimoire, she would read the passages aloud and then practice the enchantments contained within. Its promises were tantalizing: casting arcane shields, shapeshifting into beasts, and summoning powerful thunderstorms. Practicing was slow and difficult, for years had conditioned her to summon sorcerous power with impulses, not concentrated will. Fortunately, the grimoire contained more than just doctrine. It also contained meditation guides, exercises for focus, and even an ancient cinnamon sour cream porridge recipe that claimed to attune one's spiritual energies to that of the sky. Chasmira transcribed the recipe on another piece of paper and presented it to Nyell, who was more than happy to accept an archaic culinary challenge. Luthian and Chasmira detected no spiritual attunement after the first bowl of it, but they had two more bowls just to make sure.

Between her walks with Warrick and her secret sorcery studies with Luthian, Chasmira was left with little time for anything else, entirely neglecting to join Emorya in the mornings while she trained the Beastkin into proper warriors. For weeks, the two women saw very little of each other. The young warmaiden was up before the sun, gone all day, and returned while Chasmira was already up in the library. Not that Emorya seemed to miss her too badly, for on rare occasions when Emorya returned early from training, the two would cross paths at the stairs as Chasmira was about to go up to see Luthian again, and Emorya always flashed that smile of hers.

The quiet guilt over it eventually got louder, and one morning Chasmira rose early to catch up with her. She found Emorya standing at the edge of the southern reach, watching with arms crossed as the Beastkin engaged in a mock battle in the blowing snow. Much as Chasmira hated to admit it, there was something about the sight of battle that she found alluring—beautiful even. Her silent presence in the courts of warlords was painful, but it allowed her to observe the art of war closer than most are permitted.

"They are coming along, then?" she casually inquired.

"They have a long way to go," Emorya answered, her eyes scanning the pairs of dueling fighters. Observing a common weakness, she shouted above the wind, "Raise your guard! Those shields are not for decoration! If your arm is getting tired, I'm sure Argismora's warriors will be happy to cut it off for you!"

Chasmira nodded approvingly. "They have an excellent teacher."

"I have learned that they cannot be constantly pushed, annoying as that is. They are strong of body but weak-willed, which will get them killed. Discipline will save them. They are not there yet, but I'm doing my damnedest to be patient."

"I take it Guff is still being headstrong as ever?"

"You haven't heard?"

Chasmira blinked in confusion. "Heard what?"

"Three weeks ago, he was found on the southern hillside, dead. Mauled. He must have left the barracks after sundown and something found him. The sentries were questioned the next day, and one of them said that he had seen a strange black wolf prowling the treeline a few nights in a row."

Chasmira's heart sank. Something inside her chastised her for not coming to the southern reach more often. Not that anything could have been done to save poor Guff, but at least she would have seen him before that happened. "That's so sad."

"Very sad," Emorya replied, but Chasmira did not hear the same sentiment in the warmaiden's words. Emorya was not there that night on Harmony's Eve. She had no idea Guff had surrendered his resentment.

"He held nothing against you, you know."

Emorya wrinkled her nose and squinted through the blowing snow. "Why would I care if he did?" She smiled and laughed, turning her attention back to the sparring Beastkin. "Hey! Is that blood I see? That better be from his sword and not your own!"

Chasmira stared down into the cold snow. *There are few things that bring out the worst of people, like war does. The preparation may even be worse than fighting. No one could blame someone scarred from battle, but those who plan a war in time of peace? They must scar themselves first.*

ψ

The fires behind the black throne leapt high. "The Harmony Moon is past, and we are no closer to rebuilding our former power than we were at the start of harvest," Lord Maram said as he stabbed a metal poker into the coals to stir them hotter. Warrick and Wilvrey sat in this chamber with him, enduring his harsh criticism.

Warrick shrugged, "Your daughter is out there with them practically every day. They train with all manner of weapons and soon they will practice field maneuvers. Is that not enough, milord?"

"Not nearly enough," Maram snapped at him. "One of the sentries reported that they were having a fight with snowballs in the orchard yesterday."

"Are they not allowed to rest and play?"

Maram's gnarled features bent into a deep scowl. "They are *warriors*. No one in my koga or your father's ever wasted their time with children's games. They were hardened for war—broken and rebuilt." He turned to Wilvrey sitting in the armchair beside the fireplace. "Have you nothing to add? Your expertise is needed. Come summer, they will be facing a host of Argismora's soldiers."

Wilvrey mused grimly, "Yes, I wonder how many of their skulls would fit on the fireplace mantle…" His finger tapped on his chin.

"Wilvrey! Enough of your fetishes. Focus on the task at hand."

He chuckled wickedly. "My deepest apologies, Uncle. I mean not to appear absentminded while you two are sorting out the details. I'm simply excited about getting to hear that sound of bone breaking under the force of my hand. It is possibly the second most exciting thing in the world."

"Well, leave us not in suspense, Wilvrey. What is the first—"

"No," Warrick interrupted, "Don't tell us. I am more than happy to never know the answer to that."

Maram looked between his two nephews with seething anger. Did neither of them take preparation for war seriously? Warrick he could understand, for he had never ridden into battle before, but Wilvrey? Since when did Wilvrey the Serpent stare idly into a hearth on a winter day while someone else trained his warriors? There had to be a reason why, and Maram felt certain he knew what it was.

"Leave us, Warrick," Maram said. "I wish to speak with the commander of our warband alone."

Warrick stood, grumbling to himself as usual. He hated these meetings, hated speaking to his scathing uncle and his maniacal younger brother. He was happy to leave, but a bad taste still lingered in his mouth.

Maram waited for the door to close behind Warrick before speaking again. "You are distracted, boy."

Wilvrey chuckled, pretending to be amused. "What do you mean?"

"You have always been given to obsessions, Wilvrey. The war in the East consumed you for months before you even got there, before you even felt the snow beneath your boots. I had hoped it would be so with this new war in the North. However, it seems my faith may be misplaced."

"Your faith is not misplaced. The war is all I think about."

"Really," Maram sneered, "Then why are Lord Ovis' furry brutes not prepared for battle yet? You have had all winter to ready them, and yet here you sit."

"I am doing my best. I can lead them, but I cannot control them. The teaching work is better suited to Emorya, anyway."

Maram jabbed a finger at him accusingly. "Spare me your

excuses. I have seen your best, and this is far from it. The fact is you have been preoccupied. That woman, that witch, has stolen your focus. On top of that, she seems to think she owns our land. She has even invited an Ogre to live on the western sward, without consulting any of us. Beware her wiles, or before you know it she'll be leading you around like a castrated dog."

Wilvrey rose from his seat, his green eyes flaring fiercely. "Or she'll be kneeling in front of me while I sit on the throne. Do not underestimate me, Uncle."

Maram's craggy features softened a little, glad to see Wilvrey stirred by his piercing words. "It is not that I underestimate you. I am afeard that *you* are underestimating *her*."

"Well, you needn't fear. She believes herself to be free, that she can do whatever she pleases and command our servants? Then I will remind her that she lives in our house, and not the other way around."

ψ

It was just after the seventh hour when Chasmira knocked on the door to Wilvrey's chambers.

"Wil, you said you wanted to see me?"

"Yes, come in, it is not locked," he called out from inside.

She entered. The room was a bit larger than her own bedroom, but with the same vaulted ceiling and same window in the corner. Chasmira had expected the room to be cramped with weapons and armor stands, or perhaps littered with trophies and grisly souvenirs from his many battles. Instead, it was surprisingly minimal and tidy. Perhaps an expression of self-discipline, she thought, or perhaps it was a way of establishing control over his surroundings. In the corner near the window was a writing desk with rolls of parchment stacked atop it. The centerpiece of the room was the large four-post bed, complete with a beautiful cloth canopy the color of red wine.

From behind the canopy rose Wilvrey. He had been sitting on the bed and now stood to greet her. His hair was still damp from what must have been a recent bath, for the room smelt of rose, amber, and pomegranate—his favorite scents. The warm, earthy smell grew stronger as he approached, clad in a handsome, loose-fitting, black robe. He also wore a necklace of various animal fangs, and she noticed some of the sharp tips had been dipped in gold.

"You came quickly. I'm glad," he greeted her. His pleasant formality became more serious as he wasted no time getting to the point. "Lady Chasmira, are you happy here?"

She shrugged. "Happy as one can be. Though your uncle Lord Maram was very inhospitable at first, I seem to have somehow endeared myself to the household. I have friends, a library, a home with a dog… You have all afforded me the chance to make good on my words, to guide and help your family, although there are days you make it more challenging than others."

"It's true, I can be infuriating," he chuckled, opening a bottle of dark liquor. He splashed a little into a small glass goblet and held it out in offering, but she declined with a smile. He admired the glass for a moment. "But you have indeed made good on your word, and at risk to your own life."

Chasmira remembered the ordeal in Argismora and the terrible price she nearly paid on the Archvate's execution pyre. She winced a little at the memory but simply nodded her agreement.

"Still, I am perplexed. Why would a woman risk her life trying to save perfect strangers who, not long ago, were her enemies?"

Feeling uneasy being cornered between the table and the door, she casually circled him to find the middle of the room. "Ah, correction: you were the *Magnate's* enemies, not mine."

"That is true," he conceded, washing it down with the drink.

She breathed a little easier.

Wilvrey, however, was nothing if not persistent. "So there is nothing at all that *you* have to gain from this?"

Something in the way he phrased it panged her. Could she ever confess this was all for revenge? The only person who knew the truth was Hakon, who laid dead on the road in the forest. Dead like her parents, whose resurrection the Angelic dangled as bait for Chasmira to do her divine dirty work. She had not shared the truth with Warrick or even Luthian… How could she share it with Wilrey?

He approached like a looming storm cloud casting its shadow. "No doubt, the children of Mirikinin are famed in this land. What you truly seek, you knew you might find it here with us. That is why you came to make yourself friendly and invite yourself in."

"I…" she began, and Wilvrey lifted her chin with his finger.

"I have seen the time you spend with my brothers. Your long walks with Warrick. Your literary retreats with Luthian. There is something vacant in you, empty and needing to be filled."

It took a moment for her to absorb his implications. Much as she felt relieved that he did not suspect her true motive, she now had a different conflict at hand. "Wil, I assure you that you're quite mistaken about that."

He stood so close now, she could feel the warmth from his bare chest on her chin, her lips. "I certainly hope so. Why, they had you for a whole week before I ever set foot back on my homeland. I would regret terribly the lateness of my return, if you told me I'd lost you to either of them."

"Lost me? You act as if you had me already," she said, putting her hand to his chest to gently push him back. His finely-sculpted muscle was solid as stone beneath her dainty fingers, and he did not move an inch.

Wilvrey put a hand to her wrist, kneading it in his grasp. "You must think your actions have gone unnoticed, but they have not. You have a truly amazing way of answering me, answering my needs and wishes. You are not a woman easily dominated. Those moments when you choose to serve makes a man feel powerful."

She scoffed and shook her head, turning away. "Flatterer. You do not need a woman to make you feel powerful, Wil."

"But I do need one to make me feel satisfied," he said, approaching from behind and running his hands over her bare shoulders. Goosebumps rose across her skin from shoulder to wrist. "I want you. Here, now."

"No, you don't. You couldn't," she said with swallowed sullenness.

"What?"

"You don't even think I'm beautiful."

"What do you mean?"

Turning around, she tore her gaze from the floor and looked up into his intense green eyes. "In the garden behind Lord Ovis' villa. We were looking at the stars. I asked if you think I'm beautiful and you said no."

"You think I want *beauty*?" With tempest fury, Wilvrey seized her arm with one hand and her hair with the other hand. She could feel his hot breath against her face with every vehement word. "There is nothing beautiful in this world that I want. While impaling dying soldiers, I trod down snowdrifts that were once perfect snowflakes in the air. While razing castles, I have burnt fields that were once filled with perfect wildflowers. I don't want beautiful things, Chasmira. Beautiful things are of no use to me. Give me storms to hide the sound of my mount as I charge. Give me darkness to veil me as I hunt. Give me steel to shed blood till I've had my fill. Give me fire, give me war, give me chaos, but don't give me anything beautiful and perfect to look at. I want something I can use. I want something I can ruin."

Both of them stood breathless, hearts thundering, face to face. She could not take her eyes away from him. Wilvrey unwound his fingers from her hair and slid his hand down her back. She could tell he was holding back and did not want to do so any longer. His lips parted and he leaned in.

He stopped short.

"You want something to use, I'm sure you could find it in Argismora for a cheap price," Chasmira hissed, "Because you won't find it here."

Wilvrey arched his head backward slowly, for pressed to his throat was the jagged, broken blade of the blue dagger Warrick gave her. Wilvrey was far larger and stronger than her, and her sorcery did not seem to frighten him. However, the sight of a weapon was something he understood very well.

"You lay another hand on me, and I will carve your throat out."

"What are you doing? I've done nothing to you."

"Yes, and it'll stay that way," she snapped.

"There's no need for this. Calm down."

She coughed out a laugh, breath shuddering with a mixture of fear and rage. "Calm? You were certainly trying to keep me calm, weren't you? Pulling my hair and caressing my rear. Yes, how calming, Wil. The very fact of the matter is that you care nothing for others' feelings unless they can be molded to serve your purpose. That's what you do. You goad and prod and lure people in."

"It's called seduction. Can you blame me? I want you, whatever way I can have you." He almost sounded like he was pleading.

"I am not yours to have. You think that you started something that night in the garden at Ovis' villa, something you could finish tonight? You think you can find the cracks in me and slither in? Well, you've thought wrong, Wilvrey the Serpent. Your coils will never hold me, neither will your fangs break my skin."

"Don't be too sure," he dared, now sounding bolder. She pressed the blade harder against his throat, but still he added, "You know what you want. You're just denying both of us."

"You are the one in denial, not me. You think I want you? A big man with an army and a taste for bloodshed? I've known a hundred men like you, Wil. You think you're something special, that others respect you? They don't. They're simply afraid of you."

He had that look again in his green eyes. "And you are not?"

She locked eyes with him. "No, I am not."

"Who is in denial now?"

She drew in a sharp breath, fighting to keep their eyes locked so as not to show any wavering or weakness.

Wilvrey's voice was a deep purr. "I feel your fear, my enchantress. It compels you. It excites you as much as it disturbs you. You pretend it is not there, but it is real. The dagger at my throat confirms it."

She gasped as she felt his hand close around hers. The metal of the dagger felt much colder contrasted with his warm fingers wrapped around it.

"You would not hold onto it so tightly if you were not afraid of what would happen if you let go," he whispered.

"You are the one who should be afraid," she hissed back.

A sinful smile crossed his lips. "I should, but a man cannot hold fire so long as he fears it."

He was right. She was afraid what would happen if she let go. She had been holding it back this entire time, and suddenly she felt her guard go down. She could hold back no longer.

The dagger dropped to the floor.

No sooner did steel touch stone than flames burst from Chasmira's eyes. She did not care whether she missed entirely or burnt his head clean off. When the flames dissipated, Wilvrey laid on the ground, his arms crossed over his face, hands protecting his head. The fetid smell of burnt hair and singed flesh rose off him up to Chasmira's nostrils.

"Don't touch me ever again. This ends now. Do you understand? Don't touch me ever again," she repeated through grit teeth. Her entire body shook with anger, the room glowing bright red. The flower petals curled and blackened, and dark burn marks scored the side of the bedsheets. "I don't want this. I don't want you, and I never will."

She did not wait for a reply or even for him to look up at her. Every step that carried her away from his room felt like a step taken in a dream, like running against a river's current. It was hard, even painful, to run… not from Wilvrey, but from the part of herself that would have said yes to him a hundred times.

CHAPTER 27

"Wil?"

Lart ventured down the hallway, craning his neck to peer into the dining room. He thought he heard a noise and thought it might be Wilvrey. Emorya had stopped by, expecting Wilvrey to inspect the Beastkin and watch their combat drills, but he was late. She was unwilling to wait for him, especially while the obstinate Beastkin required constant oversight, so she tasked Lart to seek him out and returned to the camp.

Terror padded along at Lart's side, sniffing the air and perking his ears to help track Wilvrey down. Another clatter echoed through the dining room and Terror barked, confirming for Lart that he did indeed hear something. They ventured in but found no one at the table. However, the door leading into the kitchen was open. They took only two steps toward it before Terror whined and flattened his ears back on his head.

"Uh, Wil?" Lart asked softly.

From the doorway emerged Warrick with a bottle in his hands. His face knotted with annoyance, "Do I *look* like Wilvrey to you? What do you want?"

"Emorya's looking for him. Didn't expect to find you rummaging in the cupboards. You hungry?"

Warrick gestured to the bottle of aged brandy. "Thirsty. Now leave me alone."

"I see you are bad-humored again, Warrick."

"What are you talking about?"

"Glasses of spirits both last night and in the morning too?"

"Shut up, Lart. It is the weather that has me in a poor humor, if anything. I always feel foul at winter's peak. My knee acts up."

"Ah, right… your, um… knee," Lart nodded dubiously.

Warrick was done explaining himself. "Where are the glasses anyway? There's nothing in here but tins."

"Ain't they good enough?"

All he got was a frustrated grunt in return. Warrick shoved the bottle into Lart's hands and went back to rummaging in the kitchen. "Why is everything hidden in this blasted house? Where is Nyell anyway? Nyell!" He shouted back over his shoulder as he knelt down to search the cupboards.

"I haven't seen her."

"Well, go find her!"

Flustered, Lart spun around in place once, trying to decide whether to look outside or elsewhere in the fortress. Terror began to bark and growl. Lart was about to wonder why aloud, but received his answer as Wilvrey rounded the corner.

"Doesn't he do anything else but make noise?" Wilvrey groaned. He ambled like a man with a hangover as he elbowed his way past Lart and leaned on the dining table.

"Hey Wil, where you been? Emorya was here looking for you."

Wilvrey paused, running his hands back through his hair. A smile crept onto his face. "Oh, was she? I didn't realize. Time must have slipped away from me upstairs."

"Upstairs?"

"Mhmm," he grinned, licking his teeth. "And what a time it was. I knew the women of Dimol Gol were feral, but that little minx is something to write folktales about."

Lart nearly dropped the bottle in his hands. He glanced behind Wilvrey, who had no idea Warrick was even in the room. "Do you mean—"

"You wound me, cousin, acting so surprised! Of course I mean Chasmira. Why, she has been staring straight through my clothes since the day I returned home from Eppenhorn. Poor thing's been so neglected, it seemed she was a bit pent-up!"

"Wil—"

Wilvrey whistled and wiped his brow. "I'd dare say we loosened some of the walls of this bloody house!"

His coarse laughter was cut short by a hard right cross to the jaw. The blow threw him out of his chair and to the floor. Wilvrey looked up to see Warrick standing over him, fuming like an angry bear. "Shut. Your. Mouth."

"Big brother, what a surprise," said Wilvrey. "I did not expect you to rush to defend that filthy whore's honor."

Warrick seethed, "The only whore in this room is you, Wilvrey. Do not touch her again."

"What a pity. Father taught us the value of sharing."

Lart ran up but dared not physically step between the two men. "Pay him no mind, Wil. Warrick's not well. He's been fighting fever all day, ain't you Warrick?"

There was blood in Wilvrey's smile. "Oh, then I'll tell Nyell to prepare you some soup with herbs and mushrooms. A few hot bowls ought to help you feel less choleric."

"I'm warning you," Warrick growled.

"You're warning me?" He chuckled as he started clambering back up onto his feet. "Of what?"

Another hard right across the chin answered his question.

That was enough. Warrick rolled his shoulders a few times and then left the dining room, making for the front door. The cold would surely chill his heated temper. The fresh air and quiet would be welcome, too—his head was swimming a little from the drink and anger mixing inside him.

He got no more than ten steps into the yard before he heard Wilvrey angrily yelling taunts behind him. "You start a fight but don't stick around to finish it? Very disappointing, brother, but not surprising!" He drew his dark steel longsword from the sheath.

Warrick just stared at him. "Really?"

"Yes, really. A minute ago it was worth bloodying your fists to defend that witch, but now you will not draw sword to defend yourself?"

"Unlike you, I need not a sword to win a fight."

Wilvrey lunged, but Warrick stepped inside the thrust and grabbed hold of the longsword's crossguard. The elder brother regretted it almost immediately, however. He felt like he had an angry ox by the horns, the way Wilvrey pulled to wrench his weapon free.

The fight for the sword was only a distraction. Warrick discovered this when a hard uppercut connected with his chin so hard, his feet momentarily left the ground. Twisting his sword free, Wilvrey slammed Warrick in the face with the hilt. A few inches higher and the crossguard would have put out his eye entirely. Not that Wilvrey cared.

Warrick staggered backward, blood running from his nose and a gash under his left eye. He wiped his face with the back of his hand. Looking at the red smear, he grit his teeth and yanked his shortsword from its sheath. "You should have kept that big mouth shut!"

"Now this is more like it," Wilvrey said, his eyes wild from the taste of his own blood.

The discordant notes of steel on steel echoed through the courtyard. Warrick angrily advanced with long, one-handed swipes of his sword, knocking Wilvrey's blade aside to close the gap between them and grapple. Wilvrey, meanwhile, had already adapted to this tactic. He began evading instead of blocking, forcing Warrick out of position by letting every swipe find nothing but air.

Wilvrey ducked one broad swipe, dropping to the ground and sweeping Warrick's leg out from under him. He would have fallen, but dropped to one knee instead. It sank into the snow, and Warrick had no leverage to stand again. Seizing this chance, Wilvrey began to hammer down his sword again and again, trying to break Warrick's blade or at least his grip. His hair clung to the sweat on his face. With every swing he panted like an animal fighting for its life.

"STOP!"

Wilvrey swung in the direction of the voice. The ringing of his sword against Emorya's blade echoed through the winter air. Nyell and Chasmira stood beside her, and the three women quickly divided the fighting brothers.

"What in Avgannon is wrong with you two?" Emorya chided

them. She pointed her sword at each of them, and they backed off.

"Put your swords away. You're brothers," Nyell scolded.

"Idiots, but brothers," Emorya added.

Both men looked at Chasmira with accusing eyes.

"What? Can two men not express their feelings?" Wilvrey laughed, sheathing his sword. He licked the blood from his teeth and casually spat it in the snow, as if moments ago he was not snarling like a rabid beast. "Good fight, Warrick. Watch your low guard next time. It will save your life."

Warrick did not play along. Chasmira drew a handkerchief to tend the cut on his face, but he simply grunted and stomped away across the yard to the gate.

"Warrick—" she called after him, but he ignored her. She glared over her shoulder at Wilvrey, whose only reply was a flash of a bloody smile before he turned his back to her and went back into the house, with Lart and Emorya close behind him. Terror barked after Warrick, but he too returned to the house after receiving no acknowledgement.

Chasmira shook her head at them. She ran after Warrick, her boots slipping every step in the packed snow.

She found him just past the treeline of the woods beyond the western sward. He leaned back against a tree, holding snow against his red knuckles and cursing quietly to himself. She could not suppress a fond smile at the sight of Warrick standing there. He was so big, he looked like he would knock the entire tree over just leaning on it. He turned his head a little as she approached, hearing the crunch of her footsteps in the snow.

"You know, I cannot say I blame you," she said, breaking the quiet of the woods. "You must have wanted to hit him so many times before."

"More times than I can count."

She stood next to him, and Warrick made a meager attempt to hide his tender knuckles. Gently, she reached up to brush his hair away from his face. "You're bleeding."

"Not the first time," he grunted.

"You won't die from it, but it will likely leave a very nasty scar no matter how well we dress it."

"I don't care."

"Well, I do," she answered softly. He was still angry after the fight, understandably, and not wanting to show weakness.

He looked as if he wanted to answer. There were words behind his lips, but he bit them back. Shaking his head, he walked away from her farther into the woods.

Ouch. Piqued from his cold response, she followed after. "If you don't wish to talk about Wil, we certainly don't need to," she said, a little more harshly than intended.

He stopped dead in his tracks, sighed heavily, and then turned to face her. "No, I think we need to. You know, I would have rather found out any other way than the way I did. Servants' gossip, or Lart idiotically blurting out something he was not supposed to."

"Found out what? Warrick, what are you on about?"

Warrick grew more frustrated being forced to say it. "If you wanted to sleep with him, you could have simply told me and not gone behind my back."

She struggled to find words. "Wanted… to sleep with him?"

As soon as he heard his words from her mouth, it was as if cold water had been splashed in his face. "I overheard him in the kitchen talking to Lart. He was bragging about it, as though you were an eastern village and he had just ravaged you."

Chasmira could feel the heat from her own flushed face. She could not even bring herself to look up at him. "Well, I can assure you that did not happen."

"No?" He sounded accusatory but then added, "I hope not."

"I could *never*," she said with disgust.

"I'm relieved to hear it. The very thought of it…"

What was this she heard in his voice? It was that same earnestness she heard when he insisted they leave Argismora together. "The very thought of it?" she asked, prompting for more.

He let out a long sigh that was more like a growl. "The very thought of it makes me feel like I have that very same fire in me that you have in you. If I could kill with a look, I think I would have killed him, because it's simply *wrong*. It's wrong for you to be in his arms and not in mine."

"Warrick… Why are you saying this?"

"Why does anyone say things like this? Why does a man swordfight his brother in the middle of the bloody winter? Because I'm in love with you, damn it."

She stared up at him. "You… what?"

Those dark brown eyes, done searching the woods and the snow, finally settled upon her and did not drift away. "I said, I'm in love with you."

"Warrick," she spoke in a whisper. "How? How can you love me?"

He stepped closer, smoothing back her hair and grazing the side of her neck with his fingertips. "How could I not? You, who came in and turned our lives upside down. A sweet but firm hand in the most uncertain of times. That night at the campfire—"

"I pushed you too hard that night, I'm sorry," she blurted out. "About your father, and how much you needed him. It was too much."

Warrick blinked. "No, it was not. Chasmira, I opened my heart that night because someone like you, who guards her own heart so well… could surely know how to guard mine if I showed it to you."

Chasmira swallowed a lump that had formed in her throat. She leaned to press her face against his hand.

His arms tightened around her waist, and he stood to his full height, lifting her off the ground, eye-to-eye with him. She kicked her feet but was held very securely in his strong, irresistible arms. Chasmira ran her hands over his chest and shoulders, which were far too broad for her to wrap her arms around them. *He just goes on forever*, she thought to herself, biting her lip.

She had not time for another thought before his lips met hers in a slow, hungry kiss. Her hands found his hair, and she stroked a handful of his locks as she sighed happily, lost in their embrace.

CHAPTER 28

The amber glow on the horizon felt like the last goodbye kiss of autumn as it laid down to slumber beneath fresh snow. Winter wrapped the sun in thick blankets of cloud and tucked in the dayglow to sleep. From here until spring, the nights would have a special chill to them when one came to bed or arose too early while it was still dark.

Chasmira felt that very chill and tugged at the covers to pull them up a little higher.

"Let me," Warrick said, grabbing ahold of the heavy quilts he kept on his bed. His other arm was around her waist, his hand on her hip.

She nestled in closer, putting her head on his bare chest. He was so warm, so strong. She put her face against him and breathed him in, shutting her eyes as if creating a memory. "It feels as if I dreamt it," she said.

"Dreamt what?"

"That you are in love with me. That the words left your lips and found my ears, and both on the same day, in the same place. What an amazing coincidence."

Warrick smiled over at her and shook his head. "You are talking nonsense again."

"Well, you had better become fluent in nonsense quickly."

"Why is the burden on me? You could just as easily learn my language, you know."

"Because grunts and growls and loud sighs are for animals, Warrick," she smirked. "You might as well be in love with Terror."

"You have a point there," Warrick played along, stroking his bearded chin thoughtfully. "He's quite a catch."

"Oh stop," slapping at his shoulder.

"No, really. He's a faithful companion, loves to go hunting, takes directions well, and he and I like the same foods."

"Really?"

"Mhmm, we both love meat," squeezing a handful of her hip.

Chasmira squealed. Not only did it tickle, but she was already quite sore from a long day of lovemaking. She wrestled his hand away, interlocking their fingers. "True. Just last week he ate an entire venison leg himself."

"See?"

"And threw up afterward from eating too fast," she grimaced.

"Which I can also relate to," he chuckled.

"You're right, you two have so much in common," sighing as if defeated. "Too bad he hates whenever you're in the room."

"No. Does he really?"

She patted his arm. "Only when you're in a bad humor."

"That is fairly often."

"I think I know how to improve your mood," she said, swinging her leg over him and straddling him.

He groaned breathlessly and smiled up at her with a look of warning. "Don't start what you cannot finish."

"Oh, finishing will not be a problem at all, dear man." She

giggled and ran her hands over his broad, hairy chest. He sank his fingers into her soft, thick hair and slowly ran them through it. She sensed the gentleness in his touch, and noticed his expression had become softer, more serious. She let the playful smile fall from her face as she laid down on him, folding her hands beneath her chin and giving him her full attention. "A copper for your thoughts?"

Without hesitation, "Is it love for you too?"

That one simple question—those six words—set her mind awhirl with dozens more questions. This was not why she came here. She came not to romance the late prince's son, but to set them aflame on a path to war. She had no idea she would come to care about them so much. Did she even want a war anymore? Not if it meant endangering him. Endangering whatever this was. Was it love? The only thing she ever knew of love was her parents', the kind that sheltered her against threats from outside. This was the only love she knew, but was that enough? Was this the very essence of love in all its forms, or just a child's sentiment carried through to adulthood? She did not know, but she knew this: Warrick felt safe with her, and she felt safe with him. In a world that threatened the heart, body, and soul constantly in a hundred different ways, safety was too rare and precious a thing to give away for any reason *but* love.

Warrick watched her eyes as she was lost in thought, and he grew tense waiting. "Lart, uh, told me you said to him that you would never be with a prince."

"I said that I didn't want a prince, and I don't," she explained. "I don't need riches and power to attract me."

"You told him you didn't want anybody."

"That's right. I don't want anybody. Somebody who wants

anybody will accept just anybody. You're not just anybody, Warrick. You're somebody to me. Somebody worth making space for, and making time for, because I love you. I do, Warrick. I love you."

His smile widened again. "And I love you. I've felt like this for a long time."

She stared dreamily at him. "Really?"

"Yes," sheepishly scratching at his beard.

"Since when? And don't you dare lie and give me some line about love at first sight."

"Hardly!" He belly-laughed in the way someone does when they lie on their back, laughing a little harder and longer. "You won't believe me when I tell you when it was."

"When? Tell me."

"Do you remember when we saw the Scarrlok in the marketplace in Argismora, and you followed that troupe of women?"

She raised an eyebrow, "*That* strummed your heartstrings? Seeing me run off with a group of escorts?"

"No, but afterward I… missed you. We had spent the entire time together from the hour we left here, rode the first day, camped the first night, and rode into town together. And when you left, all I could think about was you. I was jealous for your presence. I missed the sound of your voice. I didn't even feel like talking to anyone else."

Chasmira wiped away tears that glistened in her eyes. Her face hurt from smiling as she listened to him. "I think I've loved you since the night we spent in the inn."

"We fought that night."

She quickly added, "Not when we fought, but that next morning when you told me you were not leaving without me, that we go together."

"Yes, and we do. We do go together."

"We do," she agreed, hugging her face against his chest. She felt wrapped in the bliss of this moment, warmer than any quilts or furs. She had never known love like this, where two bared hearts could speak freely and always hear each other so well.

"Will you marry me?"

She was sure she misheard him at first. "Marry you?"

At first, he seemed not to know whether to interpret her surprise as good or bad. "Yes, marry me. Chasmira, I cannot think of anyone else I could share my life with, no one else I could want more than I want you."

In those moments while he spoke, she imagined many moments of a life together. She imagined trading knowing glances to each other across the length of the dining table, past the noses of so many guests and family all talking excitedly. She imagined nights after difficult days, letting his stress melt away in her arms, his head against her bosom as he slept. She imagined his hand running through her hair while he admired the new grey streaks in it. She imagined how she would counter his every compliment with a self-deprecating jab, to help him artfully segue into his next compliment. She imagined his fussing and her fighting him over his aging, to leave more work for the servants and stop doing it all himself.

"The question asks more of you than just your love forevermore. It also means you would be Princess, a title which grants you both power and privilege but burdens you with it, too.

Heavy was the crown my father wore, and he wore it alone. I wish for us both to share the crown, for I cannot be the same man he was: overburdened by a power he refused to share."

Her heart melted a little, and she caressed his face lovingly. "Yes, to all of it. Yes, I will marry you, and I will happily share your crown. I will help you rule over your kingdom, if you will let me reign over your heart."

He began to laugh the purest, happiest laughter. He had asked, and she accepted. With one hand, he slid her up his body until they were eye to eye. "I love you, Chasmira."

"And I love you."

"Seal it with a kiss?" he asked sweetly.

"Oh, you'd better seal it with more than that," she said, biting at his lip and running her nails over his broad, hairy chest. "Remember that my reputation is on the line here. You know us Dimol Gol women, sleeping our way into places of power," she teased as she flaunted herself.

He exhaled sharply, feeling himself starting to give in to her. "Will you ever shut up about that?"

"Make me."

Warrick spent the rest of the night doing exactly that.

CHAPTER 29

It was Uliam, the third month, when Warrick and Chasmira married upon the northern highland. She took her vows of love, faith, and honor wearing a dress the color of brightest pearl, and upon the cuffs were strings of moonstone beads that shone like starlight and jingled with a sort of sweet, melodious tone with every move she made.

The wedding feast after the ceremony was jubilant and loud, almost riotous. A multitude filled the inner yard with lively chatter and song. Lord Ovis and his family attended in full force, and the Beastkin's joyous reunion with their friends and relatives only added to the celebration. Wine flowed freely, and guests danced to the rhythm of the bodhran drum. The other vassals and friends of the family attended as well, sharing their gifts and well-wishing with the newlyweds. Among them was a pan flautist, whose talents enraptured everyone as Warrick and Chasmira shared a dance alone, for a moment forgetting the thousands of eyes upon them.

Lord Maram did not attend, but he lurked somewhere in the fortress during all the festivities outside. If he was already disgusted just having Chasmira living in their house, one could only imagine his revulsion at her marrying one of his nephews. Lart was quite the life of the party, dancing so hard that he sprained his calf halfway through the evening. Emorya sat in attendance too, drinking heavily and mostly leaving the bride and groom to enjoy their day.

Anyone would have assumed Wilvrey would not attend, but they would have assumed wrong. He came tottering through the crowd, bottle in hand, dressed in his finest formal robes, complete with a flowing black cape and shimmering shoulder pauldrons. He insisted they permit him to make a speech.

"I am not sure that's a good idea," Warrick said warily.

At first, Chasmira's impulse was to have him removed from the wedding by force. She then remembered Wilvrey's impressive poise during the ball at the villa. In public, he was quite a different person than he was behind closed doors. She shrugged and sighed, "What's the worst he could say, really?"

By this hour of the evening, Wilvrey was halfway through that large liquor bottle he was nursing. He somehow managed to stand on the feast table without falling, much to the delight of the cheering guests. As he cleared his throat, the crowd hushed.

"What wonders are wrought, which pass the common understanding of man, for today my big brother is married!" The crowd erupted into cheers, banging on the tabletops for the bride and groom to kiss. The obligatory smooch was greeted with even louder cheers, until Wilvrey hushed everyone down again. "Six months ago, an unlikely visitor arrived on our grieving land. She brought with her a fire that has, in the time since, lit up the halls of the House of Mirikinin like never before. The night sky itself bears witness that I myself have never known anyone quite like her. And now, she belongs to Warrick. Tonight we toast to Lady Chasmira and my lucky brother. I know that our father toasts with us too, from Soth's table you probably assume... But I say that he toasts from the table of Naru, god of laughter! For what greater humor could there be than this: that in our darkest hour, the brightest star of all fell right into our laps. Here's to you both."

The wedding guests applauded, many of them patting Wilvrey on the back as they helped him down. Lart and Chasmira shared a surprised look across the table, and even Warrick joined in the applause. "I didn't know he had it in him to be gracious."

"I doubt anyone with that much liquor in them could remember a reason not to be," Chasmira replied wryly. She wanted to hate Wilvrey but could not bring herself to, at least not on an evening as joyous as this one. His speech reinvigorated the guests even more, and the music had risen back to an energetic tempo. These people were no longer just her hosts, they were her family. She lifted her own glass to Warrick. "To us?"

Warrick beamed with pride as he toasted, "To us."

ψ

By the fifth month, the snow had almost completely melted away. Springtime bore that timeless joy of new life, a joy Chasmira shared as she discovered she bore Warrick's child.

Warrick was stoic at first, of course, telling her that it would be best to wait to share the news with everyone. Within a single day, however, he had told everyone from Nyell baking bread in the kitchen to the farmhands planting radishes in the field. All spring and summer, the House of Mirikinin was abuzz with the news of the coming birth.

One warm, sunny day, Chasmira sat with Wisp in the green

grass, watching Morth, Warrick, and the farmhands working the north fields. She marveled that the fields were only more fertile now after the destruction wrought by Argismora's warriors more than half a year ago. Red daffodils grew all around her, raising their trumpets proudly into the sunlight. Bees hustled from flower to flower, dodging past round dinglebugs coming in to greedily gobble up nectar. They jingled like tiny bells whenever they took flight, hence their name.

"Can you *feel* it in there?" Wisp said, pressing their head to her belly and listening hard.

Peep was perplexed. "Peep peep?"

"No, not yet," Chasmira explained. "It will be a few months longer before I start to feel him moving around."

"That's so weirrrd. I was never carried around and born like that."

"You silly little thing, how would you even know that?"

Wisp looked up defiantly, "Because I'm not weirrrd!"

Chasmira laughed, lying back in the grass. She looked up at the sky, at the curled white clouds high in the perfect blue canopy overhead. Staring, she realized she could see two birds, so high up that she could only make out the tiny, white, winged specks if she concentrated on them and kept her head still. They slowly dipped past each other in a lazy, lovely dance.

So this is what it feels like. To have a home and a family. To have peace enough to rest.

She must have fallen asleep, for one minute she was looking at the sky, and the next she was looking up at Warrick standing next to her.

"Hi."

"Hi."

"What are you doing sleeping in the grass?"

"Admiring the sky. It's so beautiful."

He looked up at the sky and then back at her. "I seem to have found a more beautiful sight."

"Aww," she smiled up at his sweet comment and patted the head of the Cloven relaxing on her belly. "I had no idea you admired Wisp so much, but I can't blame you."

Warrick groaned and rolled his eyes as Wisp giggled, "You think I'm boot-iful, Warck?"

"So this is what I get for baring my heart to you, huh?" Warrick huffed as he sat down next to them, trying not to laugh too. "You're already passing off your bad habits to Wisp."

"Peeeeep!"

"And Peep."

"You'll be outnumbered soon," Chasmira said, putting a hand to her belly. "This is training for you."

"Training? Emorya goes easier on those Beastkin than this. I ought to go train with them instead," Warrick burst out laughing.

"Take that back," she laughed, swatting at him.

Warrick reached over and effortlessly pulled her up on top of him as he laid back. There, wrapped in the tranquility around them, she rested her head on his chest and shut her eyes. The air was saturated with the sweet fragrance of wildflowers and tall grass, and the delicate jingling of the dinglebugs sounded like a lullaby. Warrick's arms were warm around her. There, in perfect peace, she slept.

ψ

In a world where snow still dominated eight months of the year, the midsummer blazed all the hotter in defiance. By the seventh month, the cool, damp air of summer nights was a welcome relief.

Chasmira shut her eyes and inhaled slowly, drawing in a deep breath of that cool air. She stood on the open floor of the library, where furniture had been moved back to give her space. Planting her bare feet on the black stone floor, she focused inward, searching for the storm within her.

All her life, sorcery meant nothing but uncontrolled destruction at worst and controlled destruction at best. In contrast, Odic Sorcery held the potential to help and protect others, not frighten and harm them. Discovering this in herself meant that this was her potential as well, that her power was meant for something more than leaving burns everywhere she went and on everything she touched.

She turned around with her arms spread, one in front of her and one behind her. She raised both palms, shouting the old Odic incantation.

"Skina þromr!"

Nothing happened. She opened one eye, sighed, and shouted the incantation again. Still nothing.

Luthian called out, "Are you sure it's pronounced that way?"

She bit her lip, trying to keep focused. "An incantation is not a magic password, Luthian. It is a summoning, a communion with the primordial power. It connects your consciousness to something infinitely more powerful."

"If it's infinitely more powerful, why is it not working?"

The storms slumber deep within thy soul, ready to rise at thy command, untamed and wild, dancing to the furious drums of thunder, she recited to herself. The incantation was supposed to create a shimmering ward of sapphire energy, but days of practice had yielded not so much as a blue sparkle. Concentrating, she shouted again, "Skina þromr!"

Nothing.

"Damn it." She dropped her arms to her sides.

Luthian sat cross-legged, back resting against a bookshelf, casually flipping through the grimoire. "If it is any consolation, I believe it has started raining outside."

"It isn't any, Luthian. I'm not trying to make it rain. I'm trying to create a ward. It probably isn't even me causing the rain anyway."

"It was a perfectly clear night at sundown. That doesn't reek of supernatural weather occurrence to you?"

She sighed wearily. "You need not butter me up, Luthian. It's just summer. I saw a red sky this morning, so it makes perfect sense that it's raining now."

Luthian scrunched his nose at her reasoning. "And I suppose when a tiddalik croaks in Uliam, it means six more weeks of winter," he guessed sarcastically.

"No, it means there will be drought in the summer. A tiddalik would not croak that early in the year except to call to its mate to find water. Not all old wives' fables lack the science you crave."

He rolled his eyes and resumed flipping pages. "This book makes more sense than you right now."

She planted her hands on her hips. "Not everything you need

to know in life is in books, Luthian. Sometimes you need to get outside and learn things a book cannot teach you."

"Well, while you are ruminating on the married life of giant frogs, the secrets of sky magic seem to keep eluding you."

She pulled up a chair to rest. "Yes, and I know not why."

"Perhaps you are still having trouble concentrating. Wasn't there a passage about magic talismans that could help?"

Chasmira wet her fingers and flipped through the pages of the grimoire. "No, talismans block the enchantments of other sorcerers. You're thinking of staffs and wands, which enhance a sorcerer's power."

"Yes, could you not use of those?"

"Funny you should mention it. I just made this last week," she said, reaching down to a leather scabbard on her hip. From it she produced an ornate-crafted wand, about the length of her forearm. "Made from black oakwood, like these bookshelves. I carved it on the wood lathe, sanded it, and varnished it myself."

"What a thing of beauty! What does it do?"

She sighed. "At the moment, nothing. A sorcerer's wand is infused with arcane power to make a tool of singular purpose: destruction, restoration, or transmission. I have not been able to decide which purpose I want for it."

"Your iron staff with the sharp prongs on the top—it is infused with the power of destruction already, is it not?"

"True, but it is quite heavy to carry everywhere. Perhaps I want something more lady-like to turn people to ash."

He stared wide-eyed for a moment. "Or we could heal people…"

"Or speak to them over great distances, yes. It's very hard to choose, so I have not chosen yet," she said, putting it back in its scabbard.

Luthian rolled his eyes and began looking through the grimoire. "Well, in the meantime you have a very pretty stick, and you should be proud of it."

"Don't patronize me, *Uncle Luthian*. I'm carrying your niece or nephew," she prodded, but he continued idly flipping through the book, ignoring her. She took a deep breath, raised a hand, and shouted, "Himinnsokn!"

Bright blue light flashed in the window, and the fortress shook from the booming force of a thunderbolt outside. Luthian yelped in fright, covering his head with the book like a shelter. He poked his face out from under it. "When did you learn that?"

"Two nights ago," she beamed. "I can summon the thunderbolt from the sky, but I cannot aim it just yet…"

"Two nights ago? I was here. I didn't see you."

She heard the accusation in his tone. "I was outside in the yard."

"You practiced *outside*?"

"I was trying to call down thunderbolts. Inside the library is not the safest place to do that," she reasoned.

"That's not the point," he said, shutting the book and jumping to his feet in outrage. "This is our secret. We agreed to keep the book *here* and study *here*, in the library. We are supposed to be doing this together."

"We *are* doing this together. Luthian, calm down please."

"You don't get it." He paced in an agitated figure-eight, running his hand through his hair as he mulled over the emotions. "I wish I could explain to you. I just… I don't want to lose this."

"Lose what?"

"The only friend I have."

Her heart sank. Without hesitation, she walked up to him, slipped her arms around his slim waist, and hugged him with her cheek pressed to his chest. "Oh, Luthian. Luthian, no. That is not what's happening here. I was not trying to exclude you. You are not losing your only friend. You are not losing me."

Chasmira's tenderness melted him. He hugged her, blinking back his emotions and sniffling softly. When she finally pulled back from him, he hung onto her like a wilting flower hanging from a vase, unable to look her in the eye. She touched his cheek to bring him back and saw his dark blue eyes glitter with tears.

"I am not going anywhere. As life goes on, many things will pull at my time and my attention. I am married to your brother, the new prince, with our first child on the way, but I always will make time for you. It may not be as much as before, when life was simpler, but you will never lose this safe place. And you are right that this is our secret," she said, touching the grimoire in his hands, "I should have treated it like it was. I was just impatient to learn and thoughtless about how you might make you feel, Luthian, and I'm sorry. I promise it was not intentional."

Luthian chewed his lip. "You promise?"

She smiled up at him and caressed his face fondly. "I promise."

He hung his head and sighed, letting the emotions fall away. "I didn't realize how much it mattered to me until it felt like I was losing it," he chuckled at himself.

"Many things are like that. Also, I did not realize how much our time together meant to you. If it makes you feel any better, I think it is because it's so easy and natural, it is one of the rare things that I never overthink or doubt."

He nodded. Her openness in response to his was a profound comfort. Leaning back against a bookshelf, he slid back down to sit cross-legged on the floor. This time, she sat down with him, and he held her hands while she lowered herself to the floor.

"This may be the last time I ever do this, at least for the next five months."

He laughed, still holding her hands. "You know, I was not always the book goblin, hiding up here. Warrick and I were actually quite close when I was little, despite the age gap between us. He took me everywhere with him. I would ride with him on his horse to the river, where he taught me how to fish… I think, in a way, Warrick was making sure I had the kind of childhood he never had."

"It sounds like he was an amazing big brother."

"He was. Wilvrey, on the other hand, was always too busy being jealous of him, always looking for ways to one-up Warrick and get Father's attention. Little did he know, Father hadn't enough attention for any one of us. Wilvrey was wasting his time competing for a prize that never existed."

"So why aren't you and Warrick still close?"

"He became the foreman of the land, and adult life took him away." He was silent for a few long seconds, revisiting memories. He would watch Warrick walk away to the fields until he was out of sight, and then play alone. "I never want that to happen to me."

"You don't want to grow up?"

"Gods no," he laughed.

"You know what?"

"What?"

She smirked. "Himinnsokn."

The crash of thunder startled him so bad, he bumped his head against the shelf behind him and burst out laughing.

"I don't want to grow up either."

"Well, very clearly you are in no danger of that!" Luthian said, rubbing his head and shoving her. "Come on now, stop scaring the dogs and get back to practice. You can create quite a storm, but you had better learn how to tame it."

CHAPTER 30

Summer gave way to autumn, and autumn gave way to winter. While the cold months normally did not bother Chasmira, this time there was a deep feeling of melancholy. The third trimester of her pregnancy was a strangely difficult one, fraught with anxiety of all kinds. Her appetite failed her most of the time, much to Nyell's concern. No matter what delicious foods the housekeeper presented to the princess, nothing appealed to her, even when she felt hungry.

The worst of it was in the middle of the night. Chasmira would lie down, exhausted and ready for sleep, only to awaken in less than an hour. This persisted for weeks. Nyell insisted Chasmira try sleeping in various rooms and on other types of furniture, but nothing seemed to help.

It was Arca, the eleventh month. She stood staring out the latticed window, watching the snow falling. The sky was full of broken clouds. She felt frustrated that the sky was not either fully cloudy or fully clear, but felt further frustrated at herself for the meaningless frustration.

She placed her forehead against the cold window pane, looking out at the forest beyond the western sward. She thought back to Hakon's body still lying in the woods on the very spot the

Angelic had killed him. Why was she wishing he was here?

In the last eight months, not much had changed. She was still a filthy enchantress to Lord Maram and to the farmhands, too, even though she was now their Princess. She cringed at the creeping feeling that she was still only what she meant to others. She was a useless bother to Maram and a useful ally to Emorya. She was a hundred different things but not herself. Warrick loved her, but he did not know her the way she wanted to be known. Nobody knew her, and nobody cared to know her the way Hakon did. Not the way the armor-clad sorcerer prompted, prodded, pursued, and pieced together the bits she let slip when she was running her mouth.

The child inside her turned and stretched. She winced a little, but answered with a gentle caress of her hand. Warrick lay in bed, lost in a deep sleep. She felt ashamed for internally belittling him for the way he cared. *People care in their own ways*, she told herself and her child. *Your father is a strong, loving man. He pursued me but silently, in a different way than I imagined.* She took a deep breath, sat down in bed, and continued caressing her belly as she thought of her unborn child.

Inside her was the heir of Mirikinin. The savage royal blood of Warrick's family coursed through their veins, along with her own sorcerous might. Destructive might. Destruction itself coursed through the child's veins. From her. From it. From Chaos. She could not help but envision it like fire burning within her, warming her but also threatening to consume her. She imagined fire from the child's eyes, burning through her stomach the way she burned through the soldiers in the marsh outside Dimol Gol. She clutched her belly protectively at the thought.

The child would need discipline to use their power. Could Chasmira teach them? Did she even have any discipline to pass on? Her studies in the Art of Odic Sorcery discovered more weaknesses than strengths. Unable to focus properly, her own powers were still fueled by nothing more than her whims: the very chaos within her that burst to the surface whenever she so much as slacked her grip on its leash. With just a thought and a word, she could summon fire or create eyeballs all over a suit of armor like sprouts on a potato. Once she started, though, it was difficult to stop. Without a tug on that leash, the fire would consume everything in sight. Without her will to restrain it, a suit of armor would animate completely, sprouting spines and tentacles before consuming its wearer whole in a fizzling cloud of red foam. Chaos was easy to summon but difficult to control.

She shuddered and took a few deep breaths. Rolling over in her bed, she squinted against the light that shone in her eyes. The waning half-moon hung carelessly in the sky out her window. Unexpectedly, the sight of it comforted her. The moon's cycles never stopped. The full moon always came to term while the world watched in awe or superstitious fear.

In another month, the Last Moon would be full. She would come to full term and Warrick, newly a prince over the salvaged kingdom, would have his heir. A smile broke across her lips as she watched the moon sauntering slowly across the sky.

Before she even felt her eyelids getting heavy, she was asleep.

ψ

The arrival of their firstborn daughter brought a warm glow to an otherwise dark winter, on the twelfth day of the twelfth month. As Chasmira swaddled the newborn, admiring her through exhausted tears, Warrick leaned down beside her. He looked into his tiny daughter's little face, incredulous at the precious life created by his wife.

"Have you a name already for her?" he asked.

"I have not. I wanted to meet the child first and see if I felt inspired looking at their face for the first time."

He caressed her shoulder and planted a kiss in her hair. "So, what whispers the midwife muse to you?"

She laughed and reclined in deep thought. "Otzana."

"Otzana…" he echoed. "Now there's a name with some strength behind it. That's not commonly heard in Jacore, but more so down in the south country, this side of Gerustrom. It means 'she-wolf.'"

"It is perfect, then," Chasmira said.

"Named after someone in particular?"

She pondered his question with a smile. "It just sounds right."

As she settled in for sleep, Warrick took the infant in his arms, cradling her tenderly. "My little Otzana. I'm so glad you're here. My daughter, my little she-wolf."

ψ

"Congratulations, brother, on the birth of your daughter." Wilvrey said as he craned his neck to look over at Warrick. They sat across from each other in the private chamber behind the black throne, and upon the table was a colossal basket of dried fruits, meats, cheeses, and candies. It was by far the biggest gift sent by their vassals to celebrate the new year, but Lord Ovis had a special appreciation for Chasmira. Warrick could barely see the top of Wilvrey's head over the mound of treats.

"You almost sound sincere," Warrick replied.

"No need to be so cynical," Wilvrey said, standing to be seen more easily. "Was I against your marriage from the very start? Of course. And did I dread the day you would bring a child into the world? Naturally…"

"You are not helping my cynicism, Wilvrey."

"The point is, it has not eluded me that your entire countenance is better and brighter after the birth of baby Otzana. This is the happiest time in your life and in hers. The two of you have a family now, and without doubt that is your sole focus at the moment. You are content building a kingdom within a kingdom. Sensational."

Warrick leaned his face against his fist. "There's another edge to the blade you're wielding at the moment, I know it."

"No man shakes the foundation while he is still building thereupon, or his good work will fall apart," Wilvrey said, popping a piece of candied fruit into his mouth. "Happy people do not start wars, Warrick, and where this is no war, we need not warriors, do we? Also *wow*, this candy is good…"

"Just what are you saying?"

"I am sending my warriors back to their homes."

"What? How are we to defend our father's house? Argismora—"

"Has been silent for a year," Wilvrey interrupted as he cut a hunk of cheese and stuffed it in his mouth. "Clearly my warband crippled them, and they dare not provoke us again."

"And what if they do?"

"You have five hundred Beastkin right in the southern reach. Let them fight and make good on their lord's pledge. I will waste my army no longer. They need rest, and to comfort themselves in their own homes again. They will depart, and so will I."

Warrick stood. "You? Where are *you* going?"

"Well, I cannot very well stay here when there is nothing for me, although this cheese is very enticing. Maybe I'll take a little holiday somewhere nice, perhaps down in Holireath for a few months, until spring returns. Don't worry about me getting bored. I'm certain there's enough fresh meat in the Holireath whorehouses to keep me occupied for a while," he grinned wickedly.

"Perhaps you are right," Warrick conceded. "It may be better for you to roam about rather than stay caged here, as it were. Besides, it sounds as if your mind is already made up."

"It is."

Warrick was only too happy to see his brother go, but internally he dreaded releasing him out upon the unsuspecting world. The first sentiment was greater, in this case. Peace was definitely overdue, and easier without Wilvrey around. He held out his hand. "Then farewell, Wilvrey. Until you return, I wish you a good holiday."

Wilvrey did not take his hand. He just smiled and nodded. "Farewell, Warrick."

As Wilvrey departed, throwing his cape around his shoulders, he passed through the audience chamber. There, Maram stood in a shadow beside the throne, waiting to speak with the prince.

"Uncle Maram," said Warrick, "What brings you here?"

The wrinkled warlord watched Wilvrey cross the entire chamber and exit before he spoke a word. "I see Wilvrey decided to leave after all."

"You two have already spoken about it?"

"He asked my opinion."

Warrick leaned against the side of the throne. "Oh? And so you swayed him to leave."

"Not at all," Maram growled. "We are stronger with his army at the ready, but in his eyes they serve only him and his goals. Last year, he wanted Argismora as a bloody gift for the witch."

"Uncle, be careful how you speak."

"These are the facts, Warrick."

"*Prince* Warrick."

"You watch your tongue—"

"No, Uncle. You watch yours. I hate to remind you, but you are lord regent no longer."

"No, but I am your uncle, your flesh and blood—"

"And I am your prince!" Warrick shouted over him. "As you once insisted I respect your title at all times, you will afford the same reverence to me, and especially to my wife, Princess Chasmira."

Maram held a hard stare at him for a long time before finally bowing his head. "As you say, My Prince."

Satisfied, Warrick sat down upon the black throne, his ironwolf fur cape spreading out beneath him. The chamber echoed with the rolling clamor of pointed quills against black stone.

Maram began again, this time in a mellow, low voice. "With Wilvrey's battalion on leave, we are vulnerable. The kingdoms round about us may still seek our harm. We must maintain a show of strength."

"And how do you propose we do that?" Warrick asked.

"A writ of mandate, drafting from all our territory into our warband, the able-bodied from seventeen years to forty-five."

"You want me to order a draft? The cost in loyalty would far outweigh the gain in force," Warrick countered.

"The only loyalty soldiers have is to a strong, unrelenting leader, My Prince."

"The kingdoms around us have shown no aggression in over a year. Suddenly massing our forces could provoke them into attacking. Doing so would compromise the peace we currently enjoy."

"Peace? Do not confuse peace with quiet. If you show complacency, you open a window of opportunity for them to strike."

Warrick's expression was stony. He had already removed a bothersome barb with Wilvrey's departure, and he was not about to allow Maram to fill the position instead. "Thank you for your counsel, Uncle, but that is a chance I am willing to take."

CHAPTER 31

The sound of a blasting war horn sent Warrick's drink halfway across the table. Red wine ran down the tablecloth. He cursed and rushed from the table, with Chasmira following close behind.

Halfway to the front door, Warrick ran into Lart. The latter seemed overwhelmed, walking slowly and anxiously.

"Lart, what the blazes is going on?"

"I don't know," he answered.

"What do you mean, you don't know?" Warrick grumbled, "You're the steward of the damn house."

Already out of patience, Warrick pushed him aside and opened the front door. One step out into the courtyard, Warrick stopped. Chasmira was unable to see around his huge frame, so she squeezed around him and, just the same, stopped dead in her tracks.

Emorya's Beastkin trainees, all five hundred of them, filled the courtyard. Pure agitation wafted in the air from many voices all bleating and lowing to each other.

"The Beastkin," one of the sentries explained from behind them. "They sounded an alarm. Blew the warning horn, so we opened the front gate to let them inside like they was falling back against some enemy. Didn't question it."

"It makes no damn sense," Warrick blustered, pushing forward into the crowd. "What's all this now? What's all this?" The herd hardly had any answers for him, none that he could understand in all the noise, anyway. Instead, he pushed his way past the Goatkin that huddled together like leaves shaking in the wind, and the huge Oxkin that cowered like cats in a thunderstorm.

He clapped his hand down on the shoulder of the frontmost Goatkin, who gnawed at his fingernails anxiously. The Kin jumped from the surprise.

"Tell me," Warrick said, calmly as he could, "What's this about?"

"M-Mazigorn," stuttering with fear.

Warrick did not even ask another question. Mazigorns were monsters of myth, but for the Beastkin they were a stark, terrible reality. In the twenty days of the waxing Blood Moon, Beastkin dared not walk the night. Mazigorns lurked in the shadows, waiting to drag them away to slaughter when the moon was full and red. The Blood Moon was already long past, but these monsters craved the blood and meat of their favorite prey any day of the year. Every single Kin had fled out of pure instinct, out of the innate terror within them.

As Warrick pondered this, Chasmira arrived at his side and asked, "Is it what I think? Only one thing can frighten them this badly."

"So they say, but on a dark, foggy night like this?" Warrick listened hard for any animal call that might give the predator away. "Could be anything out there."

"I know what I heard," the Goatkin insisted. "I heard its voice."

"Then we must answer it," said Warrick.

Chasmira stepped in front of him. "No."

"You expect me not to defend my home?"

"Of course not, but such a dark creature is beyond any of you. Mazigorns feed on fear. They can smell it in your blood, and it only increases their power and hunger."

"So, what then? We hunker down and wait for daybreak while a single monster menaces our walls?"

"Would that it were so simple, but you are underestimating this foe. A Mazigorn could easily scale the walls and take its prey if it truly wanted to. No, it wants to draw out our fear. This fortress is a boiling pot."

Warrick nodded, but he already had a feeling what she was going to say next. "You are not going out there."

"I am clearly the most suited for it."

"You just birthed a child barely a month ago," he countered.

"Which proves I fear nothing," she cracked a smile.

His voice was husky and low. "Take Morth with you."

Chasmira grimaced. "It is winter, and he is still in hibernation."

"Damn it, then I'll come with you," Warrick said and started drawing his sword.

"You won't."

"I will."

"No, you won't," pushing his sword back into the sheath. "Zana needs protection. She needs her father."

He sighed. "You'll take two sentries with you, then."

She replied with a hard stare.

"Zana needs her mother, too."

Chasmira's shoulders slumped, and she nodded her agreement.

"They will be the two stoutest-hearted men I have. Indulge me, for I could not in good conscience let you go alone."

A shiver went through her. *Alone.*

Five minutes later, Warrick had chosen two of his most seasoned sentries to send with her. Gryff and Cadoc had guarded the grounds and the wall for a decade, yet neither of them had ambitions to become quartermaster or captain. They were content in their stations and stalwart in the face of any threat. Each carrying a sword and a flaming torch, the sentries flanked Chasmira as the three of them set off into the night.

Cadoc, bald and broad-shouldered, walked and talked as casually as if he were out hunting rabbits. He spoke in the thick accent of northern Jacorian tribes, with upspeak at the end of everything he said. "Quiet night for a monster. You have encountered such a thing before, milady?"

She tip-toed warily through the brush, watching and listening for any sign of danger. "No, but there was a master huntsman in the court of Dimol Gol, who claimed to have seen one."

"I've heard tales about Mazigorns," Gryff said. "Demons of the wastelands... faster than a horse, craftier than a spider, and stronger than a bear."

"Do they only eat Beastkin?" Cadoc asked. "I've heard all about the Taking, in the days before a Blood Moon."

"They'll eat anything with a beating heart," Gryff replied. "They like the taste of fear in their prey."

A sudden crash in the foliage.

All three of them spun to face it.

Just a young buck, with its antlers caught in the low, forked limbs of a chaste tree. The helpless animal, already exhausted from struggling, tugged a few times more as they approached.

"You gave me a start, poor little friend," Cadoc said, patting his chest with one hand. The bald man sheathed his sword to grab hold of its antlers. "I'll free you."

Chasmira also caught her breath after such a scare. "To answer your question though, Cadoc, Mazigorn do not gather Beastkin during the Taking merely for food. The monsters use them as part of a terrible ritual to honor their goddess."

"And they can't just use plain, dumb animals like this one?"

"No, I imagine she is a cruel mistress indeed," she replied.

Cadoc finally freed the buck, which scrambled away as quickly as it could. He wiped his hands off and clapped them together. "Makes sense. I've had a few cruel mistresses meself," he chuckled.

They had not time to laugh with him before his feet were knocked out from under him. Cadoc fell into the umbrage, and the forked tree limb caught him by the neck.

"Cadoc!"

His legs lifted up and went straight back. A terrible roar shook the air. The Mazigorn had him by the ankles. "I'm stuck! Hel—"

It pulled. Hard. Cadoc's head jerked violently out of the tree fork with a loud snap of his neck. He fell limp to the ground with a thud, and started screaming.

"I can't move! I can't move!"

Before either of them could reach him, Cadoc was dragged off into the darkness. Gryff raised his sword to chase after, but Chasmira put her hand to his chest and shook her head no.

Cadoc's terrified screaming ended with a wet crunching sound.

The crackle of Gryff's torch was the only sound as they held their breath, waiting for the monster to appear, to lunge out of the dark to snap their necks too.

Instead, two red eyes glowed in the darkness ahead, out of reach of the torch's light. The Mazigorn's voice rumbled in the night, "You are too far from home. Your blood is already bubbling with fear, I can smell it."

"Begone from these lands, monster. I do not fear you," Gryff said, voice solid as a castle wall.

"Perhaps not, but I know what you *do* fear." The Mazigorn's voice oozed with cruel glee. "The cry of your bereft wife if she ever saw your face again."

Gryff froze. The hairs on the back of his neck stood straight up.

"Yesssss... Crying angry tears as she screams at you that it's been what, ten years since you left her and the children? Did she always scream at you? Was that why you decided to abandon them and hide on the walls of a distant black fortress until time finally took you? I can hear those screams, too, Gryff. I can taste the nightmares on you like salt on pork."

The man turned to Chasmira. His eyes were wide with fright, his face pale as a ghost. His fears, no matter how deeply buried, had been found. "Forgive me, milady," as a single tear ran down his face.

The Mazigorn's growl exploded out of the night. A sliver of moonlight gleamed off something. A horn, perhaps, or a claw dashing by. She spun to follow it, but only quickly enough to see

Gryff vanish into the darkness. His faint, guttural cry ended abruptly.

Two red eyes hovered in the dark, closer now.

She backed away slowly, placing her feet carefully. If she stepped on a root or tripped over a log—if she fell—it meant certain death. The Mazigorn would surely break and tear off her limbs, and then devour her stump and head whole. Mazigorns ate their prey alive, cruel things, for they savored the taste of a still-beating heart.

Her thoughts leapt to poor Cadoc and Gryff. The monster could smell their fear, but it could do much more than that. It found the residue of Gryff's guilt and his subconscious fears, and it picked up the scent like a bloodhound. His nightmares were like tracks that led it straight to his deepest terror, dragging it to the surface.

Self-preservation asked to think back on recent nights' visions, but Chasmira denied her instincts. To do so would only invite any fears back to the surface, which was exactly what the malevolent beast wanted.

The two red eyes vanished.

Chasmira's body went rigid. She had been staring at the eyes for so long that they were her anchor in otherwise pitch-black darkness. Disorienting her would sow confusion and yield fear, so Chasmira shut her eyes and steeled herself. With her eyes closed, she controlled the darkness instead of it controlling her. If she was going to be blind, it would feel as if it were her own choice.

"You shouldn't be here," she asserted sternly. She could almost hear the echo of her own voice.

A grating baritone shook her bones. "Neither should you."

"The Blood Moon is past. The Taking is done, and your goddess honors your sacrifices no longer."

"Still, I must eat," the monster rumbled. She could hear the evil smile in its words.

"And must you terrorize this good land, and the fortress of the late Prince Mirikinin's family?"

At this she could hear the trees rustle in the darkness as if shaken by a great wind. There was a crash of tree branches, and in a few seconds she felt the Mazigorn's hot breath on the right side of her neck. "Terrorize? This land already *reeks* of fear," it slavered. "Fear seasons the meat."

Her lips curled with disgust. "And fire roasts it. Burn."

The woods ignited with bright red light. She cast a veritable wall of fire from her eyes, enough to incinerate ten men. Trees lit aflame *Be thorough. No sense in taking chances.*

Out of the blaze rose a dark shape. Chasmira faltered, blinking away fire to get a better look at it in the orange light of the burning trees. Its head appeared goatish, with a long snout and great spiraling horns, but its neck was wrapped in a thick mane like a lion. Its hulking body glittered with dark, red scales…

A gust of bitterly cold wind shook the trees, blasting the fires into nothing but faint embers. Before the forest plunged back into darkness, Chasmira saw the Mazigorn turn and lock eyes with her. Its gaze was like that of a falcon, keen and red, spotting prey from even great distances.

"You will find that to be useless. I am unbothered by fire," the Mazigorn growled out of the dark. "Yours, however, is not ordinary fire, now is it?"

Chasmira backed away slowly. Its voice was moving again. It

was either some other kind of trick, or the monster was circling her.

"*You* shouldn't be here," said the Mazigorn.

"I live here."

"And Chaos lives in you. You have no home, none that you will not inevitably burn down. Tell me, what evil have you in store for these people?"

"No evil at all," Chasmira countered. "I live here peacefully with my husband and my daughter."

"Peacefully?" The Mazigorn bellowed, now behind her. Chasmira whirled around to see its red eyes much too close for comfort. She scrambled back, supporting herself on a tree. "I know who you are, Chasmira. I found your battlefield beyond the boglands and gleaned the survivors, every one of them drowning in fear and despair. There is no greater despair than that of warriors without a war."

"There is neither war nor despair here, demon. There is safety and love, two things that I have long sought after."

It approached her. The foliage crunched and snapped with every heavy, thudding step the Mazigorn took. It came so close to her, the glow of her eyes illuminated its snout as it nearly touched her face. Its fangs were streaked with warm human blood from its meal. It inhaled deeply, savoring every scent in the air, but Chasmira knew what it was searching for. "Seems I was wrong," it growled. "The greatest despair is from losing that which long you sought and finally found."

Chasmira did not yield.

Its face sank back into the night, but its red eyes continued watching her. "We are the same, you and I… both part of the darkness. Do not deny it. You create fear, and I feed off it. For creatures like us, there is no peace."

"You're wrong."

"We shall see. When the time is right, when the fear has soaked deep enough into this place, perhaps I will return." Its eyes shrank away and vanished, and the Mazigorn's laughter echoed through the night.

PART THREE

CHAPTER 32

Chasmira snapped out of her sleep.

She shuddered for a moment, steadying herself with a slow breath before relaxing back into the bedding. Had a dream awoken her, or perhaps a chill that slipped past the warm covers? A shiver went through her body. It was the middle of Arca, and the weather was getting colder each night. Even Terror wanted to sleep in their bedroom that night, but she kept him shut out. *It is going to be a cold winter*, Chasmira thought.

Shivering again, she pulled the blankets up to her neck. Warrick lay with his back to her as usual. The thought of putting her cold feet against his back intruded on her, but she quickly shooed it off. Instead, she nestled closer and slid her arm around him. He did not feel much warmer. *Poor thing is freezing like I am.* She lifted her hand to cradle his face, and Warrick's hand brushed hers gently.

It was wet.

She pulled her hand back to look.

Blood.

She leapt up, barely able to fathom what she saw. Warrick's throat, hands, and chest were covered in red that ran freely from his neck. His skin was cool and pale, and he looked up at her with bleary eyes.

With no time to lose, she flung open their bedroom door and screamed down the hallway for help, for anyone to hear her. She had no idea what hour of the morning it was, if anyone else was even awake…

When she turned back around it was as if time had stopped. In a moment she took in the whole disastrous scene, and her mind wanted to reject everything she saw. Dim overcast morning shone in the window. A broken window, like someone had leapt through the glass panes to escape the room. *An assassin.* And there lay Warrick in blood-soaked blankets and furs, looking so strangely small and helpless.

Chasmira screamed again for help and then flung herself onto Warrick. She grabbed a handful of the blankets and pressed them to his throat to slow the bleeding. He had lost so much blood already, something inside her cried out that it was a useless gesture, but she had to do something.

"Warrick," she whispered.

His response was a soft rasp.

Behind her were voices shouting in the hall. Shouting her name. Nyell, maybe, or Lart. Someone heard her and was coming. They would be there soon. Shaking terribly, Warrick reached up and squeezed her hand.

"You'll make it through," Chasmira's voice was dry as sand.

"I won't."

"You will."

"No, I won't." He gripped her hand tighter.

Warrick's loving look became a glassy stare. His huge hand went limp. He sank back into the bed, and Chasmira grasped for him as if trying to keep him from slipping under the surface of the sea.

At first she felt nothing. Breath held, eyes fixed on him, hand still holding on. *Wake up*, she urged herself, for all she knew was that this could not be real. She was going to wake up from this and throw her arms around him while he smiled quizzically at her. *Wake up.*

Emorya's hand touched hers, holding the blood-soaked blanket against Warrick's neck. She said something, but Chasmira could not hear her.

Lart's arms wrapped around her, pulling her back from the bed to give Emorya space. The room around her became a blur, a spinning cloud, a whirlpool of numbness. She groped blindly, fighting Lart as if she were underwater fighting for air.

At last Nyell came to the doorway, and Lart shoved Chasmira into the woman's arms as he too ran to the bedside. Nyell pulled her out of the room, trying to say something reassuring to her. She could feel the hum of her voice but could not receive a single word.

In her hazy vision she saw the door to the room shrinking away from her with every step. She could not fight back. Her limbs had gone numb, even as she kicked and thrashed to free herself from Nyell's arrest.

The lithe, dark outline of Luthian came to her side, and Nyell's grip slackened while she talked with him. She could not understand a word they said. It was all incoherent mumbling to her, and she was filled with the urge to run from the sound. Chasmira tore herself free, retreating down the stairs. They would not let her back into that bedroom, and she no longer wanted to be there. That room held only pain and death, and it had killed her husband. It stole Warrick from her.

She stumbled like a blind woman, for all her senses were turned inward, clinging desperately to what she was losing. The feeling of Warrick's bear hugs filled with strength and warmth wrapped around her, that she would never feel again. The sound of Warrick's voice, so deep and brittle with annoyance most of the time, that she would never hear again. Her mind scrambled for memories as if they were pages that fell out of a book, scattered at her feet and carried away by gale winds.

She burst out the door into a soundless outside world. Not a bird sang. Not a breeze moved. The sky was a canopy of grey glass, cruel and unanswering as she screamed upward. Oh, to break the world apart with her hands, but the cold ground yielded not under her pounding fists and clawing fingers. The earth was a dull brown grave, clammy and uncaring as she screamed downward. She wanted to bid the world burn, to pour fire from her eyes and die in the blaze. She wanted to summon a blade and carve out her own heart, to let Chaos end her suffering. Yet, even as these dark whims strove within her, nothing happened. No fire rose in her eyes. No red threads appeared between her fingers to make a dagger.

Chasmira gasped and shuddered as her eyes filled with tears. She had not even the strength to sob, for something inside her had broken and died. Something inside her was left in that room with Warrick to take to the realm beyond… something she would never get back.

CHAPTER 33

Another day. The sun rose and set.

She watched it from the window.

She slept but awoke exhausted.

Another day. The sun rose and set.

The latticed window was her only companion. Nine horizontal bars spanned across the window. Between them, and between the top and bottom of the window, were metal rings about a hand's width each. In all there were ten rows of rings, and each row was six rings from side to side. Chasmira counted them every day.

She slept but awoke exhausted.

"She needs you," Nyell said.

Chasmira blinked slowly, only now realizing Nyell was there helping her pull on her robe. Her hand was up Chasmira's sleeve, holding her wrist to gently guide her hand.

"What did you say?"

"I said she needs you."

Chasmira stared through her. "Who?"

"Your daughter."

"Warrick's daughter. Warrick is gone."

Nyell folded her hands. "Your daughter Otzana is here, and

she needs you right now."

Chasmira shut her eyes. "Where is the wet nurse?"

"She's been ill all night and this morning. Stomach sickness."

"She can nurse Zana when she's well enough," she said, standing. She moved to the window as if she were dragging chains behind her until she reached the chair and sank into it. She let out a thin sigh.

"She's hungry, milady."

She laid her forehead against her palm. "You feed her, then."

"You know that I cannot—"

"What do you expect ME to do?" Chasmira snapped at her.

"You're her mother!"

"As if I've forgotten?"

"You act as if you have!"

"And *you* act as if you have forgotten her father, my husband, died a month ago."

"Milady… it's been almost two months."

Chasmira sank back into her chair. *Has it been so long already?* The days had slipped by faster than she realized. She shivered in the chair, and before she could form a thought, Nyell was already placing a blanket around her shoulders. There were none in her room, unless Nyell brought one with when she entered.

"Life has been cruel to you. None understand Tyor's ways or his goals," Nyell said, naming the Jacorian god of necessity. When pains and trials arose in life, they were often credited to him.

"I feel as if a fire within me has gone out entirely."

"What do you mean?"

She was not even truly speaking to Nyell but more so to herself, so Chasmira did not answer her. She simply stared out the window, resuming a state she had fallen into daily since Warrick's death. The latticed window was her confidant, her silent comfort. Nothing changed about it. It was always the same, and it asked nothing from her. It stood between her and the rest of the world, but it let her see it. She began counting the rings. Ten rows, and six rings on each row. Each ring had a little tuft of feathery frost at the bottom, and Chasmira began to think on how the frost forms. She thought on how the cold must creep across the glass, carefully painting each icy line before the glass realizes it is encased in it.

Is this what has befallen me? Have icy lines set upon me like frost upon glass? Beyond the glass, endless white snow bound the fields and grottos of the land. Spring had not come. *It will never come,* she thought dourly. *The world and I will rest here forever in perpetual cold, as they did in the Dragon's Winter. That would be best for all of us.*

Outside it was becoming quite dark. She nodded sadly, and rose to her feet with great effort. Chasmira reached out, brushed the window with the backs of her fingers, and slowly returned to her bed.

She slept but awoke exhausted.

Another day.

Another two weeks passed before Chasmira could convince herself to leave her room. She cracked the door and looked down the hallway. The House of Mirikinin seemed like a daunting labyrinth compared to the simple safety of the bedroom, and for a moment she irrationally despaired how best to leave a trail back to her room in case she became lost. Perhaps shreds of paper from a page carried in her sleeve, or crumbs of the loaf leftover from her uneaten dinner…

She discarded the idea, wrapped herself in a robe and fur blanket, and ventured down the hall to the stairs, eventually making her way to the dining room. As she turned the corner, raised voices suddenly fell silent. Wilvrey and Emorya stood, clearly in the middle of a harsh disagreement, and now stared at her. She stared back like a frightened cat.

The silence was broken by Terror happily padding up to her across the floor and barking happily up at her in greeting. She flinched at first. He pawed at her and licked her hand, and she absentmindedly stroked his bat-like ears as she stared at the others.

Much to her surprise, Wilvrey was the first to approach her with hurried steps. He looked as if he meant to take her hand, but refrained. "You have come back to us."

She nodded. She had not seen any of them for nearly three months, secluded in her room. If any of them had opened the door to see her, she had not noticed, lost in the fog of another day passing.

"Are you well?" he asked with concern.

"As well as one could expect," attempting a smile but failing.

He looked at her strangely, she thought, the way one looks strangely at someone whose name you are trying to remember. Had so much time passed that she was a stranger to him?

She turned to leave.

"Don't go," Wilvrey said, grabbing her hand. "Nyell has prepared wheatcakes with butter and fresh eggs for us, but even such a meal would be incomplete without you there."

She steadied her breath. Her hand was ice-cold, while his was warm as hearthstone. She wanted to pull away and flee back to her room, but could not bring herself to refuse that warmth wrapped around her fingers. Without a word, she turned back and let Wilvrey lead her to the table.

Terror followed so closely that he nearly tripped her. When she sat, he laid down beneath her seat with his back against her calves.

No sooner had they seated themselves than Lart's voice echoed around the corner. "I tell you, there's no way we could have dealt with this winter if not for that Ogre. The way he's earning his keep, soon we'll have to give him his own room in the—" He fumbled the rest of his thought the second he saw her. He would have exclaimed, would have run up and hugged her, had he not seen the cautionary glares from his sister and cousin.

Emorya set a platter of breakfast food at the spot next to her. Lart hung his winter cloak by the fire to dry it, walked somberly to the table, and cleared his throat as he sat. "Morth and Wisp are well, despite the bitterness of the cold."

Chasmira stared past him into the fire, thinking about her two friends living on the western sward.

Lart poured hot butter on his wheatcakes and then started to rummage through his pockets. "Wisp asked me to give this to you," he said, handing her a folded piece of paper. When she did not take it, he set it down in front of her.

"They wrote me a letter?" she asked with a furrowed brow.

"No," he laughed, "Neither of them can write a word. But I think I can translate their meaning."

Intrigued, Chasmira picked at the corner of the paper until it unfolded. It contained a scribbly drawing of Morth, Chasmira, Wisp, and Peep sleeping in their chairs with bowls of Morth's Sleeping Stew on the table.

"Wisp said they miss you, and they hope you can visit soon. The stew is delicious but it's too much for them to eat by themselves," Lart told her.

She smiled sadly at the drawing, but then noticed something. "Who is this fifth person sitting with us, with the curly hair?"

They looked at one another as a few silent moments passed. Emorya leaned in close, pointing to the figure on the paper. "That's your daughter Otzana."

"Otzana?" She blinked at the paper. "Zana has curly hair?"

A painful silence followed. Months had passed since she had seen her own daughter. In her deep mourning, in the deadness of her heart, she had distanced herself so far from everyone, including her own child. She could feel a familiar coldness creeping inside herself, those frostlines closing around her heart...

"Where is she?" Chasmira said louder than she should have, more to silence her thoughts than to be heard.

"In the nursery," Lart offered.

"Do you want to see her?" Emorya added.

"No, no. She is probably asleep. I should not disturb her," Chasmira answered. "She is better off without me there."

CHAPTER 34

Days slipped by like falling snowflakes. They piled at her feet similarly unheeded.

It was not a sadness that gripped her, not a pain, for there were no tears to be shed for either reason. It was not something that a single word can encompass, for it was many things all at once. Food did not tempt or excite, but hunger was a nagging nuisance that needed to be quieted down. The sound of music became like the buzzing of flies, and so she constantly sought the quiet but never stayed in one place long enough to enjoy it. A sort of restlessness overcame her often, and she would aimlessly walk through the halls, outside into the yard, and then back inside. More than once she forgot to put on her coat and cape, and so Nyell took care that they were set out with her clothes so that she wore them at all times. If she was absent-minded enough to ignore the cold until she had a bad chill, she could also be absent-minded enough to not mind the extra layers of clothing.

Her grieving took a cruel turn when Chasmira's state changed from numbness to an acute awareness of Warrick's absence. She found herself fighting the urge to say his name and see if he would answer. She wanted to call for him down the hallway, in the yard, or from the outer wall. Night became a torturous time, for she would lie awake, waiting for him to open the bedroom door and join her under the covers. The bed turned into a pit of loneliness to the point she felt in agony even sleeping there. The frustration would mount to the point that she would tear all the bedding off, hurling it against the walls in fits of wordless, soundless, panting rage. It was in these moments she truly felt that baby Otzana was fortunate not to see her in such a pitiful state, and could not stop thinking it may be better if the child never saw her again.

The thoughts started to scare her.

She began to avoid everyone who could possibly start a conversation with her. Why, she did not really know, but she only questioned it twice, so it did not matter. Part of her imagined that her fits and frustrations were plain for all to see, and so she wanted to hide herself out of shame. Another part of her insisted that all her pain was invisible to everyone else, that what she felt mattered nothing to them.

Luthian was easy enough to elude, for he rarely ventured out of the library or his bedroom, wherever that was. Books were companions they shared, but now she wanted nothing to do with them. She wanted neither to read nor be read by the books that freely touched her heart the moment she turned a page. Lord Maram—who had reassumed the throne after Warrick's death—thankfully avoided her out of sheer disgust. She could not blame him; she hated him equally. Wilvrey was far more challenging, for he seemed to lurk around every corner, intentionally placing himself in her path. Was he watching over her? Did he pity her?

She decided she did not care. He could burn and die for all she cared. Ignorant bastard. She did not want pity. She did not want sympathy. She did not want anything of theirs. She wanted something they could not give her. She wanted Warrick. She wanted to feel happy.

"But why don't you feel happy?" Wisp asked her earnestly.

Chasmira felt tears welling up, but her hand was dry after wiped at her eyes. She looked at her hand closely, scratching at the skin in search of a trace. Her tea had gone cold in the time they sat idly talking. The little Cloven was the only person she felt like talking to at the moment. There was something irrevocably innocent about them, that made them both safe and helpful.

"Why?" the little Cloven repeated.

"I have lost part of myself."

"Which part?" Wisp cocked his head to one side, and Peep mimicked the same movement.

She stared down at her cold teacup. "The part of me that felt happiness. The part of me that could laugh at things."

"Where is it?"

"I don't know. Someone took it from me, Wisp."

Wisp looked over at Peep and then stared down at the table, brow furrowed in thought. They had no concept of loss, of death, of mourning, which was exactly why Chasmira asked for time alone with them while Morth hibernated. Wisp and Peep were the only comfort in this kind of pain: a naive sort of comfort that made everything so simple.

Finally, the little Cloven asked, "I'm sorry they took your laughter. What kind of monster would do that?"

"What sort of monster..." Chasmira echoed, asking herself the same question. She was struck with a sudden sense of clarity, and her heart started to race. "What sort of monster? I know what kind."

As she leapt up from the chair, going for the door, Wisp called after her. "Where are you going?"

Flinging open the door, she answered, "I don't know yet, but I am about to find out."

ψ

The Beastkin cowered, shielding their eyes against the bitter wind that blew into the barracks. In the doorway stood Chasmira, her robe lashing in the wind, wrapped in a halo of harsh white light from the snow outside. She did not so much as move or shiver in the cold, for kindling inside her was a newfound rage.

"Lady Chasmira," said the kneeling Goatkin, the same that explained the Harmony's Eve ceremony to her a year ago. "Your presence is so unexpected. What can we—"

"Where lies the lair of the Mazigorn?" She had no time for pleasantries.

His face went pale with fear. "Why would ye ask such a thing?"

Chasmira loomed closer, her shadow falling over him. "Trifle not with me, for I am in no mood for games. Tell me where the monster may be found, so that I can kill it."

The Goatkin's jaw went slack. Here stood a sorceress of Chaos, pledging herself to killing their worst enemy. Swallowing the lump in his throat, he leaned in closer and with a shaking voice said, "We have always been told the monster comes from the southeast at sunset, and returns there each night."

"To the southeast lies the river and beyond it, Holireath."

The Goatkin nodded. "Right ye are, but between here and the river lies a great barren plain where no man lives, for it is the domain of the accursed, of the blood-eaters."

She said not another word to them. There was no time to lose. She went to the stables and commanded for her ivrit to be immediately saddled and bridled. She rode despite the protests of the sentries that sunset was only a few hours away, and night riding was too dangerous. She ignored them, setting out at a gallop right from the front gate.

Chasmira rode all night, confident that the ivrit could endure the cold, tireless journey. If it could live through the frigid siege of Eppenhorn, she reasoned, it could live through a long night in the plains. She made sure it drank water at every pool and brook, for once the barren plains began, the only water fit to drink would be the snow at their feet.

Night became day, but not a ray of sunlight could be found. The land seemed devoid of any living creatures, save for a single black vulture high overhead, waiting for her to perish. The sky was an uncaring grey, which made the journey even more numbing. Over every ridge was another plain, as if she were traversing jagged dunes in a desert of rock and snow. Other than the dark, earthen face of a boulder or a cluster of dry grass jutting from the snow, as far as the eye could see was a bleak, white wasteland.

Hours passed, until finally she saw a woodland of small, thin, bare trees: the one place a monster could make a lair in this environment. She urged her mount toward it eagerly, but as she neared the treeline, her ivrit whined, skidded, and stopped. It turned away, tugging against the reins.

"Don't worry, I won't force you to go in," said Chasmira, dismounting and looking the frightened beast in the eyes. She could not take any chances, however. "*Obey.* Do not run off without me, and come if I call you," she commanded.

The ivrit obeyed. Compelled by her enchantment, it lingered a safe distance away from the treeline and did not run when she left it alone. Chasmira ambled through the deep snow and crunched through the brittle branches scattered everywhere in the woods.

The woods were even more inhospitable than the plains. Not only did the thin trees provide no shelter against the blowing cold, the wind moaned eerily through the thousands of wiry branches. Like a choir of weeping hags, the sound chilled her to the bone, yet she continued with bitter resolve. Every step farther into the woods was accompanied by the muffled crunch of deep snow and a crackling of branches. She had nowhere to hide here, but neither did her adversary.

She paused. The sea of thin, dead trees was all starting to look the same, and the sky above was a flat plane of grey clouds. With no shadows and no markers, she had no idea where she was going or where she had been. The trek across the plains had been so long and so numbing, she did not truly know how much time it had taken or how much daylight remained. Was this what Warrick's ancestors endured in the terrible Dragon's Winter, staring at what could be their death every minute?

Breathing shakily, Chasmira whirled around to look for natural landmarks behind her, anything that she might have missed. She found none at all. Then, she noticed the trail she left in the deep snow. *Of course*, she chided herself for panicking.

Her relief was short-lived. No sooner did she turn again to step forward, she saw a dark shape standing in the middle of the woods ahead. It was no monster, but she could not discern what it was without drawing nearer. Every bit of reason and self-preservation told her to turn back, but she ignored them. This monster had to die.

What she discovered was an ominous clearing about fifty feet wide. The trees were not broken down or torn away—they simply dared not grow any closer to the spot. Chasmira had faced the carnage of war and the demons of Chaos itself, but had never felt so naked in her life as she did stepping into that clearing and facing what stood at the center.

Books were written about the abominable practices of the Mazigorns and their terrible religion, and those books were burned the moment anyone with an ounce of decency found them. Their perverse faith instilled in them a hunger to commit atrocities upon the living and the dead alike, a hunger never satisfied. Thus, no written record was ever allowed to exist. The testimony of these dark acts now stood before Chasmira in the center of the clearing.

At first, she could not conceive what she was seeing. It must have been a tree once, now carved into a pillar of petrified wood and frozen gore. Shriveled, eyeless heads dangled from the tree's branchless limbs. Fiendish runes were stained onto what appeared to be flesh stretched into fabric banners, flapping in the freezing wind. Strings of bells and bones jangled together like wind chimes. She averted her eyes when she realized what crowned this horrific monument. As she retreated, her mind staggered to forget the sight of jagged wood impaled through a human ribcage.

Her chest squeezed itself tight, and she thought she might pass out. The woods were starting to spin in her vision. She half-knelt, half-fell into the snow, grabbed a handful of it, and pressed it to the side of her neck as she sucked in long breaths. The flash of cold centered her and not a moment too soon, for a pair of huge, curled horns rumbled out of the snowdrifts behind her, and two glowing, red eyes appeared beneath them.

The Mazigorn shook off the snow, though its scales were still encrusted with ice. It stood easily eight feet tall, and its posture was like that of a great ape, with massive forelimbs thick as oak trees. Its familiar voice was like booming thunder over the wailing wind. "So, Chasmira... You have come to die."

She bared her teeth. "No, I have come to *kill*."

Chasmira screamed and attacked in a fit of rage, summoning infernal energies into rows of jagged blades wrapped around her hands. She leapt at the monster as it crouched and backed away, seemingly unprepared for this kind of aggression. The thin, bare trees of the woods toppled over without resistance as the Mazigorn backed into them, giving itself room, but Chasmira did not stop or falter. She attacked with such ferocity, such quickness, it was as if something else entirely had taken possession of her body and was using it to kill. One of her blades caught the Mazigorn across its snout, shearing off chunks of thick scales into the snow.

If it had been tolerating her to this point, it was no longer doing so. The Mazigorn lunged forward, grasping at her to rend her apart. She unleashed a swirling blast of fire from her eyes, which the Mazigorn shrugged off easily.

The fire was not intended to burn, but to block its vision as she dove behind a snowdrift. The Mazigorn growled and scanned the woods for her. It was just lifting its snout to pick up her scent when she burst from her hiding place and dug her blades deep into its side. Black blood spattered on the snow. The forest shook with a roar of pain. The monster whirled angrily, landing a backhanded blow that caught Chasmira square in the chest. With the breath knocked out of her, she glanced across the snow like a stone skipping across water. Bellowing fiercely, the Mazigorn pursued.

Chasmira snarled an incantation, and from her coat sprouted four long, segmented legs that brought her to a stop. With the gait of an insect, the new appendages lifted her above the ground and carried her in a swift charge to meet her foe. Again, red infernal energy knit itself into a weapon in her hand, this time some strange, oblong set of razor-edged whips. She did not care about craftsmanship, only that it could kill and kill painfully. The moment the Mazigorn was within reach, Chasmira slashed at it in a frenzy.

But the Mazigorn was no mere brute beast. It was the most cunning of predators, and it knew a blind rage when it saw one. It lunged inside her attacks, accepting deep lashes across its back and shoulders. At first Chasmira smiled at the lines of black gore that spurted from the wounds, but her smile fell away as the Mazigorn grabbed one of the segmented legs and ripped it off.

"NOOO!" Chasmira cried as it grabbed another leg and spun, hurling her to the snow. She landed so hard, everything went double in her vision. She saw two of the Mazigorn as it leapt onto her, tearing at the insectoid limbs she had created.

Chasmira's visceral scream was almost inhuman. She fought back with every enchantment she had. Long spikes grew from her clothing to impale the monster, but it brushed them aside as easily as cobwebs. Weapon after weapon materialized in her hands, but they were seized and broken just as quickly as she could conjure them. She doused the Mazigorn in flames over and over until the fire was pouring out of her mouth and nostrils, too...

The Mazigorn roared as it ripped off the last of the segmented legs from her enchanted coat, which then shriveled and browned as if it was a dying leaf. "You cannot win."

Fiery tears, like streams of red-hot metal, sizzled down her cheeks. "I don't care! You killed my husband! You will have to kill me too! Do it! Kill me!"

The Mazigorn stared down at her.

"You need to die! You killed him! Kill me too! Do it! Kill me!"

It was no longer fighting her. It was holding her down.

She crumbled into angry sobs. Snow began to fall.

"I did not kill your husband."

Strands of steam rose from the white ground as her tears burnt into it. "Then who did, and why?"

The Mazigorn let go of her. It stood over her, looking down at her pathetic, crumpled form in the snow. "I know not, and I care not, but I will not kill you. I have no taste for someone in such a state. You have no fear, no, not even of dying. Your heart is stale with grief, Chasmira. It is colder than any winter, with such bitterness and pain inside it."

She shivered and wept. "What do I do?"

The monster started to lumber away, snow rolling off its crimson hide. It cast one more glance back over its shoulder at her. "Make the choice that all things do: stay here, or live on."

Chasmira lay there in the snow, watching the snowflakes fall down on her and listening to the trees rattle in the wind. The fire in her eyes died. She stared skyward and waited for the Mazigorn's words to make sense. The dispassionate grey sky above had about as many answers as she did. *How does one live on?*

CHAPTER 35

Not a word was spoken when Chasmira returned home. The Beastkin saw her ride back to the fortress on her ivrit, but they knew not how to interpret the outcome of her journey. The sentries received her without questioning where she went. The servants did not even bow to her as she walked by, for they were too frightened of her haggard appearance and hollow stare. She was numb, and not just from the cold outside. She had found just enough space for her rage, and now even that had come to nought. She was empty.

She ascended the stairs with ice and snow still caked on her clothing. Dragging herself into the room, she let herself fall into bed.

There, she cried like she never had before. The pillows packed around her face were a void into which she could scream and pour out the agony that had festered inside her. Out came the despair and frustration. Out came the hatred and rage. Out came the sorrow and loneliness. Out came the wailing and sobbing, all into the void.

She resurfaced, unaware how much time had passed, if any at all. She was oblivious to the time of day when she returned. Blearily, she looked out the window and saw nighttime. Whether it was now night, or still night, she had no idea. Her limbs ached. Her eyes ached.

There was a soft knock at the door, but Chasmira had no strength to reply. The door creaked open.

"I feared you would not return," he said.

Wilvrey.

Turning around in bed felt like dragging a boulder. Bringing herself to look him in the eyes was even worse. "So did I," she said.

Worry was etched on his face. "Where did you go?"

She could not even feel the tears as they fell. "I thought the Mazigorn killed him. I went to find it."

He approached as if stepping too loudly would shatter her. "And did you find the monster?"

She nodded.

"You didn't kill it."

She shook her head.

Wilvrey brushed her cheek with the back of his hand, pulling it away in surprise. "Gods, you're like ice. Come on, let me get you to a fire."

She made no protest, no reply, as Wilvrey lifted her effortlessly in his arms. He carried her to his room, which glowed with orange light from the fire. The warmth of the room brought some color back into her cheeks, and she breathed in the sweet smell of amber that rose from scented candles on the floor.

"You look better already," he said, brushing back her hair and looking at her tired eyes. "But you need sleep. You look hollow as the new moon."

"I'm not sure I could sleep if I tried, Wil."

"When was the last time you ate?"

She sighed. "I have no use for food."

He paused, looking at her in that way only he did. His green eyes beckoned to her. "Then what do you want?"

"I… I really do not know what I want."

Wilvrey pulled her in close. He took her by the shoulders, stroking them with his strong hands.

"I do. I know what it is that you want."

"Do you?"

"Yes. To be truly unafraid."

She shuddered. "I have forgotten what that feels like."

"Let me remind you, then. It feels like having no secrets, no pretenses, no looking over your shoulder… to be truly yourself, to be truly powerful."

"You see this in me?" Her lip trembled as she spoke.

"I used to. The very first day that I met you, when I looked into your eyes and I saw unholy fire. I saw something incomprehensibly dangerous and from that moment, I knew I wanted it. Give it to me now. Give me the fire inside your eyes, the war inside your mind. Give me the Chaos in your soul."

"You know not what you ask," she said through grit teeth. Tears burned in the corners of her eyes. "You don't want that. You don't want me."

"Yes, I do."

She struggled to pull away from his embrace. "You want something you can use. Something you can ruin."

"Yes, and so do you, Chasmira."

Wilvrey's words struck her with the force of a thunderbolt.

She had ruined things by mistake over and over in her life and spent far too much time cleaning up the debris. She *did* want to ruin something intentionally, to finally stop fearing the destruction that had overshadowed her entire life to this point. She wanted to *be* the destruction, *be* the chaos.

From her depths arose a sudden heat, and she suddenly found herself breathless. "Yes."

"Yes what?"

"Yes, I want that. I want this." Her fingertips began to tingle as they found his chest under his shirt. Impatiently, she ripped the shirt open, scattering his buttons onto the floor. She paused, listening to them clatter and roll. The sounds were sharp and clear. The fog she had been living in for months, was gone.

"Why did you stop? Are you still afraid?"

When Chasmira looked up at him, her eyes burned with bright red flames. Her lips curled back in a lustful snarl. "No." Their lips met with breathless, burning passion.

Outside, the wind began to stir and shake the treetops, and thunder rumbled in the distance. Like two hungry ironwolves, Chasmira and Wilvrey clawed each other and sank their teeth into each other's skin. He tore open her dress, his hands greedily grabbing for handfuls of her. The windstorm outside intensified as thunderbolts flashed by and shook the room.

As he carried her past fragrant candles and satin veils, she slid down, placed her feet on the floor, and shoved him back on the bed.

"You're still full of tricks, enchantress," he panted.

"Am I *that* enchanting?"

"By the gods, yes."

Sitting atop him, she pressed her hand over his mouth. "Speak not of the gods. The gods are not welcome here. Here burn my unholy flames that you have kindled..."

In his eyes was lust equally unholy. "Then tomorrow let the rising sun find only my ashes."

ψ

The dawn light crept cautiously through the forest. Its warm, gentle light trickled through the morning mist and glittered on the dew. Like a skittish animal, it vanished behind the broken, black cloudbanks when they rumbled, waiting a minute before it dared shine again. As it reached deeper into the forest, the sunlight discovered many fallen trees cast down by the furious windstorm overnight.

The servants had supplied the room with fresh brandy and hot breakfast. The bedside table was almost overflowing with buttered wheatcakes, boiled eggs with paprika, smoked sausages, and candied fruit.

"Quite a feast," said Wilvrey as he piled food onto a plate. He was ravenous this morning. "But nothing like the feast I enjoyed last night, My Lady."

Chasmira lay with her head on his chest, breathing in the scent of his skin. His naked body was so warm, almost hot to the touch. Her wild bed hair clung to both their bodies in splayed curls. It was as if they were two puzzle pieces that perfectly fit against one another, she thought.

He grabbed a handful of her hair, brushing it away from her face to see how peacefully she rested. Setting his breakfast plate down on the blanket, he rested one arm across her bare back as she lay. She sighed contently.

"You have given me everything," Wilvrey said as he cut into his food. "What can I give you? Surely there is something you want."

She had no inhibitions about the question anymore. "Originally, I wanted the Guardian City destroyed. That's why I came here. I wanted it wiped off the map forever."

Wilvrey stared at her incredulously. "That's it? That's all you wanted? If that's all you wanted, you could have just told me." He did not inquire any further, not even why she wanted this. He simply washed his mouthful down with another sip of brandy.

She began to laugh, harder than she expected. For nearly two years, her need for revenge against Nandrzael had been her best-kept secret, and now that she finally let it come to light, Wilvrey cared nothing about her motives. Destruction for its own sake was enough for him.

"We need not destroy the Guardian City ourselves, you know. Our army can be put to better use than to break itself against Argismora."

She was intrigued. "How so?"

"Well, consider that the lords of Whiteshore and Farholdt rule westward, beyond Dimol Gol and the Mountain of Iron. Long did they vex our land decades ago, wishing to conquer us and then march to Eppenhorn to take it. We withstood them many times, but neither my grandfather nor my father had the strength to retaliate directly against them."

"What do you propose?"

"An offer they cannot refuse. Since they know they cannot defeat us, we will offer to them an alliance to join us in an assault against Argismora. The arrogant old bastards will inevitably want the glory, claiming the northern ridgeline—a grand prize no lord could ever claim alone."

She smiled at his manipulative genius. "Brilliant, Wil."

"Naturally," he chuckled, taking another drink of brandy. "But the invitation cannot come from me. They will never trust the extended hand of Wilvrey the Serpent, as well they should not. No, this invitation must come from you, My Lady."

"Me?"

"Of course you. You are Chasmira, who stood at court with the mighty Magnate Argolvrecht and so many others. Trusted advisor, dark seer, and survivor of the war at Dimol Gol. They know not where your loyalty lies."

"It lies with you," she replied, kissing and gently biting at the flesh of his hip.

He chuckled, running his hand through her hair sweetly. "As far as they know, you may well be standing at *their* side in another six months. They've every reason to trust you."

"In that case, I will write to them, welcoming them to join us against our common enemy. And what will we do when they are trapped, at your mercy?"

She could feel his excitement welling. Before she could even react, Wilvrey gripped her by the hips and moved her where he wanted her. The plate of food crashed to the floor, but neither of them cared. "We will crush them between our cavalry and the unbreakable walls of the Guardian City. The blood of man and beasts will mingle in the valley, red and rich. It will be a graveyard for our old enemies." He covered her mouth with his hand. A deep growl rose from his chest, and he sank back in bed to revel in the pleasure. "Then, my conquest of these lands shall begin. Argismora can keep the northern ridgeline. From the mountains to the sea, all of West Jacore will be mine."

ψ

The next two weeks went by like a whirlwind. Chasmira's letters to the lords of Whiteshore and Farholdt were some of her finest persuasion yet, she thought. To perfectly ensure their safe delivery, she asked Morth to personally deliver them to the mountain kingdoms. The Ogre dutifully accepted, departing with a troop of ivrit riders as an escort. Wilvrey had summoned back his army from their leave, and they returned rested and readier than ever for the roar of battle.

Nyell was hard at work in the kitchen when she recognized the scent of pomegranate perfume. She wiped off her hands and turned from the cooking pot to greet Chasmira as she entered.

"Morning, milady."

"Morning, Nyell! My my, the entire kitchen smells edible. What in the world are you making today?"

"Lart killed a wild boar yesterday. I've got the meat in a stew on the fire, along with garlic, rosemary, and fresh tomatoes from the fields. Should be ready in time for lunch."

Chasmira sneaked an unused slice of tomato off the cutting board, savoring a bite of the sweet, juicy fruit.

Nyell could only bite her tongue for so long. "Milady, I hope you won't mind if I speak freely."

"I never do," she answered, smacking her lips.

"Why are you allowing this?"

Chasmira's brow furrowed. "What am I allowing?"

"What, indeed. I'm talking about Wilvrey. He comes to you and takes whatever he wants, shamelessly. In the kitchen… in the yard… Really, Chasmira, stop it."

"No, you stop. I've a right to happiness as much as anyone. Sorry if it vexes you to see it."

Nyell pursed her lips tightly. "Is it happiness though?"

"Close enough," she mumbled back.

"I know it's not love."

"Well, damn it, it's something," Chasmira snapped. "Something better than a cold bed or the condemning stare of my child wondering why her father is gone. Something rather than the stupid, dead nothing I have felt for months, Nyell. At least I feel *something.*"

Nyell's eyes were full of pity. "I understand it's filling a need, but you're filling it with something harmful. You know that he's using you, don't you?. Wilvrey doesn't see people as people, he sees them as things."

"All I know is that being with him has thawed what felt like ice in my blood. I feel alive again. That's all I care about and all I need." She turned and left, slamming the kitchen door so hard that the glasses in the cabinets shattered.

CHAPTER 36

"If you had told me a year ago that I'd be married twice by now, I would have said you were mad," Chasmira said, sipping some of the dark liquor from her goblet. Wearing nothing but a white smock, she slowly rotated herself in front of a full-length mirror as two seamstresses took her measurements. She hummed the tune she learned last night, when two lutists played in the garden while she and Wilvrey made love there. She turned and tugged at the neckline of her garment so she could admire the tender bruises he left on her breasts. He had not proposed marriage yet, but she knew it was inevitable. In order to secure the throne, he would have to marry, and she wanted to be as prepared as possible.

The door to the room opened, and before the servant could announce who was there, Emorya swept into the room. She wore a plated leather tunic that, as usual, left her muscular arms bared. About her shoulders was a fur-lined brown cape, which matched the riding clothes she wore.

Seeing her in the mirror's reflection, Chasmira smiled. "Emorya dear, from your garb I would assume there is warm weather today?"

"Quite warm for spring, yes," she said, tugging her gloves off.

"Nyell told me you were having a dress made. I see she was right. Special occasion?"

Busybody, she thought. "Oh, just some new gowns. Some formal, some everyday. I lost a bit of weight over the last few months, and my wardrobe doesn't fit quite like it used to. Just look at my collarbone!"

"Of course, of course, makes sense." Emorya maintained her cool demeanor, seeing right through Chasmira's lie. "You know, it has not escaped my notice that you and Wilvrey are quite... involved. Surely it's all for cheap thrills and nothing more?"

The sorceress sighed. She waved off the seamstresses, dismissing them from the room before she finally turned around to face Emorya. The long-held eye contact between the two women told the entire story. Chasmira could see the disappointment in Emorya's eyes, and Emorya could see the confusion in hers.

"What's really going on, Chasmira?"

"I wish I knew."

Emorya sat down on the side of the bed and smiled. "I'm all ears. It doesn't even have to make sense, just start talking."

She wrestled with the words. "From the moment I met Wil, there has always been something in the way he looks at me. Seeing past my defenses, seeing his way in."

"He's devious that way."

The barb was intended for Wilvrey, but Chasmira felt it. "I wouldn't call it that. It's just his way, his strange way." She sat down on the bed next to her. "When I'm around him, things become so simple. I used to hate it, but it's so easy. You and I could talk all day about someone who brings out the good in you, but what about someone who brings out the *bad* in you… and you like it?

Emorya pinched the bridge of her nose. "Look, I'm not even trying to get on you about Wilvrey. It's not about him, it's you. I know you're trying very hard to forget about this, but Chasmira, you lost your husband to an assassin just four months ago."

The reality burned to think about. She folded her hands in her lap and sighed.

"You have been so deeply distressed in your mourning. You are suffering a pain I have not experienced. I have never married, and my father and brother still live."

"I miss him every day," Chasmira said, surprised at the stillness of her own voice. She expected herself to be shaking. "We would always tease and banter when we were together, and it was wonderful. He was never the sort of man who easily spoke his mind, but when he did it was so deep and heartfelt. There were other things too—little ways that he knew how to reach me. Little things that only he and I shared, of which only we knew the significance. Like that dagger he always used to carry around, the one with the blue hilt and the cracked blade?"

She would have gone on, but the look on Emorya's face stopped her. The girl looked pale and wide-eyed, as if she'd seen a ghost.

"Emorya? What's wrong?"

"Your dagger with the blue hilt? It was from Warrick?"

"Yes. What is it, dear?"

Emorya rose slowly from the bedside, as if moving too swiftly would shatter her into pieces. "Wait for me right here, and do not leave this room. I'll be back as quickly as I can."

She slipped out of the room while Chasmira waited in confusion. What had she said that would cause even a hardened warmaiden like her such fright and alarm? She thought about going after her, but she had waited too long. There was no way to tell where Emorya had gone now. All she could do was wait.

Ten minutes passed before Emorya returned, shutting and locking the door behind her. She hunkered down on the bed next to Chasmira, revealing a small object wrapped in black linen.

Their eyes met. Chasmira's were dark with disbelief. She lifted aside the linen folds, knowing already what she would find before she even saw the glisten of the blue hilt. Lifting aside the last bit of linen exposed the blade, the jagged crack forming that familiar diagonal edge.

She pulled her hand back from it so cautiously, one would think it were a snake wrapped in linen, not a dagger. "Where did you get this?"

"We've always had it. In our family, an assassin's blade is defiled by such treachery and unfit for war, so it is sealed away in a crypt underground, beneath this fortress. But when I heard you describe the blue hilt on the dagger you were given, I knew instantly it was the same one."

"The same as what? I do not understand."

"Chasmira…" Emorya looked down, wrestling with her next words. "When Warrick died, we took the weapon that killed him and sealed it away. I was there. I tended to him after you left. I pulled the dagger from him myself. It had been used to cut his throat and then stabbed deep into his chest."

Chasmira gawked at the dagger in shock. She could not draw a breath, as if it were now stabbed into her own chest.

"Does this mean… Warrick used his own dagger to—"

"No," Chasmira choked out the word and swatted at the tears that ran freely down her face. "Warrick has not carried that dagger since the night of the ball at Lord Ovis' villa. He gave it to me in the courtyard after you and I rode home together. How could you not remember?"

Emorya shook her head. "I remember nothing of that night."

"Oh, of course not, you're right. How would you? You were passed out in the yard from all the moonshine you drank. Warrick gave me the dagger as a gift, and I kept it until…"

"Until what?"

Chasmira began to tremble, with emotion she could not quite identify yet. "Until I gave it to Wilvrey."

"Why did you give it to Wilvrey?" Emorya asked.

It all came rushing back like a flood. Wilvrey looming over her, threatening to force her right then and there. The dagger pressed to his throat, and then him talking her down enough to make her drop it. "I did not give it to him. I must have dropped it, one night when I was there with him. I've made a terrible mistake."

Emorya's hands clenched into fists. "He's a monster. I told you, Chasmira. I warned you."

"You did, and I didn't listen to you." She put a hand on the warmaiden's fist. "I played right into his hand, saying yes to him when I was at my weakest. Now I have given myself away, and in so doing I have given him the throne, the power he always wanted."

Emorya unclenched her fists and squeezed Chasmira's hand. "So what are you going to do now?"

"What I should have done that day."

ψ

Wilvrey clambered up the black stone stairs. He could not wait to get out of his doublet. The very sensation of his clothes rubbing against his skin was an irritation after hours outside in them. The day had been long spent inspecting each of the Beastkin's armor and armaments. They were specially tailored for the things, since their size and build was quite different from a Human. He felt the need to personally inspect each of them. To him, his warband was but a single warrior made of many small warriors. Each small warrior represented a scale in a single suit of armor. Each small weapon represented a part of a single sword's edge. Wilvrey wanted no gaps in his armor, no dull parts to his sword.

When he opened the door to his room, he was greeted by the warm ambiance of candlelight. Upon every dresser and table, candles flickered like stars in the night sky. And in the midst of it all, Chasmira lay naked on his bed, a lascivious smile on her face.

He licked his lips. "How did you know I wanted you tonight?"

"Because you want me every night. The question is only when and where," she purred, rolling over onto her belly. "Take me tonight. Now."

Wilvrey's breathing grew heavier, and he began stripping down out of his clothes. As Chasmira watched, she fought hard to govern her expression. Wilvrey would see nothing but mindless lust from her, exactly what he wanted to see.

She knelt on the bed, welcoming him. "You said I would bear your heir. Make good your word now, My Prince."

Wilvrey seized her, and she wrapped her limbs around him. He was tightly muscled, every bit of him, and she felt that deadly strength every single time. It made him dangerous—the kind of dangerous she feared in the past. She had to let him have what he wanted. She needed to let him lower all his guards.

It did not take long. Her neck strained as he held her down by her hair. In the throes of passion, his hands moved to her throat. His powerful body was pressed against her, moving rhythmically. He could not wait any longer, and neither could she. Sliding her hand under the pillow, she drew the broken blue dagger from where she had hidden it. She clutched it tightly, tears throbbing in her eyes.

She slashed blindly with the dagger as hard as she could, over and over. Hot fresh blood gushed on her, running down the bedsheets onto the floor.

CHAPTER 37

Chasmira tiptoed through the corridors of the great House of Mirikinin, wearing nothing but her robe. She had discreetly sent a servant to fetch Nyell, who could hardly stomach the scene of horror before her eyes.

An oath was taken. Whatever assassin had killed Warrick, had returned and killed Wilvrey too. That was the story, the story Nyell was oath-bound to tell forever more, no matter who asked her. She even repeated the story to Chasmira as she helped her scrub the blood from her body, perfuming her and wrapping her in a house robe.

"Do not linger here. I will take care of it," Nyell assured her, and Chasmira stole away out of the room.

Her whole body trembled, still reeling from the shock. She did not tell Nyell that Wilvrey had finished making love to her when she drew the dagger. There was no water that could scrub off the filth she felt. It clung to her, as did the smell of hot blood. Supporting herself against the wall every step, she tiptoed not to her room, but to the only place she felt truly safe: the library.

"Chasmira. Are you alright?"

Luthian.

She did not know why she was surprised to see him, but in

this state anything would have startled her. He stood from his chair, setting down the book he was reading and putting it in the cabinet. There he was, her last refuge. The last son of Mirikinin.

Unable to get a word out, all she could do was walk to him, wrap her arms around him, and hide her face against his chest.

"You're holding me so tightly," he said. "What's wrong?"

She looked up into those dark blue eyes, full of so much soul and quiet sadness. She had no idea what he saw in hers. Did he see unholy fire? Did he see the blood on her hands that she still saw? Did he see the pieces of her heart she had sharpened into weapons? Did he see the Chaos in her soul?

He squeezed her tightly in his arms. His heartbeat echoed in her ear, in the hollow halls of her mind. All he said was, "I'm here."

"I need you more than ever."

"Anything you need," he smiled down at her.

"Your kingdom needs an heir. Take me. Take me tonight."

He stared slack-jawed. "What? No. No."

"I need you, Luthian."

Luthian put his hands on her shoulders, gently creating space between them. "No. I can't, I'm sorry."

"Don't say that. You are all I have. We are all we have."

"What are you talking about? What about Wilvrey? You and he clearly are ready to—"

"He's dead."

A harsh silence hung in the air.

"Dead?" Luthian's eyes widened. "How?"

"He killed Warrick." The words were stony. Unfeeling.

"What? No. He wouldn't."

"But he did. Driven by that jealousy he has always had against him. Wil was denied your father's good favor his whole life, and then he was denied me when I married Warrick. The consequences of his vile actions have come back on him, and Warrick's memory can finally rest."

Luthian began to pace, biting at his nails. "So my oldest brother took the throne, my middle brother killed him to take the throne, and now it is down to me."

"You are the last one left. This is your chance, Luthian. Our chance to end the madness and set all of this right. It's you and me now."

"I can't."

His rejection burned. Chasmira backed away, biting back bitterness as much as she could. "Sorry, in my absence have you become an Ædant? A vow of abstinence is not a good look for you, Luthian."

"It's not that. It's that I-I—"

"What?"

"I don't want to be Prince!" His voice echoed around the room. "I have no desire to sit upon a throne and judge matters of war and law. That… that is not for me."

"You had better warm up to the idea, and quickly. You are the only heir this kingdom can accept. This responsibility falls to you."

"I don't want it. Let it fall to someone else."

She nearly seized him by the collar. "You have no idea what you are saying. This is not a book you can set down and pick up at your leisure. You would forfeit the entire legacy of your father and grandfather. You have a responsibility, Luthian, to that legacy and to me. I came here to restore your father's kingdom after his fall, and I will not see all my hard work undone because of you!

Do you have any idea what I have sacrificed?"

"What if I leave?"

Her heart ached at his words, but Luthian did not even notice as he paced the room, feverishly spinning his plan.

"What if I go, right now, down to the stables and ride an ivrit off into the southern plains, never to return?"

She could hardly believe what he was saying. "Don't leave. I need you here. You can't turn your back on me, on my daughter!"

He backed away from her, seeing the raging flames in her eyes. "Surely there would be another they might choose instead of me. What about Lart?"

"Lart? He cannot even rule his own dog. Luthian, please!"

"All I want is to be left alone to my books, to my peace. I do not want power and I do not want war. I do not want to become my father!" His shouting echoed in the library. He expected his voice to be one of resistance—even resolve—but all he heard was his own fear.

Chasmira could hardly take any more. She put her palms on the table and took a few shuddering breaths.

Luthian knelt at the side of the table to look up at her face. "I'm sorry. I know that I'm a coward for saying all of this. Perhaps there is another way. Why do you not just rule the kingdom yourself?"

Chasmira let herself fall backward into the chair. "If I could, I would, but according to the laws of your father and grandfather, a woman cannot inherit the throne alone. When Warrick died, the throne returned to Lord Maram until the next of Mirikinin's sons marries. If all of them forfeit the throne by death or disappearance, Maram will keep the throne, and Lart will become Prince after he dies. In short, I have no power myself, and neither does my daughter," she groaned, cradling her forehead in her palm.

Luthian threw the candlestick off the table in frustration. "Idiotic law! It binds both you and me. It should never have been made."

Chasmira slowly lifted her head in realization. "Then change it."

"What do you mean, change it?"

"The Prince is the only one with the power to change the laws of the kingdom. Marry me. After we get Maram's blessing, you will become Prince and you can change what was written in stone before you."

"I would be able to alter the laws of succession…"

"Yes. You would even be able to delegate your full power to me, to rule in your stead as you while away your time here in the library. You need only wear the crown, and I will go handle the matters of war and law for you."

"Yes… Yes, that would work." He ran his hands back through his dark locks, finally able to catch his breath. "So long as I can give you the throne, I will marry you. I am not cut out for that kind of responsibility."

"Not all men are," she said, squeezing his arm. She could feel the tension already leaving his body. "That does not make you any less of a man."

He put an arm around her. "Thank you."

She sighed in relief. There was no time to lose.

"We will make plans after I speak to Uncle Maram tomorrow."

"We'll make our plans right now." Chasmira shoved him back with both hands, sending him toppling down onto the table.

Before he could get back up, she was straddling him.

"Chasmira—"

Luthian put his hands on her to lift her off, but a passionate kiss smothered any notions he had about resisting her. When she breathlessly parted their lips, dark red fire kindled in her eyes. He panted as her fist closed around his hair and held him down. "We are not leaving this room until I am done with you. I came here to bear your heir and that is *exactly* what is going to happen."

CHAPTER 38

It was Marb Sod, the sixth month, when Luthian and Chasmira married upon the southern hillside. She took her vows of love, faith, and honor wearing a dress of deepest crimson, and upon each seam were tiny metal spikes that hung like tassels and jingled a sort of quiet, macabre tune with every move she made.

The wedding feast after the ceremony was pleasantly quiet, almost somber. About a hundred guests attended, most of them vassals of the House of Mirikinin. Without doubt the guests had many questions surrounding Wilvrey's recent death, but most of them accepted that where family politics were concerned, there would be no asking and no answers. This was a joyous occasion, and a necessary one, for Luthian was the only heir of Prince Mirikinin that remained. Some even went so far as to attribute this marriage to an ancient rite that a brother should marry his brother's widow, and said that Warrick would be happy.

Luthian and Chasmira took the opportunity to present his first written proclamation, altering the laws of succession to make Princes and Princesses equal rulers. In the event of one's death, the other could retain the throne as long as they liked before passing it to whichever of their children they wished. All it would take is one press of the signet ring to make a new future.

Several times, she caught herself resting her hand upon her belly, sensing new life deep within herself like the flickering of a newly lit candle. *It is Luthian's*, she told herself almost hourly. If only saying it would make it so. If only life had such reassurances, but it does not. The only thing Chasmira could be sure of, was that she could not be sure of anything.

By sunset, Chasmira was growing more and more agitated. Luthian did not even have the chance to ask what was troubling her before she excused herself and returned from the southern hill back to the fortress. The most important task was still incomplete.

She was alarmed at how loudly her own footsteps echoed in the audience chamber. No servants tended to the house, for all were outside accommodating the wedding feast. Upon the black throne sat Lord Maram watching her from the shadows as he did the very first day she arrived. As he did with her first wedding, he had shunned the ceremony and the feast out of sheer protest. Not that he had been invited anyway, but he clearly stated his refusal before getting any offer.

Chasmira came forward, already seething at his stubbornness and arrogance. "It is done according to your idiotic custom. Luthian and I have wed. Give me the blessing."

Maram stared stonily at her, unanswering.

She was out of patience for this old man."Give it to me."

"My blessing is for my brother's sons," he said, voice darker than the new moon, "Not for usurping whores."

Chasmira's eyes glowed with anger. "I have done more for this family than you or anyone else in it! You sat unawares on the brink of ruin at the hands of betrayers and backstabbers who would have killed you *all.* At the very least, the bloodline of your brother persists because of me. He will have heirs now."

"Heirs of what? Destruction? I was right about you. From the moment you entered this house, I knew that you were poison. I should have let you walk out of that door. Instead, foolish, arrogant old man that I am, I let your seducing lies crawl into my ears like worms. You lured us into fighting your war, witch. There will be no blessing."

Chasmira's fists tightened, and she began to slowly ascend the steps toward him. "I warn you, I have been denied blessings by higher powers than you, and they met with a disastrous fate."

As ever, Maram did not so much as flinch. "You killed my brother, and you've killed two of his sons already. I will not let you take the third."

And from the darkness, there came a roar of primordial force.

No.

Chasmira's world went white before her eyes.

She felt the hard stone of the floor against her back and her side, sliding until she hit something equally hard. Her eyes burned. Flashes in her vision cleared away, and blurry images became clear. At the top of the steps was the black throne and the pale, haunting face of Maram rising in that cloud of darkness as he stood.

She could not feel her fingers. She lifted them and saw they were white as ash, wavering numbly at the ends of her hands. Indeed, they were ashen, for one of her fingers crumbled partially away into dust. She gasped. By sheer force of will, she had resisted the power that could have turned her into powder, but she was doubtful she could do it a second time. Against such magic the mind is strong, but the body is fragile.

Out of the darkness gleamed the three sharp prongs of the iron staff. It rumbled with destructive might, and Chasmira could feel the vibration in the stone beneath her.

"So, this is what it feels like to hold death itself in your hands." Maram said, breathless with both awe and glee. "Our dark executor Hakon described it to me many times, but nothing compares to actually wielding it myself."

Her back was against one of the pillars of the audience chamber. The flowering vines on it trembled. *I have to get out of here.*

Maram's gravelly voice called her attention back to him. "You will plague us no longer, witch. By the very power you have borne into this house shall you be destroyed."

She leapt up and lunged behind the stone pillar. *He must see me to use it on me,* she reassured herself. That terrible roar once again filled the chamber, and the walls flashed brightly with cold, white light. Silt trickled down from the ceiling as the fortress shook.

Too close. She needed to take it out of his hands, but if he saw her it would take little more than a thought to summon the power of the staff. She would die instantly. Her eyes darted around the room vainly, for any attempt to ascend the steps to reach the way out would mean Maram seeing her.

He must see me to use it on me, she repeated, this time hearing herself and forming a desperate plan. The room was lit by two hanging braziers of burning coal, one on either side. With a whispered word, she summoned infernal energy in her hands and formed it into two discs. She grasped them as tightly as she could, for she could barely feel anything in her fingers…

"Face your fate!" Maram's voice echoed. He was close. "There is no escape."

There was no margin for error. Spinning to one side, she hurled a disc at the brazier, cutting the chains that held it to the ceiling. It fell with a crash, and flaming coal and ash scattered across the floor as that side of the chamber went dark.

She spun, keeping her momentum, and let go of the other disc just as she met Lord Maram's eyes between the pillars.

"THERE you are!"

A roar of primordial power.

A crash of metal and coal.

A bright white flash in the darkness.

Maram's laugh was a breathless snarl. He was no sorcerer. Sorcerers were gifted with force of will beyond that of normal mortal beings, enough to comprehend the primordial tongues and summon arcane power with ease. Maram was a warrior his whole life, with his will steeled against pain, blood, and the fear of death. Coupled with his hatred, his will was sufficient to call forth the power of the iron staff, but his head throbbed from the effort. His gnarled hands tightened their grip. The staff was growing hotter after each use. White strands of smoke, thin as spiderwebs, trailed from the staff's three sharp prongs. Maram squinted hard, searching for her. The faint red glow of the scattered coal was the only light.

"You make darkness your ally? No surprise. Come out, creature, and face your ending." His voice was like the noise of a tree branches against a roof in a storm. Maram circled the pillars, staff at the ready for the moment he found her.

She came leaping out of the darkness behind him, grabbing hold of the staff to rip it from his hands. He spun, nearly throwing her off her feet as she clung to the weapon. When she stood up straight again, she pressed her back against Maram to place herself between him and the staff in his hands. He was stronger than she expected. Thin and gnarled with age as he was, Maram had been a warrior in his youth. She pushed as hard as she could to break his grip but could not, for her fingers were still numb from repelling the staff's power.

They struggled, running into the pillars and nearly falling down to the floor. Maram now pulled the staff much tighter to himself, and Chasmira realized he was trying to get it under her chin to break her neck. She fought back, but another of her ashen fingers folded and crumbled away.

The staff was smoking, with glowing white cracks along its surface. It needed to cool down between uses, but Maram did not know that.

There was nothing else she could do.

"Burn."

Fire poured from her eyes and onto the middle of the staff in front of her face. Squinting, Chasmira changed the fire from a bright yellow blaze into two focused, blue beams. The iron quickly started to flake apart as white light shone out of it...

It cracked in two in a tremendous blast. Strands of bright white energy arced outward, painting themselves on the floor and walls like bands of glowing liquid silver. Chasmira went spinning across the floor, totally disoriented in the darkness. Pieces of the staff clattered loudly across the stone, and dead silence followed. She groaned. Her back was in splitting pain. Slowly, she rolled over and clawed the stairs to climb out of the audience chamber.

Her head jerked back as Maram's hands clamped around her throat. His foot slammed down into her back, holding her down, and he pulled back on her neck to break it. She gagged and strained, purple veins flashing under her clenched eyelids.

She kicked her legs wildly, and one kick took Maram's foot out from under him. He fell on top of her, grabbing a fistful of her hair and smashing her face onto the marble step. She tasted blood from her now split lip.

Instead of pulling away, she arched her back and slammed Maram's face with the back of her head. Once, and then again. She heard his nose break, and at last he let go of her.

She rolled over and crawled backward a few steps. Her vision was spinning from the blow to the head, but she could make out white glowing shapes scattered across the floor. *The shards of the staff,* she realized. Chasmira lunged forward, half-running, half-crawling. Her knees and the heels of her hands stung from hitting against the black stone floor as she searched. At last she saw it: the three-pronged end of the staff.

She could hear Maram approaching behind her, panting and moaning in pain. She did not even look back. Scrambling forward, she fell on top of the staff shard, grabbed it with both hands, and rolled on her back just in time to see him lunging down at her.

A short gasp echoed in the audience chamber. Lord Maram collapsed to the floor, the three prongs of the iron staff piercing through his chest and out his back.

Chasmira trembled like a leaf in the wind as she tried to stand. Her head throbbed and her back seized, sending her crashing to the ground. Her hands were numb and missing fingers. The room was spinning, and she was quickly losing her battle against an irresistible urge to lie down and sleep. Her heartbeat pounded in her ears, but it sounded like distant echoes under murky water.

She locked her elbows and bit her tongue, using the pain to stay conscious as she crawled to the pillar and clutched the flowering vines. "No… No… This is not how I die."

Chasmira gasped, and the castle rumbled like a quaking mountain. All at once the vines shriveled away and crumbled like dust as she sucked away their life to heal herself. She stretched her back cautiously, feeling it pop once or twice. She sighed in relief, but then was struck with a stab of panic.

Slowly, she raised a hand to her belly and touched it. The tiny fire inside her still glowed persistently, and Chasmira could finally catch her breath. She flexed her hand, happy to see the missing fingers had been restored as well. She rose with both hands clenched into fists.

A blast of white-hot fire reduced the fallen Maram to a mere memory in seconds. Where he once laid there was nothing but a crusty pile of ash that she disdainfully kicked aside until she unearthed the signet ring. She picked it up and admired it in the light of her own eyes.

The throne seemed to beckon to her. She ascended the steps—each hewn from the blackest marble—and took her place there upon the seat of power.

Hakon was right. This view is splendid.

CHAPTER 39

The very next morning, in the sunlit yard of the House of Mirikinin, Prince Luthian sealed his first proclamation into law. Immediately after, he made his second proclamation: that Princess Chasmira would possess the throne and the full ruling power over the kingdom. After sealing it into law, Luthian ceremoniously removed the signet ring from his hand and held it out to her.

"Princess, I believe this belongs to you," he said as he placed it on her finger. They sealed it with a kiss under the flawlessly blue summer sky, while baby Otzana—now six months old—poked at the shiny black and gold ring.

"Looks like she already wants her turn," Chasmira joked.

"Now now, give your mother a chance. She'll do fine."

The vassals laughed and applauded, amazed at the changes that had come so quickly into Prince Luthian's reign. Before they departed to return back to their land, each of them complimented the Prince on what humility and courage it took for him to ensure the protection of his ruling bloodline.

When they had all gone, Luthian and Chasmira were only too happy to have their solitude back again. Under the shade of the poplars in the east yard, they finally relaxed. The past month had been nothing short of tempestuous, and there was still more to do.

"More?" Luthian said, slumping down on a couch.

Chasmira rocked Otzana in her arms to soothe her after all the excitement of the morning. "Unfortunately, yes. The lords of Whiteshore and Farholdt may be coming here, if they have accepted a very persuasive offer I sent them."

"Whiteshore and Farholdt? Are they not our oldest foes?"

"They are," she said, wincing as Otzana pulled on her hair. "It is a ruse. I told them we would all attack Argismora together, but the plan is to let them charge and then turn on them, trapping them in the valley."

He weighed the odds in his mind. "Argismora to the north, and us to the south. Nowhere to go. It's not a bad plan."

"It's not, but the mastermind behind it is no longer here to lead his army into battle," she sighed.

"Wilvrey."

"Yes."

He wrung his hands. "Well, what do we do?"

"The warband will be demoralized to hear of their commander's death, but I'm sure Emorya is more than capable of leading them. She fancied herself their second-in-command. Perhaps they did, too."

Luthian rose from the chair, walking out into the sunlight like the weight of the whole world was on his shoulders. Chasmira laid little Otzana in the bassinet under the poplars, where she could nap in the shade. She gently placed the cover over the top before joining him.

Luthian looked off into the summer sky. "What a mess he made. He could not simply leave well enough alone. What happened?"

"Jealousy rotted his heart, as it does to all hearts."

"I knew it was bad, but I knew not it was that bad. How did you ever discover that it was he who killed Warrick?"

She grimaced at the remembrance of it. "The evidence spoke for itself, sadly. He was murdered with a dagger that Wilvrey took from me. It was found in Warrick's chest and assumed to be an assassin's dagger."

"Why did you say nothing about it, all this time?"

"I myself knew nothing of it until recently. The dagger was stowed away according to your family's laws."

At this Luthian paused. "What laws?"

"The laws concerning the weapons of manhunters, that they are considered cursed objects for being an affront to the art of war," Chasmira explained.

"We have never had such a law."

Her brow furrowed and a lump formed in her throat. "You do not seal such things away from the sun in an underground crypt?"

He looked more confused than ever. "I have never heard of such a tradition or tenet. Certainly not in my family. The crypt under this fortress has not been opened since Warrick was entombed."

Chasmira's heart pounded in her ears. This could not be.

"Who told you this, anyway?"

She was shaking visibly. "Where is Emorya?"

"Emorya? She's not here. No one has seen her all day."

"Where is the crypt?"

ψ

The smell of musty air and cold stone was the only welcome to the crypt. Not a sound rose from the dark entryway as Chasmira stepped through it. She expected to hear something: the sound of vermin scuttling or the fortress stone settling, but no. As soon as she stepped over the threshold, a profound silence enveloped her.

Here and there along the ceiling, dim blue lights moved slowly along. Graveling spiders emanated a soft blue light from their abdomens as they lazily rested in fuzzy webbing that striped the ceiling and archways. They were not true spiders, but bulbous fungi that mimicked arachnids while scavenging for corpses and coffin flies.

Along the walls lay dozens of great stone coffins, filled with the remains of Mirikinin's ancestors. The largest coffins stood upright, each of their lids displaying the image of some creature carved into the stone.

"Wilvrey…" a voice called out of the dark crypt.

Chasmira froze. The voice was Emorya's.

"Wilvrey the Serpent…" she continued, "Normally the great princes of the family line are named with the likeness of a beast after they die, when their deeds can be measured by those who survive them. Wilvrey could not wait, so he named his own likeness and spread the word. Ironic, don't you think? It is as if he were dead already long ago, and he knew it."

"Is that how you were able to sleep at night?" Chasmira fumed. "Did you tell yourself they were just dead already?"

A bit of silence. Chasmira rounded a corner, certain she would find Emorya but only found a dead end instead.

"No, just Wilvrey," Emorya replied with a laugh, echoing from far across the crypt.

Chasmira grit her teeth, stalking through the crypt in the direction of her voice. "And what about Warrick?"

"Warrick had to die."

Those four words alone felt like daggers themselves, stabbing deep into Chasmira's chest. She staggered forward, bracing herself against an archway as she gasped. "It was Wilvrey you wanted dead, not Warrick. Not Warrick!"

"Yes, I wanted Wilvrey dead, but killing him would have changed nothing. Warrick was already on the throne, and you were beside him, very content to let him rule over you. You, his happy little wife, bearing him children to take the throne next. Killing him could change everything and look, it did."

"Warrick meant everything to me."

Emorya's words dripped with contempt. "Yes, he meant too much. It clouded your vision, your true purpose! We did this together, you and I. We have changed the world. The laws of succession have been rewritten. The old ways are gone, and a new path lies before us… for me, you, and your daughter. To stand in the shadows no longer but rather in the sunlight, fully and gloriously. Is that not what you wanted?"

Chasmira could hardly believe her ears. "You paved your way to the throne with my husband's blood? I trusted you!"

"And I could not trust you," Emorya answered out of the darkness. "I told you to stay away from Wilvrey, and then I found your dagger in his chambers, lying on the floor. Your dagger, the one Warrick gave you."

"How did you know it was mine? You passed out in your own

vomit in the courtyard the night he gave it to me."

"You thought," she gloated.

Chasmira growled in frustration. "So you're a warrior and an actress too. You planted the dagger so that I would kill Wilvrey for you. Am I supposed to tell you how brilliant you are for this vile scheme?"

"I cannot take all the credit. The hands that held the dagger were mine, but this entire plan was *her* idea."

"Whose?"

"Nandrzael."

Chasmira felt the fire in her veins go cold. She turned slowly and saw Emorya standing at the end of the corridor. In the dim blue glow of the graveling spiders, she was a figure made of pure shadow.

"When at first I saw how Wilvrey was with you, I despaired that he would take you for himself. However, the heavens sent me grace in the form of a glorious Angelic. She reassured me that while Wilvrey was not meant for me, he was not meant for you either. She told me my divine purpose, Chasmira. She told me the future."

"What future?"

"She saw the black throne with me upon it, ruling the House of Mirikinin. It could only be possible with your help, of course, marrying the correct son… the weakest son."

The realization knocked her breathless. "Luthian. That's why you were so pleased whenever I was with him."

"We only needed the other two out of the way, and here we are. We've done it, you and I."

Chasmira's head was spinning. Any grief inside her was

kindling now for a fire that grew hotter with every passing second. "Damn her… Damn her and damn you."

"Damn me? You should be thanking me, Chasmira, for saving you from a life that was never meant for you."

"Not meant for me? I had a husband! I had love and safety! I had a home for the first time since I was eleven years old! You burned it all, and now you will *burn* with it!"

The corridor lit up brightly from the flames that shot from Chasmira's eyes. She snarled with rage, pushing the fire hotter, but soon realized she had lost sight of Emorya. With nothing to consume, the flames died down immediately, and darkness returned to the crypt.

Emorya's laughter echoed from behind her. "Love? Safety? You found a comfortable place to sleep, laid down, and started dreaming. You know that you cannot do that. You need to evolve. You need to stay hungry and keep moving, Chasmira. When the lioness couches down to rest, that is when the hunters catch her and pull out her teeth. Stay on the prowl, and they will never catch you."

She had heard enough. "BURN," she shouted, filling the chamber with fire again. Out of the flames a dark shape leapt toward her. Not Emorya, but a black lioness with claws reaching to tear out Chasmira's throat.

The swipe of the lioness' claws sent her tumbling to the floor. They missed her neck, but they tore deep, bloody lines through the flesh of her left cheek. When Chasmira looked again, she saw the silhouette of the black beast circling back at the end of the corridor. To her great surprise, the lioness then rose up and shifted back into the cloaked shape of Emorya.

"You're a sorceress," Chasmira gasped.

"I'm disappointed all this time you never figured it out for yourself, but it was high time that I come clean. How did you put it once? 'What is greater than blood and glory? Greater than they both is the truth'?"

A chill went through Chasmira. "How-How could you know that? You were not even there."

"One could say, I was a fly on the wall."

Her eyes widened at the realization. "You *were* there. The black firefly at the ball… the black wolf in the yard… the black vulture in the plains… and let me guess, your father Maram's little messenger raven too?"

Emorya shrugged and bowed like a flattered stage performer. "The old arts of Odic Sorcery. Father said that as a child, I would talk in the Odic tongue when I slept and summon rainstorms when I dreamt."

Chasmira had heard enough. The rage inside her finally cooled into simmering indignation. "You will need quite the rainstorm to extinguish the blaze I am about to start. Thank you for telling me who is responsible for all of this, Emorya. Now, if you will excuse me, I'm going to burn Nandrzael's city to the ground." With that, she turned and left. There was no reason for mercy any more. She would pour out upon Argismora the sort of Chaos the Angelics once feared would consume the whole world.

She reached the exit, but when she stepped over the threshold, she suddenly found herself standing in the middle of the crypt again. It took a moment for her to absorb the familiar sight of coffins and wandering graveling spiders around her.

"What illusion is this?" she called out, hearing the anger in her own voice as it echoed in the corridors. She trod through the crypt again, a little disoriented, in search of the exit.

"Burn Nandrzael's city, Argismora? I'm afraid I can't let you do that," Emorya's voice answered distantly.

Chasmira followed the sound. "Oh? Just try and stop me."

When she rounded the next two turns, she found the corridor leading out. However, standing between her and the open doorway was the cloaked figure of Emorya. A wedge of faint blue light fell across her face, illuminating one eye and the circular scar that seemed more prominent in the strange glow.

"I don't have to try," Emorya grinned wickedly.

Chasmira charged at her, summoning a long, serrated sword out of infernal energy. Emorya stepped backward, hands clasped calmly at her waist, out the exit. Chasmira wound up to plunge the sword through her, but when she stepped over the threshold, she again found herself instantly transported to the middle of the crypt.

With an angry scream, she threw down her infernal weapon, which vanished into red smoke when it hit the ground. Through the cold, musty crypt, she could hear Emorya's cackling laughter.

"All your might, and yet you are foiled by a simple enchantment of imprisonment," she laughed.

Chasmira's mind began to race against the panic welling inside her. She had read about this enchantment in the Odic grimoire. She was trapped, possibly forever, or so long as Emorya lived. "Emorya… Some warmaiden you are," attempting to goad her back. "I never thought you were one to flee from battle. Come here and end this," Chasmira growled.

"Oh I will, after a few weeks. If you're not dead by the time I get back, fret not, I will finish what I started. It is best you disappear anyway, since you are standing between me and my future. Although, come to think of it, so is your weak husband and your little daughter too..."

"No! Emorya!" she shouted over and over, but her captor was gone. Like a caged animal, Chasmira rushed to one wall and then to another. Everything in her wanted to run for the exit, but she knew it would be useless. She was a fly caught in an inescapable web. Her thoughts went in frantic circles, grasping for a solution, only to arrive at the same dead end every time. In the eerie silence, the only sound was the voice in her head berating herself for her own naivety, her trust in the one who had lured her into this wretched tomb. Emorya had baited her into eliminating Wilvrey for her, and now she had baited her into this trap too.

In the dim, sepulchral light, she crumpled down onto the ground, her heart aching as she clutched her chest. Then, her fingers brushed against the leather holster still hanging from her belt. In it was the blackwood wand, the wand whose potential power was yet to be unlocked. A spark of hope remained.

The choices she had considered for its power—destruction, restoration, transmission—now seemed like distant memories of another life. There was only one choice, and she knew it with a stark clarity.

With trembling hands, she drew the wand from its holster. Her fingers traced its contours as she began the process of imbuing it with her sorcerous energy. It required only a few minutes of meditation, but in the deafening silence of this prison, with little Otzana's very life on the line, it felt like an eternity. She cursed and concentrated harder.

As Chasmira's consciousness delved deep into the well of ageless arcane power within her, it began to feel like grappling with forces that had long slumbered, untamed and unforgiving. The sensation was surreal: a melding of her very essence with the wand, like intertwining veins of energy. It was as if the wand itself also had a heartbeat. Each pulse of her life essence resonated with the hum of the arcane. Like a dark symphony, it surged and waned, and in these precarious minutes Chasmira played the role of a sorcerous conductor, coaxing the power out of the depths of her being and into the willing vessel of the blackwood wand.

Sweat beaded on her head and trickled down her neck. She could not let her concentration waver, not even for a moment. With every passing moment, her daughter was a heartbeat closer to death. The beastly visages upon the coffins bore witness as the battle for her daughter's life raged against time within the confines of her own will.

CHAPTER 40

The midsummer breeze gently rocked the poplars. Under the shadow of the trees, the bassinet rocked just as gently.

One of the poplars rustled. From its branches emerged a huge black gallowsbird. They were also called noosebeaks, for after catching prey they would land and dangle it in their huge, crushing beaks, before finally breaking their prey's neck and eating it.

Emorya could not have chosen a grislier creature for this.

The bassinet crunched under her clawed feet as she fell upon it, stomping it down. She viciously tore into it with her beak, shredding through linen and wicker weave in search of tender flesh.

"How strange," said a voice behind her. She whirled around to see Luthian standing across the yard, with baby Otzana swaddled in his arms. "I've never seen a black gallowsbird before. Poor thing must be some kind of freak."

Spitting out the remains of the empty bassinet, Emorya shed her beast form and returned to her Human state. She glared at him under the hood of her black cloak. "Clever. How did you know I was coming?"

"A little bird told me," he winked.

"Very funny. What's even funnier is that you've saved me the trouble of hunting you down. Now I can kill you both right where you stand."

"You'll have to kill more than just us."

An arrow struck the poplar right in front of Emorya's face. Luthian had alerted the sentries on the wall, who now loosed arrow after arrow at her.

She lunged behind the cover of the nearest tree, hugging herself against the trunk as one arrow pierced her shoulder pauldron. "Not much of a challenge!" She mocked them with scornful laughter, and began chanting in the Odic tongue.

From nowhere, dark clouds unfurled in the middle of the perfect blue sky. Fierce winds began to gust, and the arrows of the sentries curved off-target.

"Pitiful," she cried over the rush of the wind. "You have no idea what you are facing! Storms slumber deep within my soul, ready to rise at my command, untamed and wild, dancing to the furious drums of thunder!" The wind intensified, ripping the sentries off the walls and killing them on the rocky hillside.

Luthian knelt down, covering baby Otzana with his body as the winds threatened to pull him off his feet. He felt a sharp sting on the side of his ear, and another on the back of his neck. In the grass around him, white hailstones bounced as they fell.

Emorya cackled her incantations to the sky, beckoning it to grow even darker. Thunder burst forth from the growing clouds as bright flashes leapt overhead. The winds and hail beat down with increasing fury, battering Luthian as he shielded the infant in his arms. The hail was starting to leave cuts and gashes on his head and neck.

He shivered from the cold and the pain as the storm laid down its punishment on him, but he called out, "Yes, you can create quite a storm, but you have no idea how to tame it, do you?"

Emorya watched in shock as Luthian, crouched in the midst of the furious storm, raised his hand to the sky.

"Let me show you!" The wind whipped the blood from his stinging wounds across the lawn like red raindrops. Hugging baby Otzana close, he grit his teeth, shut his eyes, and spoke with a voice like thunder itself:

"HIMINNSOKN!"

The earth shook with the force of the thunderbolt. It roared down in a brilliant blue flash, splitting the poplar into two twisted, smoldering halves. Blackened roots reached out of the smoking crater left at its base. The hailstorm stopped immediately, and the winds died down to a cold breeze. Thunder still rumbled hesitantly in the sky, and the black clouds softened to a somber grey as they continued churning overhead.

"Nyell!" Luthian shouted, and the housekeeper came running across the yard to take the wailing infant from him. "Get her inside and somewhere safe. This storm is not over yet."

She lingered only a moment to ask, "But what about you?"

"I will check the damage."

While she scurried inside with the baby, Luthian stood and trudged to the edge of the crater.

There lay Emorya, shattered and burnt. She groaned weakly, barely able to move her head to look at him. Her voice was a broken, dry croak. "You fool… She is born from the very womb of evil. The same dark fire burns in her... She has her mother's eyes."

Luthian stared coldly down at her, blood trickling in thin streams down his face and shoulders. "No, she has Warrick's eyes," he said as he turned his back on her and walked away.

He had gone about ten steps when he shouted over his shoulder, "HIMMINSOKN!"

After the second thunderbolt fell, the day sky returned to its normal placid blue, and the warm sun shone again.

ψ

An hour later, Luthian laid face-down in his bed, bandages thoroughly wrapped over his back, neck, and head. The hailstones left a hundred painful, bruising, bleeding welts all over him.

"So, when were you going to tell me you could read Odic?" Chasmira asked, sitting in the armchair nearby.

"Sometime when I wanted to show off," he laughed, wincing.

"Why did you not just tell me?"

He pondered the question for a moment. "I was scared. When we opened the grimoire, what once looked like unintelligible magic runes scribbled on old pages when I was a little boy, suddenly made sense to me. It spoke to me on a deeper level, a level I was not prepared for yet."

She nodded. "Growing up is like that."

"I suppose it is."

"So you watched me practice instead?"

"I did. I read the entire grimoire over and over again when you were not there, and after you married Warrick, I began practicing the meditation and incantations by myself."

"Even though I struggled, you still learned?"

He laughed a little at his answer before sharing it. "I think I learned *because* you struggled. I didn't just watch the way you concentrated, or the way you spoke the Odic tongue. I watched you overcome the doubt and disappointment that comes with discovering something new about yourself, something uncertain. I watched you overcome fear."

She smiled at the irony. "And it helped you overcome your fear?"

"Yes, I think it did."

"I'm glad to have inspired you," Chasmira said, getting up and kneeling down at the bedside to look him in the eyes. "And thank you for saving my daughter."

He smiled at her. "If not for you warning me, I would not have been able to. You finally decided to make it a wand of transmission, eh?"

She lifted the blackwood wand and admired it. "It wasn't my first choice, but circumstances being what they were, the decision made itself for me."

"I admit, having you in my head was pretty frightening at first."

"Get used to that. We're married now."

Luthian groaned. "You had to remind me. Where's the grimoire? I want to see if it's possible to self-thunderbolt."

Chasmira laughed, and kissed him on the cheek. "Well, you ruminate upon the possibilities, Luthian dear. I will leave you to rest until the healing potions are prepared."

"Where are you going?"

"Me? I have a lot to do now as a wife, mother, and princess. I need to check on Zana, approve the dinner menu with Nyell, and probably speak with the farmhands about planting a new tree," tapping her chin in thought. "Oh, and tomorrow I'm going to destroy Argismora."

CHAPTER 41

Morth's hut was still. No stew bubbling on the fire, no rumbles of snoring from the bed, no clouds of pipe smoke swirling in the rafters. It was empty save for the tiny pale figure of Wisp sweeping the floor. Their little broom was nothing more than a cluster of bird feathers lashed to a small stick, yet Wisp diligently chased the dirt and dust into the corners.

A warm breeze rolled in the front door as it swung open. Soft dawn light cast itself over Wisp, but a shadow replaced it just as quickly. Chasmira loomed like a ghoul: her hair wild, her eyes aglow. Her dark silhouette bristled with spikes, for she wore the ironwolf fur cloak that Wilvrey had gifted her. When she moved, it rang softly with the noise of a hundred knife blades rubbing against each other.

"I told you, you should leave."

"We have to wait for Morth," Wisp said.

"Peeeep," Peep agreed.

She sighed and swept into the room, stepping over them. "You do not understand. This is a time of *war*, you two. We cannot know who will come back, who we can wait for. Morth has been away for weeks."

Wisp giggled, "Oh, Morth will come back, he wouldn't forget

about us. He was just delivering your message."

"Peeeep."

Chasmira pinched the bridge of her nose and knelt down. "It hasn't anything to do with forgetting. In war, not everyone returns home. Where we are going, many will not return. We know not what all awaits us, nor if we are enough."

"Then why are you going?"

"Peeeeeep?"

"Because we must," she said. "I thought I had taken a better path by letting the past lie. But I realize now it never truly laid down. It waited for me to forget it, and then it followed. The fact is that the past will never lie down and die. You must kill it. You must hold it down and run it through over and over again and then burn it. You must be relentless in killing the past, or it will haunt you. It will take everything from you if you let it."

Chasmira's own voice sounded strange to her. It sounded heavy with the losses she had suffered, dark with the pain she'd endured. Here she stood wrapped in iron quills, in the skin of an untouchable beast. Her eyes filled with bitter tears and she clenched her teeth trying to fight them back. "My sweetest friend, what have I become?"

Wisp looked up at her. "Exactly what you needed to."

"You cannot stay here. If I fail, Nandrzael's wrath will fall upon this place and all herein."

Wisp reached out for her hand. Chasmira hesitated, as if touching them would somehow stain them like wine on a white dress. Wisp stepped forward and wrapped their soft little hands around her fingers. "Then make sure you come back. Peep and I'll be waiting right here for you, like always."

Her gaze fell, and she nodded somberly. There was innocence yet to protect at home: Wisp, Peep, and her precious little Otzana. She looked up and tried to smile, but she could not find it in herself to do so. Instead she gave one last lingering look down at them before she turned and left.

As she walked from the hut, war drums pounded louder and louder. The warband had assembled outside the walls.

"Princess," the quartermaster said with a bow.

"Is the koga ready?"

"Yes, as you commanded. Every one of them girded and armed."

They strode out of the front gate together. Her ivrit was waiting for her, with gleaming black armor around its head and neck to protect it in a cavalry charge. She mounted the beast, getting comfortable for the long ride northward.

She glanced over at the nearest mounted warrior. He was a nightmare of iron scales, black fur, and spikes, topped with a helmet cast in the shape of a wolf skull. The morning light shone in the warrior's eyes, shimmering briefly like silver in the dark recesses of his morbid helmet. Hundreds more stood in rows upon rows, waiting for her to ride. *How fitting,* she thought, *that once I thought commanding a fierce beast with a single word was power. Now I lead an army of beasts without even a single word spoken. That is real power.*

She had barely taken the reins when the long, low blast of a war horn echoed in the air. The ivrits all raised their heads alertly at the sound. Chasmira noticed the beasts all looked westward. Following their gaze, she saw a massive force approaching in the open plains along the border of the forest. The dawn light fell across the thousands of white-armored footsoldiers that marched in formation. Hundreds of riders on huge flightless birds strode beside them. Wooly warbeasts plodded along behind them, carrying siege engines on their backs.

"Princess, are they invaders?" one warrior asked.

"They are," she replied, smiling at the streaming banners of Whiteshore and Farholdt. "Just like us. Let us not keep Argismora waiting."

CHAPTER 42

Nandrzael cursed, tucking back the lock of her pearly hair that kept falling out of place. *Everything must be perfect*, she repeated to herself. *Everything must be perfect.*

She floated horizontally, using the flawless mirror of the lake water to check her appearance. It was a momentous day—the day that Oczandarys' trust in her would be restored. Twenty-two months had passed since her disgraceful failure at the fall of Dimol Gol. All her careful planning, anticipation, and manipulation was about to pay off.

He is coming.

Oczandarys would be there soon. She had dreamed for years about what it must be like to see him shear through the sky, his golden aura leaving a trail lingering behind him. In all her life, she had never seen him in flight. Few had, for Oczandarys moved with speed unmatched by most Angelics, and all but incomprehensible to mortals. She wanted to see it. She wanted to see what nobody else was graced enough to see. She had earned it.

He is coming.

She looked off across the lake, scanning the shore and sky. Nandrzael had been there for hours. *Or have I missed him?*

She frantically snapped back toward the Criterion dome, her

pearl hair falling out of place where she had painstakingly tucked it back. *Is he here already?*

When she arrived at the forecourt, she panicked momentarily. *I cannot enter the dome. Who can tell me if he is here?* She then noticed a familiar Angelic sitting cross-legged on a stone bench, reading from a book.

"Vametheon," she greeted him, dropping down in front of him.

His eyes sparkled as soon as he saw her. "Ah, Nan. I should have known you were not far behind."

"Behind what?"

"Oczandarys."

Her heart hammered at just the sound of his name. "Is he—"

"Inside already? Yes, he is."

Her heart sank, and her wings drooped. "I was hoping to have caught him before he entered into the hallowed chamber. Today he will see that I have corrected the threadline, and all is as he hoped it to be. Today is my redemption, Vam."

He smiled. He loved the way her affections moved so swiftly from one to the next and back again. She was like a leaf on the wind, stirred by every movement. "Words cannot express my relief. I have watched you spinning your web for a long time. Have you caught your fly?"

Nandrzael laughed. "Indeed I have. The sorceress is trapped in a tomb, waiting to join her lovers in death, and my faithful follower has no doubt slain the last of Mirikinin's whelps."

"Peace at last," he complimented her good work.

She beamed proudly. "All I need do is wait."

Vametheon shut his book, stretched his wings, and looked

back at the dome. "Our mighty prince has not been inside long. I wish I could wait with you, but I must carry out my missions."

"Thank you, my friend, but I am more than happy to wait."

CHAPTER 43

It was an hour past sunset when the great bells in the Oracle of Ædant Aculus began to ring. It was not the familiar knell that called them to prayer every Faderdyd at sunrise, nor was it the lively midnight chime of a holiday's observance. It was the clamor of all the gilded spires' bells at once: a full alarm for the city.

Soldiers scrambled to their armories to gird themselves. Those already upon the wall cried out for the city gates to be shut, barred, and barricaded.

The army had assembled in the south forest under the veil of waning daylight, in the hour when shapes are hardest to distinguish. In the dark they moved out into the clearing, displaying what a formidable force they truly were. One by one, torchpoles lit across the front lines. There was no need for ambushes, no point in maintaining an element of stealth. They wanted Argismora's guards to see the glint of steel armor and the cold breath of their mounts. This was pure intimidation.

At the front line was Chasmira, cooly watching as more and more soldiers appeared along the walls of the city.

"They are unprepared. We should charge the gates now," said a warrior beside her, panting with excitement for the battle.

"Your eagerness will be rewarded soon," The sorceress

reassured him. "First, I must speak with the people of the Guardian City."

From her cloak she drew her wand of twisted black oakwood. She shut her eyes, held the wand out toward the city, and took a deep breath. It glowed like a hearth log, crackling with red glow from within. When she opened her eyes, both they and the tip of her wand lit up with bright red flame.

In the sky above the city, a spark quickly grew into a floating fireball. It took shape until it resembled Chasmira herself, fashioned out of fire and speaking with a voice as fearful as a rumbling volcano. Thousands gawked up at the fiery figure hovering in the sky.

"People of Argismora! Where is your divine guardian? Call upon her now, in your hour of need. Go to your Oracle and summon her here to deliver you… or have you already? Have you already called, and she not answered?"

The soldiers upon the wall simply stood in baffled horror, as did all inside the city.

"I am Princess Chasmira, of the lands and legacy of mighty Mirikinin. Look upon us! Look from your rooftops and walls southward. Look upon the army that has gathered, poised to destroy you for her sake. All of us that stand before you, she has taken something from us. From the House of Mirikinin she has taken a father, a son, and a sister. She has taken from me my friend, and last of all my heart. And we will be repaid… for we will break down your walls and take from you your fathers, your sons, your sisters, your friends, and last of all we will take your hearts. We will tear them out of your chests and feed them to our war dogs. There is, however, one way to escape this fate. Renounce her. Renounce the Angelic who blindly you serve. She has abandoned you, now abandon her. Burn the Oracle! Burn it, and when I see the flames burning in the night, we will stop our assault. If you do not renounce her—if you keep your faith—I know it will not be out of love or reverence. It will be out of fear… fear of her wrath. I used to fear it too, but no more. I invite it. In fact, her wrath cannot come swiftly enough for me."

A soft rumble went through the ranks of Argismora's soldiers. A mass shiver at her words, perhaps, or at the urge to run and do as she bade them.

Chasmira waited and watched. She looked from man to man as they stood along the walls, down to the end and then back again. Yet, none of them moved a step from their post. Not one of them yielded. Not a word from the stoic Guardian City.

As she fixed her gaze upon the towering gates of the walled city, an ominous silence descended. With eerie calmness, she said, "So you still abide by her. Very well then. Since you will not be convinced, you will *burn*."

The cataclysmic torrent of Chaos fire she released from her eye sockets was like twin infernal suns. It tore across the field, engulfing the main gates in a massive firestorm. Dozens of the soldiers who lined the battlements recoiled in terror, their faces etched with dread as the flames voraciously licked at the stone walls.

The very foundations of Argismora quaked under the fury of her unleashed power. Its deafening roar echoed through the city's heart. A sense of helplessness washed over all those who stood watching, the sheer magnitude of the sorceress's wrath beyond anything they had ever witnessed. Some unfortunate souls, in their awe and panic, lost their footing and plummeted from the battlements, their cries swallowed by the maw of the relentless firestorm. In that moment, it was not just the city's gates that shook, but the very souls of those who dared to defy her. She stood as an embodiment of vengeance before a city that now trembled in the face of such dark sorcery. Chaos had arrived at their door, and its last offer of mercy was gone.

The firestorm began to die down. Chasmira had sustained it as long as she could, like a singer holding a single note until their breath ran out. She shut her eyes, and smoke streamed from her eyelids. Between her and the gates now lay a field of grey brick, streaked and cracked like ocean waves frozen in place. The earth, once clay and soil and grass, was now a hellish road paved from her army to the city.

The gates of Argismora still stood. The portcullis had melted away entirely, and red flame danced along the face of the blackened doors, but they stood. The soldiers dared to breathe a sigh of relief.

Their relief would be short-lived, for the night air began to fill with the sound of thousands of chanting voices. The soldiers exchanged dark, fearful looks, and someone called for the tower guard to tell where it was coming from. It was not from Chasmira's host, but from the east and west. Out of the shroud of darkness, the armies of Whiteshore and Farholdt closed in on the city from both sides. Great siege towers, already loaded with chanting white-armored warriors, appeared out of the dark, pushed along by massive sloth-like warbeasts.

Hundreds of Argismora's soldiers rushed through the streets and along the walls to reinforce the east and west. Their defenses were spread thinner by the minute, and the commanders knew it. There was no time to mount a more thorough defense: the invaders had not come to encamp and bombard the city for weeks and months, trying to break it. No, they had come to force every soldier in the city to face their mortality this night. This was a fight to the very last man.

Chasmira's voice erupted in a war cry, followed by the thunderous roar of her army as they charged.

The ivrits moved with blinding speed, outpaced only by the storm of fiery arrows that launched over their heads, peppering the wall of the city. Soldiers crouched behind the battlements, watching their fellows fall around them like wilting flowers. The roar of the army grew louder and louder.

Behind the wall, a phalanx of Argismora soldiers watched, crouched with shields raised and spears ready. Behind them, rows of archers stood waiting with bows drawn, ready for the warriors of Mirikinin to begin ramming. They had watched the firestorm scorch the gates and melt the beams. The moment so much as a crack opened in the gates, they would greet Chasmira and her warriors with a hailstorm of arrows.

Instead, they were greeted with an explosion of wood and a thick cloud of ash. The captain screamed his command, and the archers filled the cloud with arrows. When the billowing ash cleared, they saw only a lone figure standing: a towering Ogre covered head to foot in iron scale armor. Just one battle charge, and Morth had shattered the burnt-out gates. Their mouths fell agape, and they looked to their stunned captain for his next command.

He lumbered forward, and the archers panicked to release

another volley that simply bounced off him.

One soldier called out, "Captain—" but it was too late.

The soldier's head was torn off by the first ironwolf that lunged from the ash cloud. Dozens more followed, shrugging off the spears of the phalanx as they charged the shield wall. Morth waded into the fray, crushing anyone unfortunate enough to challenge him. Soldiers screamed and blood gushed upon the streets, but the siege had only begun.

The siege towers had landed on the eastern and western walls, dumping hundreds of bloodthirsty warriors across their drawbridges. The warriors slung explosive blast potions, lighting up the city with rippling rows of red shockwaves. Plumes of smoke began to rise all over.

Chasmira and her cavalry breached the main threshold of Argismora, crossing the charred remnants of the once-formidable gates. She rode at the forefront, her eyes aflame with malevolent power. With each thundering heartbeat, Chasmira unleashed streams of fire that incinerated anything in her path. The city's defenders, overwhelmed by the onslaught, scattered in terror, but their cries of fear and desperation were quickly swallowed by the war cries and blaring horns of the invaders. Hundreds of ivrits' hooves pounded against the cobblestone streets as they surged forward.

The civilians who had not fled cowered in their homes as they bore witness to the nightmarish arrival of their conquerors. Soldiers were torn to shreds by packs of ironwolves, while buildings smoldered and crumbled under the relentless assault. The sorceress's fiery gaze searched constantly for anything that moved, and anything she found was reduced to a black, charred scuff with a single thought. Her infernal fire was her whip upon the back of the Guardian City, a punishment exacted for their blind faith. Every lash cast the shadows of her warriors and warbeasts upon the walls like flickering, malevolent silhouettes that danced over the devastation.

CHAPTER 44

The shadows of the white willows upon the paved forecourt were entertaining for a while. A leisurely walk around the perimeter of the island occupied her for a while longer. Not that Nandrzael counted time when it came to Oczandarys.

She sat at the top of the stairs, knees tucked to her chin, her wings trailing down the steps behind her like the grand train of a bridal gown, but woven out of ten thousand crystal prisms. There she waited, watching the door to that secret chamber of the Criterion, where Oczandarys studied the threads of time.

She imagined him there: his hands, strong as steel and gleaming like bronze in sunlight, playing along the timelines like they were ephemeral strings, and he the musician. She imagined his eyes shut in perfect concentration, and she imagined her lips kissing each eyelid with the gentleness of a spider's footfall.

Time is your preoccupation, and yet it is your plaything too, as am I, she sighed. *While you sit amidst the threads of time, you look outward to see every possible future. You are a scribe of destiny, a high priest of the divine will that goes before us where we cannot follow. Yet, while you judge how best to connect the myriad futures, it eludes you that all futures connect to you. You, who have seen the beginning of all things and possess all knowledge. You, whose very handprints are upon the sculpture of lifekind's worst tragedies and greatest salvation.*

I know that cold, golden stare of yours, and how you are unimpressed by dull, mortal creatures whose mundane lives slip into the same sad, predictable tropes. You deserve something new, something to brighten those eyes again, something worthy of your time.

You watch mortal lives pass like the falling leaves. Would that I could stand with you hand in hand, watching the leaves grow only to fall all over again.

A great rushing noise ripped her from her thoughts. She turned around to see the white leaves of the willows spinning through the air as if they were hurled by a cyclone.

"Nan." Vametheon floated above her, having just arrived with the greatest of speed. "Your redemption may not be as near as you hope. The Guardian City is burning."

No.

The perfect lake water split down the middle as Nandrzael streaked across it like a sunbeam. Clipping the tops of the white trees, she thundered toward the nearest cloudbank that would give way to the night sky below. When she reached it, she closed her wings behind her and dropped like a javelin, falling straight down to the earth.

The mountains and valleys of Grimmgard far below grew closer and closer with every excruciating second. No force could move her quickly enough. Something had gone terribly, terribly wrong.

Smoke from the northern ridgeline bled up into the sky.

No.

She's alive.

CHAPTER 45

Like whispers on the celestial winds, the distant cries of anguish guided Nandrzael towards the city. As she broke through the clouds, a wave of dread washed over her.

She hovered amid plumes of rising smoke darker than the night sky itself. Below, her ever-faithful Argismora was engulfed in a nightmarish maelstrom of death and blood. The siege, so swift and brutal, had left the streets awash with crimson that gleamed in the light of a hundred raging fires. The Oracle of Ædant Aculus—her beautiful, glorious Oracle—was in flames. Its polished stone towers billowed with smoke, and the winding vines burned along the ancient walls. Around it, the city was a barren, scorched hellscape. The thunderous charge of Chasmira's army left the earth striped with pockmarked trenches and pools of blood in their wake.

Nandrzael hung there in the air, staring in stunned awe. Her jade eyes, once filled with the hope of saving her beloved city, now glistened with tears of grief and rage.

She hurtled earthward. They would pay for this. She would rip the heads off every single warrior and make a pile of them, with Chasmira's at the very top. It was the only punishment for blasphemy this foul. She announced her arrival with a blast of searing brilliance. When the light faded, hundreds of the invaders blinked blearily up at her. Nandrzael lowered herself to the ground with the softness of a feather. She leaned down to see the mangled, charred remains of Argismora's soldiers all around her.

She drew her sword, a long blade of shining, frozen vapor. The air shuddered as she spoke. "None of you will leave here alive."

Before she could move, red, wiry tendrils wound around her legs, wriggling like tentacles to tighten themselves. Nandrzael shrieked, for they sizzled painfully against her skin like hot irons. Before another word could leave her mouth, she was yanked through the open archway into the Oracle.

They threw her down in the middle of the chapel before unwinding themselves from her. Smoke rose from blistering, crisscrossing lines they left on her legs. Seething with anger, Nandrzael leapt up, nearly running face-first into the brass statue of herself set upon a stone pedestal. Firelight danced against the etched walls and marble pillars that stretched high up to meet the domed ceiling. The chapel tapestries and furniture were nothing but kindling in the devastation all around her.

She watched as the thin red tendrils snaked away, scraping noisily across the polished stone floor. They soon retracted back into the open hands of a fiery-eyed sorceress standing at the Oracle's shattered altar. All manner of holy books lay scattered across the floor, their pages burning.

Nandrzael's jade eyes flared with rage. "You!"

Chasmira only replied with a grim smile.

"What have you DONE?" she screamed. "Did you come here thinking all of this would get you justice?"

"Justice?" She scoffed and wiped the ash from her face where it mixed with her sweat. "Oh, no, no. No. *You* took away everyone I loved. So *I* came here and took away everyone who loved you. Call it not justice, Nandrzael. Call it what it is... Revenge."

The Angelic was shaking with fury. She glanced down at her vaporous sword on the floor, and in the blink of an eye, it was back in her grasp. "My mistake was not having you killed first."

"Why did you not?"

Her knuckles whitened. "I wanted to see you suffer, sorceress. You deserved it. You humiliated me."

"And I'm enjoying humiliating you again," Chasmira retorted with a snort.

Nandrzael's attack was so quick, it was as if she vanished entirely. Her stab was aimed for Chasmira's throat, to spear her skull from beneath and rip it clear off her body, but the tip of the sword stopped inches from the mark. A hundred red infernal threads knit themselves into a sheath around Nandrzael's weapon. Her jaw hung open in surprise and disgust as she tried to yank it free, but it was stuck fast.

A smug smile crept on Chasmira's face. This was not the same woman that frantically spewed flame at Nandrzael in the forest that morning two years ago. The infernal forge within her created only the finest craft now: not just crude blades, but any tool of war she could imagine.

A hiss escaped Chasmira's lips as she raised her blackwood wand in her other hand and aimed it squarely at Nandrzael. The Angelic's jade eyes widened with fear as a bright arcane bolt flashed from the wand's tip. Wrenching her blade free, she lunged aside. The bolt sizzled through the air, blasting a sizable chunk off one of the chapel's pillars and sending an explosion of hot gravel through the air.

Nandrzael moved through the air at tremendous speed, but the firelight gleaming off her crystalline wings gave away her movements. Chasmira spun, her Chaos energies knitting together a serrated blade to parry Nandrzael's lightning-quick strike. The vaporous sword met the crimson blade with a violent clash, igniting sparks of primordial power that seared the air.

Where once this sacred building echoed with psalms and prayers, it now thundered with blasphemous battle. Chasmira's unbound power and Nandrzael's unearthly speed kept them locked in a fierce stalemate, each striving to find a gap in the other's defenses. The Oracle itself quaked—an unwilling, tortured witness to this deadly contest.

The Angelic's voice dripped with scorn as they fought. "I was right when I said you were murderous scum."

"Killing my husband while he slept is murder," Chasmira replied with hate in every word. "This, Nandrzael, is *war*."

A fiery burst from her eyes forced Nandrzael to retreat into the air under the intense assault. She then unleashed a barrage of arcane bolts from her wand, sending Nandrzael hurtling out of the way. The barrage pounded the walls and pillars like lightning strikes mere inches behind the Angelic's speeding outline. Chasmira's other hand, dripping with infernal power, wove a writhing whip and lashed it at the Angelic.

Stepping off the wall to change direction, Nandrzael accepted the challenge head-on with swift, precise counterstrikes, her vaporous blade slicing through each sinewy lash with uncanny precision. Each hunk of the Chaos whip that fell, broke on the ground with the sulphuric squelch of a rotten egg.

An agonizing cry echoed through the burning chapel as one of Chasmira's arcane bolts found its mark. Her wing, once shimmering with pristine brilliance, now bore a jagged wound, the feathers shattered like shards of glass. Yet, Nandrzael's hatred burned even fiercer than the pain. She screamed back into battle, her injured wing hampering her speed but not her determination. She would make Chasmira pay for that, and for everything else she had done.

The chapel's foundations shuddered as their battle continued. Chasmira's fiery gaze intensified, blazing with an even fiercer fury than before. With a scream, Chasmira forged a colossal hammer, swinging it in a devastating arc. Nandrzael did not hesitate. The Angelic recklessly met the onslaught with such a powerful strike of her own, the vaporous sword sheared straight through the hammer and split it apart in a chaotic explosion. The blast hurled both women to the floor, and the chapel ignited with a flash of kaleidoscopic light. Red infernal shards peppered the walls. Some of them burnt bubbling stains that oozed with sparkling, oily pus. Some sprouted blossoms of otherworldly whispering flowers with petals like raw flesh. Others left splotches of puckered glass that shone like mirrors.

The Oracle groaned like a dying beast. Cracks began to stripe the stone walls, and the marble floor buckled. Both women gawked upward as boulders rapidly caved into the chamber from above.

Chasmira crossed her arms over her face. "Sníka—"

In seconds, darkness closed its jaws around them.

CHAPTER 46

Chasmira slowly uncrossed her arms from over her face, looking down at her hands in the strange sapphire light. She looked around at the barrier she had cast around herself, made of that same light. The words to the Odic ward enchantment had come to her lips instinctively to save herself from the collapsing Oracle.

Overhead, between the chunks of rubble that lay atop her ward, she could see flickering red light: the smoky air aglow from nearby fires. She breathed a sigh of relief that she was not buried beneath tons of collapsed stone. Backing herself away from the center, she squeezed herself against the side and lowered the ward. The dome of sapphire light vanished, and Chasmira hugged herself to the wall to avoid being struck by the debris that dropped in next to her.

She emerged out of the crater her ward had left, surveying what was now a desolate boulder field covered in the ashy fog of war. Without doubt, the collapsing Oracle had crushed many other buildings in its wake. In the ash cloud, she could hardly see more than fifty feet in front of her. The sounds of the siege—thundering hooves, snarling ironwolves, shouting warriors—seemed almost imperceptibly distant.

Ahead of her, a hunched silhouette appeared in the firelit smoke. Chasmira squinted through the smoke and dripping sweat that stung her eyes.

From the smoke cloud emerged Nandrzael. She limped forward, dragging her broken wing next to her. Her Angelic blood glittered like molten diamond from deep gashes on her head, arms, and one of her legs. "I should have gone straight to the House of the Mirikinin and wiped them out instead of coming here," she shouted, blood trickling from her mouth. "Their bloodline needs to die."

"Even that would be futile," said Chasmira.

Nandrzael sensed the soul of the child within her. Another heir. Her lip curled back in disgust. "Mother of evil, there is no curse to tell how I hate you."

Chasmira stood tall. "If you hate me, it is because I defy the fear you live under. I take fate in my own hands while your fate depends upon others, on the slaves you create. You enslave mortals using our greed, fear, and guilt, the way you enslaved me… But that enslaved you to me as well, for you can do nothing for yourself, and that terrifies you."

"Shut up," Nandrzael hissed.

"If you had to write your own future instead of what's been written for you, could you? If you had to fulfill it yourself, could you? Or do you fear being alone? Could you live without someone else giving you your purpose? Or do you fear having no one but yourself to say your life has any purpose at all, because what if you are wrong?"

"SHUT UP!"

A wry smile crept onto Chasmira's lips. "The truth is, you are a slave who fears to be free."

And in this moment—like it had been chipped away bit by bit, little by little, over a long time—something snapped inside of Nandrzael. Her pain and injury became meaningless compared to her rage. She launched herself forward with such speed that loose shards of her broken crystalline wing blew in the air behind her as her hands closed around Chasmira's neck, slamming her to the ground. Nandrzael screamed unintelligibly, her golden blood spattering down all over Chasmira as she choked her. Had she the use of both her wings, she would have dragged the sorceress straight up into the air and let her fall to her death. This was much better: killing her enemy with her own bare hands.

Chasmira's vision blurred from the strain. Nandrzael was squeezing so tightly, she could feel her windpipe collapsing. She attempted to summon fire, but could not get the word out. She clawed at Nandrzael's hands and arms, drawing blood with her nails, but could not make her let go.

Her arms flailed as she reached for anything she could use. Her wand was long gone, and apparently so was Nandrzael's sword, but a sizable rock would do plenty of damage, too. She did not find a rock but rather one of Nandrzael's broken wing shards. Grabbing it, she swung it for Nandrzael's temple as hard as she could. The Angelic saw it coming, but refused to break her chokehold. She tried to lean away from the strike, but it crossed her face instead, slicing her cheek and smashing her nose.

Chasmira felt the death grip loosen. Grabbing hold of two fingers, she wrenched them back and heard the snap when they broke. Nandrzael finally let go, but not before sending a hard kick to her chin. There was a *crunch*, and Chasmira tasted blood.

"So I was right," Chasmira chuckled as red seeped between her teeth. "Now I know I have seen what no one else has: the real you."

"The last thing you will ever see," Nandrzael said through grit teeth. She spread her arms and her wings out wide and uttered a single word in the divine tongue, and from the Angelic burst forth light brighter than the mind can imagine.

There was no time for Chasmira to react, to even blink. Not that it would have helped, for so intense was the light, it would have made her closed eyes feel as if they were wide open. Her eyes seared with pain that shot through her head all the way to the back of her skull. Reeling from shock and anguish, the sorceress tumbled backward down the rubble. She lay like a worm squirming against the daylight, writhing blindly. Not even tears rose to soothe her, for her eyes were swollen and blistered from the blast.

A winged shadow fell over her, and Nandrzael's mocking, shallow laughter echoed from above. "It burns, doesn't it? Look at you now, Princess Chasmira… Helpless. How pathetic does your infernal flame feel compared to the glorious light of a purer being?"

She was answered with a deafening crack of thunder and a shockwave that sent her hurtling backward. When she looked up again, bright arcing strands of red energy streamed from the crater. Nandrzael limped to the edge and looked down, expecting to admire Chasmira's crumpled body. Instead, she backed away in horror.

Chasmira rose like the sun. Not the sun that nourishes and gives, but the sun that burns, withers, consumes with its heat. All traces of her flesh were gone. All that remained now was bone and fire. Her hair was a cloud of billowing smoke and her eyes were the hearts of volcanoes. Fire surrounded her like a veil, a bride finally wed to the power within her.

Red energy arced around the shape of a rip in the air itself, a torn-open portal darker than the blackest night. From it, there echoed a distant howling of a thousand unearthly voices, a haunting choir of Chaos from a forbidden realm. Chasmira levitated in the air halfway in this doorway, resting against its surface as if floating on her back in a pool of dark water.

Her voice was echoed by the monstrous voices behind her. "The infernal flame dwells in all living things, Nandrzael… even in you."

"NO!" Nandrzael screamed, her silhouette turning pure white as she unleashed another onslaught of searing light. As quickly as she summoned it forth, it dissipated like smoke in the wind, sucked into the black void around Chasmira. Hot angry tears streamed freely down the Angelic's face. "Blasphemous wretch! I am of the heavens themselves! I am an immortal child of the starlight! I am divinity itself! I am *perfection*! What are you?"

Chasmira laughed, and the sky echoed her laugh as it thundered. "I am all that you are not. You are but one perfect note while I am a symphony of discord. You are but one unerring brushstroke while I am a spectrum of clashing color. You are but one arrow in a bullseye while I am a hailstorm… You are an immortal child of the starlight, but I am death in a million forms. I am everything unexpected. I am all things imperfect. I… AM… CHAOS."

From the portal, hundreds of segmented, spidery limbs stretched out to embrace Chasmira. As they gripped onto her, energy pulsed through them and into her body, intensifying the flames and the wild, flashing red energy.

"From this moment forward, you shall haunt my family no longer. For the rest of your days and with every ounce of my power, I curse you. I curse you! BE GONE!"

Out of Chasmira's chest burst forth dark red tendrils that snaked through the air in all directions. They pierced through Nandrzael like needles, skewering her flesh and shattering her wings. Blood and crystalline shards scattered together across the ground. Nandrzael's mouth gaped in wordless agony. The jade shine went out of her eyes as they clouded over.

A wave of bright, crackling, red energy surged out of Chasmira's heart and through every one of the tendrils. When the wave struck the helpless Nandrzael, both she and the tendrils were instantly vaporized, disintegrating into red powder that scattered away on the wind.

With an otherworldly shriek of victory, the limbs retracted into the portal, and the abyssal doorway slammed shut. Chasmira dropped to the ground, panting and soaked in her own sweat. She could hardly raise her head to look up.

When she did, she could not believe her eyes.

In the sky above the carnage, a figure floated, glowing like the sheen of brass in firelight. Chasmira crawled forward like an animal, blinking hard to restore her vision and see clearly.

The figure in the sky descended, and she could see two dreadful, outstretched, black wings. He stared down at her with eyes as bright and brilliant as gold, yet dispassionate as stone. "You know who I am?"

"There is not a soul alive that does not know of you, Oczandarys."

He mumbled a vague acknowledgment and lowered nearly to the ground, yet did not touch it. "You know then, that I can see all things future… all things fated."

She nodded. "I know our actions have natural consequences. They have logical ends."

He stared a moment, as if pondering her answer, before looking out across the battlefield. "Once, I looked upon this land and all that dwell herein, and the future I saw was filled with centuries of war and death. I saw the lords of these northlands slaughtering each other in an endless cycle: one bloody conquest followed by another bloody conquest. Destruction."

Chasmira's eyes widened. "Magnate Argolvrecht."

"He needed to fall, for he was paving the way for an even greater threat to come. But when Mirikinin fell with him…"

"Another bloody conquest began," Chasmira said wearily, clinging to a boulder of rubble to lift herself upright.

"So I thought."

"Whatever do you mean?"

Oczandarys hovered idly, looking across the burnt-out battlefield in macabre admiration. "It is simple to observe mortal lives and know their future. Like leaves of the trees, they bud, grow, fade, and fall. It is predictable, because, as you yourself said, actions have natural consequences and logical ends. However, Chaos obeys none of them. It neither bows to natural consequences nor yields to a logical end. I expected the House of Mirikinin to become the newest bloody conqueror, and Argismora its conquest. But something happened that I could not predict.

Something I could not see changed the future."

"What changed it?"

His piercing golden eyes fixed upon her. "You did."

"I did? I do not understand."

"Then I will illuminate it for you. The lords of Jacore have always been at each other's throats. One calls for surrender, the other resists, and war begins. However, when *you* called to the kingdoms around you, you called not for their surrender but their aid, and united the kings of the mountains and the lords of the forest against a singular foe..."

"Against Nandrzael," she finished the thought for him.

He smiled at her as if she were a child showing him a shiny rock. "No. She was never your true foe. Destiny will reveal itself soon enough."

"What will become of her, then?"

"She will again revive, but you have nothing to fear from her."

"Doubtful," Chasmira said, crossing her arms. "If anything, I have doubled her hatred of me."

"Nandrzael has lost her Oracle and the faith of all who put their trust in her. She has nothing left to fight for, not even her pride. She has only acted as I bade her, so upon my word she will vex you and your house no longer. Her failure was necessary and served its purpose."

"Necessary? Purpose? You *have* foreseen this all, haven't you? You've planned it," she accused him.

Oczandarys laughed through the nose. "I wish that were so, but no. You are a fire, and fires simply burn wherever they will. I was content to stoke the fire and watch it burn."

"So… you used Nadrzael for kindling."

A gust of hot wind tore across the battlefield, sending ash clouds swirling in long trails around them both. Red embers pelted them like sizzling rain, trickling across Oczandarys' tattooed flesh and black wings. As he hung there in the air, totally unbothered, Chasmira thought she saw the trace of a smile in his eyes. It was the only answer she would get.

Her chapped, cracked lips widened into a grin. She looked up at him and cocked her head to one side. "So what now, mighty prince?"

"Now I depart," said he, spreading his wings wide. His shining aura glowed more brightly, and it was as if the clouds opened to welcome his return. "You have worked diligently these last few years to build a new kingdom for yourself upon the grave of the old one. As if a great castle fell, and from the rubble you made a throne. I sincerely hope you will be equally diligent in protecting what you have built, as you were in building it."

"I will, provided I may do so without any divine intervention."

Oczandarys looked down on her with what she swore was a smile in his eyes. "I will be watching, but *only* watching. Some people, it seems, are bigger than fate can control."

CHAPTER 47

How quickly a year passes.

How quickly the land forgot Argismora after its destruction, becoming little more than a fleeting memory. The name of Ædant Aculus was lost along with his Oracle, as was the name of the Angelic who failed to save it. They of the Northern Wilds told a new tale around their bonfires, how the mountain ridges screamed with red, unholy fire for one night and then were silent forever after.

How quickly children grow, for little Otzana was already walking that next summer, exploring the grassy fields full of red daffodils. She giggled when Wisp put the flowers in her curly hair, and she clapped and pointed whenever a dinglebug would float lazily past them. The child picked handfuls of sweet-smelling clover and then delivered them to Morth, who sat nearby to watch her. The Ogre was appointed her personal protector, for there was no one more precious in all the kingdom than the firstborn heir to the black throne.

The sound of the front gate grinding open attracted Morth's gaze. He motioned Otzana and the Cloven to come to him, and they sat in his huge shadow as he looked upon the new arrival.

In strode a black winged horse, whose flesh was the shade of midnight, matching the long cloak of its rider. The horse snorted like the growl of a lion, baring sharp teeth that could tear and devour flesh. The rider dismounted, and the guards cautiously escorted them into the black stone fortress.

Inside the audience chamber, the guards stepped aside and allowed the cloaked rider to stand before the throne. There sat Princess Chasmira. The metal scales of her armor suit glistened in the firelight. A massive, black, feather cape flowed off the sides of the throne across the floor, and one could not tell where it ended, merging with the cold stone as if she were part of the fortress itself.

The cloaked figure neither knelt nor bowed.

"Whence come you, rider?"

From beneath the black cowl came a guttural, croaking voice. "I bring Your Ladyship salutation from the new King of the West. I am his herald. The King wishes you good health after the birth of your son Lucen, and furthermore extends His blessing to you and your house."

King of the West? Chasmira thought back to the rumor she heard in the Prefect's tower almost three years ago. If a new power had risen in the lands beyond Jacore, it was best to be gracious. "Yes, against all odds, the House of Mirikinin still stands and evermore will stand. Tell your King that I thank Him for His blessing. I, Princess Chasmira, welcome you to enjoy dinner with myself and my husband, Prince Luthian. You may stay the night as our guest."

"Thank you, Your Ladyship. Think me not rude for declining, but I have not hungered in three years." The herald lifted back his cowl, revealing a fleshless skull, mottled brown like burnt leather. Its dark eye cavities at first appeared empty, but flickered with faint, familiar flames like candlelight. "You misunderstand me,

Your Ladyship. This land and all therein are now a part of the Volgoth Empire, ruled by the great and immortal Ever-King. Come with me and bow yourselves before His Infernal Majesty. Receive your blessing in like manner as I have, for your destiny is to rest in His almighty hand."

Chasmira's eyes glanced skyward with fire in them. *Destiny revealed, indeed.*

The herald stared out of the hollows of its skull. "What say you?"

She rose from the throne, her cape flowing at her sides like billowing waves in a storm. "What say I? I say that I must decline the gracious blessing of your Ever-King. This family has not survived the Dragon's Winter and an Angelic's game, only to become darkened slaves in a kingdom of Chaos. If this land and all therein are truly destined for His hand…"

Something gleamed in her grasp. From beneath her cape emerged the three-pronged head of the iron staff.

"Then I say let Him come and take it Himself."

ACKNOWLEDGEMENTS

My gratitude goes out to so many people who have been with me on the journey writing this book. Thank you first of all to my family and friends who watched me sacrifice many hours of sleep working to turn my dreams into reality the past two years.

Next, my heartfelt thanks to the Grimmgard fandom, for your obsession with this fierce world I have created. You keep coming back for more, and I am eternally grateful for you.

All my love to the Bookstagram community and thank you for all the love you have shown me back. Special thanks to M.A. Leon and Abigail Hair, whose books inspired me to keep raising the bar.

Thank you to Hanne Merete, Amanda Milwood, Ingrid Sigfridsson, and Rachel Fields, all of whom took their turns helping me refine this book from the earliest concepts to the final edits. I could not have done this without you.

To Tiffani, my Stardust—Keep showing every day how light persists even out of deep darkness. You inspire me daily.

Lastly, thank you to Jordan Dickinson, fellow writer and one of the best men I have ever known. Thank you, brother, for all your help during this journey, but most of all for your enduring friendship that means the world to me.

Made in the USA
Coppell, TX
17 January 2025